MW00513960

LIKE FATHER

LIKE FATHER

Nicholas Day-Lewis

Library of Congress Control Number:		2022915618
ISBN:	Hardcover	978-1-6698-3149-5
	Softcover	978-1-6698-3148-8
	eBook	978-1-6698-3147-1

Rev. date: 08/29/2022

To order additional copies of this book, contact:
Xlibris
AU TFN: 1 800 844 927 (Toll Free inside Australia)
AU Local: (02) 8310 8187 (+61 2 8310 8187 from outside Australia)
www.Xlibris.com.au
Orders@Xlibris.com.au
843449

We are never so defenceless against suffering as when we love.

—Sigmund Freud

CHAPTER 1

1961–1979

My earliest memory was the sound of crying. That and shouting. I was possibly around three years old at the time, though it's hard to know since that same sound kept haunting me in later years. My mother, as she cuddled me, would often have red eyes, tear-stained cheeks, and bruises. I didn't understand at first, though it wasn't long before I understood that my father was the cause of her hurts. I began to recognise his bellows of rage, and when I was too small to move around unaided and therefore to hide, I began to realise that all I could do was shut my eyes and pretend to be asleep. It seemed to deflect my father's anger. I didn't realise it at the time, but I was simply withdrawing into myself, my only method of hiding myself away.

I should tell you a little bit about the Maddens. I guess you would call us a working class family. My father, John Madden Senior, is a tram driver, and my mother, Flo, is a housewife. My father runs the family with a rod of iron, taking no nonsense from either his wife or his two children, me and my elder sister, Barbara. In fact, Dad is a bit of a tyrant, a domestic abuser I think it's called these days, and Mum was often the recipient of a slap or a punch. So was I, but somehow Barb always managed to avoid the worst of his angry outbursts. My sister is three years older than me. She was canny enough to see a threat before it arrived, and she always did exactly as she was told, and, unlike me, she never answered back. She managed to escape the confines of home as soon as she was twenty-one and could stick it up to Dad. In fact, she went one better and married one of the first guys she'd ever gone out with, an easy-talking character called Paul, who promptly easy-talked Barb into bed only the second time they'd met and got her pregnant, the silly girl. But more about that later; I don't want to get too far ahead of the story.

Anyway, my early days weren't always so grim. There were happy times as well, times when there was laughter in the house and an atmosphere of well-being. I remember my sister's tenth birthday for my father came home with a huge doll's house for her. Barbara was his favourite. As I said, she was always polite and did his every bidding, never questioning his authority. Little did I realise at the time that this was her way of deflecting his anger onto someone else, usually my mother but sometimes me. And I learnt never to cry in his presence, even after a beating, because tears were responded to with further violence. I was particularly prone to bed-wetting, and Dad's reaction just made matters worse, so I began suffering from nightmares. 'Your little runt has pissed himself again!' he would shout out to Mum.

I remember one occasion, horrific in its intensity. I must have been about six at the time. My father came home one evening in a particularly belligerent mood. He was unsteady on his feet, and his speech was slurred. The three of us were in the lounge room, and my father started picking an argument with me for some misdemeanour that I've long forgotten. Mum immediately took my side and told him to lay off me. He bellowed at her, accusing her of pampering me, and then, after more swearing, he grabbed her and threw her onto the couch. He started ripping her clothes off. 'No! Stop!' she shouted a couple of times. 'Not in front of the children.' But he didn't stop, and Barbara took my hand and dragged me out of the room. I now think that my father used to rape Mum a lot, perhaps every time he came home drunk. But at the time, I had no idea what was going on. To me, it was just something else to be avoided.

I developed the ability to scan for the warning signs. I even became attuned to Dad's inner state: subtle changes in his facial expression, voice, and body language, so I could begin to decipher signals of anger or intoxication. And when I saw such signals, I would go and hide. I found many hidey-holes in the house, my favourite being the laundry cupboard. I could just fit in there when I was small. I would continue to sit in there, quivering with fear, until it seemed safe to emerge. Sometimes, I'd be hiding for an hour at a time. And when I emerged into a now silent household, my father, if he was still there, wouldn't have noticed I'd gone missing.

A lot changed when I was old enough to go to school. Barbara had been at the primary for three years before I went, so she walked me there every morning and back in the afternoon and guided me through the early weeks of this strange new life. It was at school that I first discovered that the Madden household was much poorer than most others. There was little money for books or proper uniforms, and certainly none for outings and school excursions. I was teased unmercifully by the other children when I came to school, usually dressed in very second-hand-looking and ill-fitting clothing. And if I ever lost anything, or more likely had it stolen, there was yet another excuse for my father to administer a thrashing.

Sometimes, I wonder how I survived. Looking back on my primary school years, I think there were two things that helped me to endure: my sister and my teachers. I had a series of wonderful teachers, mostly women, and mostly people who understood poverty and how it affected children. Whenever they could be, they were supportive and made sure my disadvantage did not hinder my progress through the school. As a result, though I wasn't a brilliant student, I did manage to hold my own. Nevertheless, it was with a sense of shame that I walked to school every morning, often hungry, and always fearful of the day ahead. I particularly remember Miss Snow. I thought she was pretty old, but I later found out she was still in her early twenties. She was my form teacher in year two, and she always started the day with arithmetic, and not just the ordinary kind, but *mental* arithmetic. She'd read out a series of numbers, which she would make us add up in our heads, sums that occasionally included a bit of multiplying, dividing, or subtracting. I had a hidden aptitude for numbers, and I adored Miss Snow, probably as a result. And I retained my love of maths throughout my school years.

I struggled with the other subjects; though with Barbara's help, I had learnt to read at an early age. So in the early years, until other subjects were introduced, I managed to keep up. The time came, however, when my sister had to move on to high school, and at the same time, everything got a little harder. Without Barbara to protect me, the school bullies took their chances. My schoolwork suffered as I spent increasing amounts of time trying to escape their attention. I cannot even remember half of the indignities I was subjected to. They have blurred together in my memory, but many were the times I returned home in tears, vowing never to go to school anymore. Mum would do her best to jolly me along and persuade me to keep trying. She was a saint, I often think now, judging by everything she had to put up with from Dad, and having a snivelling little urchin for a son wouldn't have helped.

One thing I do remember well occurred when I was in year four. It was the turn of our class to go on a school camp that summer, but, as usual, my parents couldn't afford the fees, so I had to stay behind. Even though there were no classes, I was still required to attend school, me and one other boy whose parents must have suffered from the same problem. Unfortunately, Trevor was one of the nastier bullies, and as we were left alone together in the otherwise empty classroom, he could have been particularly unpleasant. However, we had been set some maths to do, and Trevor was something of a dunce for anything to do with numbers, so he actually asked me to help him. I was only too glad to show off my knowledge, especially if it could improve relations with someone who always seemed to look down on me. I guess the reason I remember this episode so well is that this apparent act of friendship was so unlike my other school experiences. He actually blushed when he had to ask me for help, and he even said thank you afterwards, once I had virtually done all his sums for him.

Another memory from primary school happened in my last term. For some reason that is now beyond me, our class was shown a short movie describing the workings of an internal combustion engine. I think the teacher must have been unable to think of anything to teach us or had just run out of ideas, so showing a movie was a way to fill in time. For most of the class, the movie was acutely boring; but for some reason, I found the subject fascinating. The operation of the pistons in their cylinders, the timing of the fuel injection and the spark plugs firing, and all the other little bits and pieces that go to make up an engine, all enthralled me. Afterwards, the others were saying how boring it was, how they couldn't understand any of it, that the movie was stupid. But I stuck my neck out, for once, and said I thought it fairly simple, that it made a lot of sense. They all rounded on me, telling me I was a liar and saying I was stuck up. However, that movie had made a huge impression on me. I now knew what I wanted to be when I grew up.

The important thing about high school was that I would be reunited with Barbara. So I looked forward to it with slightly less apprehension than I would otherwise have done. My year six at primary had ended with an orientation visit to the new school, a much larger establishment than the one I was used to. We were shown around various buildings and had a short lecture from the new principal, a rather fierce-looking lady whom everyone seemed a little wary of, and who told us that whatever else we did, or didn't do, it was of paramount importance to keep in touch by regularly looking at notice boards. At least I think that was what she was saying. So, at least on my first day of year seven, I thought I would easily be able to find out where to go and how I could find out which classroom to attend and when. At least that was the theory, though in practice it took many weeks before I arrived on time at the right place for every class.

The second thing about high school was that I was eventually able to make a few friends. There was one boy in particular that befriended me. Hudson Little was in the same class for maths. He was every bit as good as I was in the subject, and we set up a fair rivalry. In fact, in the end, we went right through most of high school together in the same maths class, though he was well ahead of me in other subjects. Unfortunately, some of the more obnoxious boys from primary had also been elevated to my new school, and they tried to take up where they had left off in year six. It started with the usual name-calling and the surreptitious hiding or stealing of books and other possessions, but one lunch break, as we were milling around outside, two of them became quite belligerent. Teachers were patrolling the yard, but they were out of sight at the time.

However, Hudson saw them threatening me and came to my rescue. Hudson Little wasn't little at all. He was a tall boy for his age, and he had a forbidding presence when aroused. 'You can cut it out!' he shouted at them, raising his fists. By that stage, unlike me, his voice had already broken. His man's voice, already quite deep, had authority. It did the trick, and I was never accosted in such a way again. 'Bullies are actually cowards,' he said to me afterwards. 'They won't trouble you anymore.' Although I hardly knew Hudson at the time of the altercation, he became not only my friend but also my guardian. I was immensely grateful to him, and from then, I began to accrue a little more self-confidence. It was wonderful having someone other than family to confide in, and once I'd got to know him better, I told him much about my situation at home. 'I thought as much,' he said. 'You always look a bit under the weather when you get to school. A bit sad too.'

Often, when events got a little out of hand at home, Hudson and I would hang out together, and a couple of times I stayed over at his house. He was always a kind and gentle soul, though he teased me about my voice, which when it started breaking, it couldn't make up its mind as to the correct pitch. For months, it would suddenly squeak in the middle of a sentence, something that caused great mirth in class.

In the years to come, once my voice had settled down to a normal tenor and tufts of hair began to grow where they should, my increasing self-confidence also became reflected in my home life. A couple of times, I stood up to my father and didn't flinch when he threatened me. We came to an uneasy peace, and I even managed a conversation with him about my future. He suggested a couple of big motor repair shops where I could apply for an apprenticeship once I had left school, and I spent a bit of time over my school holidays beginning to sound them out. One in particular, the local Ford dealer, sounded quite promising. The maintenance manager told me I should at least complete my year ten and preferably my year eleven. I'd be seventeen by then, and I'm sure ready to enter the workforce.

And so my school years dragged to a close, and with only a short break over Christmas, I started my apprenticeship at the Ford dealer in the New Year. I don't know what I expected, perhaps an instant introduction to what would be the tools of my trade and immediately getting to work on the latest high-tech motor-car engine. It certainly wasn't as glamorous as that. I hadn't realised that a first-year apprentice is the lowest form of human life. For the first few weeks, I was simply a gopher, running around at everyone's whim, trying to find things for them, spares or tools I didn't know the names of, or even what they looked like. And I was given all the jobs of cleaning filthy engine parts that no one else would touch. But I kept my cool and my eyes open, ready for an opportunity to shine. I eventually caught the eye of Barry Weston, an oldish mechanic with untidy grey hair and a winning smile. He took me under his wing and started me helping him on some of the more basic tasks. He told me that the mechanics treat all new apprentices the same way, testing their mettle, seeing how they react. He said I had survived my initiation pretty well, but not to get above myself, as he put it.

I was surprised to find a girl working alongside the men. I had never realised that girls would ever want to become mechanics, so I guess I'd been guilty of gender stereotyping. Nola was a third-year apprentice, and I was soon to discover that she was Barry Weston's daughter. He had persuaded to try her hand at his trade, and, according to Barry, she was enjoying every minute of it. Initially, I got talking to her because I wanted to discover the difference between first and third years as regards apprenticeship training. I continued talking to her because I liked her. I had never had a regular girlfriend at school, and only occasional dates, so it was high time I got more interested in the fair sex. She seemed quite amenable to being chatted up. I even asked Barry if it was OK for me to ask her out to the movies.

'Don't ask me,' he said. 'Ask her.'

'I will, but does she have a boyfriend already?'

'She did,' said Barry, 'but she gets through boyfriends so quickly that I'm not sure if she's still seeing the current one.'

So, at the first opportunity, I cornered Nola and in great trepidation popped the question. 'I was just wondering whether ....' She was looking at me with such a strange expression that I stopped.

'Wondering what?' she asked me.

'Well, you know, whether you'd be free sometime.'

'Free for what?'

'To come on a date with me.'

She shook her head at me, a pained look on her face. 'I can't, John. Sorry.'

'Already have a boyfriend, do you?'

'Something like that.'

In a way, I was actually quite relieved. I realised I was out of my depth. 'Ah, well,' I said, 'you can't win them all.'

'No, you can't.' She still looked a little unhappy at having to refuse me. I realised that, had she not had a boyfriend, she might well have agreed to see me outside work, so I was quite buoyed by her response. And she might even be able to help me with a project I was planning.

The last time I had visited Hudson, his father had mentioned something about ditching his ancient car. He'd had his old Volkswagen Beetle for fifteen years, and it had been sitting in his garage for the last six months gathering dust. He'd already bought a new Mitsubishi Colt and wanted to sell the old car.

'How much do you want for it?' I asked him one day.

'Oh, it's not worth much. It's falling apart. It won't start anymore.'

'I might be interested,' I told him, 'if it's not too much.'

'For you, John, fifty dollars.'

'Are you serious?'

'Of course. It would probably cost me fifty to get it taken away to the scrapyard. So I'm not going to lose any sleep over it.'

'Well,' I said, 'I don't earn much, but if you give me a couple of weeks, I'll try and find the cash.'

'OK. It's a deal,' he said, and we shook hands.

I had previously discovered that Barry Weston and his family lived only two streets away from the Maddens, and the next time I had a chance to have a chat with Barry, I told him about the Beetle and how I wanted to do it up. Could he help me? I was overjoyed when he said that he'd be happy to assist. He had a big double garage, and his family only had the one car, so he only used one half of it. But if I took up his offer of the space, he wanted Nola to be a partner in the overhaul of the car. That seemed fair enough to me, and she was as keen as me to get started. Barry found me the name of a company they used for towing broken-down cars, and in two weeks, everything was ready. I gave Hudson's father his fifty dollars and had enough over to pay the trucking company. I met the tow truck driver at Hudson's house on a Saturday morning, and once the front of the Beetle was lifted and made secure, I got into the truck's passenger seat. Hudson's father came to see us off, and he looked quite composed and happy as he waved us off down the road. I directed the driver to the Westons' house, and in fifteen minutes, my car was safely ensconced in Barry's garage. He and Nola, as well as Barry's wife, Charlene, came and inspected my new purchase. Nola introduced me to her mother, a lady who smiled a lot but remained silent the whole time.

We had pushed the car in nose first so that the engine faced the garage entrance, giving us more natural light. None of us had ever worked on a Beetle before, so it would be something new for everyone. I saw that there was a small workbench at the back. 'Can I use that?' I asked Barry.

'Sure,' he said, 'but you'll need to hire one of those small mobile cranes to get the engine out.'

'Where should I go for that?' I asked him.

'You could try Coates. There's a branch in the next suburb.'

'OK. I'll contact them next week.'

'And you'd better get yourself all the necessary tools. Have you received your tool allowance yet?'

'No.'

'Go and see the boss first thing Monday. He'll fix you up.'

'Thanks.'

'And you'd better see if you can get hold of a manual for the car. Perhaps Volkswagen can help with that, you know, one of their dealers, or they can give you the name of someone to contact in their head office. Tell them it's a training exercise. That should help.'

I was beginning to get cold feet. Now that I'd taken delivery of the vehicle, I realised that this was going to be a fairly complicated, lengthy, and arduous job, as well as an expensive one, but I could never turn back now. I'd feel such an idiot if I did. The die was cast, and at least I had all the advice and help I would need to get the old jalopy back on the road. Even then, it would most likely take me at least six months to get her roadworthy, and I'd have to work on it just about every weekend. Someone once told me that nice girls only went out with boys who have a car, so perhaps in six months, I would get lucky. As I contemplated the months ahead, Charlene suddenly broke her silence and invited me into the house for a cup of tea.

'Thank you,' I said and followed the Weston family as they trooped inside.

In the end, the overhaul of the Beetle took nearly a year. Just about everything that could go wrong did. For a start, Nola wasn't a great deal of help. She wanted to spend much of every weekend with her man, and I could hardly blame her for that. Barry himself was, of course, a great help and was always on hand to advise me. One of the main problems was finding the necessary spares. They were expensive and, in some cases, unobtainable, so I had to go fossicking around in old scrapyards to find them second-hand. It had already taken two months to find a manual for this particular model, something I eventually sourced through a copy of the *Trading Post*. My one really big drawback was that I was pretty green when it came to the details of internal combustion engines. After all, I was only a first-year apprentice, so I was forced to learn as I went along. But I do have an aptitude and very slowly began to make progress.

Events at home didn't help. My sister, Barbara, was already twenty that year and becoming more independent. She had a job at a pharmacy and was meeting all sorts of interesting people, mainly men, and being invited out to parties and dinners. My father could see his family disintegrating and was at pains to try and keep Barbara at home with threats and warnings of all the terrible things that could befall her if she met the wrong type. And my being out every weekend as well didn't help. My mother was very supportive of what I was doing, but I had to give her a fair chunk of my wages every week, as Dad was mean with his, and that also slowed down progress on the car. Sometimes, I had to wait a week or more before I could afford a part. Dad continued to berate me for wasting my time. 'You should save up and buy yourself a proper car if you really want one,' he kept telling me, 'not waste your time messing about with that old junk heap.' He just didn't understand the satisfaction of fixing something up, doing a job one could be proud of.

One day, towards the end of my first year as an apprentice, Barbara came home and told her mother she was pregnant. It was only two weeks before her twenty-first birthday, and she announced that as soon as she reached that milestone, she and Paul were going to get married. She loved him and he wanted to marry her, and that was her decision so Dad had better back off and not get in their way. She was sure he would try, and so it turned out.

'You're a fucking whore!' Dad shouted at her when she confronted him with the news. I'm sure Dad still considered Barbara a compliant sixteen-year-old, and not a grown-up.

She simply walked up to him and slapped him in the face. 'How dare you call me that!' Dad got such a shock, he just stood there, unbelieving. 'If you don't apologise, I won't ask you to my wedding,' she added, and she walked off with her head held high.

I was never privy to how the confrontation was settled, but two weeks later, Barbara and Paul were married at the local registry office, and Dad was in attendance. He'd actually put on a suit for the occasion, though he remained somewhat grumpy throughout the ceremony. Paul had persuaded a couple of his friends to come along, possibly with the promise of a feed and booze-up at the local pub afterwards. His parents were there as well, and Mum and me, so there were nine of us in all. Barbara had insisted there be no speeches, but we drank the health of the couple at least three times during the meal. One of Paul's friends got rather drunk and started telling dirty jokes, mostly aimed at Paul. The bridegroom had made no bones about telling everybody that he'd got Barbara pregnant. That started an argument, and Paul's father came round the table, grabbed the drunk man by the scruff of the neck, and ushered him out.

Once the meal was finished, we bade farewell to Barbara and Paul as they set out on their honeymoon. Barbara went round to everybody, even Dad, and dispensed kisses all round. When she came to me, I asked her where she was going, but she said she didn't know. Paul had decided to make the destination a surprise. Mum gave her a big hug. She appeared quite relaxed until the happy couple got into their car to leave. Then the tears started.

'Stop snivelling, woman,' said Dad in a loud voice.

'I'm crying 'cos I'm really happy for them,' answered Mum through her tears. 'That's plain stupid,' said Dad.

Everyone waved to them as their car pulled away, and then we returned to our humdrum lives.

The first year of my apprenticeship was drawing to a close. I took two weeks leave over Christmas, a time I expected to spend finishing the overhaul. I hadn't realised that Barry and his wife were taking the same two weeks, and were going off for a camping holiday, so there would be no help from that quarter. However, Nola wouldn't be joining them, so I thought that *she* at least would be available. The first day I went round there, it was after ten o'clock in the morning. Her boyfriend must have got there first, or probably he'd been there all night. I was just about to knock on the door to see if Nola would come and help when I heard a series of moans and grunts coming from an open upstairs window. The moans were definitely female and the grunts male, and the cries were increasing in intensity. Obviously, Nola was busy, so I refrained from knocking and went to the garage to start work.

I had never met the boyfriend. I was keen to see who it was that Nola found so important in her life. They emerged together an hour later. They were very affectionate, kissing passionately and clutching each other in a farewell embrace, and it was only after they separated that I could see who her lover was. James Chase was one of our new car salesmen, and I happened to know that he was married. Nola was somewhat flushed and seemed surprised to see me.

'Hello, Jimmy,' I said. 'I didn't expect to find you here.'

He blushed, his eyes jumping from me to Nola and back again. 'I ....
I ....,' he started.

'It's all right, darling,' interrupted Nola. 'John's working here, on his car.'

'I see,' said Jimmy, and with that, he raced off down the drive as if the very devil was after him. Then he turned and waved, and Nola blew him a kiss.

'You do know that Mum and Dad are not here, don't you?' said Nola.

'You do know that Jimmy is married, don't you?' I countered.

'Yes.'

'And a yes for me too,' I said. 'That your parents are away, I mean. I knew *you* were still at home, though, and I hoped you would help me.'

'I would, John, but I'm exhausted.'

'I'm not surprised.'

'Look. Yes, Jimmy is married, but he's very unhappy. He's promised to leave his wife and marry me as soon as I'm out of my time. We love each other.'

'I can see that, but do you really believe him?'

'I do, but please, John, don't tell anyone, especially my parents. They'd kill me if they knew.'

'OK, but one good turn deserves another.'

'What?'

'Give me as much time on my car as you give Jimmy in your bed.'

'Deal,' and we gave each other high-fives.

So life wasn't humdrum after all. Nola and I made good progress in between her trysts with Jimmy, and the car was all but ready for a roadworthy by the time her parents returned from their trip. The near completion of the Beetle allayed some of the fears that Barry might have had that his daughter had got up to mischief during his absence. Nola must have been working hard.

Events at home were also back on an even keel to a large extent. My parents were both feeling the absence of my sister, and when Mum set the table for our traditional Christmas dinner, she mistakenly set a place for Barbara. When Dad discovered what she had done, his comments were a lot less snide than usual. In fact, he made quite a joke of it. Barbara and Paul came back from their honeymoon and were staying with Paul's parents while they looked for an apartment. She came round once to visit while Dad was at work, and she was positively blooming.

'Pregnancy suits you,' Mum said more than once. And I could just see the slight bulge my sister carried around with her. She somehow looked more mature, more ready for life, and she was very much in love.

In February, as my second year got under way, the Beetle was ready. I decided to do some extra work on the inside, buying new seat covers and generally making the car more habitable. I also bought new tyres. I'd had a few driving lessons over Christmas and now sported my L plates as Barry and I drove the car off to get it tested for a roadworthy certificate. I was pretty nervous, but the inspector knew Barry well, and there was no trouble. Then we drove round to my parents' home for them to see it. We shovelled them into the somewhat cramped back seats and took them for a drive. They were a little nervous as we started out but soon settled down and were quite complimentary, even Dad, who had up to then been quite scathing about my ability to do anything useful.

My second year continued much like the first, though two events made it notable. In July, Barbara gave birth to a daughter. She and Paul named her Florence, though she was always referred to as Florrie. Paul had found them a small apartment in the city, and there they went to live with their little girl. They seemed blissfully happy. I was quite envious; I still had trouble finding a girl I liked well enough to want to marry. I had even started frequenting bars in the hope of meeting someone. I still had lustful feelings over Nola, but that avenue had been closed a long time ago.

The second notable event concerned her. In September, Nola went to her mother with the news that she had fallen pregnant. Then the whole story came out. Barry confronted Jimmy at work and gave him a severe beating. Eventually, his colleagues managed to drag him off, and the pair of them were paraded in front of the general manager. Both were fired for their part in the fracas and for bringing the dealership into disrepute in front of some of the firm's customers, though Barry was later reinstated once the whole truth had been laid bare. Nola promised never to see the man again, and Jimmy went back to his wife, who, surprisingly, forgave him.

What with all the angst in the Weston household, I kept well clear. I therefore had no idea how they handled the situation, and I didn't want to get involved. Barry became very introverted at work. He hardly spoke to anyone, unless spoken to first, and I for one kept well clear of him. Under the circumstances, Nola was granted leave of absence and was told she could return at a later date to complete her final year. I missed her presence in the workshop for I still had feelings for her, and as the year proceeded, I often thought about her predicament. She and I had spent a fair bit of time together as we worked on the Beetle, and many were the times I wanted to take her in my arms and kiss her. I thought about her a lot. Perhaps, if I'd envisaged the emotional roller coaster that awaited me at TAFE the following autumn, I would have forgotten her much sooner.

*   *   *

CHAPTER 2

1980

I was nineteen when I first saw Helen. She was doing some sort of secretarial work at the TAFE, where I spend two days a week studying. That day, the day when we came face to face, she was taking registrations at the start of my third year, and frankly I was bowled over, not only by her looks but also by her confident personality and her silky voice. She had a cascade of blonde hair that framed her pretty face and a light-blue dress that accentuated her generous bust. My eyes were glued to her as I edged forward in the queue, and when it was my turn, she smiled at me. I always remember how she leant over the counter as she took my details, giving me a good view of her cleavage. She smiled again when she saw me looking, and my face turned a bright red, I suspect. Mind you, I was never good at sussing out women. If truth be told, I was terrified of them, probably because, while being both attracted to and excited by girls, I was at the same time petrified at the prospect of rejection. They invariably aroused in me a sexual need but left me frightened to make a move. Even with Nola, I had been far from confident in the way I had approached her. I would have liked to have talked to my sister about my feelings for women but was always too shy.

My mother wasn't much of a role model, being so timid, I felt, and Dad didn't help in my dealings with girls. He just scoffed every time I mentioned the name of one I liked, belittling me with his ridicule, so I just kept my thoughts and my cravings to myself. I hoped that my whole approach to womankind would never be coloured by my father's behaviour towards Mum. He continued to lift his hand to her every time he felt something was wrong, making her feel guilty for perceived misdemeanours, especially if he didn't like a meal she'd cooked. And I vowed, many times, that I would never sink to his level of disdain or treat a woman with contempt as he did my mother. For instance, when I was little, she used to take Barbara and me to church on a Sunday, but Dad was forever disparaging her faith, laughing at what he called her stupidity and ignorance for believing the rubbish they preached. I was seven when Mum had finally had enough, and we stopped going.

So, when I first saw Helen, I was struck dumb with puppy love. My tongue seemed to be glued to the roof of my mouth, and when I finally found my voice, I just muttered something about the course I was doing and wanting to re-sign for. With what seemed an indication of her efficiency, she went straight to a nearby filing cabinet and found the necessary forms. I quickly signed and hurriedly left. Quite frankly, I was in a state of alarm. No one else had ever had such a profound effect on me, but I could see that she was in a different class to the Maddens, so I just tried to put her out of my mind. But I couldn't. At night, I dreamt of her and all the things I would love to do with her. It took me another three weeks before I plucked up enough courage to speak to her again. I had often seen her in the canteen at lunchtime and decided that was the best time to make myself known to her. With considerable trepidation, I approached her table and stood there, hovering, holding my tray of food. I stood for quite a long time, wondering what to say. Eventually, she stopped eating and looked up at me.

'Do you want to come and sit?' she asked in a kindly manner.

'Thank you,' I replied and took a chair opposite her.

'My name is Helen Sykes,' she told me. 'And you are John Madden, aren't you?'

'You remembered me, then.'

'How could I forget? I thought you were going to melt that day.'

'Really?'

'Your face was on fire.'

'Sorry. I do blush easily.'

Helen smiled and went back to her food. 'Your lunch is getting cold,' she added between mouthfuls. So I started eating, though my appetite had somewhat disappeared. 'You are doing the motor mechanics course, aren't you?'

'Yes.' I began to realise that if she remembered all this about me, then she must have taken an interest in me from the start, so I was encouraged to try my luck. 'Do you perhaps already have a . . . you know, like . . . a boyfriend?' I asked her, my voice trembling with anxiety.

'Not at the moment. Why do you ask?' She seemed completely unfazed by my question.

'Well, I was wondering if you'd like to go out with *me* sometime.'

'To do what exactly?'

She sounded faintly aloof, as if she was testing my resolve, so I hesitated. 'Well, what do you like doing?' I asked her. She just looked at me, silently studying my face. Eventually, I thought I had better suggest something. 'A movie perhaps. Or dinner, or just a coffee somewhere. You know, away from here, I mean.'

'Can I let you know?' she enquired as she rose to her feet.

'Sure, Helen,' I answered as I also stood. I felt that the meeting had not gone well, that she must have decided I was not the right type of person to be seen out with. After that, I went back to frequenting bars and anywhere else where there might be more of a chance of meeting unattached girls. I even started approaching other girls in the TAFE canteen.

Two weeks passed after I'd abandoned any hope regarding a date with Helen, then suddenly everything changed. One afternoon, she stopped me as I was leaving the classrooms to go home. 'Have you decided where you would like to take me?' she asked. She smiled up at me in a way that told me she was game for a date after all. I got such a surprise that I was suddenly struck dumb. 'Wherever it is,' she added, 'my father wants to meet you first.'

'Doesn't he trust me?' I asked her.

'Perhaps you should ask me if *I* trust you.'

'OK. Do you?'

'I don't know yet, do I?' she said with a grin. 'Anyway, my parents are a bit old-fashioned. I'm nearly twenty-one, but while I'm still living at home, they want to meet everyone I go out with.'

'Fair enough, I suppose.'

'They actually prefer me to go out with older boys, so I didn't tell them your age.' I didn't know what to say to that. She continued. 'But I did tell them that you are quite mature and have your own car. And that you have your P plates now.'

'You seem to know a lot about me,' I said.

'I've spent two weeks asking around.'

'Sounds like you've been snooping.'

Helen laughed. 'Just a bit,' she agreed.

'Is Saturday OK, then?'

'Depends where you want to take me.'

'A movie would be good. Maybe a coffee after.'

'That's cool, John.'

'Tell me, what does your father do for a living?'

'He's a cop. Why do you ask?'

'I guess I'd better be on my best behaviour, then.'

'Absolutely. Come round to my place at six. Here's the address. And my phone number's on there as well.' She gave me a slip of paper, and with a cursory nod of her head, she left.

When I got home that evening, my dad was still out on shift, and Mum was preparing the tea. I told her that I'd got a date for Saturday night. 'Where's she from, then?' Mum asked.

'She works at the TAFE.'

'I hope she's not as scatter-brained as your sister.'

'Of course not.'

'Don't want any more illegits in the family.'

'It's not like that, Mum.'

'Of course not. Never is, until the hormones start rattling around in your head.'

Mum returned to her task of chopping carrots for the soup she was preparing, and I escaped to my room with a newspaper I'd picked up on the way home. I needed to see what was on at the local cinema and find a suitable movie for Saturday. I had just finished making a list of the possibles when I heard the front door slam downstairs and my dad's voice booming in the kitchen. He was obviously angry about something. His voice was as loud and drunken as Mum's voice was soft. Consequently, from the safety of my room, I could only hear one side of the conversation.

'What's this, then .... . I don't want fuckin' soup .... . Well, I won't eat it. I want a proper meal, something I can get my teeth into .... . What do you mean there's nothing else?' and so it continued for what seemed about five minutes. Then I heard Dad utter a loud expletive, and there came the sound of something metal crashing to the floor. The front door slammed again, and I could make out a wailing sound coming from the kitchen. I waited another couple of minutes before venturing out. Mum was crouched over the workbench. On the floor around her, the remains of her soup covered the floor, pieces of vegetable in a sea of brown liquid. She lifted her head as I entered, one eye looking at me balefully while the other was closed, a bruise forming on her cheek below. Of course, it wasn't the first time I had been a witness to my father's temper, but I still had no idea how to handle it. I didn't know what to say. I had no idea how to defuse the situation. I just stood, gawping. Many seconds passed as I surveyed the remains of our meal, but eventually Mum straightened up and looked at me. I could see that she was trying to smile, make the best of it, but her face wasn't cooperating. Frankly, it was embarrassing.

'I'm sorry, John,' she said in mournful voice. She bent down to retrieve the saucepan that had fetched up in a corner. 'There'll be no tea tonight. I hope you're not too hungry.'

'I'm OK,' I answered, even though I was feeling far from happy. I knew that I wasn't as sorry for my mother as I should have been but still felt the need to lend a hand if I could. 'Let me help you clear up,' I said.

'It's all right,' she answered. 'Get yourself down to that Indian place down the street and get yourself a takeaway.'

So I quickly took her at her word and escaped.

My excitement mounted as the weekend approached. Even Dad, once he'd got over his tantrum, was supportive when I raised the subject of my upcoming date. In fact, he sounded quite pleased, especially when I told him Helen's father was a cop. 'That'll keep you in order,' he said, and he slapped me on the back. 'Make a man out of you. I hope she's not one of those dumb blondes,' he added.

'Well, she is a blonde, but she's far from being dumb,' I told him.

'Glad to hear it. Just don't let her fuck you around, that's all.'

'What do you mean, Dad?'

'Don't let her be the boss. You've got to wear the pants, keep the womenfolk in their place, or you'll be in trouble later on.'

I didn't really understand my father's point of view, and his attitude had me a bit worried. However, I'd forgotten our conversation by the time that Saturday eventually arrived. Along with it came a September day as sunny and warm as anyone could have hoped for. I went out in the morning and bought a big bunch of daffodils for Helen. That was Mum's idea. I was spruced up as best as I could be and not a little nervous as I walked up the path to Helen's house at six o'clock. There was a low brick wall along the road boundary, and the house was set well back, leaving a big expanse of garden. On either side of the drive and a path of regular paving slabs that led from it to the front door were narrow beds of flowering annuals and, beyond them, a lawn and shrubs. They all looked well cared for. The house itself was a fairly modest two-storey place. It was tucked away at the end of a cul-de-sac, which, with Helen's instructions, I had found quite easily.

I walked hesitantly up to the front door, clutching the flowers, and rang the bell. Nothing happened at first. I thought for an awful moment that I'd come on the wrong day or that Helen had changed her mind, but then, just as I was about to turn away, the door opened.

Instead of Helen, a shortish and slightly dumpy woman stood there looking at me. She had an untidy mop of blonde hair and was dressed casually in a pair of dungarees. She wore a pair of glasses with a multicoloured frame and lenses that looked like a sort of bottle glass, so thick that it made her blue irises enormous. I stared at her, a little spooked, for despite the strange spectacles, I could see so much of Helen in her. I was just about to say something, tell her my business, when she got in first.

'You must be John, Helen's friend,' she said. She had a pleasant, fairly cultured voice, and she smiled at me in a kindly way. 'I'm Myra, her mother. Come in,' she added. 'Helen won't be long.'

'Thank you,' I answered.

Chalk and cheese, that was the difference between the Madden house and the Sykes house. In mine, you could never find anything, and cleaning was an irregular happening. The sagging furniture looked old and gloomy, and there were gaps in the ancient wallpaper. There was always a pile of dishes and cutlery awaiting Mum's attention, as well as heaps of washing. On the other hand, Helen's house was impeccably tidy, just like the garden. Everything seemed to have a place, the wooden floors gleamed, and there was a smell of polish. Somehow, I immediately sensed that it was a happy house, though why I thought that I had no idea.

I was led into the bright well-lit lounge room. It was furnished with two large settees facing each other and a couple of other chairs in the same upholstery. There were a variety of pictures on the walls, a large television at one end of the room, and an upright piano at the other, a nest of music sitting on its stool. As I entered, a man rose from an armchair and walked over to greet me. 'I'm Peter,' he said. Helen's father was the opposite of her mother. He was tall and a little gangling, and he looked down on me with sharp eyes that seemed to take in and assess everything about me. In fact, he seemed to tower over me as he shook my hand. Meanwhile, Myra had taken the flowers I'd brought and had gone out looking for a vase.

'Take a seat,' Pete instructed me, and I quickly obeyed. 'We like to meet all of Helen's friends, so it's good of you to come round and see us.'

'Of course,' I answered, not having a clue what to say.

'Helen tells me you are doing an apprenticeship and studying at her TAFE.'

'That's right. Motor mechanic.'

'Very sound choice. How's it going?'

'Well enough. Less than two years to go now.'

'And then what are your plans?'

That got me rattled a bit. I didn't really have any plans for the future. It was enough just to keep my nose clean for the present, but I realised I would need to say something that would raise my shares, make me a suitable escort for his daughter. 'Well,' I eventually answered, 'I would like to get into the maintenance of heavy earth-moving equipment. One day. Something like that.'

'And what does your father do?'

'Public transport,' I answered and was relieved when the door opened and Helen walked in, so I didn't have to expand on my reply. I jumped to my feet. She was looking ravishing, dressed in a short-skirted dress in various shades of green. I stared at her, frantically blushing and not wanting to tell her how fabulous she looked, at least not in front of her father. We just stood, both smiling at each other. I was hoping that we could say our goodbyes and leave as quickly as possible, preferably before I had to answer any more questions.

Just then, Myra also entered the room. 'Just look what John brought for you. Aren't they lovely?' she said, holding out the vase with the daffodils in. 'Oh,' said Helen, 'yes, they're beautiful. Thanks, John.' And she walked up to me, stretched up, and planted a kiss on my cheek. As she had come close to me, I experienced a waft of some delicate perfume that was distinctly provocative. By then, I must have been the colour of beetroot, but Myra immediately stepped in, wished us both a pleasant evening, and herded us out of the room.

As we left, Pete called out after us. 'Have her back by eleven, won't you?'

'Yes, of course,' I answered. 'Good to have met you both.'

'Come on,' said Helen, and she took my arm and ushered me out of the house.

As we walked down the path to my car, I wanted to tell Helen how absolutely gorgeous she looked and smelt, but I was unable to find the words to describe my feelings, so I remained silent. We reached my car, and Helen stopped dead.

'Is this it?' she asked, looking a bit worried.

'It's quite safe,' I said. 'It's got a roadworthy.'

'I didn't think they still made these cars.'

'They don't. It's fifteen years old, but I've done it up.'

'OK,' she said in a querying voice.

'New tyres, and I've overhauled the engine.'

'Clever you,' and she smiled at me.

'I'm actually quite proud of it.'

'As well you should be, John.' I unlocked the passenger side door and opened it for her. 'Thank you,' she said as she slid into the seat. She sat demurely with her small handbag on her lap as I went round to the other side and got in. 'I can see that you've been working on the interior as well,' she said. 'It's nice and wonderfully old-fashioned,' and she laughed. 'Now, where are you taking me?'

The movie we saw that evening was a sort of love story, a bit soppy to be honest, but Helen seemed to enjoy it. Afterwards, I suggested we try the pub across the road and get a bite to eat. 'Or perhaps you've already had your tea,' I suggested.

'Actually, no, I haven't,' she answered.

'OK, then.'

We walked across the road to the hotel. The bistro was busy, being a Saturday evening and still only a little after eight o'clock, but we found a table for two and settled down. I collected a couple of menus, and once Helen had decided what she wanted, I went to the counter and ordered, returning with our order number fitted into a stand. We sat for a while, not having much to say, then suddenly she looked at me with a frown.

'I don't understand you, John. I mean, you aren't like other boys I've been out with.'

'How so?'

'Well, you never tried to touch me, feel me up. Usually, when I'm sitting in the dark, in a cinema or wherever, with a boy, I'm having to fight him off. They're onto me like a rash.'

I didn't know what to say. I didn't dare tell her that all the way through the movie, I had been itching to put my hand on her leg or even just hold her hand, but every time I thought about it, I had started panicking, expecting a severe rebuff. 'Sorry,' I said eventually, and when I thought about it a bit more, I added, 'I suppose I've put you on a bit of a pedestal.'

'Oh, John, you mustn't do that.'

'I can't help it. Sorry.'

'And do stop saying sorry! I like you a lot, or I wouldn't be here. And I'm just a normal girl with no pretensions, not some "lady of the manor". So stop treating me like one.'

Again, I was at a loss for words. In, fact I was just about to say sorry again but just stopped myself in time. Instead, I looked down at her hands as they rested on the table between us, clasped together. They seemed to me very delicate, and she had painted her nails a soft shade of pink that I found enchanting. I had an irresistible urge to touch them, so I simply reached out a hand across the table and placed it over hers. She gripped my fingers tightly for a brief moment, smiled at me, then withdrew her hand. That brief touch was something I would never forget. It was then that I found my voice, my confidence returning, but, first, I had to make a confession. 'It may surprise you,' I said, 'but you are the first girl I've ever been out with, I mean on a date like this.'

'Wow!'

'So I'm not sure what to do.'

'Well, John, you're doing very well, then, considering.'

'Thanks, Helen. And I like you too, very much.' She smiled again as I spoke, and I noticed a very faint blush in her cheeks. Just then, she looked up. A waiter arrived with our plates of food, a bowl of fettuccine marinara for Helen and a chicken Parma for me. It was then that I realised that I'd completely forgotten to ask her if she'd like a drink from the bar. When I eventually got around to it, she just wanted a glass of water, and that suited me. Funds were running a bit low. While we were eating, the tension that I had been experiencing all evening started dissipating, and we were able to talk freely. She told me about her job at the TAFE and the difficulties she was having with other members of staff, and she told me about her parents, whom she loved, even though her father was rather uptight.

'My mother's eyesight is very poor,' she told me, 'so she struggles with everyday things.'

'That must be very difficult for you all,' I answered.

'We manage.' She paused, looking intently at me. 'So tell me about your family, John.'

'You don't want to know about *my* family.'

'Oh, I do. I want to know *all* about you.'

So I plucked up courage and told Helen about the dysfunction that ruled my life. I told her about my controlling father, his temper, his abuse, and my mother's subservience. I described something of the somewhat shambolic household I lived in, and I made a bit of a joke about my sister, Barb, and her novel method of breaking free from the family. I wasn't looking for any sympathy. I just wanted her to know a little bit of my background, even if it turned her away from me. She would have to know sometime if our budding relationship was to go anywhere.

She didn't speak for a full minute after I'd finished. She opened her mouth a couple of times as if about to say something but then seemed to think better of it. 'That's so awful,' she said at last. 'Thanks for telling me all this. Was your dad like that right through your childhood?'

'Much of it,' I answered.

'I mean, did he belt you up a lot?'

'Sometimes.'

'Oh, John,' she whispered, and she gave me a tender look that warmed me right through. 'As I said, my dad can be a bit uptight, and he's a bit of a snob sometimes, but he would never raise a hand to us. He's a lovely man underneath his stern nature.'

It was a happy evening for both of us, I think. We'd cleared the air a bit, and when we finally left, we held hands as we walked to my car. Holding hands was the ultimate contact for me on a first date, and I was elated as I drove her home. When we reached it, I parked the car and told her I would walk her up to the house. I quickly went round to her door and opened it for her.

'Thank you,' she said.

'My pleasure,' I replied.

'Always the gentleman,' she answered. 'That's one of the reasons I like you so much.'

'And I like to be appreciated,' I said, 'though I'm not sure I'll always be able to behave like a gentleman.'

'Don't worry. I enjoy a bit of spirit in a man'—she paused—'once I get to know him really well, that is.'

'I'd like to get to know you *really* well, Helen.'

'Me too,' she replied, giving me a coquettish grin. I took her hand in mine as we sauntered slowly up the path to her front door. It occurred to me that our conversation had marginally touched on our sexual expectations, and I was curious as to how far Helen would permit me to go. So, as we walked to her door, I wondered if I would be permitted a kiss. However, I didn't wish to impose myself on her, for I was still a little shy and didn't want to spoil the evening by doing something that one of us would later regret, much as though my physical longing was threatening to boil over. But as we reached her door, she turned up her face to me, and, after a moment's pause, she spoke to me in a whisper. 'Kiss me, John,' she said, so I did. That kiss unleashed a hunger in me that must have been building for some time. I had never kissed a girl in such a way, and I must have been somewhat clumsy in the way I did it. I rather lost control of myself, especially when I felt her breasts shoving into me. Finally, Helen broke away. She laughed quietly. 'Wow! That was some kiss,' she said, breathing heavily. 'Thank you.' And without another word, she rummaged in her bag for her key and opened the door.

'Goodnight,' I said once I had found my voice.

'Goodnight,' she answered. 'And thanks for a great evening.'

I sat in my car for a long time before driving home. I thought about our evening and its delightful culmination: that extravagant and erotic kiss, together with the electrifying sensation of her breasts pushing into my chest. And I thought that now, more than ever before, I was truly under Helen's spell and that I was even more determined to make her mine.

Further, as I approached my home, I reminisced about the conversation we'd had about my childhood. There were many things I *hadn't* told her about my early life. The worst memories were still all too raw. I didn't know if I would ever be ready to talk about them.

*   *   *

CHAPTER 3

1980—continued

It took me the rest of that year, the year in which I had met Helen, to fall in love with her, really fall in love like she was the only person in the world, the one person I wanted to spend the rest of my life with. What I thought was love when I'd *first* met Helen was, of course, unbridled lust, and it remained an unrequited lust. Our abstinence wasn't due to any lack of opportunity but rather on my part not knowing how to break the ice. On TAFE days, Helen and I spent just about every lunchtime together in the canteen, though sometimes in the summer and autumn, after we'd known each other a whole year and the sun was shining, we would walk out to the local park. There we would lie in the shade of a tree and eat the sandwiches we'd brought, and we'd kiss and talk and kiss some more. By then, I'd learnt to kiss gently, subtly, and Helen responded in the same way. But sex was out. Helen seemed to value her virginity, and if my hands should ever stray below her waist, she would gently move them away again. I was still not game to go against her wishes. But it was difficult. My body kept telling me that I was ready.

And we began spending many weekends together, but we always separated to our respective homes at night. Helen's parents became very friendly once they could see we were both serious about each other, and I spent many evenings round at her house, watching television or just talking. And, often, Myra would invite me to dinner. They had dinner at their house, not tea, so I had to remember the distinction and to call the evening meal by their preferred moniker. They never ate before 7.30, after the ABC news was finished, so I often got quite hungry waiting. Tea in the Madden house was usually around six o'clock, though it was a bit of a movable feast, depending on Dad's shifts or Mum's inclinations.

One evening, as I arrived at their front door, I heard the tinkling sound of the piano being played inside. I am not a very musical person and didn't particularly like the piece of music that was being played. However, I stood there for a time wondering which member of the family was the pianist.

Whoever it was, they kept stopping and then replaying a phrase a couple of times, trying to get it right, before continuing. When I'd had enough, I rang the bell. It gave a loud peal from somewhere in the house, and the music suddenly ceased. Helen herself opened the door. 'Oh. Hello, John,' she said as she gave me a quick kiss and then stood aside to let me in.

'Was it you playing?' I asked her.

'Yes. Just practising.'

'It was good.' In fact, I had no idea whether her playing was any good, but I felt it did no harm to give her praise. 'Don't let me interrupt you,' I added.

'It's OK. I was just about finished anyway.'

'How long have you been playing?' I asked her.

'I started learning at school.'

We walked into the lounge room, and she went to the piano to close the lid and return the music into the piano stool. Once again, I found myself admiring the comfort and orderliness of the room. Helen never came to my house, largely because I never invited her there. Somehow, I didn't think she'd fit in with the ad hoc way my parents lived. In fact, I thought she would be disgusted by the whole set-up, and frankly I was terrified she'd want to walk out on me if she saw our house and witnessed the goings-on.

One event that cemented my opposition to having her round had happened the previous year when, on Christmas Eve, my sister, Barb, and her husband, Paul, brought Florrie round. Dad had still not accepted the way she had left us, so my sister was still trying to make peace with him. Mum was happy to have the whole family around her, and I thought Florrie a rather cute as she looked around her in an enquiring manner. We hadn't been talking for more than a few minutes when she started getting fractious, and Barb decided that the child needed feeding. She undid her top, unhooked her bra, and moved it clear of her breasts. I had only once ever seen my sister topless, and then she was just a teenager and her breasts were quite small, but now they seemed enormous. And I had never witnessed a woman breastfeeding a baby, but Barb was entirely open about it and not in the least bit embarrassed. Unlike me. I tried to look away, not entirely successfully, and I couldn't help thinking about Helen, whose breasts I'd never been permitted to see.

Dad wasn't in the house at the time. He came in a bit later, slightly tipsy. He was, as usual, in a belligerent mood following a Christmas piss-up at work, one organised by his bosses. Barb was still feeding Florrie as Dad entered the lounge room, and he stopped dead when he saw her. Then he went absolutely crazy. 'What the fuck are you doing!' he shouted at her. 'You can't come in here waving your tits around. This isn't a brothel.'

Then Paul tried to mediate. 'She's only feeding our baby,' he ventured in a somewhat timid voice.

Dad rounded on him. 'It's gross. This is my house, and I won't have it.'

'It's OK, John,' said Mum. 'I agreed to let her.'

'You trying to turn us into a knocking shop?' he shouted at Mum.

'What's a knocking shop?' asked Paul.

Dad ignored the question but turned on him again. 'You seduce my daughter, carry her off, and then come here and try and tell me my business. Well, you can fuck off. You're not welcome.'

'And why not?' Barb asked him. Her voice was quiet, but her voice cut right through the hostility in the room. She spoke as if she really wanted to know the answer, but my father just looked at her, shaking his head. The tension lingered on, but suddenly there was a loud pop as Florrie, now replete, let go of Barb's nipple. Some of us giggled self-consciously when it happened, but Dad just looked daggers at everyone and stormed out. Paul and Barb left soon afterwards with Florrie, leaving me and Mum to enjoy what remained of our Christmas festivities. It was no wonder that I refused to let Helen witness scenes like this.

Helen's birthday was on September 20, and so her twenty-first was later in that first year of our acquaintance. By then, we had got to know each other well, and I asked her what she would be doing to mark the occasion. Evidently, her father had booked a local church hall for the evening, and he promised that some of his fellow officers would be on hand to prevent any gatecrashers or bad behaviour, as he put it. And he had hired a band for dancing and a catering firm to look after both solid and liquid refreshments. Helen was an only child, so her parents wanted to make a big show of it.

I managed to persuade Helen's parents to allow me to pick her up from home and take her to the hall in my car. 'On one condition,' decreed Peter. 'I want to check on you at the end, make sure you're safe to drive her home. So you'd better not drink too much.'

'Fair enough,' I replied. He was very protective of his daughter. I liked that. Actually, I wasn't a heavy drinker anyway and never became one. I had suffered too often from Dad's drunken rages, and on the only occasion when I had become quite tipsy, I had thrown up on the way home. Helen was, as usual, looking a dream when I picked her up for the party. She was dressed in an ankle-length white dress with a low neckline that looked a bit like a wedding dress, and she wore a necklace made of some glittery stuff that matched her beautiful eyes. I told her that she looked so gorgeous that she would light up the evening. She smiled at me as I took her hand. 'Thank you, John,' she said. 'That was quite poetic.'

Her parents had gone on ahead to check everything was ready, and by the time we arrived, most of the guests were already there, and the band was tuning up. There were two burly-looking cops in plain clothes guarding the door, and they greeted Helen with big smiles. I was feeling pretty nervous as, hand in hand, we entered. Immediately, the band became silent, except for the drummer, who started playing an extravagant drum roll. The guests broke into applause as Myra came up to us and led us to our places at their table.

The hall had been decorated with streamers and flowers, and it looked very festive. The tables surrounding the dance floor were also decorated with colourful tablecloths and small vases of flowers, and a big silver "21" hung from the ceiling over the band stand. There was a bar at the opposite end of the hall from the band. A queue of people wishing to order drinks was already forming in front of an overworked barman. We had no sooner sat down than the band started playing.

'You and I must lead off the dancing,' Helen told me.

'Do I have to?'

'Yes, you do. Come on,' and she rose to her feet, grabbed my hand, and dragged me up. I felt very exposed, having everyone's eyes on me, watching my every move and my relative ineptitude as a dancer. But my embarrassment didn't last long. Helen made up for my failings, and the floor quickly filled.

After an hour, the meal was served. Up to that time, there had been a swarm of men, some of my age but many a lot older, all wanting to dance with Helen. Frankly, I was getting a little uncomfortable with all the attention she was getting, quite annoyed in fact. After all, she was *my* girlfriend, but I was getting sidelined. Over the meal, she came and sat with me, and Peter gave a lovely speech between courses, full of praise for his daughter, interspersed with accounts of her youthful foibles. During her father's speech, Helen held my hand under the table. I felt a little better after that, but once the band had restarted, the queue of dance partners reformed, and my irritation increased as the evening progressed. Peter had bought us a bottle of wine, which we'd all shared over the meal. There was still a little bit left, so I helped myself and finished it.

At midnight, the last dance was called. Helen came over to me and beckoned me to join her, but I just shook my head. 'Ask one of your other boyfriends,' I told her. She just looked at me; her face said it all. It was full of pain and humiliation. I realised that I'd spoken to her in a resentful way and that I'd hurt her feelings, but I didn't care. She'd hurt mine. She'd ignored me most of the evening, and I wanted her to see my indignation. Anyway, she just came and sat next to me, refusing to say anything. We remained silent until the band finished the last number with a big flourish from the drummer. Then Helen got up and went touring the other tables, saying her farewells as other guests began to leave. Her parents had also left the table and were standing at the door, shaking hands with people as they left. I continued to sit, wondering at myself, thinking that maybe I had been a bit harsh, but somehow, when Helen finally reappeared, I found I couldn't apologise.

On the way home, we maintained a resolute silence, and our rift lasted until we turned into Helen's street. Then she suddenly turned to me. 'Why are you being so perverse, John? What the hell's got into you?'

As soon as she spoke, I pulled into the side of the road and stopped. 'You ignored me all evening,' I said, turning to her.

'That's nonsense. Of course, I didn't.'

'You must have danced with every man in the place.'

'Are you jealous or something?'

'Of course not,' I claimed, though, of course, I was.

'Well, it was *my* twenty-first. The people I danced with are all friends of the family, people I've grown up with. You've no right to dictate to me.' She paused, and I could see a tear forming in her eye as she turned away. 'Now take me home, will you?' she added quietly, her voice breaking. 'You've spoilt my whole evening.'

Helen and I had made arrangements for the following weekend, but I decided to give it a miss. I somehow still felt distanced from her, feeling that if I gave her time, she would come round and see my point of view. Instead, I went off to visit my friend Hudson. He was now studying with me at TAFE but was doing a different course, something to do with IT.

Consequently, we saw little of each other during the day. He had stayed at school right through to year twelve and had done very well in his final exams.

He and I continued to keep in touch, though I'd seen little of him for the last year and a half, firstly while I worked on my car and latterly while my attentions had been focused on Helen. The times that I did visit his home were usually occasions when I felt the need to get away from the ill feelings and anxiety at home. Sometimes, I even had meals there at his house, and this time, Hudson's mother again asked me if I'd like to stay for tea. After we'd eaten, he asked me up to his bedroom for a chat. 'I've always wanted to ask you something, Johnny,' he said somewhat tentatively. 'What's it like, you know, having sex?'

I was startled by such a question. 'I've no idea,' I answered eventually.

'What! Don't you and Helen have a screw every now and again?'

'No.'

'Christ. Why not?'

'She doesn't want to, that's all.'

'Doesn't she fancy you enough?' he asked.

'I think she does, but I'm not sure.'

'But you do love *her*, don't you?'

'Of course, I do.'

'And have you told her you love her?'

'Not really.'

'Oh, Johnny, you sound really undecided.' I didn't say anything, and Hudson continued to dissect my relationship. 'Anyway, perhaps she's just religious or something.'

'I don't think so.'

'You don't seem to know much about her,' he said, shaking his head. 'Perhaps she just wants to get married first,' he added. 'Have you popped the question yet?'

'No.'

'Shit, Johnny, you're fucking slow. She's stunning. You should grab her before someone else does.'

'I want to be qualified before I can support a wife.'

'But that doesn't stop you from making plans.'

'I guess not,' I answered. 'Anyway, I don't think we'll ever get married.'

'Why not?'

So I told him about the tiff we'd had at her twenty-first. 'She spent the whole evening dancing with other guys, left me sitting there like a spare part.'

'Well, whose party was it?'

'Hers, I guess.'

'Well, then, get real, Johnny. You should be proud of her, the way she got all the attention, not complaining about it.'

'Maybe,' I said. 'Yes, I suppose that's one way of looking at it.'

'It's the only way, Johnny. You'll lose a lovely lady if you don't look out.'

I felt a bit uncomfortable talking to Hudson like this. It was all too personal and not something I should be discussing with him, even if he is my best friend. I had often thought that I should have been more persistent with Helen, but I'd let her take the lead and hadn't pushed the issue of sex. People, Hudson included, seemed to assume that because we were together so much, we must be lovers. That made me even more sure that I was missing out on life.

That conversation with Hudson weighed on my mind, and I realised I would have to apologise one day, and the sooner the better. Even though Hudson had no more experience with women than I'd had, he made me feel that I had a lot to learn. I did love Helen. In my moments of introspection, I had often visualised our being together for a lifetime of happiness, but I didn't know if I was clutching at straws. I *had* put her on a pedestal, and I was terrified she was not as committed to our relationship as I was. There was only one way to find out, even if I lost her in the process of declaring myself. I'd eat humble pie, buy her a bunch of roses, and write her a letter of contrition to go with it. I'd go round and leave it with her mother one day when I knew Helen would be at work. And I'd have to explain my non-appearance at the weekend. So I penned the letter, telling her that I now realised how spiteful I had been at her twenty-first, how awful I felt afterwards, knowing how badly I had behaved towards her, and asking for her forgiveness. Then I told her that I had fallen sick, which was why I hadn't been able to keep our date, and finally begging to see her again soon. It took a lot of time, soul-searching, and torn-up copies of my letter before I felt I'd finally gotten it right. I didn't tell her that I loved her. I wanted to tell her that to her face at an opportune moment. The sickness was, of course, a lie, but she was hardly likely to check up on me. I left the workshop one lunchtime, hopped in my car, and took the roses and the letter round to Helen's house. Her mum answered the door.

'Oh, hello, John,' she'd said. 'We were all wondering what had happened to you.' Her voice was a little unfriendly to say the least. 'What can I do for you?'

'Sorry, Mrs Sykes, I ....'

'Do call me Myra.'

'Yes, sorry, Myra, I was sick and couldn't make it.'

'Oh, dear. Are you better now?'

'Yes, thanks. Please, would you mind passing these on to Helen for me?'

'Certainly, John.' She sniffed the roses, then looked up at me. 'Lovely scent,' she said. 'Are you not at TAFE today?'

'Not till Tuesday next week now,' I'd replied. She'd already gone in and shut the door as I'd turned away and left.

And now it was Tuesday. I was on tenterhooks. I had no idea what Helen's reaction would be, and I would have to wait until lunchtime before I'd have the chance to see her. But perhaps she might not come to the canteen. I was half hoping she wouldn't be there so I wouldn't have to meet her. At the same time, I knew I had to get it over with.

She *was* there, sitting at a table on her own, though she had no lunch in front of her. She must have seen me as I walked in the door. She stood up as I walked over to her. She was looking as gorgeous as ever, but her face was expressionless. I couldn't decipher how she felt about me from her looks or what her reaction would be when I approached her. She continued to stare into my face, and I wanted to tell her how lovely she was, but I was too overcome with emotion to say anything. We stood facing each other for a time, and then she spoke. 'Let's go outside. There are too many people in here.' I didn't answer but followed her out into the garden. 'I liked the roses, John. They were lovely. Thanks.' She seemed a little stiff, formal almost. We sat on the steps outside the canteen. The atmosphere between us seemed to be thawing, just a little, and I was beginning to hope that I'd been forgiven. 'Now, John, your letter.'

'Yes,' I said, hoping for the best.

'Did you really *mean* everything you said?'

'Everything.'

'Well, I hope so. I don't approve of lies,' she said sternly.

'I promise you, I meant every last word.'

Helen didn't say anything for a time, and I, too, remained silent, wondering what else I could say to make things right between us. When she spoke again, her voice was softer, more pensive. 'Do you realise how angry you made me that night?'

'I'm sorry, Helen. I wasn't thinking straight.'

'I didn't tell you beforehand, but I had arranged a surprise for you after the party.' I again remained silent, so she continued. 'I'd planned to give myself to you that night, if you know what I mean.'

'I'm not sure I do,' I said.

'I was going to …. you know, invite you upstairs after the party.'

'Oh.'

'I obviously needed to get my parents' permission, and when I broached the subject, my father wasn't at all happy about the idea. I wanted to be completely open with them, not sneak you in behind their backs.' I remained silent, absorbed in my disappointment over the lost opportunity. 'I told them that if they didn't agree, I'd just have to take you somewhere else, to a motel or something, if you weren't welcome in my room, and they finally relented.'

'I never realised that you loved me enough to do that.'

'Perhaps I didn't, but I loved you enough to take a chance on you.'

'Oh, Helen.'

'Now I'm twenty-one, I can do what I like, within reason. I could before, but I feel I've passed a milestone. I can do what I want with my body now, and I wanted a life with you. After your behaviour at the party, I was no longer so sure. You'd gone and spoilt everything.'

I was awestruck by her admission of love but felt contrite regarding my behaviour and the effect that it had had on her feelings and on her beguiling proposal. She must have found it so difficult to pursue her plan when confronted by Peter's initial objections. In the past few days, following my conversation with Hudson, I had been rehearsing in my mind what I would say to Helen about my feelings when the time arrived. I could wait no longer. The time was here, my win-or-lose moment. I spoke carefully. 'You do realise, don't you,' I said, my voice beginning to shake with emotion, 'that I have loved you for a long time, but I've been too afraid to say anything. As you know, I come from a very working class family, and I was terrified that if I told you how I felt, you would just laugh at me. I'm aware that you accepted me just as I am, and I remember you telling me never to put you on a pedestal, but I can't change the way I feel about you. I guess I just don't know how to say what's on my mind sometimes. Or show you how I feel. I'm sorry I've made such a hash of it.'

She stared at me for a time with a quizzical expression. 'You really must stop running yourself down, John. You are not some "down and out" that I've been befriending, and I do not consider my family any better than yours.' I didn't say anything, and after a few moments, she continued. 'You made your point, but I can assure you that I have been aware of your feelings for a long time. And I have reciprocated them.' Helen had largely put my mind at ease, and I took her hand in mine. 'So, you do love me?' I queried.

She squeezed my hand and smiled. 'I did, and I can do so again.'

'That's all I can ask for now.'

'Look me in the eye, John, and tell me truthfully. Do you really love me, or do you just want to sleep with me?'

'Actually, I want to marry you, eventually, so I can do both,' I answered with a grin.

She sighed and shook her head. 'I'm not thinking of marriage yet. Just give me a bit more time, enough time to get over my hurt, and the time I need for you to prove your love for me.'

'I understand—I'm on probation.' I realised that I would have to be careful how I asked the obvious question. 'In the meantime, can we reconnect?' I said. 'You know, start again?'

'Yes, of course,' she answered. 'Come round tonight and make your peace with my parents. They could tell how upset I was after the party and thought it must be your fault.'

'So it could be a bit hairy?'

'Yes, it could.'

'No worries. I'll be there at six.'

The atmosphere in the Sykes household was somewhat strained to start with that evening, but when Helen greeted me with a kiss in front of her parents, they began to loosen up. I was grateful to Helen for doing that, and I felt that I no longer needed to apologise to them for my behaviour at the party. It was now a closed subject. I was soon accepted into the family circle, and in the end, we all had a pleasant evening.

'Would you like to stay for dinner, John?' Myra asked me.

'I would, thank you.' I had told Mum that I was hoping for such an invitation, so I wasn't expected at home till late.

'I hope you like curry,' she added.

'Yes, indeed.'

We sat together in companionable silence watching the ABC news, and after the weather forecast, we all trooped into dinner. The Sykes household didn't drink wine at meals except at weekends, for which I was grateful. There would have been nothing worse than me getting tipsy just as I was working my way back into the fold. I really needed to keep my wits about me. After the meal, Helen and I had a chance to have a bit of time alone together. It appeared that I'd been forgiven, she told me, and accepted back into the family. I felt much better. We made arrangements to meet again at the weekend. We would take in a movie and a meal, just as we had done on our first date, and I hoped I wouldn't be quite as gauche this time around.

The Saturday evening outing went as well as I had hoped, and at the end of it, Helen and I kissed at her front door. I knew that it wasn't time yet for me to push my luck, so I didn't feel her up or anything like that. But she was definitely more relaxed, and we agreed to meet again in the morning and go for a drive. She said she would organise a picnic. Perhaps we could go down to a beach somewhere and have a swim. 'Sounds good,' I said, "but I never learnt to swim.'

'My goodness me,' she replied. 'Really?'

'My parents never took me to the beach or a swimming pool, so I never had the chance.'

'You should learn, John. Everyone should.' I remained silent, slightly embarrassed by my confession. 'So, you won't have a cossie?' she added.

'A what?'

'A swimming costume.'

'No.'

'Tell you what,' she added, 'you get yourself a pair during next week, and the following weekend, we'll go to the pool and I'll teach you to swim. How's that?'

'Sounds good, as long as you don't drown me.'

'I'll try not to,' and she laughed. 'The weather's warming up now, and the pools have been open for a month.'

We still went to the beach on Saturday, however. It was a lovely cloudless day, and by eleven o'clock, it was getting hot. We drove to a place near Rye, down on the Mornington Peninsula. It was a beach that was largely deserted. Helen had a very sexy blue-and-white bikini, which she had put on under her outer clothes, and before we had our picnic lunch, she slipped off her dress. Then she tucked her blonde curls into her bathing cap, ran down the beach, and plunged into the waves. At that stage, I had never seen her in anything so scanty, and I was visibly aroused, though luckily she didn't seem to notice. I kicked off my sandals and followed her down to the water. There was little wind, and the waves were minimal. I paddled in the shallows as I watched her swimming. She went a fair way out before returning to shore, and by the time she had emerged, my body had settled down. She rubbed herself down with her beach towel before laying it down on the sand and lying on her back to soak up the sun.

I couldn't take my eyes off her. 'You look a treat,' I told her.

'Thanks, but it's still looking only.'

'As long as you don't *mind* me looking.'

She just laughed. 'Are you hungry?'

'I'm always hungry,' I answered, staring at her body.

'I noticed,' she said, laughing even more. 'Anyway, I think we should eat before the sun dries out our sandwiches. I've made us egg and cheese, and there's plenty of fruit.'

After our meal, we put everything back in the car and went for a walk along the beach. The sand was now too hot for bare feet, but the tide was on its way out, so there was an area of wet sand to walk on. I took her hand in one of mine and held my sandals in the other. She looked up at me and smiled. Helen looked so absolutely adorable that I stopped dead in my tracks. I put my arms around her and gave her a long and deeply satisfying kiss. Then we walked on. She looked happy and contented, and I realised we were over the worst of our troubles.

The following week, I kept imagining myself swimming alongside Helen, splashing around together in the waves, then meeting up, holding hands, looking into each other's eyes, and kissing. But, first, I would have to learn how to swim. I went shopping for a pair of trunks and at the same shop bought myself a large, colourful beach towel. On Saturday morning, I collected Helen and drove to the local pool. When I emerged from the change room, I was shivering, though not from the cold.

Helen was waiting for me. 'Are you nervous, John?'

'Yes,' I admitted. I saw that Helen had a different costume on, not the bikini but a one-piece that covered a lot more of her. That was undoubtedly a good thing.

'You won't drown,' she promised.

While we were still on dry land, she made me move my arms as though

I was doing the breast stroke. Then we headed down to the shallow end, and I followed Helen down the steps. She grabbed my hand and walked me up the pool till the water was past our waists. 'Now lie down in the water, on your front, while I hold you under your middle. Then move your arms like I showed you.' I just had to trust that she wouldn't let me go. I got into position, feeling her arms supporting me, and tried moving my arms as she had taught me. 'Now move your legs in the same way,' she instructed me.

I felt a bit embarrassed. A number of people were standing on the side of the pool, staring at my efforts, probably wondering why a grown man needed such a basic lesson. I was determined to get it right, and once I had the rhythm, I felt Helen slowly loosening her hold on me. I started panicking and swallowed a mouthful of water. I got back on my feet, choking from the chlorine. The second time we tried the same procedure, I found myself actually making progress towards the side of the pool. When I reached it, I heard clapping from the onlookers. Helen joined in. She made me swim the width of the pool a couple more times before she was satisfied.

'There you go,' she said. 'You can swim. It's not difficult, is it?'

'I guess not,' I replied.

'Next, you must try freestyle.' She showed me the hand and arm movements and how I should try and move my feet. Then she swam across the pool and back, showing me how to breathe. 'You won't get it all the first time you try, but I'll support you again while you give it a go.' We spent another half hour while I attempted to emulate my teacher. By the end, I thought I'd mastered it a bit better, though, of course, I was far from swimming either as fast or as smoothly as Helen. I decided we'd had enough for one session, so we called it a day.

We repeated our excursion to the pool every Saturday morning for a month. I gained in confidence and skill, and by early December, I could manage two complete lengths of the pool. I even learnt to dive. I was no longer frightened of the deep end or opening my eyes and swimming under water. Helen and I started having a lot of fun together, swimming between each other's legs and diving into the pool in tandem. 'You've passed all your tests,' she said to me one morning. 'Now we must go back to the sea and swim among the waves.'

'You must wear your bikini again, then.'

'For you, of course,' and she laughed heartily.

So we repeated our trip to the beach near Rye. I was hoping that it would be just as deserted as last time, but it was crowded, and even parking was at a premium. However, I was at least now able to join her as she mixed with the throng of other swimmers. Afterwards, we drove home full of sun. Helen put her hand on my knee and looked at me with a contented smile. 'John,' she said, 'what are you doing over Christmas?'

'I hadn't thought much about it,' I replied.

'Would you like to go away somewhere? Maybe for a few days.'

'With you?'

'That's the general idea.'

The road was thick with cars returning from the peninsula after the weekend, and I nearly ran into the one in front of me when I realised what she was suggesting. 'Sounds great,' I said.

'I've booked a motel room just outside Cowes.'

'Wow!' I could hardly believe my ears. 'Phillip Island. I've never been there.'

'The second Tuesday in January. Just for three nights. Can you get leave?'

'Don't worry. I'm due for three whole weeks.'

'What about your parents?' she asked me.

'They won't mind.'

'I think I should meet them, don't you?'

'My father's a bit of a tyrant.'

'I'd still like to meet them.'

'OK,' I said, though I was not happy at the prospect. Then I thought of something else. 'Does this mean I'm totally forgiven?' I asked her.

'Yes, it does.'

*   *   *

CHAPTER 4

1981

It was late morning as we drove out through Tooradin and headed towards Phillip Island. I thought back to the evening, just before Christmas, when I had introduced Helen to my parents. I had no wish to introduce her to the abject conditions we lived in at home, not while there was still a chance that she could change her mind about me, so I had arranged for the four of us to meet for a meal at the local RSL club. I'd been told that the food at RSL clubs was always good and not too expensive. I had hoped that Dad would moderate his drinking and would refrain from his normal rudeness.

'So you're John's lady friend,' he'd said to Helen on being introduced. 'Often wondered what you look like,' he'd continued. 'John's been rabbiting on about you for months. He's chosen well, hasn't he, Flo?' he added, turning to Mum. In fact, Dad was quite stricken with Helen and didn't seem able to contain his effusiveness but talked to her most of the evening. And he seemed content with a couple of beers. Mum hardly spoke at all the whole evening but smiled at Helen a lot and seemed very grateful to be included, though she didn't eat much of her dinner. We had parted company at around nine o'clock, and I had called a taxi to take my parents home. I had wanted to have Helen to myself for a time. As I drove her home, I told her that I'd thought the evening had turned out pretty well.

'I can't think why you say your father is a tyrant,' she'd said.

'It's when he's on the booze,' I answered. 'He was on his best behaviour tonight.'

'A bit of a rough diamond, I thought. That's all.'

I'd let it pass. The last thing I wanted to do was to have an argument with Helen, let alone detail the worst of his intemperate behaviour. So when we'd reached her house, I'd simply walked her up to her door, where we'd exchanged some passionate kisses before saying goodnight.

Helen had brought sandwiches, so halfway down, we'd stopped at the side of the road for lunch. We had driven on, all the way down to the Phillip

Island turn-off when Helen spoke her thoughts. I guess we had probably both been thinking about our first night together, how it would pan out. It was a prospect about which I was highly excited but equally nervous. I was wondering how she felt about it.'Are you still a virgin, John?' she suddenly asked me.Helen was always very outspoken, but this was right out of the blue. 'Yes, I am,' I admitted.'I've always guessed as much.' She paused a moment. 'I'm not.'

'Oh,' I said, a little surprised. 'That I *didn't* guess.'

'I hope it doesn't matter to you.'

'Why should it?'

'Well, some men seem to want their women to be pure and innocent,' she replied.

'And you're no longer the virginal little girl I imagined you were.' Helen laughed at the way I spoke. 'Do you want to tell me about it?' I added.

'Yes, I should. It may help to explain a few things.'

'Like what?'

'Like why I've perhaps seemed a little cold towards you sometimes or not permitted you to touch me in places where I know that you've wanted to.' I reached out and put my hand on her leg but didn't say anything, and she eventually continued. 'It all happened about five years ago, when I was in year ten. There was a boy in year twelve I'd gotten to know. He seemed nice enough, and I was starting to get an interest in boys, so when he invited me to his house, I accepted. I thought I was going to meet his parents, but they'd gone out. I realise now that he knew they were out and that he'd therefore have the house to himself. Anyway, he took me upstairs to his bedroom. I was petrified. I had no idea what to do and little idea what *he* was going to do.'

'I can guess what's coming,' I said.

'I struggled, but it was no use. He was much too strong for me. He pushed me onto his bed, pulled off my panties, and raped me. There was no loving, no affection of any sort, no lead up. He hurt me badly. I felt so used.'

'That's terrible. Did you tell your parents?'

'I didn't dare. And when my next period was a couple of days late, I was terrified. But, luckily, it did arrive eventually. I never felt more relieved.'

'I bet. What a total bastard.'

'He left school afterwards. Apparently, I wasn't the first, or the last, and someone finally dobbed him in.'

'Good riddance, I say.'

She looked up at me with a concerned expression. 'You'd never do anything like that to me, would you, John?'

'Of course not.'

We were silent again for a long time, and then Helen spoke again. 'You know, I don't have to worry about pregnancy now. I'm on the pill.'

'That's good,' I said, feeling very relieved but thinking about the dozen condoms I'd brought and would no longer be needing.

'I've always loved the idea of sex, even dreamt of it, especially after hearing from friends at work what a joyful experience it can be, but that schoolgirl episode left me frightened of men. Perhaps you'll understand me better now.'

'Of course.'

'I started taking the pill before my twenty-first, just in case.' She paused a moment. 'For you actually.' I ignored the implied criticism of my behaviour that evening, but, more than ever before, I now understood the extent of her disappointment and the rejection she must have felt. 'You must treat me gently, John. You will do, won't you?'

'I will try.' I had never known Helen to sound so vulnerable. She always seemed to be so totally in charge of everything round her, so confident of her abilities, always on top of everything. She was the one who had arranged this holiday, and here I was almost feeling sorry for her.

By this time, we were driving down the main street of Cowes. 'Turn left here,' Helen instructed. 'There's the place, on the right, the Princes Motel.'

I pulled into the parking area in front of the Reception sign, and we went in together to fill in the register. 'Room 15,' said the young lady as she handed me the key. I saw her glance at Helen's hand. 'Are you not married?' she asked.

'Not yet,' I answered. 'Is that a problem?'

'Sorry. Of course not,' and I could see her blushing as she turned away.

Back in the car, I drove on and parked outside number 15. Helen was smiling to herself. 'Not yet,' she echoed my words. 'You haven't even asked me yet.'

'Well, no, I haven't.' I paused, thinking that now's my chance. 'OK, then,' I said, 'will you marry me?'

Helen looked at me, a serious expression now on her face. 'I love you John, but I can't answer that, not yet.'

We grabbed our bags and went in. The first thing I noticed was the queen-size bed, which seemed to take up half the room. I'd always slept in a single bed at home, so this one looked enormous. The room was painted a rather grubby cream colour. There was a television set attached high up on the wall opposite the bed and, below that, a counter long enough to put our bags on. It had a small cupboard underneath with a kettle, cups, and saucers. Next to it was an even smaller fridge that was empty except for a minute carton of milk. And there was just enough room for one easy chair and small tables on either side of the bed. A door led through to a tiny bathroom that had just enough space for a basin, shower, and toilet.

Helen looked a little saddened as she watched me surveying the room and its facilities. 'I couldn't afford anything better,' she said.

'It's quite opulent compared to our house,' I replied. 'Anyway, I don't expect you to pay for everything. We should go halves.'

'Fair enough. We'll sort it all out later.'

'What do you want to do first?' I asked her.

'Same as you,' she replied, laughing, 'but I think we should first explore the town. Go on down to the beach. Then it'll be time to find something to eat.'

It was quite a long way to the beach. We passed a number of quite posh restaurants and a couple of cheaper-looking cafes that looked suitable, one of which we decided to revisit later. But, first, we walked onto the Cowes pier. We watched a small ferry arrive and then leave again on its way back to French Island and Stoney Point. We explored the beach in both directions and sat for a while on the sand. Then it was time to return to our cafe.

It was only a little after seven when we got back to the motel. It was still broad daylight and hardly bedtime, though I was more than ready. Luckily, Helen seemed to agree; the moment we were in the door, she gave me a kiss and said she was going to have a shower. She was in there a long time, at least ten minutes after the sound of water ceased, but eventually she emerged. She was wearing only her bra and knickers but glowing and smelling incredibly seductive.

'Your turn,' she said. 'I need a bit of time on my own.'

I didn't ask why. Some sort of women's business, I guessed. So I had my shower, and afterwards, I put on a new pair of boxer shorts. I had no idea what I should be wearing on such an occasion, but I thought boxers were a reasonable choice. I wondered if the women's business was complete, so I opened the bathroom door only slightly and called out, 'Can I come in now?'

'Of course, silly.' Helen was sitting up in bed. She was now wearing a lemon-coloured nightie that showed a deep cleavage. I could feel my body responding. She smiled at me and patted the bed next to her. What happened next is a bit of a blur in my memory. I remember slipping into bed with her, leaning over, and kissing her. I pushed my shorts down to the bottom of the bed. Then she pulled me over her. She was a bit tense, and she was shaking. She had her eyes shut, and she had a slightly worried look on her face as I scouted her body. My emotions were so pent up with excitement that when I eventually managed to find the right place, I immediately ejaculated. It was embarrassing.

'Gee, that was quick,' she whispered, giggling to herself. She sounded quite unconcerned.

'Sorry. I couldn't stop myself,' I muttered. 'I should clean up a bit.' I started climbing out of bed to fetch a towel, but she stopped me.

'You mustn't worry,' she said. 'Premature ejaculation can happen to anyone the first time.' I was surprised that she knew so much about men. 'Just calm down,' she added. 'Then we'll try again.' She sat up and lifted her nightie over her head, exposing to me for the first time her fabulous body. When she lay down again, she took my hand and moved it onto her breast. Just the sight of her naked body and the feel of her nipple under my hand had me aroused again very quickly. By now, she was more relaxed, though she still seemed anxious and her body remained tensed. Her eyes opened wide as I once again moved over her and found the spot. I tried to enter her gently, but she flinched slightly as I did so. I imagined that she was still thinking about the boy from her school and the pain of her first sexual encounter, but suddenly she smiled up at me and relaxed completely. 'That feels so good,' she said. She tightened her arms around me and pulled me deeper into her. This time, it took me much longer, but once again I felt the pressure mounting. So I stilled my body for a few moments before slowly moving once more. I heard her breathing speed up as she gave little cries of pleasure. I realised I had once again passed the point of no return and couldn't hold back. I erupted even more powerfully than the first time. Helen looked lovingly up at me, her eyes wide and sparkling.

'That was beautiful.' she said. 'I love you, darling.'

She had never called me darling before. It sounded so right. 'And I love you too,' I responded, 'my lover,' I added, kissing her deeply as we snuggled down in each other's arms.

It was now quite dark outside. We lay there together for what seemed a long time, still clutching each other. It was such a strange new feeling having Helen lying naked next to me. I was almost overcome with the joy of it. There had been so many times that I had envisaged such a blissful union, and there were times when I had thought it would never happen.

We spent the next two days exploring the island. We visited the wildlife park, walking around the various exhibits, and were particularly intrigued by a couple of baby wombats that appeared out of an underground lair and started playing. There were many different types of kangaroos, some of which stared at us, totally unconcerned by our presence. One evening, we visited the penguins, watching them waddling ashore after their day out at sea. There was a busload of Japanese tourists sitting with us on the tiered seats, and though everyone had been told not to use flash with their cameras, for fear of frightening the little animals, the Japanese completely ignored the instruction, much to everyone else's indignation.

On our last afternoon, we decided to return to the Cowes beach for a swim. Helen was wearing her sexy bikini again, and I saw a few of the other bathers ogling her. When we came out of the water, we spread our towels and lay on our backs to dry off. I must have dozed off, and when I partially surfaced, I could feel Helen's hand touching the front of my bathers. I realised she wasn't just touching me but gently rubbing me. I woke fully and turned to her. 'Somebody will see us,' I chided.

'John, darling,' she whispered, 'I've got the hots.'

So had I by then. 'Let's go,' I said.

We jumped to our feet, quickly gathered our possessions, and ran to the car. I heard a man's voice behind me, 'Where's the fire?' followed by a woman's laughter. I drove back to the motel rather faster than was entirely safe and nearly collected an old codger who was jaywalking across the road in front of us. He gave us a two-fingered salute as I beeped him, and Helen started giggling. In fact, she was still giggling when we arrived at number 15, and I was laughing too. It became a race to see who could get undressed first, and even though she had two pieces of clothing to remove, to my one, she beat me by a second. We were still laughing, and it took a couple of minutes of kissing and fondling before we could be serious.

After our first two nights of intimacy, we were getting more used to each other's body language, and this time, there was no gentleness about our lovemaking. Helen was more than ready for me as I plunged into her with little warning. Almost immediately, I felt her body stiffen, then spasm as she gave out a loud cry. I thought I must have hurt her in some way, but as she relaxed again, she had the most beatific smile on her face. 'Wow,' she said. 'That really *was* quick,' she added, echoing her earlier comment.

'Did you come?' I asked her.

'And how,' she replied, 'I've often played down there on my own, but it was never as good as that.' I knew very little about the female orgasm, but I felt proud of myself having the ability to produce such ecstasy. 'Now it's your turn,' she said once she'd got her breath back. So I continued moving, slowing down when I felt I was getting close, then speeding up again. It was something new to me, this control of my body. Helen continued little cries of pleasure, until eventually I could wait no longer.

We didn't go out again that night but remained with our arms around each other in a tight embrace. We watched the light slowly fade outside, and I was nearly asleep when I heard Helen's sleepy voice. 'I never did answer your question.' I hadn't heard her properly, so I asked her to repeat what she'd said. 'That question you asked me when we arrived, I never answered.'

'So?'

She turned to face me. 'The answer is, yes, darling, I *will* marry you.'

'That's great,' I said, 'but why couldn't you answer on Tuesday?'

'I wanted to be sure we were compatible.'

'Like in bed?'

'I feel it's so important.'

'Yes, I'm sure it is,' I said, but I don't know if she heard my last sentence. She was breathing steadily by then. While Helen slept, I remained awake for another ten minutes or so. I think it was about that time that I began to have second thoughts—well, not exactly second thoughts, more a reassessment of my life. Yes, the sex was good. In fact, it was bloody marvellous, even better than I had expected or hoped, but Helen was my first experience. Wouldn't sex be great no matter whom I was with? And wasn't I bit young to make such a life-changing decision? Next month, I would be twenty; my life was still in front of me.

And there was another thing that was worrying me. Helen had been entirely free with her body, not in the least bit shy when parading her nakedness in front of me. She welcomed me in and was quite comfortable when I suggested trying different positions, but I sensed that there was a line in the sand and that there were things she would never allow in our sex life. There were acts that were permissible and others that were not. She had once or twice dismissed certain acts as perverted and had stopped me going any lower when I brushed my lips over her stomach. I had obtained many ideas from watching porn videos and had been hoping to try them, but I soon realised they were not welcome.

Then I thought how much I loved her, that it was my idea, my wish to have her as my wife from almost the first moment I had met her. These were still early days, so perhaps, in time, she would come round to my way of thinking. My doubts receded, and I was finally able to get to sleep.

The next day, we returned home. On the way, we made a plan that I would drop Helen off at her house and then return at six o'clock, when her parents would both be there so we could jointly tell them about our engagement. And then we would go out the following day to buy a ring.

'What's your parents' reaction going to be like?' I asked her.

'They'll be fine. They like you. What about your parents?'

'Mum will be happy. Don't know about my father.'

'Anyway, I don't want you to put any money towards our holiday,' she said. 'Keep it and use it for the ring.'

When we reached her house, we had one more lingering kiss. Then I carried her bag up to her front door, where we had another. I returned to the car, and we waved as she disappeared inside. I drove home and parked in the road outside our house. Our garage used to be full of junk, but I had managed to get rid of enough of the old broken furniture, defunct white goods, and other bits and pieces that were there so that I could squeeze my car inside. But for now, I'd left it in the road as I would need it later. I grabbed my bag and walked to the door, only to find it locked. It was only ever locked at night or when everyone was out, so Mum must be away shopping and my father still at work. I found my key and went inside, deciding to drop my bag in my room before heading to the kitchen to make myself a cuppa.

As I passed the door of the lounge room, I became aware of a pungent smell. The door was slightly open, so I pushed it wider and went in. I stood for a moment, transfixed by the scene in front of me. Mum was lying there on the floor, lifeless, and, at first, I thought she was dead. I could see bruising on her face, and there was blood on the carpet. One of her eyes was closed, though the other focused on me as I stood there. The smell was coming from her inert body, for there was a puddle of dried vomit next to her face and the carpet was soaked in urine. At first, I was too shaken to speak. I just looked at Mum, horrified. My first thought was that my father had done this to her. 'What happened?' I managed to say at last.

Mum didn't speak at first. She tried to smile but instead gave out a soft groan. 'You're back, then,' she whispered eventually.

'Did Dad do this to you?' I asked her. I then saw that there were bruise marks round her throat as well. 'Did he try and throttle you?'

'He was very drunk,' she managed to say after a number of attempts. Her voice was croaky, and I could see it was painful for her to talk.

I was angry and probably not thinking too clearly. 'The bastard,' I said. 'When did this happen?'

'I don't remember. Last night, I suppose.'

'Have you had anything to eat or drink?'

'I don't think so.'

I went to the kitchen, found some bread, and spread some Vegemite on two slices while the kettle boiled. Then I made a cup of tea and took it all back to Mum. When I returned, I realised that she couldn't even sit up, let alone drink her tea. I tried lifting her, but she cried out in pain, so I decided to leave her where she was. I didn't know what to do, but then I thought, Helen will know. I went to the phone in the hall and dialled her number. Her mother answered the phone, and I asked to speak to Helen. I heard footsteps then the phone being picked up. 'Hello, darling. Mother says you wanted me.'

'Actually, it's my mum,' I said. 'She's in a bad way.'

'What's happened?'

'She's hurt. My father has given her a beating. She can't even sit up.'

'Oh my god. Are you sure it was him?'

'She says so.'

'That's terrible. I think you should call an ambulance,' she advised.

'You're right, but if she goes to hospital, I should be there for her.'

'Of course.'

'So I probably won't make it by six o'clock.'

'I understand, John. Do what you have to.'

I phoned emergency, who put me through to the ambulance service, and they promised to be with me in twenty minutes. In fact, it took less than fifteen. Mum was not happy when I told her she would have to go to hospital, but the paramedics said I'd done the right thing. After they had inspected her, they injected her with a painkiller. Then they put her on a stretcher and carried her out to the waiting ambulance. One of the paramedics returned and spoke to me. I explained how I'd come back from a few days away and had found her like this. 'Who would do a thing like this?' he pondered. 'It's absolutely savage.'

'My father is a violent man,' I said.

'Your father? So you think it was him, then?'

'Who else?'

'Could be a police matter,' he suggested.

'Which hospital are you taking her to?' I asked him.

'It'll be the Alfred,' he replied.

After they left, I was in two minds whether to follow the ambulance or stay and confront my father. I was still shaking with anger at him, but, first, I went to my room and repacked my bag with some clean clothes. I was determined not to stay the night in the house with my father. He was now a complete anathema to me. I hated him for what he had done. I went back outside, undecided as to my next move. I stood leaning against my car and considering my options when the matter was taken out of my hands. I saw my father striding up the road from the bus stop. He had his head down and didn't see me until he was about to enter the driveway.

'Oh, hello, John. Back from your holiday, then?' he asked me in a jovial voice.

How could he be so laid-back after what he'd done? He sounded so relaxed and uncaring, carrying on as though nothing had happened, but I somehow had to keep my cool. 'About half an hour ago,' I replied in an aggressive tone. He didn't appear to notice, and he continued as before.

'How's Helen, then?'

'Good, thank you.' He made a move towards the front door. 'You won't find her in there,' I added.

'What do you mean?' he asked me, frowning.

'Mum's in hospital.' I was trying to maintain some calm, so I was still speaking quietly.

'Hospital? Why?'

'You may well ask,' I replied, my voice now rising in fury. As I contemplated my father's guilty frown, I managed to conjure up a moment of reckless bravery. 'You've gone too far this time!' I yelled at him. 'You nearly murdered her. I'm so fucking angry. And I'm telling you now that if you ever do so much as touch a hair off Mum's head ever again, I'll kill you.' I knew instantly that I would never be able to carry out my threat, but it stopped my father in his tracks. He just looked at me, his mouth opening and shutting like a fish on dry land, as if he wanted to say something but kept thinking the better of it. Finally, he went inside, and I breathed a sigh of relief.

As I drove to the Alfred, I pondered on my father's behaviour. Was it possible that because of his drunken state, he had not been aware of the damage he'd caused? Can drunkenness deaden one's recollection to such an extent that one's memory is obliterated? I just couldn't believe it. I still can't.

*   *   *

CHAPTER 5

1981—continued

Mum was asleep when I arrived. A nurse led me to a bed in the Intensive Care Unit and drew the curtain around her. I pulled up a chair as close as I could and took her hand in mine. The nurse had told me that she was heavily sedated, so I didn't expect any reaction. A gentle sigh escaped her as she felt my touch, but that was all. Her head was heavily bandaged, her one eye being completely covered, and the nurse had told me they were going to let her rest overnight as her indications were all normal. They would take her for X-rays in the morning, as there was a possibility of damage to her eye socket. Also, her blood pressure was a bit low, and there could be some internal bleeding, but it hadn't gotten worse since she was brought in. I settled down to wait.

When I'd arrived at the hospital, I'd found a pay phone in the foyer and had called Helen. I told her I was at the Alfred and that I had no idea how long I would be. And I also told her about the ultimatum I had given my father, so I couldn't face going home tonight. She'd informed her parents about the situation, she told me, and I was welcome to stay the night, whatever time I arrived. So my mind was put at rest as far as that was concerned.

I sat watching Mum for nearly an hour before she suddenly cried out and her head started shaking. Then she started panting, and her whole body began quivering. She cried out again. I thought she might be having a nightmare, and I clutched her hand more tightly. Just then, the curtain was drawn back, and the nurse reappeared. 'I heard a cry,' she said.

'Mum was calling out in her sleep,' I told her. 'A bad dream, I think.'

'OK,' said the nurse as she withdrew. 'Let me know if it happens again.'

A few moments later, Mum suddenly opened her one good eye and stared at me. She looked at me as if she had no idea who I was, but then her mind must have cleared. 'Where am I?' she asked.

'In the Alfred, Mum. The ambulance brought you.'

'But, why are *you* here?' Her voice was still a bit croaky.

'I wanted to check on you, see that you're OK.'

She subsided back into the bedclothes. 'You're a good boy, John.'

'Do you remember what happened? Back at home?'

'I'm beginning to.' She was silent for a time, her puzzled eye travelling round, taking in all the medical equipment that surrounded her, but then, hesitantly and in unconnected sentences, her story emerged. Evidently, my father had come home earlier than usual. There had been a mix-up with the shifts, and he hadn't been required at the depot, so he'd spent most of the day in the pub. When he'd got home, he could hardly walk, and he'd arrived home while Mum was still out visiting Barbara. He'd said many times that she was never to visit my sister, who, according to him, had brought so much shame on the family. When she eventually did get home and he'd found out where Mum had been, he flew into a rage and attacked her.

'I don't remember much after that,' she added. 'He'd knocked me out, and when I came to, I was on my own and it was dark. He must have kicked me when I was on the floor, 'cos my back hurt and I couldn't move. I don't remember what happened next, except I was sick. He'd hit me in the stomach as well as punched me in the eye.'

'Are you still hurting now, Mum?' I asked her. She sighed and moved a hand to the bandage covering her eye. I saw a bell hanging next to her bed and pressed it. Soon, the nurse reappeared, and I asked her if Mum could have more painkillers. She was given another injection, which put her to sleep again almost immediately, so I told the nurse I'd leave now and return the next afternoon.

'There'll be different nurses on tomorrow,' she said.

'I realise that,' I answered, 'and thanks for all your help.'

'No worries,' she said, smiling. 'You can see your way out OK?'

'I hope so,' I replied.

It was nearly eight o'clock when I arrived at Helen's house. I would have been earlier, but I'd stopped again on the way out of the Alfred to phone Barbara. She had been understandably devastated when I told her what had happened, especially when I explained the reason for my father's frenzy. 'I'll be coming to visit her again tomorrow,' I told her, and she said she felt she ought to be there too. 'Better come on your own,' I said. 'The ICU isn't the place for children.' Helen came to the door as soon as I knocked. She was looking worried as she gave me a quick kiss. 'Hello, darling. How is your mother?' she asked me.

'Still in a lot of pain,' I replied. 'I left her sleeping.'

'We're just finishing dinner,' she said as she gave me a kiss and led me inside.

'I don't want to interrupt anything,' I said.

'It's OK. Mother's kept yours warm, so come and join us.'

'Have you told them yet?'

'No. I was waiting for you.'

'Thanks,' I said. It was only when I smelt the food that I realised how hungry I was. I was welcomed by Peter, who stood and shook my hand, while Myra went off to fetch my dinner.

'I hear you had a good time,' said Peter.

'It was great, thanks,' I replied.

'But your mother's had a bad accident,' Helen tells me.

I realised then that Helen had not said anything about my father's hand in this. I was grateful for her silence and decided to play it down myself. 'Yes, I've just been to see her at the Alfred. She's resting at present.' Soon, I was sitting in the family circle and tucking into a delicious dish of chicken piled high with all the trimmings. Helen and her parents must have realised how hungry I was, so they didn't speak to me till I was finished. 'That was lovely,' I said when it was all gone. 'Thanks so much.'

'You're welcome,' said Myra, and Helen smiled at me.

After the meal, we went into the lounge room. Helen came and stood with me next to the sofa. She waited until her parents were settled in their armchairs. She then took my hand and made her announcement. 'John and I have something to tell you,' she started. 'We're engaged to be married, though we won't tie the knot till John completes his apprenticeship.'

Both her parents jumped to their feet. 'That's wonderful,' said Myra. 'Congratulations. We were hoping something would come out of your holiday.' She came over and gave us both a big hug.

Then it was Peter's turn. 'Yes, my congratulations as well. Welcome to the family.' He shook my hand warmly and gave Helen a long hug. 'This calls for a toast,' he added. He left the room, returning quickly with a bottle of Oz Fizz, as he called it, and Myra went to fetch glasses. 'Splendid news,' Peter added. 'We hope you'll be really happy together.'

'Thank you both,' I said. 'You've both always made me feel very welcome.'

Once again, I became aware of the strange dichotomy in my life. I asked myself whether Peter, in particular, would have been quite as effusive if he had known the full details of the 'accident', the extent of my father's abusive behaviour, or even the state of my parents' house. He'd probably have been horrified, but for now, at least the family was all smiles and good will. In fact, we had a good evening together, and after a couple of glasses of bubbles each, we were more than happy. I tried to put the memory of my mother's inert body lying on our lounge room floor out of my mind, but it was not easy.

There was much discussion about our marriage. Peter wanted to know what we were planning. I told him I'd be out of my time by the end of the year, so it could be a December wedding or early next year. Helen and I hadn't decided. 'In the meantime,' said Helen, 'I want John to spend his weekends here. As much as possible, anyway. Starting tonight.' At this, her parents looked at each other anxiously as though they were unsure what to say. I remained silent, but Helen continued speaking. 'I don't want you to feel uncomfortable about it, but we *have* shared a bed for the last three nights, so it's nothing new.'

'Of course, dear,' said Myra. 'We don't have any objections, do we?' she asked, turning to Peter.

'I guessed you're engaged now, so I'm happy. You're committed to each other. That's what counts.'

'Thanks, Dad,' said Helen, and she went to him and kissed his cheek. 'We're going off to get the ring in the morning—make it official.'

It wasn't long before Peter again jumped to his feet. 'Well,' he said, 'I've got an early start in the morning, so I'll be off to bed. Good night.'

'Me too,' said Myra, and she followed Peter out. I thought they'd probably moved out quickly to give us space and to save us from the embarrassment of slinking off to bed together in front of them.

'You must be tired too, John,' said Helen. 'It's been a long day, especially for you.' I'd left my bag by the front door and picked it up as we made our way upstairs. I was nervous, in a strange sort of way, for I had never been in Helen's room before and had no idea what to expect. However, there was one thing I was sure of long before I ever got there. It would be a lot better furnished and more comfortable than my room at home. Indeed, it was, and very feminine. This is where I would be spending just about every weekend night for the next ten months at least. As with the motel, the first thing I saw was the bed, but this time a double bed, and covered with a colourful mauve, green, and white patterned bedspread. It was not a big room, but Helen had furnished it with a small armchair, a dressing table and mirror, and a bedside table and lamp. There was also a big chest of drawers and a row of built-in cupboards on the side opposite the window.

'What a lovely room,' I said.

'I've cleared a drawer in the chest for you,' she said, 'and I've made a space in the cupboard in case you want to hang anything. So if you want to leave clothes here, you're welcome to.'

'You must have known I would be staying,' I said, laughing.

'I was certainly hoping so,' she said. 'I had to be prepared.'

'Thanks, my love. You think of everything. Now, where's the toilet? I'm bursting.'

'Yes, of course, the geography.' She took me out into the passage and indicated the doors opposite. 'That's the bathroom, and that's the toilet,' she said. 'Mum and Dad have their own en suite, so these are ours. And, of course, there's a toilet downstairs as you know.'

By the time I returned from the bathroom, Helen was already in bed. She was wearing the same nightie she had at the motel, and I had on the same boxers. 'Snap,' I said.

'I just want you to hold me tonight, unless you're feeling the need for sex,' she said once we were tucked up in bed.

'That's fine,' I replied. 'I'm actually exhausted and need to sleep.' So we had a long kiss, and then I wrapped my arm around her, cupping a breast in my hand, and in a few minutes, I was asleep.

The next morning, I was awakened by the sun and the sound of birds. When I opened my eyes, Helen was already awake and sitting up. She bent over and kissed me. 'I thought you'd never wake up,' she said, laughing. 'Now, would you like a cup of tea?' 'Yes, thanks,' I answered. Helen jumped out of bed, put on the dressing gown that hung on the back of the door, and headed downstairs. While she was out, I lay back, surveying the room and glorying in the relative luxury of the furnishings. I was comparing her lifestyle to the austere one I enjoyed at home, and that started me thinking about my father. I wondered what he would be doing, whether he'd be sorry for his brutal attack on Mum and whether he would ever mend his ways. And I wondered whether he would clean up the mess in the lounge room or just leave it for someone else, that someone else probably being my poor mother. If he left it to her, he'd have to live with the mess, and the smell, for a long time. Mum would undoubtedly have to remain in hospital for a few days, perhaps weeks, because I thought her condition could be much worse than the hospital had admitted. I'd have to go back, on Sunday evening at the latest, so it could well be me that would have to clean up. The idea didn't appeal to me one bit.

I was just ruminating on the visit I would make to Mum that afternoon when Helen walked in carrying two mugs of tea. When I asked her if she would like to join me at the hospital, she readily agreed. I told her that she would probably meet my sister there, and as soon as we had drunk our tea, we got dressed and went to the kitchen. Myra was already there. She said that Peter was working over the weekend and had already left. We sat down to a simple breakfast of cereal, toast, and coffee and then set off for the local jewellers. I had little idea how much I would have to spend on an engagement ring, but I wanted Helen to have something she really wanted, so I was prepared to spend big on my credit card. I thought a ring with a single diamond would be good, but in the end, after much hesitation, she chose one with a cluster of small diamonds set in silver. It looked fabulous on her hand, and it didn't cost as much as I expected.

Once I had paid and we were ready to leave, she was lavish with her gratitude. 'Thank you so much, John. I shall wear it forever and with great pride.' And she gave me a very loving kiss to the amusement of the shop assistant.

'I hope you'll be very happy,' he said, bowing slightly.

As we left, Helen turned to me again then looked again at the ring. 'I love you, darling,' she said. 'Thank you again. It's lovely.'

'My pleasure,' I said as I took her other hand, and we walked to the car.

She smiled all the way as we drove back to her house, and when we arrived, she ran in to show her mother. 'Look, Mum. Isn't it gorgeous?' she said.

'That's beautiful,' said Myra as she held Helen's hand up the light. She gazed at it for quite a long time. 'Reminds me of *my* engagement,' she said, looking into Helen's eyes. 'Lots of sparkle. You're a lucky girl.' She gave us both another hug and went off to prepare the lunch.

It was nearly three o'clock as we entered the ICU. We were immediately stopped by a nurse. She asked if I was John Madden because the doctor in charge wanted to see me. She led us to an office and bade us enter. The doctor, a tall thin Asiatic man with a moustache, rose from his chair and beckoned us to sit.

'I'm Dr Tan,' he said. 'You are John Madden?'

'That's right, and this is my fiancée, Helen Sykes. I hope it's all right if she joins us.'

'That's fine.' He paused while taking a look at some notes. 'Well, John, the news is not too good. Her left eye socket is definitely cracked, though we think we can save her eye. And her spleen has been partially ruptured, though it seems to have healed itself inasmuch as the bleeding has stopped. However, any movement could open it up again, so your mother will have to remain bedridden for quite a few days while the healing process becomes more advanced.'

'I understand,' I said.

'She's been given a blood transfusion, and her blood pressure is now back to normal,' added the doctor. He paused, looking intently at me, before continuing. 'Now, John, I have to ask you a few questions concerning her injuries. She's obviously been beaten, and we've had to contact the police. It's a requirement in cases of assault. Perhaps you can tell me what you know.' So I repeated what I had told the paramedic. 'I take it you're not fond of your father,' he said when I had finished. I hadn't thought that he would interpret my account in that way, so I was a bit surprised.

'I'm scared of him actually,' I said.

'Well, the police will be here this afternoon, so would you mind waiting for them? I'm sure they would like to talk to you as well as your mother.' I looked at Helen, who immediately nodded. 'No problem,' I said. 'Can we go and see my mother now?'

'Of course.'

We walked back into the ICU and approached her bed. She looked little changed from last night, though she had been freshly bandaged and seemed more alert. She smiled as she saw us. 'I see you've brought Helen,' she said. Even her voice had lost some of its huskiness.

'We've got news for you, Mum,"' I said proudly. 'We're engaged to be married now.' Helen showed her the ring, and her smile became almost beatific.

'How lovely. I'm so pleased for you both,' she said. 'I'm sorry I can't sit up and give you both a kiss, but the doctor says I mustn't move.' She gave a little chuckle as, first, Helen and then me, bent down and kissed her cheek.

We chatted for about ten minutes, mostly about our holiday, and then

I heard heavy footsteps approaching, and two police officers appeared, a man and a woman. 'I'm Sergeant Burrows, and this is Senior Constable Jameson,' said the male officer. 'We'd like a few words with you if we may.' Mum looked quite fearful while she was being questioned. She repeated what she had told me, and, in turn, I told my side of the story. After we had finished, they went back over a couple of details with us. The sergeant had done all the talking, while the senior constable made notes, and after they had finished, he said they would be reporting back to a senior officer but would return the next day.

When they had gone, I spoke urgently to Mum. 'You know you've got to leave him. He's dangerous.'

'Oh, John, you don't understand. I wish I could. I've often thought about getting out, but it's impossible.'

'Why?' I asked her.

She looked puzzled. 'How can I? Where would I go? I've got no money of my own, and he'd no doubt follow me wherever I went. And then he'd bash me up for leaving him. I can't win.'

I thought about her predicament. 'You are probably right,' I said. I didn't know what else to suggest. I didn't expect that the warning I had given my father would have any effect, though I would try and back it up when I saw him again. I just wished I could protect her better.

'You won't bring him here, will you?' she said, looking fearful.

'Of course not. I haven't told him which hospital you are in.'

'Good. I need time to myself.'

'Very understandable,' said Helen.

'The doctor said I would probably be moved to a ward tomorrow,' Mum announced. 'But I won't be able to leave hospital for at least a week.'

'Don't worry. I'll hold the fort till then,' I said, 'but I have to be back at work on Monday. My leave is finished.'

We were just about to say goodbye when Barbara walked in. She was brought in by a nurse, who told us that patients in ICU were only allowed two visitors at a time.

'We were just leaving,' I said, but, first, I had to make the introductions.

While Helen and Barbara were shaking hands, Mum piped up. 'They're getting married.'

'Oh, wonderful,' said Barbara. 'When, may I ask?'

'Not till the end of the year,' said Helen.

The nurse was waiting patiently for us to leave, but we finally said our goodbyes, and, following a general pecking of cheeks, Helen and I made our move. 'See you again tomorrow,' I said. It was only as we got outside that we felt the late afternoon heat. The hospital was so well air-conditioned that the change in temperature was quite dramatic, and the little Beetle didn't help because it had no such luxuries as temperature control.

'Fancy a swim to cool off?' asked Helen as we drove off down Punt Road.

I tried to remember whether my trunks were still in my bag. Probably, I thought, so we headed for Helen's house to get changed. She was already quite comfortable being naked in front of me, so when we went to her room to don our costumes, she stripped right down to the buff before fossicking in a drawer for her bikini. I wasn't quite so sanguine regarding my own nakedness, though I was certainly enjoying the view.

We lazed in the swimming pool till it closed at six then went home to enjoy one of Myra's lovely dinners. But, first, we had showers to wash off the smell of chlorine and freshen up after the heat of the day. Peter was working late, so it was only the three of us sitting down to the meal. Helen and I did the washing up, and, afterwards, Myra had a programme on television she wanted to watch, so we made an excuse and went upstairs. There was to be delay. Neither of us could wait, and we ran the last few steps to her room. Helen had told me she wanted to experience lovemaking in her own bed and in her own room. I didn't understand the motivation behind this need. After all, a bed is a bed wherever it is, but I knew I had a lot to learn about women, and about Helen in particular. No matter where or what, I was eagerly looking forward to our night together.

We didn't even get into the bed the first time. We just stripped off and lay naked on top. Our coupling was even more exciting than it had been during our holiday, but once we'd finished, both covered in perspiration, we threw off the bedclothes and snuggled together with just a sheet to cover us. She said that we were celebrating our engagement. Neither of us wanted to sleep, and Helen kept wanting more. She had incredible stamina. She was insatiable, but in the end, we were just too tired to go on.

In the morning, she again went off to make us cups of tea. After we'd drunk them, we lay back in bed. We started touching and caressing again, slowly arousing each other. Finally, we indulged ourselves once more, and in a way that was considerably more sedate than anything that had happened the previous night. By then, I wasn't just satisfied; I was exhausted. I quickly dozed off again. In fact, it was after eleven when I finally woke. I lay there for a time as Helen was still fast asleep, and I didn't like to wake her. I contemplated the day ahead. I would visit Mum in the afternoon, and then I would have to go home and confront my father. I was not looking forward to it. I expected that I would find him in denial and grumpy as ever, and I wondered how I would handle the meeting, whether he would be angry at me for what I'd said to him.

It was another thirty minutes before Helen woke. She opened her eyes, at first simply staring at the ceiling, but then she saw me looking at her, and her face broke into a loving smile. She positively glowed, bright as sunshine. 'Good morning, my darling. That was some night, that was,' she murmured.

'And morning,' I added.

'Yes, of course, that too,' and she snuggled her head into my neck.

'You obviously enjoyed it, then,' I said, laughing.

'Can't complain,' she said, and she was laughing too.

We showered, dressed, and went downstairs. Peter had come in late the previous night but had already gone back out to work. Myra was in the kitchen doing some ironing. She smirked when she saw us and shook her head in mock disgust. 'Good morning, you early birds,' she said with a smile. 'Too late for breakfast,' she added, 'unless you want to make it yourselves.'

'Don't worry, Mum,' said Helen, colouring a little. 'I'll make brunch for the two of us.' She went to the fridge and took out the ingredients for a cooked breakfast. Soon, there came the seductive smell and sizzle of frying bacon. She asked me to put some bread in the toaster, and soon everything was ready. I was ravenous. After we had eaten and cleared up, Helen wanted to buy a Sunday paper, so we walked to the newsagent on the corner of her street. There was a cafe next door to it, which was open, so we went in there for another coffee before walking home. We discussed my father and what I was going to say to him, plus a dozen other things, mainly to do with the year ahead. Helen had off till nearly the end of January, after which she would return to TAFE, and she wished me luck as I started my fourth year the next day. And she asked me to give her love to my mother when I saw her later.

Then it was time to leave. I went in to fetch and repack my bag and say goodbye to Myra, thanking her for everything. Helen clung to me as I left her. 'You will come next weekend, won't you?' she enquired.

'Of course.' What else could I say? I was surprised that she would even contemplate my not wanting to visit. Had our new-found love made her feel more vulnerable than before? I wondered. 'I'll phone during the week, let you know what's happening at home.'

'That would be good,' she said and gave me another kiss.

I eventually freed myself and walked to my trusty Beetle. I waved to her as I drove off. I had a strange feeling as I left, partly of relief. I had thoroughly enjoyed my time with Helen and the hours we had spent at her house, but in an odd way, I had felt hemmed in, out of my comfort zone. Her house was sometimes a little claustrophobic. I needed my own space, time to breathe and make contact with my old life. For some reason, I thought of Hudson. I hadn't seen him for a while and decided to visit him sometime over the coming week.When I got to the hospital, I went in search of Mum, but she had already been moved to a ward. It took me a while to find her in the maze of corridors and rooms. She was as usual lying prostrate and motionless, but she smiled when she saw me. There were four beds in the ward, only two of the others being occupied. A woman Mum's age was asleep in one, and in the other was a younger woman reading a magazine. She glanced up at me but otherwise completely ignored me as I walked in.

'That sergeant came to see me this morning,' Mum said. 'He asked me if I wanted to press charges.'

'And?'

'I told him no.'

'Why not, Mum? They could put him away in prison, do him good.'

'Then what? He'd lose his job, and what would we live on?'

I considered the problem for a moment, realising that there was little we could do about it. 'So you're caught between a rock and a hard place,' I said.

'We've just got to get over it, John—somehow.'

I was silent for a few moments, wondering how it would be once Mum came home. Then I remembered I had to give her a message. 'Oh, yes, Helen asked me to give you her love.'

'Thanks. Beautiful girl your Helen. You've really landed with your bum in the butter, haven't you?'

'I spent last night at her place, but I've got to go home tonight. I hope he's not there, to be honest.'

'Well, I wish you luck anyway.'

'I think I should bring Dad round here before you get discharged.'

'Whatever for!' she exclaimed. 'I told you I don't want him near me at present.'

'He should be made to see what he did to you, that's why.' I could see that she was shivering at the thought of seeing him, so I held her hand until she relaxed.

'Perhaps,' said Mum, 'but not for a few days.'

'OK, then.'

The young woman who had been reading a magazine in the next bed had stopped reading and appeared to be listening intently to our conversation. When we stopped talking, she picked up the magazine again, but she didn't look at it. Instead, she spoke quietly, almost as if to herself. 'Some people have all the luck.'

'Sorry?' said Mum. Now she turned to us. 'Visitors,' she said a bit louder. 'I never get visitors.'

'Don't you have anyone?' Mum asked.

'My man won't come near the place. Says he hates hospitals.'

'That's no excuse.'

'Tell *him* that,' she said angrily.

I didn't want to get involved in this conversation and felt it was time to get home anyway, so I bade Mum farewell, kissed her cheek, told her I'd visit again the following evening, and left. The voices of the two women followed me out. They had started discussing their ailments, so the ice seemed to have been broken, and I was happy to leave them to it.

I had a feeling of intense trepidation as I drove up to our house. I had no idea what I would find, but I was prepared for the worst. I left my bag in the hall and walked slowly to the lounge room. I stood in the doorway and looked in. The room was in darkness, and the smell was still there, though not as pronounced as when I'd left on Friday. I went to the window and drew back the curtains. My father was sitting in his usual chair, blinking at the light now flooding the room. He gazed up at me. He looked very old as though he'd aged many years since I'd last seen him. Neither of us said anything for a long time, but eventually he cleared his throat and spoke. 'I'm glad you're back, John. I was expecting you yesterday.'

I had been prepared for my father to be belligerent, angry even, after the way I had spoken to him on Friday, but I wasn't prepared for him to be quite so passive. I even felt a little sorry for him, though that feeling quickly left me. 'I spent two nights at Helen's,' I told him.

'I don't know how long I've been sitting here,' he said.

'I've just been to see Mum again.'

'Oh, yes.' He was silent again for a few seconds before asking, 'How is she?'

'She'll live,' I answered sarcastically. I, too, was silent for a time, wondering how much I should tell my father. Then I thought, he needs to know everything. 'She's got a cracked eye socket where you hit her and a ruptured spleen where you kicked her.' I saw that he was shaking, and when I looked closely, I realised that he was quietly sobbing and there were tears in his eyes.

It took him a while to get himself under control again. Then he looked up at me. 'I've made a promise to myself, a pledge. I'll never take another drop ever again.' I didn't say anything, because, at first, I just didn't believe him. I couldn't. But then he started talking again, explaining himself. 'I know I can't control myself when I've had a few.'

'That's no lie,' I said, again in a contemptuous tone. I still couldn't believe that he was as remorseful as he sounded, not entirely.

'I'm sorry,' he muttered quietly. This time, he sounded so apologetic that, against my better judgement, I began to believe in his anguish, to feel his distress and sympathise with him for the shame he obviously now felt. Perhaps the ultimatum I'd given him had worked after all. 'I tried to clean up a bit,' he added, 'but I'm afraid the carpet is ruined. I'll get it replaced before Flo gets back. She is coming back, isn't she?'

'Yes, Dad, and you'll be glad to hear that she isn't going to press charges over your assault.'

'Thank you, son.'

'But she doesn't want to see you. Not yet.'

'Is she really going to be all right?'

'She's out of emergency now, but the doctors say she won't be discharged for at least another week.'

'I'll make it up to her, I promise. A week will give me time: clean the house properly, fix the carpet, get some flowers in for her, make her welcome.'

'OK, Dad. I must get back to work tomorrow, but I'll help when I can.'

'Thanks, John.'

'Now, have you had anything to eat lately?'

'I haven't felt hungry.'

'I'll see what we've got and make us a meal. Then I need an early night.' In fact, once I'd had a good look, I realised that the cupboard was somewhat bare, so I made us a cup of tea and then went out shopping, coming back with enough to make a big fry-up as well as a loaf of bread and other essentials. By then, it was getting dark, and my father had done a bit of tidying, both of the lounge room and himself. In fact, he was looking a little more like his old self.

We were both somewhat reserved over the meal, having little to talk about. My father told me he wasn't on shift again till Monday at three, so he'd have plenty of time in the morning to start doing some housework. And I reminded him that I would be starting my fourth year as an apprentice the next day. There would be a small increase in wages, and I'd been promised a more independent role as a mechanic in the Ford workshop. He seemed interested in what I was saying, but I sensed that he was miles away, thinking about his own life and what he should do to get himself back in Mum's good books. It was only as we eventually went our separate ways to bed that I realised I had not told my father that Helen and I were now engaged to be married.

*   *   *

CHAPTER 6

1981—continued

It was nearly two weeks before my mother was discharged. My father had been as good as his word, much to my surprise. He had spent every spare minute sprucing up the house. He'd engaged a carpet layer to replace the damaged one; he'd tidied the place up, throwing away things that were damaged or never used; and he'd bought a huge bunch of roses to welcome Mum home. And at my persistent urging, my mother had finally agreed to allow him to come with me when I collected her from hospital. She had refused to see him while she remained in a vulnerable state, but by the time of her discharge, she had become more mobile. As each day had passed, she had exercised more and more, creeping up and down the corridor outside her ward, initially on crutches before graduating to a single stick. Once the stick was gone, Dr Tan gave her the all clear, and one warm Thursday evening, I took my father in the car up to the hospital to fetch her.

I didn't know what would happen as they saw each other again. It worried me, but in the end, their reunion was a relief, astonishing in its unexpected lack of trauma. A few days before Mum was ready to go home, I had told her what my father had said about his drinking and his promise to stop, but she remained wary. And when she first saw him, as he stood waiting for her in the hospital foyer, she looked at him with an expression of alarm, her body stiff, but he spoke gently to her and held out his hand to her. She began to unwind. When we reached home and Mum saw what my father had done to the house and she had smelt the roses he'd bought for her, she relaxed even further, much to his obvious relief. Then, after a few days of patient acceptance, they started behaving as though they'd just got married. I even heard the occasional term of endearment. I was overjoyed at the change, and in my lighter moments, I envisaged Mum accepting Dad into her bed with the same enjoyment that she must have had all those years ago, as indeed Helen continued to welcome me every weekend. I suppose that these thoughts only occurred to me because of my relative youth. I actually wondered whether my parents still made love or were even capable of enjoying sex.

I even thought it might be safe to invite Helen over to our house once in a while now that there was peace at home but decided that I should take a wait-and-see approach. Give it time, I thought, it could still turn ugly. Of course, Mum also remained a trifle sceptical regarding the apparent change in my father's temperament. It seemed that she just couldn't believe in his transformation, so it took a while for her confidence to return. But when nothing happened day after day, when he continued to return from work with a smile and an absence of booze on his breath, she began to believe and we all began to relax. My father even started looking after our minuscule garden and making plans for it, which was a miracle.

My fourth year at the Ford workshop started much as the third had ended, though I was treated with a little more respect and given more difficult jobs to attend to. The biggest change at work was that the workshop foreman had retired at the end of the previous year and Barry Weston had been promoted to the position. He had always been a great mentor to me, so I felt comfortable with him in charge. With his promotion came the return of Nola to continue her apprenticeship. I was happy to see her back, though her recent experience had put years onto her complexion. In fact, her face was quite lined. She had put on a lot of weight and seemed to have lost much of her verve. However, she wasted no time in cornering me one day as I was leaving.

'You heard what happened, didn't you?' she asked me.

'You mean about your lover boy?'

'And me having a baby?'

'Yes, why?'

'Well, I've had the baby now. She's been adopted. I couldn't really cope without the father, and he went back to his wife.'

'Well, I'm sorry to hear about that.'

'The thing is I'm free now.'

'And?'

'Well, you did want to date me once.'

'Yes, I did, but ....'

'But what?'

I realised that I still found Nola a very attractive girl, and she would be more than happy to have another man in her bed. I was sorely tempted, but my new-found relationship with Helen, indeed my engagement, stopped me from doing anything quite so nefarious. 'I'm engaged to be married now,' I said. 'That's what. I'm sorry.'

'Oh,' she said. She turned on her heel and walked off, swinging her hips.

I immediately thought of Hudson. He'd shown himself to be somewhat highly sexed and so far without a partner, so he might be interested. Two days after my talk to Nola, I went to see him after work. He was glad to see me, and I wasted no time in broaching the subject. However, before I'd got very far, he stopped me.

'How long is it since we met up?' Hudson asked me.

'A few months, I guess.'

'Well, you're behind the times, Johnny. I now have a girlfriend. It happened over Christmas.'

'Nice. What's her name?'

'Carol. Sister of a friend. I didn't like her very much to start with, but I think she must have been rather lonely. She came on to me like I was the last man on the planet.'

'OK. So what's she like?'

'Plump and boisterous, with a huge arse. And she's bloody hot.'

'So, you've had your leg over already?'

'And, wow, she fucks like the proverbial rattlesnake.' Hudson grinned at me. 'Anyway, what about you, Johnny boy?'

'I took your advice.'

'What advice?'

'Don't you remember telling me to make my peace with Helen?'

'Oh, yes. So, what happened?'

'We're engaged.'

'Wow. Congratulations.'

'And we've just been on holiday together. Phillip Island.'

'Just the two of you? No parents getting in the way of true lust?'

It was my turn to laugh. 'And I'm staying with her every weekend till we get married.'

'And when will that be?'

'Not till I'm out of my time.'

'I guess that answers all my questions.'

'Will you be my best man when it happens?'

'It would be an honour. And my pleasure.'

'Thanks, my friend. But, what about you? Are you going to marry Carol?'

'She's a fabulous fuck, but I don't think I want to spend my life with her.'

'I hope she knows that.'

'Oh, yes. I told her right from the start, but she's one of those girls that just enjoys sex without strings attached. A rare breed.'

Hudson had always been like a breath of fresh air in my life. He was a wonderful friend. I hoped he would remain so for the rest of my life. He invited me to stay for tea, and, wanting as much of his company as I could possibly have, I agreed, but, first, I asked him if I could use his phone. I needed to warn Mum that I wouldn't be home till late. Hudson's father met me as we joined his parents.

'I see my old car outside,' he said. 'How's the old jalopy going?'

'Like a dream,' I answered.

We all had a pleasant evening, and it wasn't until after ten that I got home. The house was at peace, and as I walked past my parents' door, I heard low voices and then a quiet giggle. I stopped to listen for a moment, just to witness their happiness, but there were no further sounds.

During the summer, Helen and I spent most weekends together, and some Saturdays we went off swimming, either at the local pool or at one of the many beaches that dotted the Mornington Peninsula. Sometimes, we set out without any clear idea of where we were going, and one time we drove across the peninsula from the Rosebud side and finished up in the little coastal village of Somers. As we walked down to the beach, we came across an excited group of people in the shallows and saw there were a number of dolphins swimming among them. As few of the peninsula beaches had changing facilities, we always put our bathers on under our other clothes, so we were able to strip off hastily and join the throng.

We hadn't been in the water more than a few seconds when a dolphin swam straight at us, turning at the last minute. Neither of us had ever seen dolphins up close before, so it was a particular delight. There were shouts of laughter all round us as the dolphins continued to play, and one little girl screamed in fright as a dolphin swam through her legs. Eventually, the pod must have got bored for they all suddenly left us, swimming further out to sea. Helen and I went back and stood on one of the sand dunes that backed onto the beach to see if we could spot them again, but we were disappointed. After we had eaten our picnic lunch and had enjoyed another swim, we went home. Peter and Myra were fascinated by our story, and we resolved to go back to Somers one day and see if the dolphins were a regular occurrence.

That summer brought a big resolution, this time regarding my father and my sister. Despite his apparent new-found change of heart, and behaviour, my father was still adamant that Barbara had brought shame on the family. One evening, Mum brought up the subject once again, mentioning that she would love to see her again soon.

'No way,' Dad said forcefully.

'Why do you keep saying that she brought shame?' I asked him.

'Bloody obvious,' he answered. 'She went whoring.'

'No, she didn't,' I argued. 'She and Paul were in love.'

'But she got herself pregnant.'

'You mean she brought shame because she fell pregnant, not because she followed her instincts and slept with the man she loved?'

'Exactly.'

'So she made *one* mistake. Does that mean that anyone who makes a mistake in their life should be banished for ever?' I asked him. He looked uncomfortable but didn't say anything. 'We've all made mistakes. You too, Dad.' My father looked away, unable to argue any further. 'Anyway, it's Paul's mistake as much as hers. He could have taken precautions.' My intervention eventually seemed to have done the trick. After further heated discussion, he finally agreed, albeit with much hesitation and ill humour, that Mum could visit Barbara whenever she wished and that his daughter would be welcome to visit us. Mum wasted no time, and the following week, they were all invited to a meal. My father was even persuaded to welcome Paul and shake his hand. It was a welcome change to have the whole family together again.

As autumn gave way to winter, I had a call from Hudson. He asked me to come round to see him. He had a problem he couldn't discuss over the phone, so after work the next day, I went round to his house. 'Carol's pregnant,' he announced. 'The silly bitch stopped taking the pill without telling me.' He paused. 'Now she says I must marry her.'

'What did you say?'

'I didn't say anything. I can't marry her. I don't love her.'

'Are you sure it's yours? She sounds the sort of girl who could be playing the field.'

'I assume it's mine.'

'Never assume anything,' I advised. 'Have you told your parents?'

'Not yet. They'd be devastated.'

'You should. Do it now.' I thought for a moment. Poor Hudson looked terror-stricken. 'Would you like me to come with you?'

'Thanks, Johnny. You're a good friend.'

Of course, his parents *were* deeply saddened by the news, but once they'd got over their disappointment, they became more supportive. His mother said she'd never really liked Carol, and they agreed that Hudson didn't have to marry her if he was absolutely set against the idea, but they would have to support the child once it was born. Hudson might even change his mind once he'd met his child, if he was prepared to do that. I was obviously not privy to Hudson's next meeting with Carol, but he told me all about it afterwards. Apparently, she had gone somewhat ballistic when he'd told her that he could never marry her, and she threatened all sorts of mischief. But after she'd calmed down, she said that she couldn't have a child without its father in her life and would most likely get an abortion. She thought there was nothing more depressing than being a single mum. She hadn't told her parents about her pregnancy either but knew how these things could be arranged without her parents being told. She was over twenty-one anyway, so it was her decision.

Hudson never saw her again, but as a result of the episode, he became a wiser man overnight. He had the impression that Carol had only gone off the pill just to snare him into marriage, which was pretty underhand, he reckoned. I thought of raising the subject of Nola after all, offering her as an easy replacement, but decided that he seemed more than able to find his own partner and, anyway, wouldn't fancy another manic nymph in his life.

Halfway through my final apprenticeship year, I started seriously thinking about my future. Firms were never keen to continue employing an apprentice after they had completed their time, and I didn't believe it would be any different for me. Anyway, I was interested to see what other prospects were out there. I was still interested in working with earth-moving equipment or even modern farm equipment and had started an extra course on hydraulics at TAFE. So I started looking through the yellow pages, just hunting for the names of companies that advertised earth moving as their primary activity. There weren't that many in the Melbourne area, but I picked out a few and noted their addresses. Helen helped me prepare a curriculum vitae, though there was little to put in it, and a covering letter. These I sent off, requesting an interview should they have any vacancies, though explaining that I wouldn't be available until next year.

It was already well into August when I started getting replies. Three companies offered me an interview, though none of them were currently recruiting mechanics, so I phoned each of them in turn and made appointments, all for early September. It's necessary to get your name on their books, everyone told me, so that if and when a vacancy arises, you'll be the first cab off the rank. In the event, all three interviews were satisfactory, though, of course, none of them could make any promises about hiring me next year. At least I had three options open to me when the time came. With leave both accrued and due, I would be leaving the dealership by the end of November, and we were planning to marry in December. We had settled on the first Saturday, and I was hoping to start work in a new job in late January. Plans were already well advanced for our wedding. We would hire a marriage celebrant and be married in the Sykes garden. And we would have the reception at the same venue that Peter had secured for Helen's twenty-first. Neither the Maddens nor the Sykeses were churchgoers, and these arrangement seemed the best under the circumstances. The garden was big enough for the ceremony but was too small to hold the reception. Helen's parents wanted a proper sit-down event with a band in attendance for dancing, and Helen had agreed. I wasn't properly consulted over the matter but was presented with a fait accompli. I was annoyed but managed to hold my peace.

However, it wasn't long before all our plans were thrown into disarray. It was late October, and I was at TAFE the day that the accident happened. It had been a warm sunny morning, and I thought it nice enough for a walk in the park at lunchtime, so I went looking for Helen in the office. There was no sign of her. Di, one of the other staff members, told me Helen had gone home at ten o'clock. 'She was in a hell of a hurry,' said Di. When I asked her if she knew *why* Helen had left, she couldn't tell me. She just said that Helen had just received a phone call. 'She went very pale while she was on the phone,' said Di. 'I think it was a call from home, but she didn't say. She just walked out.'

I was in two minds whether I should try her house straightaway or leave it till after classes. I was worried. I wouldn't be able to concentrate during the afternoon without knowing, so I found a fellow class member, asking him to cover for me, and went off the Sykes house. I rang the bell a couple of times, but there was no answer. Obviously, Helen had been called to go somewhere other than home, so I left a note for her to phone me when she got back from wherever she was and returned to my class. Later, I returned to the house, but there was still no answer, so I drove home, now in a state of extreme anxiety.

When my father was at home, which he was that evening, he and I would sit together at six o'clock to watch the Channel 7 news, while Mum got tea ready. The first item of news was a report on a traffic accident in which two police officers had been struck by a car. They were both in hospital, one male officer with life-threatening injuries, and the other a female officer whose injuries were minor. She was currently stable and likely to be discharged in a couple of days. As the newsreel quickly moved on to other stories, I thought no more about it. We had our meal, and I was helping with the washing up when the phone rang. I remembered the note I'd left for Helen and ran to pick it up.

'Hello,' I said.

I could hear heavy breathing on the other end then a sob. 'Oh, John,' said Helen. 'There's been a terrible accident.'

'Oh my god!' I exclaimed. 'So, it was your father?'

'How did you know?'

'It was on the news. What happened?'

'He was helping on a police line, checking for drunk drivers. He was just coming to the end of his shift when some drunken teenager in a stolen car tried to jump the queue to avoid getting stopped. But instead of getting past, he drove straight into him—him and another officer. Luckily, *she's* not hurt too badly.'

'And Peter? Which hospital?'

'The Alfred again.'

'The ICU?'

'He may not live, John. The car hit him really hard. He's in a bad way.'

'I'm sorry,' I said. I felt badly shaken. This was terrible news, and I had no idea how to comfort her. I waited a moment before speaking again. 'When did it happen?'

'In the early hours of the morning. The driver had a whole load of other teenagers with him, and he just sped off afterwards. He didn't even stop.' I heard another sob

'I hope they caught the bastard.'

'They've tracked him down now, thank God,' she said, but then I heard her weeping. I waited a moment, and then I heard a faint 'sorry' over the phone.

'Would you like me to come round?' I asked her.

'Please, John.'

I quickly told my parents what had happened and scampered out to my car. Mum called out after me, asking me to pass on their condolences. It was normally a fifteen-minute drive, but I must have done it in ten that night. I didn't even ring the bell when I arrived but went straight in as their front door was unlocked. I found Helen sitting next to Myra on one of the settees. They were clutching each other in their grief, and both looked up as I walked in but didn't say anything. I didn't know what to say either. It was obvious they had both been weeping, for their eyes were red and they looked desolate.

I just perched myself on the other settee and waited for someone to say something. I was wondering how to start a conversation, break the ice as it were. I finally decided to go and make us all a cup of tea. By then, I knew my way round their kitchen, so I just got up and went in there without asking them. When I emerged later with three mugs of tea, they still hadn't moved; but when I put the tray down in front of them, they both looked up again. 'Thanks, John,' said Myra. 'That's very thoughtful of you.'

'No worries,' I said, and Helen tried to smile up at me.

'Have you been at the hospital all afternoon?' I asked.

'Dad's been put in a coma,' said Helen. 'He was hit with such force that he was thrown against one of the nearby cars. It cracked his skull.'

'How awful,' I muttered. I couldn't think of anything to say that would help to alleviate their pain. So I kept silent, all the time wondering how anyone could possibly have survived such a horrific accident.

'His neck is broken as well as everything else,' Helen added. 'They think he could be a paraplegic for the rest of his life, even if he does recover.'

I nodded absently. I was beginning to brood over our future, Helen's and mine. 'In any event, it looks like we'll have to postpone our wedding,' I said at last.

'I'm afraid so,' said Myra.

The weeks dragged by. There was little or no change to Peter's condition. Myra and Helen went regularly to the hospital and sat with him, and sometimes I joined them, though not often. I found the visits incredibly depressing. We all did, but I found excuses to keep away. Helen managed to get compassionate leave from her job, so I saw nothing of her during TAFE days. And I saw little of her at home either. She didn't seem so keen on me coming round every weekend, and when I did, she was always distracted and never wanted to do anything with me outside her home. Even our sex life was all but finished. On the few occasions that she allowed me to make love to her, both her body and her mind seemed to be somewhere else. She had lost all her enthusiasm. And often when I visited, she spent a lot of time playing the piano, and it bored me, listening to her endless repeats. I could understand the reason for her apparent rejection of all that used to be dear to her, but I began to wonder whether we could still have a life together when it was all over.

There didn't seem much chance of life returning to normal anytime soon. November came and went, and I received a good send-off at work. I had been saving most of my wages, and now that I would be a fully fledged 'tradie', I decided to sell the old Beetle and buy a proper work vehicle, one I could store my tools in. So I visited used car yards, looking for something suitable, and eventually settled on a two-year-old ute with a large tray. It had a large built-in lockable toolbox on the tray and seemed perfect for me. I was sorry to see the end of the Beetle. It had served me well, but the salesmen gave me a good price, at least more than I'd originally paid for it.

With no job in the offing and my marriage on hold, I was now at a loose end and reapplied to the three companies that had interviewed me. Again, none of them were looking for mechanics, but two of them said they might have a vacancy in January. I spent many evenings with Hudson. He was as footloose as me, now also having a long period of leave, and we often talked long into the night. He was also very saddened by the state of my relationship and suggested we go away together somewhere, just for a break, to recharge our batteries as he put it. He asked me if I'd ever done much walking. It was not something I'd even wanted to do, but he seemed quite keen and said he'd always wanted to visit the Grampians again and walk among the hills.

'Have you been there before, then?' I asked him.

'Once, when I was still small,' he answered. 'My parents loved it there. We walked a lot, and I remember how Dad put me on his shoulders and carried me whenever I got tired.' A break seemed like a good idea, and I couldn't think of anywhere better to go.

It was close to the date that had originally been set for our wedding, so I decided to go and see Helen and tell her of our plans. She was still in a gloomy frame of mind when I spoke to her, but she perked up a bit when I told her that Hudson and I wanted to go away for a bit.

'Yes, John. You must go,' she said. 'I'm sorry I've not been myself lately.' Then she put her arms around me and kissed me. It was unexpected but made me feel so much better.

'Are you sure you don't mind?' I asked her. 'It'll only be for five days.'

'Of course, I don't mind. It'll do you good, both of you.'

'OK. Thanks,' I said. And I gave her another kiss before leaving.

By then, Hudson had bought himself a car as well, a second-hand Volvo, and he insisted on taking it. I'd left him to make all the arrangements, and he'd booked us a cabin at the Halls Gap Caravan Park. 'I hope you don't mind sharing a room with me,' he said when we met.

'Not at all,' I answered.

'It's only got one bed.'

'Oh. You're not turning queer on me, are you?'

He began laughing at me. 'Of course not, Johnny, but the big family cabins with extra beds are much more expensive.'

'Well, OK, then, as long as it's a *big* bed, but don't suddenly start getting friendly with me.'

Hudson picked me up early one sunny Sunday morning. He drove us out of the city onto the Ballarat Road then on to Stawell, where we stopped for a bit of lunch. I'd never been in this part of the state and thoroughly enjoyed looking at our surroundings, especially the last leg of the journey as we approached the mountainous scenery of the Grampians. We arrived in Halls Gap at around three o'clock and found our way to the caravan park. I don't know what I was expecting in our cabin but probably something very basic. It turned out to be quite well appointed, with many comforts and a queen-size bed. I immediately thought of Helen and our Cowes holiday and felt sad that it was Hudson and not her who was with me. There were cooking facilities on one side of the main room and a door led to an en suite. It was all entirely satisfactory.

'I've brought all the necessary to make breakfasts here,' said Hudson, 'but I thought we might want other meals out.'

'Sounds good to me,' I said.

After we had settled in and had unpacked some of our clothes, we started on our first walk. In the grassed vicinity of the cabin, a dozen or so kangaroos were grazing or lying sleeping. They took no notice of us as we walked among them. We set off up a sloping path, along a stream that meandered down from the hills ahead. The weather was very warm. There were late spring flowers everywhere and tall trees that gave us plenty of shade. We passed a few other walkers, exchanging cheery greetings with everyone we met. The path eventually led us to the Venus Baths, a group of huge rounded rocks in the stream bed itself. They'd been worn smooth by the current and were warm from the sun. We sat on one of them for a time, listening to the sounds of the cascading water, and we plunged our hands in to get a drink. I don't think I'd ever tasted water so pure, cool, and fresh. It was a wonderful feeling, relaxing in such a stretch of unspoilt nature, but after thirty minutes, it was time to turn and make our way back.

That evening, we found a small restaurant to have a meal. We were served by a young and very attractive waitress that Hudson took an immediate shine to. The girl had a badge on her uniform that told us her name was Christine. She was very chatty. 'You two on holiday, then?' she said as she gave us menus. 'Haven't seen you around before.'

'Just here for a few days. Doing a bit of walking and sightseeing,' answered Hudson.

'Where are you from, then?'

'Melbourne,' I said.

'So, where are you staying?' She seemed to want to know everything about us.

'Cabin up at the caravan park,' said Hudson.

'That's nice,' she said, but then she was called away by a couple at another table.

When she came back to take our orders, she continued where she'd left off. 'We get a lot of customers from the caravan park. But school holidays haven't started yet, so we aren't too busy.'

And when she returned ten minutes later with our food, she continued. 'Do a lot of walking, do you?'

'Not as much as I'd like,' answered Hudson.

'They say this is a fab area for walks. Enjoy.'

'It would be good to ask her out,' said Hudson once Christine was out of earshot.

'Where?' I asked him.

'I don't know. Maybe on a drive or something.'

'Are you getting horny, or what?' I asked him. Hudson just laughed. While we ate, we discussed what we would do the next day. I thought it would be nice to go for a drive somewhere—find different places to walk.

'What about MacKenzie Falls?" I suggested, having seen the name on a map in our cabin. 'Do you know where it is?'

'I think my parents took me there all those years ago. A waterfall somewhere. That's all I remember.'

When we had finished eating, Hudson called Christine over to bring the bill. 'Do you get days off?' he asked her.

'We're closed on Mondays, so tomorrow's off.'

'Fancy a drive?'

'OK,' she answered doubtfully. 'Where to?'

'Johnny here wants to see MacKenzie Falls. Then we might go on to Zumsteins and Wartook. Find somewhere for lunch.'

'OK.' She still sounded doubtful. 'I'm not doing anything else tomorrow.'

And so it was settled. Hudson arranged a meeting place and a time, and we went back to our cabin. I didn't think he would have much luck with Christine, but I didn't want to pour cold water on his enterprise. In any event, I think that she had smiled more at me than at him, and, to be honest, I wasn't that interested.

The next morning, Hudson banished me to the back seat of his car as he welcomed Christine to come and sit next to him. And he ignored me most of the time as he drove up the road towards the falls. Christine, on the other hand, hardly stopped talking. She prattled on about the Grampians, the restaurant, her family, and other people we'd never heard of, and after a few minutes, I just switched off and looked out at the scenery. I wished Helen was with us instead of this chatterbox. I was sure she would have loved these picturesque surroundings.

We eventually reached MacKenzie Falls, or rather a sign at the side of the road that pointed to the path that led to the falls. As Christine emerged, I realised that she was hardly dressed for a long walk. For a start, she was wearing totally inappropriate shoes. It was a long and rough path that we followed. She took every opportunity to complain. 'Didn't you realise we were going walking?' I asked her.

'No,' she answered. 'I thought we were just going for a drive. And lunch.'

'I think we'd better go back,' said Hudson. 'You can't walk far in those shoes.'

So we turned round. Luckily, we hadn't gone far. It was evident that Christine knew very little about the Grampians even though she'd lived there most of her life, and, in fact, she wasn't that interested. The day didn't improve much. We drove on to Wartook, a pleasant little village where we took a short stroll and eventually found a cafe where we had a bit of lunch. Afterwards, we drove back and out to Dunkeld, returning a different way. I was relieved when we finally dropped her off so Hudson and I could have time to ourselves. We agreed that it hadn't been the best idea to take her along and decided to go back to the falls the next day and see them properly. In fact, it was Hudson who suggested that we give her restaurant a wide berth for the rest of our stay, so he had obviously found her as wearing as I had. In return for this dispensation, I said I would cook us a couple of meals in our cabin since we had all the necessary facilities there. It seemed a good idea to use them.

The rest of our time in the Grampians were thankfully spent on our own. Each morning, we prepared sandwiches and visited the supermarket for fruit and cold drinks to take with us. The first day, we revisited the falls, a magnificent spectacle after all the recent rain, and on succeeding days found a number of fascinating walks after parking at a spot on the way to the MacKenzie. There was the Grand Canyon, a narrow cleft in the rock formation that we had to squeeze through, and beyond it the Pinnacle and Splitters Falls. Often, we just stopped and looked at the amazing views. It was all delightful, and every day we returned to the cabin exhausted. But I did carry out my threat to cook evening meals for us, though it was simple fare. After our exercise, we were both hungry enough to eat anything. On the Friday morning, we left tanned, content, and feeling better for our holiday. I realised that I had often thought about Helen while we were away, especially when, on one of our walks, we had come across a particularly lovely panorama. *Helen would have loved this*, I often said to myself. I had indeed missed her. I was now ready to accept her grief into my life, to be there for her and give her all the support she needed.

I hadn't seen a newspaper all the time we'd been away and hadn't thought to watch the news on the small television set in the cabin. So I hadn't been aware that Helen's father had died. Hudson dropped me off at home, and as soon as I walked in, Mum told me. 'It was on the box yesterday,' she said. 'I'm so sorry for poor Helen.' I decided to go straight round to her house. There was a police car outside in the road, and as I approached the front door, it opened, and two officers emerged. They were in uniform, and I could see they were very senior, judging by all the braid. As soon as their car had driven off, I went straight in. I didn't know what to expect: probably Myra and Helen grieving even more than before, but in the event I found them, both were quite at ease. They looked up at me as I entered the lounge room, and Helen even managed a meagre smile.

I smiled back. 'I'd just returned home when Mum told me the news,' I said. 'I'm so sorry.'

'It's all right, John,' answered Myra. 'It's a relief that it's all over. At last.'

'We knew the end was coming,' added Helen. 'But the waiting was killing us.'

'Still, it was still a bit of a shock, of course, when he finally went,' said Myra.

'I'm sure,' I said. 'I'm sorry I couldn't be here for you.'

'Don't fret,' said Myra. 'There was nothing anyone could do. I'll go and make us some tea if you would like.'

'Yes, thank you,' I said, and as I watched her leave, I reached out and took Helen's hand.

She gripped mine in hers and gave me another fleeting smile. 'Anyway, how was your holiday? You look quite bronzed,' and her smile broadened.

'Actually, it was brilliant,' I replied. 'We did so much walking.'

'Well, you're looking fit. And you haven't kissed me yet.' So I did, and her lips were loving and moist, and I was so aroused that in any other circumstances, I would have grabbed her and carried her straight up to her room. But Myra appeared with the tea, so I dropped Helen's hand and sat down. She had also brought in a plate of chocolate biscuits, so we sat in near silence while eating and drinking. I had been about to ask them when the funeral was to be when Myra spoke. She must have been reading my thoughts.

'Did you see those two police officers leaving, John?'

'Yes. Why?'

'They came to talk to us about the funeral. It's to be on Tuesday morning, at St. Paul's, and they are arranging everything. There will be a big police presence in the church, and they are providing the pall-bearers and a cortege to take the coffin to the cemetery.'

'Apparently, they do this for all police officers who die on duty,' added Helen.

'And so they should,' I said. 'Give them a proper send-off.'

'Guess what I've been doing while you were away?' Helen quizzed me. I couldn't think of anything and shook my head. 'I'm learning to drive.'

'That's great,' I said.

'It was Mum's idea. Dad's car's been sitting in the garage all this time, and she doesn't like driving anymore with her bad eyes. I've already had my first two driving lessons.'

It was then that Myra asked me if I'd like to stay for dinner, and when I told her that I would love to, she left us, shutting the door behind her. I quickly phoned Mum and then settled down to talk to Helen. I thought we'd talked about death and funerals enough so told her a bit more about our holiday. 'Have you ever been to the Grampians?' I asked her.

'Can't say I have. What's it like?'

'Very hilly, mountainous almost. Beautiful scenery and so much to see.'

'Sounds good. And the accommodation?'

'Fairly spartan.'

'And, how was your friend Hudson?' So I told her about his attempt at seducing Christine and the rather awful day we'd spent with her. I made a bit of a joke about it but suddenly realised that Helen was showing signs of jealousy. 'You didn't have anything to do with …,' she started, but I cut her off.

'No, I didn't. It was his idea from the beginning. He was the one that invited her.'

'So, was she pretty?'

'She was, but she suffered from verbal diarrhoea. Never stopped.'

'She doesn't sound very appealing.'

'I didn't like her at all,' I said. 'It was all Hudson's idea, and even he was glad to be rid of her by the end of the day.'

'That's all right, then.' Helen got up and went into the kitchen to see if she could help her mother, and when she came back, she asked me if I would come to the funeral.

'Of course,' I said.

'That's good. I'd like to have you next to me.'

'So, what's the plan?'

'A police car is coming to pick us up at nine o'clock. There'll be room for you as well.'

'I'll be here in good time, but that's still four days away. I'd like to see you again before then?'

Helen laughed. 'Of course, you can. Come round tomorrow and stay with us till Tuesday. Just remember to bring suitable clothes.'

The funeral was an impressive occasion. I was quite overawed by it, though Myra and Helen seemed to accept everything in their stride. St. Paul's was already quite full when we arrived. There was a solid contingent of police in uniform, both men and women, as we were ushered to a pew at the front. To one side, I saw a discreetly placed television cameraman. There had also been a similar one outside. Helen was to give a eulogy for her father, along with the assistant commissioner of police, and she was understandably nervous. We were each given a printed 'order of service', and the bishop of Melbourne himself was present in all his finery. I had not realised the esteem in which Peter was held by his colleagues, but it became apparent as the service proceeded. Both Myra and Helen held up well, and Helen gave a moving account of their family life when it was her turn to speak. I learnt much about my late father-in-law-to-be and was sorry that I'd never got to know him better.

Soon, it was all over. We followed the coffin out, walking slowly behind the pall-bearers. There was the fluttering sound of camera clicks from assembled journalists and members of the public in front of us, while behind us the thunderous roar of the organ continued unabated. Outside, the sun was shining, though the steps of the cathedral were in shade. The coffin was placed in the hearse, and the pall-bearers stood back and saluted as it moved off. The three of us were in the car immediately behind the hearse as we made our way to the cemetery. There were only a few of us, Peter's more intimate friends and a few relations, at the graveside, and as the coffin was lowered, Helen finally broke down with a despairing cry. Both Myra and I tried to comfort her, but she was still sobbing as we once again got into the police car for the drive home. It was a sombre journey, though I felt quite proud of myself: an impoverished boy from a shabby and abusive home rising to mix with all those powerful people. It was something I never expected, nor would it ever be likely to happen again.

*   *   *

CHAPTER 7

1981–1982

It turned out in the days following the funeral that Myra would be extremely well off. Peter had invested in a substantial life insurance policy, and as a member of the police, his widow was due further sums as a result of his early death. But there would be no immediate change in the lives of the Sykes household, and life settled down slowly. I started visiting them every weekend as before, and gradually Helen became more and more accepting of life without her father. She continued with her driving lessons, going out twice a week, and in no time she had taken and passed her driving test. It was with some pride that she mounted her P plates on her father's car.

Once she was more amenable, we began to talk once again about our wedding. Of course, it couldn't be on the scale of what had previously been planned, and Myra said that with fewer numbers, we could perhaps now have the whole event at her house. With this change, there were no restrictions on dates, and when I looked at the January calendar, I realised that my twenty-first birthday fell on a Saturday. I suggested we could kill two birds with one stone, so January 23 it would be. The other decision we still had to make was where we would live once we were married.

'Would you mind terribly if we lived here?' Helen asked me. When I looked a bit doubtful, she told me that Myra had agreed to move out of the room she'd shared with Peter. 'Mum says that it holds too many memories, and it's too big for one person,' Helen added. 'Also, my mother is becoming a little frail, and with her bad vision, she really needs someone with her in the house.'

'Well, putting it like that, it makes a lot of sense, I suppose.'

'You'll love the big room, with its lovely en-suite bathroom. And there's a queen-size bed in there,' she added with a slightly lecherous smile. 'We'll be in my old room on the night of the wedding, but Mum will move everything over while we are on our honeymoon, so we'll have the big room when we return.'

'And Myra's entirely happy with that?'

'She is.'

It was in the third week of December that we made the decision regarding our wedding date, so it gave us a month to prepare everything. However, if we were to have any sort of honeymoon, it would mean I couldn't start work until the start of February, just supposing I had found a job by then. Once again, I wrote off to the two firms that I had preferred as a result of the interviews, telling them about my marriage plans and saying I would now only be available from February 1. That would allow us a week away, which Helen thought enough, since she was also due back at TAFE on the same day. There was a quick reply from one of them, Thompson Earthmoving, offering me a job. I was overjoyed and phoned back to accept. Thompson's was a small company based in a back street of Mordialloc, so not too far to travel. It was run by the owner, Bill Thompson, a man in his fifties, and it was Bill who had interviewed me back in September. He had seemed at the time to be an honest and hard-working man, someone I would be happy working for.

I managed to book a hotel in Lakes Entrance for the week of our honeymoon, but I left all the arrangements for the wedding, including both the celebrant and the caterers, to Helen and Myra. And I largely left the guest list and the printing of invitations to them as well, though I was later roped in to help with their distribution. It was decided to limit the guest list to fifty, the most they could comfortably cater for in their garden. From my side, there was only my family and, of course, Hudson and his parents, while at the last moment, I added the Westons and included Nola. There was some discussion as to whom Myra should get to give Helen away, and they finally settled on her uncle Frank, who lived in Sydney but who was persuaded to come down again for the weekend. He'd previously been down for Peter's funeral, and I had met him then, but this time he would bring his whole family. There was no problem with my best man. I went round to see Hudson as soon as the date was fixed. 'I hope Helen will have a bevy of beautiful bridesmaids,' he said. In fact, she had decided on having only one. She would ask her friend Di from the TAFE office.

We still had to get through Christmas. Mum had decided to ask Barbara's family for Christmas Day, and she really wanted me to be there as well, if only for lunch. 'Only if we ask Helen and her mother as well,' I insisted. 'Otherwise, they'll be on their own.' My father wasn't too keen, worrying that it would be too crowded, but Mum insisted that she could manage. So there would be eight of us in total, and if we put a small table up against the existing one, we would be able to seat everyone. We'd have to find extra chairs, so it would all be a bit of a mishmash. I spoke to Helen the next time I visited, and she was pleased to be invited. I warned her that things at home were never as orderly as in her household, so she and her mother shouldn't expect anything too grand. She just said they were looking forward to meeting my whole family, regardless of the surroundings or what might happen.

Christmas Day fell on a Friday that year. I spent the previous week at home so I could help with the preparations and had arranged to fetch Myra and Helen on Christmas morning, take them back after our lunch, and stay with them over the weekend. Mum and I, and to some extent Dad, had to do a fair bit of planning for the feast. We decided on having a cold lunch: platters of prawns, sliced turkey and ham with various salads. Of course, my father said it wouldn't be Christmas without a plum pudding, so we included that, as well as an alternative of fruit and ice cream. And we must have enough crackers and a Christmas tree in the corner of the room with plenty of baubles and presents for everyone underneath. And, lastly, Mum and I decided not to have any alcohol in the house. Thankfully, my father made no objections when we told him.

The week before Christmas was spent in something of a panic: buying and storing food, buying and wrapping presents, and buying and decorating a tree. At times, it was bedlam, as it always is when one leaves everything till the last minute. But, finally, all was ready, Christmas morning arrived, and I went off to fetch our guests. Helen was looking gorgeous in a light-green summer dress, and Myra, too, had dressed up for the occasion. There was only just enough room for the three of us in the cab of my ute. When we arrived at our house, Barbara, Paul, and Florrie had already arrived. The child was walking now and, being of an inquisitive nature, had made a beeline for the presents under the tree. Barbara was having a problem keeping her from pulling on the branches and destroying the decorations. I think Mum and Dad were a bit in awe of Myra. Conversation was somewhat stilted and subdued at first, but my sister and Helen, although they had only met briefly once at the hospital, hit it off immediately, and that seemed to break the ice. In fact, Helen took Florrie over, holding her and playing games with her.

Soon, it was time to bring in all the food that Mum had laboriously put together, and we sat at the table. Helen and Barbara positioned themselves on either side of Florrie's high chair and fed her pieces of meat. Everyone was highly complimentary about the spread and enjoyed it, eating themselves to a standstill. Then it was time to pull the crackers, read the rather silly riddles printed inside them, and don the paper hats. Finally, we distributed the presents. Florrie had the most, but everyone received something, and soon the room filled up with torn wrapping paper.

I had been sitting opposite Helen at lunch. I had enjoyed watching her as she made short work of her food, but as we finally left the table, she looked distinctly pale and worried. She took me to one side and whispered in my ear, 'I'm not feeling too good.'

'In what way?'

'A bit sick.'

'Do you need to get home?' I asked her.

'Yes, please.' I noticed that my father wasn't looking well either, and Paul had gone off to the toilet complaining of a stomach ache, so I quietly told Mum we had to leave.

'So soon?' she said.

'Sorry. Helen's not well.' I spoke to Myra, and the three of us, after saying our thanks and goodbyes, headed for the car. But I hadn't driven more than a kilometre when Helen suddenly shouted, 'Stop the car!' Luckily, there was little traffic, so I was immediately able to pull into the kerb. Helen just managed to get out of the car before being violently sick.

By that stage, I wasn't feeling the best myself, but I think that was because I'd caught a whiff of Helen's vomit. 'It must be something we ate,' I said.

'Those prawns were a bit funny,' said Myra, 'so I only ate one. But I think Helen had a lot more.'

Just then, she gave another heave and brought up the rest of her lunch. She sat back on the seat, leaning out through the door, and groaned. I thought back to the purchase of the prawns and the fact that our refrigerator was so full that they'd been left out for a time. I realised it was my fault. I felt so embarrassed. It took a couple of minutes for Helen to recover, but she had ruined her dress. We opened all the windows as we drove on, and when we reached the house, I left them open. Myra took Helen inside, and I followed them so that I could phone home. Mum answered, and she was in tears. 'Your father and Paul have both been sick,' she said. 'And none of us are feeling well.'

'I'm sure it was the prawns, Mum,' I said. 'They weren't properly refrigerated.'

'I'm so sorry. Please apologise to the Sykeses for me.'

'I will, Mum. Luckily, I don't think Florrie ate one,' I said.

'It was supposed to be such a special occasion. And now it's all ruined.'

'Please don't worry, Mum. We'll all get over it.'

'And your father is angry as hell.'

'Should I come back? Try and keep the peace?'

'Please, John.'

So I went to find Myra, to apologise on Mum's behalf, and mine as well. 'Helen wasn't the only one who was sick,' I added. 'And now Mum wants me home to pour oil on troubled waters. Dad's being difficult.'

'You'd better go, then. I'll take care of Helen.'

'And I'd better stay home tonight and come back tomorrow.'

'OK,' said Myra.

When I got home, the rest of the party were still there. Strangely, neither Barbara nor I had been badly affected, though we had both eaten prawns, so there must have been some good ones among them. My father was still going on about the lunch. He'd recovered enough to be belligerent. 'What's Helen going to think of us?' he said. 'Mum's really stuffed up.'

'Don't blame her. It was *my* fault.'

'*She* was in charge of the food.'

'Yes, but I bought the prawns. And I left them out of the fridge.'

My father simply grunted, so I left him and started tidying up some of the detritus from the party. Mum and Barbara had already cleared the table and were busy washing up, Florrie having been put down for a sleep, so when I had finished packing away all the cardboard and paper, I went into the kitchen and talked to my sister. I had realised from looking at her that she was expecting another child, although nothing had been said over lunch. 'Congratulations,' I said.

'Thanks, little brother,' she replied, 'but it wasn't meant to happen quite so soon.'

'When's it due?'

'July.'

Paul had recovered as well by now, and we all sat down to tea and Christmas cake, and afterwards they left. It was a miserable evening, though nothing more was said about the lunch debacle. We consigned the rest of the prawns to the bin and had a meal off the remainder of the leftovers. We went to bed early, and I lay there unable to sleep for some time. I kept thinking of Helen and the pitiful spectacle of her in her vomit-covered dress as Myra had taken her inside. Then I thought of tomorrow when I would see her again. I visualised her coming to me, now clean and smelling fragrant, taking her clothes off for me, and then playing with me until I found relief. Only then did I sleep.

Hudson's parents threw a New Year's Eve party and invited me and Helen. There were nearly thirty of us there. They had arranged a barbecue out on their patio, and they had cleared and decorated their big double garage for dancing. We'd taken along a bottle of Amiri, a New Zealand Sauvignon Blanc, which we'd found in Peter's stock and which Helen was particularly partial to. She was very pleased to meet Hudson after hearing me talk about him so much, and the three of us spent a long time chatting. And it was good to meet Hudson's other friends as well. At midnight, we all sang 'Auld Lang Syne', and Helen and I had a long and highly erotic kiss. We were surrounded by catcalls and applause long before we had finished. We left soon afterwards, returning to her room for a considerably more private way of seeing in the New Year.

The three remaining weeks till our wedding seemed to drag. One day, I decided to run down to Mordialloc just to get the measure of the Thompson premises and make myself known to the other staff. There was a small reception office at the front of the building, reigned over by a formidable-looking but nevertheless friendly lady whom I discovered to be Bill Thompson's wife. 'I'm Donna,' she said when I introduced myself. I explained who I was. 'Ah, yes, the new mechanic. It's good of you to come down and see us.' She offered to show me round the workshop, as Bill himself was out on a job. There were two men working there: Nigel, who turned out to be Bill's and Donna's son; and Greg, an older man with a mop of grey hair and twinkling eyes who, Donna told me, was due to retire in a couple of months. She told me that Greg would only be staying on long enough to show me the ropes and would leave as soon as I was up to speed. When introduced, Greg wiped his hands on a piece of cotton waste so he could shake mine and smiled. 'Good to meet you,' he said. 'You'll like working here.' He and Nigel were working on a big excavator, but most of Thompson's equipment, what were not currently in use out on a construction site, were housed in a large shed at the back. After we'd had a brief look in there as well, Donna invited me back to the office for a cuppa and to write down all my details: address, phone number, tax file number, and so on. 'It'll save time when you start here,' she said.

'You do know I'll be married by then, don't you?'

'No, I didn't,' she said, giving me a winning smile. 'Congratulations.' As Donna was speaking, I realised that she wasn't quite as formidable as I had first thought. It must have been a front she just put on for travelling salesmen and others that wasted her time. 'We look forward to seeing you next month. And the best of luck with your wedding.'

'Thanks,' I said. I left feeling glad that I'd made the effort to come down.

There was one other event that sticks in my mind from those January days. One evening at home, about a week before the wedding, Dad sat me down for a fatherly chat, as he put it. 'You know, son, marriage isn't easy.'

'I don't expect it to be,' I said, 'but I love Helen very much. We'll be all right.'

'Love is never enough on its own.'

'Why not?' I asked him.

'It wears off after a year or two.'

'Ours won't,' I said hopefully.

'Anyway, you must call the tune, right from day one. I've watched you, son—you're not firm enough in your dealings with Helen. I reckon she's twisted you round her little finger. You follow her round like a little lapdog.'

'I don't.'

'You do. I can see that she's a strong character. She's used to ruling the roost, and you just let her dictate everything.'

'So what?'

'There can never be two bosses in one family. You've got to take control right from day one, show her who's in charge.'

'No. We want to be equals. Make decisions together.'

'That doesn't work. Marriage can *never* work like that. There's no such thing as equals, so you must lay down the law, right from the beginning, or she will make your life a misery.'

'That's ridiculous.'

'It's not. You'd better get it into your head that you've got to be the leader, not the follower.'

By this time, I was getting uneasy. What if my father was right? It was obviously the way he behaved in his life, though he'd obviously taken his philosophy to extremes. I had no real experience of the world and how things should be between a man and his wife. Perhaps my father was *not* being ridiculous. In any event, I decided to stop arguing and at least pretend to agree with him. In the years that followed, his words never left my mind, not completely anyway.

In the final week before the wedding, we revisited the jeweller to buy wedding rings. Helen had persuaded me to wear one; she really liked the idea of exchanging rings as part of the ceremony. This time, we opted for two identical gold bands, identical except in size, for her fingers were slimmer than mine. The jeweller remembered us, and after the rings were bought and paid for, he again showed us to the door, shook our hands, and offered us his congratulations. We stored the rings away in Helen's room till the big day.

Myra thought we should all meet the celebrant she had chosen, mainly to discuss the form of ceremony we wanted to have. Mary Pearson was a middle-aged lady with dark-brown hair cut short. She was quite plump and matronly. She wore glasses in a thick red frame and had an air of self-assurance that I found a little off-putting. She came once, early in the week, for the initial discussion, then again the day before the wedding for a rehearsal. By this time, Helen's uncle Frank was down from Sydney, and Hudson could join us as well. Also, the caterers had been in to erect a small marquee on the Sykes lawn and bring in the chairs and tables. It all looked very festive and fit for the occasion. Then, after the run-through, Hudson and I were politely told to make ourselves scarce until three o'clock the next day. Helen was a stickler for correct etiquette. We must not meet for the twenty-four hours before the wedding. To see each other during that time would bring bad luck. So I kissed her, thanked her mother, and left.

I felt at a bit of a loose end for the rest of the day but suggested to Hudson we should go out together for a meal. That was when he told me he'd arranged a bit of a stag night with some of the young blokes I'd met at his New Year's Eve party. 'OK,' I said, 'but don't you dare get me drunk. A hangover on my wedding day is the last thing I need.'

'Don't worry, Johnny. We'll all just go to a bistro for a meal. And only a couple of drinks.' It turned out to be quite a subdued get-together. There were five of us, and because I didn't know the other three well, they didn't try and ply me with alcohol. I bought a round, and so did Hudson, but that was it. Two of them were in fact already married themselves and didn't stay beyond nine o'clock. And the remaining three of us finished up before ten. I was grateful to Hudson for organising the stag do, and he arranged to pick me up, together with my parents, the next day at two thirty. I went home to spend my last night in my lonely single bed. Mum and Dad were still up, making sure, they said, that I got home safely. They were very solicitous, making sure I had everything I needed for the wedding and the honeymoon. I only had one suit, the one I had bought for the funeral. I had asked Helen if she thought it would do for the occasion. She said it would be fine, but she refused to tell me what she would be wearing. 'It will be surprise,' she'd said.

I had purchased two suitcases, one large and one small, and spent the next morning packing just about everything I owned, the large one to remain at my new home and the smaller one to take on honeymoon. As I heaved them into the boot of Hudson's car, dead on two thirty, Mum started going on about Christmas again. 'Do you think they've forgiven us?' she kept repeating. My father didn't have much to say on the matter, but I tried to reassure them both that all had been forgiven weeks ago, so please stop worrying. Hudson ushered them both into the back seat and held open the passenger door for me.

'You're being very gentlemanly suddenly,' I said.

'As befits the man of the moment,' he answered.

'Thanks, my friend.'

'Nervous?' he asked me.

'Yes,' I said. 'Very.' I wasn't sure if I was petrified or just overexcited. Perhaps both at once.

Hudson drove us slowly the Sykes house. There were already a number of cars in the road, so we had to park some distance from the house. Mum and Dad settled into two of the chairs in the marquee as Hudson and I carried the suitcases into the house. Knowing I mustn't see Helen before she appeared at the ceremony, I made my presence known with a loud yell. If Helen had been downstairs, she would have heard me and gone into hiding, but there was silence in the house, so we simply put the bags down in the hall. Hudson stayed inside, but I returned to the marquee to talk to other guests who were now arriving. While we'd been inside, my sister and her family had arrived, as well as Hudson's parents. I remember welcoming the Weston family and introducing them to my parents. 'And, who is this?' said Nola, pointing to my best man, who had just re-emerged from the house. I introduced her to Hudson and could see there was going to be a measure of chemistry developing, so I left them to ogle each other. Within minutes, the seating was all but full. I dragged Hudson away from Nola, and we took up our positions next to Mary Pearson.

A distant clock announced that it was three o'clock, and I turned to face the guests. Everyone seemed to be holding their breath, and the silence was absolute. The front door opened, and I heard, rather than saw, the bridal party walking down the path. They soon appeared at the back of the marquee. First came Myra, who scuttled up the aisle between the chairs and took her seat in the front row. Then behind her appeared Helen with her arm in the crook of Uncle Frank's arm. The guests turned as one, and there was a loud gasp when they saw the bride. To say that Helen was ravishingly beautiful and radiantly happy would be a huge understatement. I was so struck that I felt quite dizzy. She was wearing a lovely blue dress in some soft material, long in the hem but so low-cut that her cleavage was more than prominent. She wore no jewellery apart from her engagement ring, and her blonde hair had been swept up off her neck. She had the mildest of red lipstick on her mouth. Somehow, that seemed to make her look younger than I'd ever seen her. As she walked slowly towards me, she kept her eyes on my face. She smiled the whole time, and I sensed that she was fully aware of the effect she was having, not only on me but on everyone present as well. Behind her, and to one side, walked Di. She was dressed in a similar fashion, in a blue outfit made from the same material as Helen's, and though she appeared more attractive than when working at the TAFE, she was so completely outshone that hardly anyone noticed her.

Helen came up to me and took my hand, and Mary started speaking. I regret to say that once Helen and I were standing together, hand in hand, the whole ceremony became a complete blur to me. I remember none of it, just Helen's presence. But I must have made all the right responses at the right time, and Hudson must have produced the correct rings when asked, because I do remember hearing Mary saying, 'I pronounce you man and wife', and being told we could now kiss. And I remember her lips were warm and giving, and when we finally broke apart, there was prolonged applause.

Later, everyone was ushered out of the marquee so that the tables and chairs could be rearranged and the tables covered with white cloths, cutlery, and glasses. Then, once everything was ready, we were called back. When we were all finally sitting, Uncle Frank rose to his feet. Myra had appointed him master of ceremonies, and he announced that a buffet had been set up at the back and was now ready. And there was a bar in one corner if anyone was thirsty, but please allow the happy couple to go up first. I wasn't particularly hungry; nor was Helen, but we rose and went to the buffet. Uncle Frank went straight to the bar and collected a bottle of red wine and one of white for our table.

The meal had progressed for nearly forty-five minutes when Uncle Frank rose once more. The moment I had been dreading had arrived. There would only be two speeches: Uncle Frank first then me. He spoke for about fifteen minutes, first commenting sadly on his brother's death and how much Peter would have loved to have been here today, but the rest of his speech was spent extolling Helen's virtues and commenting on some of her youthful indiscretions. It was almost a repeat of the comments Peter himself had made at her twenty-first. Then it was my turn. I got up, my legs feeling like jelly, and looked out at all the faces turned towards me. Then I felt Helen's hand grip mine, and I felt a little better.

'Thank you all for coming,' I started. 'I, too, am really sad that Helen's father could not be with us today. He was a great mentor to me, and he and Myra have produced a daughter that surpasses all expectations.' There were calls of 'Hear! Hear!' as I continued. 'Talking of mentors, Helen herself has been an even greater mentor to me, and I want to thank her and her mother for everything they have done for me. They taught me to call tea dinner,' this comment greeted by laughter. 'They showed me empathy before I knew what the word meant,' more laughter, 'and the true meaning of both harmony and tenderness, for the Sykes house is exactly that, a house of harmony and tenderness. I know that Helen and I will always be happy together for we share a love that is unbreakable.' Again, I felt Helen squeeze my hand. 'But I am a man of few words, so I will end there. Thank you.' As applause rang out, I sat down again, hoping that I'd never have to speak in public again.

It was another hour before the guests began to leave. Once there were only a handful left, the catering and bar staff started packing everything up, leaving the marquee and furniture to be picked up the next day. By this time, Helen and I were standing together at the top of the drive, farewelling people as they left. My parents, together with Paul, Barbara, and now a sleeping Florrie, came to say goodbye. As expected, Mum was quite tearful and kept telling me she hoped I would still come visiting whenever I could, and my father told me not to forget what he had told me. I saw Hudson slip away with Nola when he thought I wasn't looking, but by then, he had already been to say goodbye and to wish us both well. When the last of the guests had gone, it was already dark, though it was still warm outside. Helen and I went in to look at the various wedding gifts that people had left. Most of them would be of little use for a while, and some of them only when we had our own house. Myra said she would make a list while we were away, so we could write our bread-and-butter letters when we returned, and she would store them all somewhere safe in the meantime.

I supposed it was normal for a married couple to change from their wedding garments at the end of the reception before saying their farewells and driving off into the future, but because we were not going anywhere that night, Helen was still in her wedding finery. It was still relatively early, but it seemed that neither of us could wait to consummate our marriage, so we said goodnight to Myra and quickly mounted the stairs to Helen's room.

'I want to pretend it's the first time we've been together,' she told me as soon as we were inside.

'OK,' I said a bit doubtfully.

'Like we've never seen each other naked before.' I didn't say anything, wondering how I could possibly pretend that, so she explained further. 'I want you to undress me. Slowly. Then I want to undress you.'

I had been intent on ripping all her clothes off without delay but realised that wasn't Helen's plan at all. She wanted everything slowed down. I looked at her clothes, thinking, just for a brief moment, that it would be a pity to disrupt such a beautiful outfit. She still looked stunning, and to remove any one item would spoil the whole effect, though I knew she was even more perfect in her birthday suit. 'So, where do I start?'

She turned her back on me. 'The zip.'

I found it and tugged it down, exposing her bra strap. 'And now?'

She turned back. 'Lift the dress over my head. Carefully.'

I managed to accomplish that safely, and then I lowered her petticoat, leaving her standing in her bra and a very brief pair of blue knickers. By this time, the bulge in my own trousers was quite significant. I had heard of men who were adept at undoing a bra with one hand behind a girl's back, but I needed both hands, and I needed to see what I was doing. Helen turned again. I loosened the clips and bared her breasts. As usual, I was totally riveted by their gorgeous shape and size. I was getting more aroused by the second. I couldn't wait but took one of her nipples in my mouth. She sighed with delight, put her arms round the back of my head, and held my face against her. 'One more thing to go,' she said once she'd finally loosed her hold on me. I knelt in front of her and slowly removed her last bit of clothing. I wanted to plunge my face into her pubic hair and breathe in her smell, but I felt her hands on my head, preventing me. It was that line in the sand again. She left them there for a moment before speaking again. 'Now it's my turn.'

My jacket was easy, and my tie, and she asked me to take my shoes and socks off myself. Then she pulled the shirt out of my trousers and threw it onto the floor. She slowly undid my belt, undid my zip, and lowered my trousers. I stepped out of them. She looked up at me smiling. 'There's something in there trying to escape,' she said, and she gently pulled my underpants clear and down. My erection stood out between us. 'You're already leaking,' she said.

'I'm not surprised,' I replied.

She took it in one hand, and with the other, she cupped my balls. 'These are all mine now,' she proclaimed. 'No one else is allowed to see or touch. Now, my darling husband, I want you to pretend I'm a virgin. Would you do that for me?'

'What do you mean?'

'I want you to plough me slowly, like it was the first time ever. For both of us.' I'd never heard that expression before, but I knew what she meant. I put one arm around her body and the other under her legs and lifted her onto the bed. And I entered her as slowly as I could, which, considering the urgency I felt, was not very slowly at all. And it wasn't long before the heat and the joy of the moment had me pumping furiously. In seconds, the room rang with our ecstatic cries. Soon, Helen wanted me again, almost immediately, though I myself needed a short pause. Only once I had fully recovered, and we were about to start over, did I ask her about the euphemism she had used for sex.

'I guess it's an old English expression,' she explained. 'Like what farmers do, you know, plough a furrow and plant a seed.'

'I like that,' I said. 'It makes sense now. You have a well-moistened furrow, and I've certainly planted the seed.' Helen laughed, but the conversation had got me thinking. 'I suppose you'll want to come off the pill now we are married. Start a family.'

'How do you know I'm not off it already?'

'What!' I exclaimed.

'It's all right. I was only joking. I think we should wait a couple of years, make sure we're well settled before having children.'

'I'm sure you're right,' I said. 'And now, Mrs Madden, I think I'm ready for a bit more ploughing.'

*   *   *

CHAPTER 8

1982

We took Helen's car on our honeymoon. It was a lot more comfortable than my ute, and she needed all the practice she could get. So I let her drive us out of Melbourne, only taking it in turns behind the wheel once we were out in the country. Helen drove well, as she did everything well, so I was able to relax and look out at the passing scene. I thought back to last night, how she had seemingly programmed everything to suit some preconceived idea of how wedding nights should proceed. And I had gone along with it all, to the letter. It was a wonderful night, one I would never forget, but in retrospect, I now wondered whether there was truth in what my father had said. Was Helen twisting me round her little finger? Was I her little lapdog, jumping to her call? And why not? I asked myself. The night was perfect, so why should I quibble? Was I not just being the sort of person that I am, and possibly will always be?

When I had woken in the morning, I had felt distinctly groggy but wonderfully contented. Helen was already up and about, singing to herself and busy packing the last few things into her suitcase. The clothes we'd left strewn all over the floor were already put away, and a mug of tea awaited me. I went to my case to take out some clothes for the journey, only to discover a package, wrapped in brown paper, that had been slipped into it without my knowledge. Helen watched me as I unwrapped it. 'What is it?' she asked me.

'It's a book. Oh my god.' I could feel my face burning with embarrassment. It had a soft cover, was no thicker than a magazine, and was called *Sexual Positions for Newlyweds*. There was a titillating colour picture of a nude couple on the front. 'You didn't put this in my case, did you?' I asked her.

'Of course not. Is there a note with it?'

I turned to the first page. 'I should have guessed,' I said. 'It's from Hudson, and *to* us both.' There was a message written there, wishing us a happy and *eventful* honeymoon. I wondered how and when he'd accessed my case, the sly bugger.

'Let's have a look,' said Helen. She grabbed the book and started paging through it. 'Wow,' she said, laughing. 'We're going to have an exciting time.' I tried looking over her shoulder, but she closed the book. 'Put it away for now. We'll have plenty of time later.'

Now, as we headed towards Warragul, and our first stop, I was itching to sneak a look at Hudson's gift, one that I realised had been given us with his typical tongue-in-cheek mischievousness, but it was safely stashed away in the boot. As we had left the house earlier, after a somewhat rushed breakfast, Myra had come out to the car to wish us a safe journey. She had risen before us and had prepared a packed lunch, for which we were grateful. She'd looked tired as she sent us on our way. I think the wedding had drained away her energy, and as we drove away, Helen repeated her hope that her mother would be all right on her own. Myra had become rather forgetful lately.

Apart from one day, the weather remained cloudless for the whole of our week in Lakes Entrance, and mostly it was hot, so we were grateful for the air-conditioning in our hotel room. At night, we tried out some of the suggestions in Hudson's book and, as Helen had prophesied, they were exciting times. And during the day, we explored much of the town, on a couple of occasions driving further afield. There were a number of brochures in our room that advertised eating places and various entertainments. One of the brochures told us of a place called Metung, further back along the coast, where one could hire rowing boats and kayaks. Neither of us had any experience of rowing or kayaking, but it sounded fun, so we decided to make the trip. We set out after breakfast one morning, dressed in our bathers and with our other clothes on over the top.

Metung is at the eastern end of Lake Victoria and, in those days, was little more than a jetty with a few houses and shops. On the beach, a number of kayaks were drawn up. They were supervised by a young bearded man who asked us if we'd ever done any kayaking before, and when we said we hadn't, he proceeded to give us a five-minute lecture, detailing all the things that could go wrong. Helen listened intently, though I was distracted by a flock of seagulls that were fighting over some discarded food further down the beach. We hired a double kayak for a two-hour period, as well as the mandated life jackets. Then we stripped off down to our bathers, and, leaving our clothes in the car, we set off.

Helen climbed into the front seat, and I pushed the kayak into the water, running alongside until it was well afloat. I then tried to climb in myself. I thought that would be the easy part, but as I swung a leg over, I nearly capsized the craft, losing my paddle as I did so. The beach shelved quite steeply, so by the time I managed to find my lost paddle and make another attempt to get on board, I was more than waist deep in water. I could no longer lift my leg high enough to get in, so I just threw myself onto the craft before it disappeared out to sea. I must have looked quite a sight, belly-flopped over the kayak, my legs waving frantically as I tried to swing them into the boat, *and* keep it on an even keel at the same time. It was a struggle. I was panting with the effort and embarrassed at my ineptitude, but I eventually got myself settled into the rear seat, though I brought a flood of water in with me as well. Helen just sat there, doubled up with laughter.

I was angry, with both her and myself. 'I don't like being laughed at,' I said sharply.

'Sorry, but you looked so funny.'

'Well, it wasn't the least bit amusing.' What made it worse was that I'd just looked back at the young bearded man, and he, too, was laughing at my predicament. I was seething.

'Anyway, are you on board at last?' she asked. She was still giggling, which added to my chagrin.

'Just,' I snapped.

'Good. Let's go, then.'

We each had a double paddle, and, at first, we made a total hash of keeping in time. In my annoyance, I kept hitting Helen's paddle or missing the water altogether and was about to suggest that we should cut our losses and go back in. But just then, a very experienced-looking couple in another kayak came flying past us, their paddles biting into the water in unison. We watched them closely, quickly realising what we had been doing wrong and how we should paddle the kayak as a team. After that, we slowly got our act together, and once we had found our rhythm, we began to make some progress, even though I was guilty of occasionally splashing Helen on purpose. We paddled for some time in uneasy silence before Helen suddenly stopped. Our paddles collided again.

'I can feel your eyes boring into the back of my head,' she said, turning round with a querulous stare. 'Please don't be annoyed with me. Now, let's try again,' and she dug her paddle into the water, expecting me to follow suit and join her rhythm. I remained silent, but after a couple of strokes, I fell into step. Slowly, the shoreline receded, along with most of my tantrum. We manoeuvred closer to the lea of the north shore. Here, the water was less choppy, there being a fairly gusty north wind blowing, and after twenty minutes or so, we found another beach that was secluded and deserted.

'Let's go ashore,' Helen suggested. 'Have a rest.'

'OK,' I replied. My arms were getting quite tired. 'I think I'm exercising muscles I didn't know I had.'

'Me too.'

So we ran the kayak up onto the beach and climbed out, pulling the craft up onto the dry sand. We tipped the boat over to drain the water that had collected then sat for a time, basking in the sun and watching another flock of seagulls as they came towards us, hoping for titbits. There was still an atmosphere of tension between us, so we remained largely silent. I was still uptight as a result of Helen's attitude and didn't know how to put things right between us. She needed to apologise before I would be able to loosen up and forget the indignity. It was while I was considering Helen's lack of sympathy that I noticed a band of grey cloud coming in from the west. I pointed it out for it seemed to be moving swiftly, and growing. We watched it for a time, and then suddenly the sun disappeared behind it, and the wind, which had died, started to swing round to the west. It was reaching us in little gusts, which came and went as though it was building up to something stronger but couldn't make up its mind.

'We'd better be moving, hadn't we?' Helen asked me. 'It feels like there's a change coming.' So we pushed the kayak back out into the water. This time, we got in from opposite sides at the same time, and the craft remained reasonably stable. We paddled out into deep water, and as we did so, we started feeling the increasing strength of the wind. By the time we had the Metung beach in sight ahead of us, the waves had started building up. We started digging our paddles in quicker and quicker, and though the wind was coming from behind us, it was also blowing slightly from the side. Consequently, the waves seemed to be coming at us from all angles, and as both the wind and the waves increased, the kayak began bobbing around like a cork. Our paddles kept missing the water, or clashing, and we completely lost our rhythm. And my bathers still being damp, I started shivering with cold. To be honest, I was quite scared. It was a hairy experience, and the shoreline seemed to take an age to reach us.

When we finally arrived and clambered out, I could hardly stand up. My legs felt like jelly, and Helen didn't look much brighter. The young bearded man was looking quite worried. 'Thought you weren't going to make it,' he said.

'Nearly didn't,' I replied.

'You shouldn't have gone so far out,' suggested the bearded man.

'We couldn't know that the weather was going sour on us,' argued Helen. 'Anyway, is there anywhere round here we can get a hot meal? We're both frozen.'

'You could try Danny's Fish and Chips,' he answered. 'Just over there,' he pointed.

We handed back all the hired equipment and returned to the car, got ourselves dried and dressed, and headed off to Danny's. By then, the sky was covered in grey cloud, dark in places, and rain threatened. We found the cafe. It had a clock on the wall, which told us that it was nearly midday, so we must have been out for at least an hour and a half. There were no other patrons, so we just sat at one of the tables with a view out over the water. We ordered two fillets of fish and minimum chips and a cup of coffee each while the fish was being cooked. We were silent for a time, then Helen looked up at me. She stretched out her hand across the table towards me and spoke quietly. 'I'm sorry if I upset you when I started laughing at you, John.'

I realised I had to say something. 'That's OK,' I replied grudgingly.

'Well, it's not OK, not really. I know you can be very sensitive, a bit brittle sometimes, but I thought you would still be able to see the funny side. I really didn't mean to make you angry, John.' Helen always calls me John when she's being serious. I knew she was being sincere, but I still couldn't completely let go of my bad temper, so I remained silent. 'I often think of your childhood and sometimes wonder if your family ever made fun of you?' she continued. 'Or perhaps it was school? Is that why you can't take a joke sometimes?' Helen can be so blunt at times. Memories of some of my school-day experiences came back to me then: the many times my classmates had laughed at me, shaming me for my appearance, my old frayed clothes and anything else they could find to taunt me with. Perhaps that was the reason I was so ill at ease now. Perhaps it explained why, even after all these years, I was so put out by someone laughing at me, and especially by the person I love. Helen frowned at me, shaking her head. 'Talk to me,' she said at last. 'Please. I hate seeing you so down in the dumps.'

I felt better after thinking about my past now thankfully put behind me. So I smiled at Helen and took her hand. 'Yes, to all of the above,' I said. 'I was teased unmercifully, especially at primary school. I guess that's made me oversensitive to criticism, and especially to people making fun of me.'

Just then, our coffee arrived, courtesy of a young waitress. 'Your fish will be ready in five,' she said as she put our cups down. 'Vinegar on your chips?' she asked us.

'No thanks,' I answered. 'Just salt.'

Helen waited till the waitress was out of earshot before speaking again. 'It must have been very difficult with your family being the way it was. The poverty. I do understand.'

'Thank you. I don't suppose I'll ever really get over the hurt. Not completely.'

Helen was just about to say something when a sudden squall hit the window next to us. The rain came sheeting down. We watched it for a time, and then the wind and rain subsided together, leaving rivulets of water continuing to run down the glass like tears from a weeping sky. Suddenly, the sun re-emerged, and at the same time, our waitress arrived with our meal: huge platefuls with a separate small bowl of salad, which was in effect simply a nest of lettuce with a few small pieces of tomato mixed in. We were both ravenous as we tucked in.

Something had happened that day, some almost imperceptible shift in our relationship. It wasn't anything that drove us apart, or brought us closer together for that matter. Nevertheless, something had changed, and I couldn't place it. Perhaps it was simply that there was now a better understanding between us. Maybe we had just gained a little more respect for each other and each other's feelings, a little more empathy. Or perhaps we had just grown up a little, become more mature. Anyway, I was happy with the change, and I felt Helen was too.

When we got back to our hotel, it had started raining again, so we decided to have our evening meal in the hotel for a change, though neither of us was particularly hungry after our huge lunch. And that night, our lovemaking was also different. It was as if we had both started thinking of each other's pleasure more than our own. Probably as a result, our loving was long-lasting and wonderfully enjoyable. There was no hurry, and we stretched it out over a long time. It had a gentleness and a timelessness, and it left a feeling of contentment, which I remembered long after our honeymoon was over. We had two more full days left, and our changed relationship continued. I think we were more in love than ever before, more considerate. I hoped it would last for ever.

We drove back to the city exhilarated and ready for the challenges we knew lay ahead. During our week away, Helen had phoned her mother a couple of times, even though I'd told her it was totally unnecessary. After all, this was our time and nobody should come between us. But she phoned anyway, and Myra said everything was fine, so we expected the house would be all ready for us. We arrived home at about three o'clock and parked in front of the Sykes garage, though, of course, it was now the Madden garage. My ute was already in there, and it being a double garage, there was plenty of room for Helen's car too. I had been given a set of keys sometime before, and I went in first with the suitcases, while Helen opened the garage and stowed her car away.

I called out as soon as I got into the hall. Myra came running downstairs. 'Oh,' she said, 'I wasn't expecting you back till tomorrow.'

'We always said we'd be back on Saturday,' I answered.

'Is today Saturday?'

'What day did you think it was?' She didn't have time to answer me before Helen arrived.

'Welcome home,' said Myra. She and Helen exchanged hugs, and as they broke apart, she added, 'You both look well.'

'We had a great time,' said Helen.

Myra had a worried frown on her face. 'I'm afraid the rooms aren't quite ready.'

'Don't worry,' said Helen. 'We'll come and help.' But, first, we moved into the lounge room, and Myra went off to make tea for us. Over tea, we talked about our holiday, and Helen gave an edited and quite humorous account of our attempts at kayaking. Then, after twenty minutes, she got up. 'Let's see what has to be done upstairs,' she said, rising to her feet. I got up too, but Helen decided I should stay downstairs for now. 'It's women's business,' she claimed.

After a further half hour, Helen called down to me. She wanted me to carry two heavy suitcases out to her car. 'These are all Dad's things,' she explained. 'Mum didn't know what to do with them, so I've packed them all up and I'll take them to an op shop next week. Then you can bring our cases up. We're just about ready.' I didn't say anything; I felt a little peeved the way I was being ordered around, but I carried out the instructions. When I returned upstairs with our cases, I went straight to our new room. I had never been inside before. It was certainly a lot bigger than Helen's old room, and full of light. The queen-size bed, complete with polished wooden head and tailboards, was covered in Helen's and my clothes, ready to put away in the built-in cupboards that lined one wall.

Myra was busy removing the last of her things. 'I seem to have so much,' she complained. 'I don't know where I'll put it all.'

'Don't worry,' said Helen. 'I'll come and help you,' and she left me to go back to her old room, giving me the chance to explore. There was one big window, which overlooked the garden, and above it a reverse-cycle air-conditioning unit. The window was framed by thick curtains, light blue with a yellow pattern, and the walls were painted a very light cream colour. I looked out into the garden, now in serious need of some maintenance. The grass had been mowed the week before our wedding but was already in need of another haircut, and there was a lighter patch where the marquee had stood. That brought back memories. I guessed it would fall to me now, as the man of the house, to look after the garden. The door to the en-suite bathroom was open, so I went in. It was big, complete with a bath, toilet, and a separate shower with ornate glass walls and sliding door, and it had his and hers handbasins with plenty of cupboard space above them. There were still a lot of items in the cupboard, including Peter's shaving kit, hairbrushes, and a myriad of bottles and packets that needed clearing out.

Helen came in as I was looking. 'Oh, dear,' she said, 'I forgot about those. They'll have to be thrown out.' She went and collected a cardboard box from downstairs and filled it with her father's bits and pieces before lugging it down to the rubbish bin. Then she returned with a cloth and a bottle of cleaning fluid to wipe out the shelves. We remained busy for the next hour, bringing in stuff from the other bathroom, unpacking and putting everything away. Meanwhile, Myra had filled another case with clothes she never wore, and this, too, I carried down to the car for later disposal. Finally, all was ready, or ready enough for us to call our new room home, and we traipsed back downstairs. I was still somewhat put out by the fact that so little had been done during the week we'd been away. Helen must have been reading my thoughts. 'It was too much to expect that Mum would be able to get everything done on her own,' she said. 'It was a lot of work, and it must have been too difficult for her, having to go through all Dad's gear. You know, John, she's still grieving.' I had to back off and agree with her.

The next morning, after a comfortable night in our new bed, I resolved to make a start on the garden. The previous summer, Peter had bought a new four-stroke mower, and cutting the grass was a relatively easy job. When I stopped, I could hear Helen on her piano, so I decided to stay outside. The mower and all the garden tools were kept in a small shed attached to the back of the garage. I found a small weeding fork and set about clearing one of the beds that ran down the side of the drive. Myra came out to see what I was doing and thanked me. 'I'm afraid the garden has got a bit out of hand,' she said. 'Peter loved gardening. It was his pride and joy. It's good that you are taking over. I can't do much these days.'

'Well, I'm not much of a gardener,' I replied. 'My parents don't have much room for growing things, the garden being tiny, and Mum used to look after what there was.'

I could see that Myra was listening to the piano. Helen came to the end of the piece she was playing, and in the silence that followed, Myra smiled and pointed at the house. 'She's really quite talented, don't you think, John?'

'Oh, yes,' I said, thinking that it was better to lie than to upset her. Because I'm not in the least musical, I had no idea whether Helen was talented. And I didn't like to tell Myra that I didn't even enjoy the piano. After a few moments looking out over Peter's handiwork, she sighed, shook her head, and went back inside. The piano restarted, and I went back to the weeding.

Thompson's start work at seven thirty. It would not have gone down well to be late on my first day at work, so Helen and I had worked out a simple schedule. I had previously timed the trip to Mordialloc at around twenty-five minutes, so I had to be up at six and away by seven every morning. I was used to this schedule from my time as an apprentice, but it would be difficult for Helen. She would have to get up an hour earlier than she was accustomed to. She insisted on providing me with a cooked breakfast every morning, and she could hardly ask her mother to make it, so she would have to be wide awake in good time. And bedtime could be no later than ten o'clock to allow us our eight hours' sleep. That first Monday morning, we bounced out of bed as soon as the alarm clock told us to. In fact, we'd been awake for some time in expectation of its jagged wake-up call. I went for a quick shower, while Helen donned her dressing gown and headed for the kitchen. As I returned from the bathroom, I could already smell bacon cooking.

'Don't rush it,' ordered Helen as I sat down to a plate of fried bacon and eggs. 'There's plenty of time.' I looked at the clock; it was only six twenty. She already had two pieces of bread in the toaster, and the kettle was boiling for coffee. And she was busy preparing a packed lunch for me. It was a splendid breakfast, and I wondered if I could expect the same treatment five days a week for the next forty years or so. I smiled at the thought. It was only ten to seven when all was ready. A bag containing work overalls, boots, and lunch was in my hand as Helen ushered me out. 'Good luck with your new job,' she said. 'Love you.'

'Love you too,' I replied. She gave me a wifely peck on the cheek and shut the door behind me.

I must have been driving very slowly when I'd timed the trip previously, as I arrived at Thompson's somewhat early. No one else was around, and the place was still locked up, so I sat in the car and waited. Ten minutes later, Bill and Donna arrived, and I emerged from my ute. 'Got a proper car now, I see,' said Bill. He shook my hand and led me inside. 'The rest'll be in soon.' I grabbed my bag and followed him through the office and into the workshop. There was a door on one side I hadn't noticed before, and it led into a small change room with a shower, a line of half-a-dozen lockers, and a table. One of the lockers already had my name on. 'You've already met Greg, I believe,' said Bill.

'That's right,' I answered.

'I'll leave you here, then.'

I got changed into my overalls and sat at the table, but I didn't have to wait long. Within minutes, Greg and Nigel arrived, and my first day at Thompson's was under way. I discovered that my first job wasn't to be in the workshop after all. Greg told me there was a problem with an excavator that was working out south on a pipeline trenching job. There was a company LDV fitted out with all the necessary tools and spares, and in this we drove down to the site. When we got there, the operator was standing next to the machine looking helpless. Before Greg asked him what the problem was, he introduced me. 'John here will be taking over when I leave,' he said. When the operator said the bucket wouldn't lift anymore, Greg went straight to a cover plate on the side of the machine, checked the size of the nuts holding it in place, and went to the LDV for tools. He gave me a spanner, told me to loosen off the plate, while he climbed into the cab to check the controls. I had the cover off before he returned, so we were able to look inside at the various mechanisms.

There was a maze of hydraulic equipment in there, together with a host of flexible hoses and other pipes, and there seemed to be a lot of fluid on the ground below the machine that had evidently leaked from one of them. 'See that one there,' said Greg, pointing. 'It's the one that carries the fluid to a hydraulic cylinder operating

the bucket. We'll take it out and check it.' So we did and found that it was indeed the culprit. 'They are well reinforced, but sometimes the continual flexing weakens them,' he added. He went back to the LDV, found the necessary replacement, and we had the excavator back in service in no time, though, first, we had to replenish all the fluid that had been lost.

'Thanks, Greg,' said the operator, giving me a nod as well.

'No worries, mate,' answered Greg as we made our way back to the LDV. 'I'll let you drive us back,' he told me. 'We often have to use this vehicle for site jobs, so you'd better get used to it.' As I drove back, we discussed the work and the various jobs we might be called on to do, and it was lunchtime when we got back to the workshop. I was looking forward to what Helen had prepared for me, and when I opened my lunch tin, I found a small package on top. It was a chocolate wrapped in a piece of paper, and on the paper she'd drawn a heart with an arrow through it, an *H* and a *J* pencilled in at the two ends. Below the heart, she had just written 'ILY'. I smiled but hid the piece of paper before anyone else could see it. I realised my face was burning.

It was four months before Greg announced that he believed me ready to take over, and at the beginning of June, he retired. Bill called me into his office, told me they were very satisfied with my work, and offered me an increase in my hourly rate, in view of the added responsibility. I was really chuffed. Bill, Donna, Nigel, and I, together with a handful of the drivers and operators, joined Greg at the Mordialloc Hotel for a farewell drink. We were joined by a number of the men's wives, most of whom seemed to know each other. I had asked Helen, but as she only finished work at five, she declined.

By the time Greg left us, I was pretty well versed in the various idiosyncrasies of the equipment, but nevertheless I was nervous about doing everything on my own. What made it worse was that I never really got on with Bill's son Nigel. In fact, I thought him an arrogant little bastard, but because he was the boss's son, I held my peace and put up with his tendency to cut corners. And on the occasion of Greg's farewell party, I discovered that he was a bit of a boozer as well. The whole party was being paid for by Bill, and Nigel certainly drank more than his fair share.

Life at home continued happily. Surprisingly, Helen had maintained her splendid start, always providing cooked breakfasts and creative lunches, and she did much of the cooking in the evenings as well.. She had returned to work as planned at the start of February but told me it had taken her a long time to get used to being addressed as Mrs Madden. There was only one aspect of our life together that I found difficult. I was becoming increasingly resentful of Myra's presence. Of course, I couldn't say anything. After all, it was her house, and we were there on sufferance. And it was costing us virtually nothing other than what we spent on food, plus a two-thirds share of the rates and utility bills, so we were saving most of our incomes. Added to that, Myra continually went out of her way to make sure we were comfortable and had everything we needed. But in a way, it was like living in a hotel. Myra wandered round the house silently, like a ghost sometimes, and I never knew where I might bump into her next. She always seemed to be at a loose end, not sure of anything, lacking a focus in her life with Peter gone, though I suppose *we* were her focus now. The whole set-up sometimes gave me a feeling of claustrophobia.

The only times Helen and I could be sure of being alone together was in our room, but even that privacy was breached a couple of times. Once, when we had gone to bed early and were in the throes of making love, the door suddenly opened and Myra walked in. It was a warm night, and we'd thrown off the bedclothes. Myra seemed in a bit of a daze. She walked right up to the bed, apparently without seeing us, then she suddenly stopped, as we had also done, though now we were scrabbling for the sheet to cover ourselves. She stared at us through her thick bottle glasses. 'Oh,' she said, 'I'm sorry. I forgot.' And she quickly backed out.

'Coitus interruptus,' said Helen, laughing. In fact, she thought it very funny, though I failed to see the joke. In fact, I was bloody angry.

'Coitus *what*?' I barked.

'Just a bit of old Latin, I think, but it's probably been anglicised.' With the interruption, she had completely lost the urge to continue, much to my annoyance. She quickly settled down to sleep, though it took me a while to regain my equilibrium.

However, a couple of weeks later, almost the same thing happened. I had just emerged naked from the bathroom after a shower when Myra again marched in without knocking, though this time she realised quickly that she was in the wrong room. 'Sorry. I keep forgetting,' she said as she turned and went out.

'I'm getting sick of this,' I told Helen rather forcibly.

'I'm sorry, darling.'

'I sometimes feel she's snooping on me.'

'Of course she isn't. She'd never do that.'

'Perhaps we should put a sign on the door, one saying "private" or something, in big letters. Something she couldn't fail to read.'

'Please give her a bit of slack, John. She's been living here for over twenty years. This room was part of her life.'

'So, how long is this going to go on for, then?' I snapped at her. Helen just shook her head, and I decided not to pursue the matter. I'd made my point. 'At least let's put a bolt on the inside of the door,' I added.

In fact, Myra was continually forgetting things, often important things like appointments, and she was forever losing items or misplacing them. I could see that it was worrying Helen, for her mother had called her at work a couple of times, and she'd had to rush home.

'I think I must take Mum to a doctor,' she told me one day.

'Do you think she's sick?' I asked her.

'I'm beginning to wonder if she's developing early-onset dementia.'

'Really?'

'Perhaps it can be brought on by grieving. I don't know.'

'How old is she?'

'Only fifty-five. She was already over thirty when she married Dad and thirty-three when I was born.'

'Surely she's far too young to have dementia.'

'I don't know. That's why I want her to see a doctor.'

A week later, Helen took Myra to see their GP, who, after a fairly cursory examination, gave her a referral to a specialist, a Mr Masters. She managed to get an appointment for the following week, and soon the worst of Helen's fears were confirmed. Mr Masters told Helen that her mother was indeed a little young to have Alzheimer, but he knew of others, some as young as young as forty-five, who had contracted it. Currently, the disease, the slow death of her mother's brain cells, wasn't yet far advanced, but there was no cure, and Helen would soon need to start thinking about the future. The specialist said that Myra would eventually need to have a full-time carer and, in a few years, might well have to go into a nursing home.

Helen was horrified at the prospect of consigning her mother to a home. She resolved to employ someone to come in five days a week while she was at work. However, she soon discovered that the cost would eat up most of her salary, so she thought it best to give up her job and look after her mother herself. She thought about it for some time but didn't seem ready to discuss it with me. Perhaps she thought it was *her* problem and only hers, but eventually, as we lay awake one night in bed, she unburdened herself. 'What do *you* think we should do?' she asked me.

In fact, I had never been entirely happy with her being back at work after we were married. I still harboured the old-fashioned idea that the man of the house was the breadwinner and the woman's place was in the home. That was the way it had always been in my family, and I saw nothing wrong with it. And I was now earning enough to keep us both. I wanted her to be here all the time, looking after me and our home, not gallivanting around at TAFE, being ogled by all the spotty-faced kids studying there. No, I was *not* being jealous. At least I didn't think I was. I just wanted Helen to myself and not be sharing her with anyone else. So I didn't have to think about my answer. 'Yes,' I said in as kind a voice as I could muster. 'I think you should give up work. Your mother will be much happier under your care.'

It was coming up to the end of June. Helen had to give a month's notice, so she would stay at TAFE until the end of July. Myra herself didn't seem too upset by the changes that were about to be made in our lives, though she continued to claim there was nothing wrong with her. But she seemed to sleep a lot, much more than she usually did, and Helen often noticed, on returning from work, that Myra had left the stove on, or the front door was wide open with Myra nowhere to be seen. And we often found things in odd places, like the milk in the crockery cupboard or the coffee jar in the fridge. It was nothing serious, but I realised that the sooner Helen stayed home, the better.

The other July event was an addition to the family. I had rather neglected my old home, only visiting my parents a couple of times since the wedding, but the birth of another child to Paul and Barbara was something I had to acknowledge and show an interest in. Amy was born on July 12, and the next day, Helen and I went to the hospital to greet the new arrival. Paul was already there, and Mum and Dad arrived soon after we did. Everyone cooed over the new baby, saying how beautiful she was, though for my part she looked a wizened little creature. And she looked so incredibly vulnerable. I had never seen a newborn baby before, so it was quite an eye-opener. I wondered how long it would be before Helen wanted one; she was going quite gooey-eyed over Amy. At one point, I took Mum aside and asked her if my father was still behaving himself, and she just smiled and said it was all good, which was a relief. I told her about Myra and the changes we would have to make at the end of the month. She said she felt sad for poor Helen, and then she asked me when *we* were going to start a family. I said I didn't think the time was right for that, and Mum agreed.

So, from August that year, Helen stayed at home. At first, she didn't seem to mind. It would give her more time to concentrate on her hobbies, she hoped, though I'd never realised that she had any, apart from the piano. That was when she told me she used to do a fair amount of knitting and hoped to make time for it. She might even knit something for little Amy. A few days after relinquishing her job, she went out and bought a stack of new music and even got a man in to retune her piano. As for Myra, she seemed a lot happier with Helen in the house all day, and there were no signs that her dementia was getting any worse. In fact, she and Helen started taking it in turns to prepare our evening meal. It became a sort of competition as to who could provide the best dinners. I was, of course, the main beneficiary of this.

The months passed. Winter turned to spring, and spring to summer. As the weather warmed, we took to taking Myra out for drives into the country, often visiting one or more of the beaches where Helen and I had done much of our courting. Myra wouldn't come swimming with us, but she enjoyed the outings. We even visited Somers, but there were no dolphins there that day. As December approached, Helen suggested that we invite my parents over on Christmas Day, as well as my sister, Paul, and the children. Myra, too, was enthusiastic, and I was given the job of issuing the invitations, all of which were gratefully accepted.

We decided to have a barbecue, or rather the ladies did, but as none of us had ever cooked on one, and as we didn't even have the wherewithal, we had to go off one Saturday morning to purchase the necessary equipment. We went to a shop on the Nepean Highway, one that advertised a huge range of barbecues. It had to be a fairly big unit, one that could cater for everybody, and we selected one that looked capable of doing the job. I persuaded the shop assistant to help us load it onto my ute, together with a large gas bottle and the connecting hose. Getting it off again at the house was another problem, but Helen managed to prevail upon a neighbour to help us, and soon it was all set up ready to use. In the shop, they'd shown me how to turn on the gas and operate the controls, so I decided to light up straightaway, just to make sure it was all working. And since it was nearly lunchtime, Helen went in and fetched a packet of lamb chops. Once they were on the grid, she left me to the cooking and went inside to prepare a salad.

We had a barbecue every weekend in the lead up to Christmas, trying out different meats and making sure I knew exactly what I was doing. Apart from the odd burnt sausage, I managed quite well and felt confident of my ability to feed the hordes on Christmas Day. The other problem was that we had insufficient garden furniture to sit everyone, so on a later trip, we purchased a large table and eight chairs. This had to be delivered, my ute being too small to carry everything. Paul had bought himself a new 'people mover' so he would be able to pick up Mum and Dad and bring them along.

On Christmas Eve, the weather forecast for the next day was not good. A cold front was on its way and showers were expected. We decided to remove the cars from the garage and set up both the barbecue and the table inside, so that if it did rain, we would at least be under cover. It was just as well. The first drops of rain and our guests' arrival coincided. But after half an hour, the rain stopped, the sun came out, and everyone's spirits rose. Even my father was smiling, though I think that was largely because I had agreed *not* to cook any prawns. Mum was just surprised I was going to cook anything. Helen renewed her friendship with Barbara and her broodiness over Amy. Myra smiled at everyone, sitting Florrie on her lap most of the time, and Paul came and helped me with the barbecue. And the party lasted until it was almost dark.

*   *   *

CHAPTER 9

1983–1984

It was only a few months later that Helen told me she thought it was time we started a family. It had occurred to me sometime before that she was often looking bored or at a loose end. I didn't want her suggesting she should go back to work, so I agreed straightaway. 'Good idea,' I said.

'Well, I'll come off the pill, then.' She smiled and gave me a kiss.

'Can't wait,' I said and kissed her back. 'We'll start trying tonight if you like.'

'OK.'

'And every night thereafter,' I joked.

But it wasn't that easy. We'd been told that the after-effects of the contraceptive pill, especially if taken over a long period, were such that it could often take time before a woman became fertile again. It was fun trying, but month after month, Helen's periods arrived with clockwork regularity, and she became a little despondent. She even suggested we both go off and get ourselves checked. I was not impressed with the idea that my manhood was in doubt, and, at first, I refused, but after three more months of the same, I relented. The doctor gave me a small container for a sample, and when I returned it, duly hidden in a plastic bag, he sent it away for testing. 'I'll have the result by Friday,' he assured me, and when I phoned him three days later, he told me my sperm count was entirely normal. Meanwhile, Helen had also been cleared of any problems, though she would never tell me how they had tested *her*. So it was back to square one: keep trying, and if at first you don't succeed, never give up.

In the event, it was a little over a year later when the logjam broke. I came back from work one cold June afternoon to find Helen all smiles. 'I've got something to tell you,' she said.

'You're pregnant,' I replied jokingly.

'How the hell did you guess?'

'I didn't. I was just trying to be funny.'

'Well, I am. At least I think I am. My period should have come five days ago.'

'And it didn't.'

'No. Are you pleased, darling?'

'Of course. Let's celebrate. I'll slip out and get a bottle of Oz Fizz.'

'No alcohol, John. If I am pregnant, it will damage our child.'

'OK, if you say so.'

'But we can still celebrate in bed. We can still make love. It'll be months before we need to be careful on that score.'

'I'm glad to hear it,' I said, laughing, and I put my arms around her and gave her a hug.

By then, there was another matter that was occupying Helen's mind. Myra's dementia was becoming worse by the day. She would often start a sentence and then forget what she was going to say, so the half sentence would hang in mid-air. Helen would always try and help her out by repeating the half sentence she had uttered in the hope of jogging Myra's memory and getting her to finish what she had hoped to say. That sometimes worked. When I witnessed one of these scenes, I became embarrassed, mainly because I didn't understand what was going on inside her head. I'd heard of, and been aware of, both long-term and short-term memory loss in people, but this sort of instantaneous memory loss in the middle of a sentence was something I couldn't take. I became apprehensive, wary of becoming involved, and I started avoiding Myra even more than before.

Then one day, when Helen had to go to the doctor for her monthly check-up, Myra found her way out of the house. I suppose she must have had some idea of where she was going, or at least wanted to go, but when Helen returned and found the house empty, she panicked. First, she tried to get me on the phone, but I was away on a job that morning and so missed the call. Then she phoned the police. She explained about her mother's dementia and said she'd had to leave her alone that morning to visit her doctor. The officer who answered her call promised to put out a general appeal to all cars that happened to be in the vicinity, asking them to keep an eye open for her mother, but Helen decided to go out looking herself. She searched everywhere she could think of but an hour later returned empty-handed to find a message on the answering machine. It asked her to call back to the police station. Evidently, Myra had walked a few streets away, entered a cafe, and ordered a toasted sandwich and a cup of coffee.

When she had finished them both, she just got up to leave without paying. The owner had caught her, and when he asked her for payment, she denied she'd ever had a toasted sandwich or a coffee. In fact, she made no sense at all, and the owner decided to call the police and report the matter. Luckily, he spoke to the same sergeant that had taken Helen's call, and he had put two and two together.

Helen went straight round to the cafe, apologised, paid the owner, adding a significant tip, and took her mother home. Later that evening, Myra seemed to have forgotten the episode completely. Helen had told me all about it when I got home, describing her panic at finding the house empty, the phone calls to the police, and the possibility of her mother being arrested. I felt we'd reached a turning point. Myra was no longer safe if left alone. Helen and I were discussing the matter later that evening, and Myra must have heard us talking about her. I was flabbergasted when she suddenly interrupted us, denying that she'd ever left the house. I couldn't believe my ears. 'That's just so bloody stupid!' I yelled. 'How can you claim you never went out? Everyone was out there looking for you.'

She looked at me as though I had hit her, cowering under my onslaught. 'I …. I …. didn't ….' she started to say, and then Helen interrupted.

'That's not fair, John. Mum doesn't remember things. You know that.'

'I do know, but this only just happened—this afternoon, for God's sake. Has your mother completely lost it?' I was angry, and the resentment I felt at Myra's presence in the house returned. 'She's a danger to us all,' I added. 'You never know what she'll do next.'

Helen stiffened, looking at me sternly. Her eyes narrowed, and her lips quivered in anger. 'I'm sorry, John, but you'll just have to leave this for me to deal with. Just go away. We'll talk later.' While Helen and I were arguing, Myra was looking at us both with a puzzled expression, as though she couldn't understand what we were arguing about, or even that she was the subject of our altercation.

It was later that evening when I managed to catch Helen alone. I felt a bit of a heel, talking to her mother the way I had done, so I thought I'd better apologise. 'I'm sorry I got so angry, but we can't go on like this,' I said.

'I know,' she answered, shaking her head.

'Well, what are we going to do about it?'

'What do you mean *we*? This has to be *my* decision.'

'OK. Then what are *you* going to do about it?'

'I'm not sure yet.'

'Perhaps we should put deadlocks on all the doors. Lock her in when you go out.'

'And if she starts a fire or something, she's trapped.'

'Well, as you say, it's your decision, but if it was me, I'd get her into a home, someplace where they understand Alzheimer, where she can be looked after *properly*.'

'You sound as though you are blaming me for what happened.'

'No, I wasn't.'

'Anyway, I can't do that.'

'Why not?'

'I can't put my own mother into a home. It wouldn't be right.'

'I think you should at least consult someone: a doctor or a specialist, and get their advice.'

'I guess you're right.'

'And take her with you this time.'

Before any of this could be done, however, Helen realised there were some legal matters that would need to be attended to. She wondered if her mother had ever drawn up a will, and if there was going to be a problem with her dementia, Myra would need both a financial and a medical power of attorney to supervise her affairs. Luckily, her mother's memory was still good in one way at least. In a moment of clear-headedness, she was able to tell Helen the name of the person who had handled their matters in the past, a lawyer called Candice Maybury. Helen found the number and phoned for an appointment. Yes, there *was* a will, and the lawyer already had a copy of it on her desk when they arrived, but it was sadly out of date, having been made when Peter was still alive. They spent an hour discussing the required changes, and Myra said that she was quite happy to give Helen the necessary powers of attorney. They also discussed the matter of Myra's finances. Candice told Helen that they had a financial consultant attached to their practice, and he would advise them what to do. And now that she had financial power of attorney, she could take her mother's money out of the bank account where it had been sitting since Peter's death and invest it in whatever the consultant advised. It was a substantial amount.Three days later, they went back, and everything was signed, though Helen was never sure that her mother really understood what she was agreeing to. And she didn't discuss it with me either, not before it was all signed and sealed. Finally, the three of us down together, and Helen told us what she had done. Myra seemed happy, if somewhat puzzled by it all, but it made sense to me, and I complimented Helen on her obvious business sense. I was also pretty buoyed up by the thought that my wife now had control over so much money, though my mind was seething over the way she was doing everything without consulting me. She had explained a great deal about her family's finances, but, as I was much later to discover, she had not told me everything. However, for the most part, I managed to hide my chagrin, planning on the day I would take full control as was my right as head of the house.

Helen phoned our GP the following day. She asked him for a referral to Mr Masters, the specialist who had originally assessed Myra. She told her mother what was being planned and, on the day of the appointment, drove her to the specialist's rooms. He gave Myra another battery of tests but told Helen he wouldn't discuss the results in front of her mother but would rather phone her the next day. However, he did give her a list of four nursing homes he could recommend, ones that catered for patients with dementia, should Helen now deem it appropriate to place her mother into one. But they needed to have their phone conversation first. Helen had asked Mr Masters to phone at two o'clock. She said her mother would be resting in her room at that time. The news was not good. The specialist ran through a number of items, quoting figures and norms that Helen understood little of. But in short, he simply told her that Myra's condition had worsened to the extent that she could no longer be held responsible for her actions.

'You mean it's gone beyond the point of hiring a full-time nurse to look after her at home?'

'I'm afraid so. Yes.'

'So a nursing home is the only option?'

'That's correct.'

I could see that Helen had been crying when I got home that day. Her eyes were red, and she sobbed as she clung to me. 'It's the end,' she said. 'I can do nothing more.' I had to hide my joy at the prospect of having the house to ourselves at last, so I said nothing. 'We must take Mum on a drive at the weekend,' she added. 'Go round all these places on the list. See what's best.'

'Of course,' I replied.

On the Saturday morning, Helen brought Myra out to the car. She thought it best not to tell her mother what was being planned. 'We're just going to look at some houses, Mum,' she announced. She was trying to sound cheerful, but I could see she was deeply unhappy. We drove round to all four places on the list, stopping at each for a short look. Helen decided that the second one we looked at, a nursing home called Beechwood Gardens, looked the nicest, so we returned there. At any rate, it had the best setting of the four: well-kept lawns and a scattering of trees, shrubs, and flower beds surrounding a number of low brick buildings. The whole area was bordered by a high wire fence, but this was largely hidden by a tall hedge that rendered it less of an eyesore. The fence was obviously designed to keep the inmates from escaping, which seemed appropriate. From the road, one entered through a gate, which automatically opened as one approached, and the drive led to a large parking area. Helen drove us in and parked close to a building that was marked Reception. 'John, darling, please take Mum for a walk while I go in and talk to them,' she asked me. Once again, I was being sidelined from any negotiations, though this time I was happy not to get involved. 'Won't be long, Mum,' Helen added as she walked off and left us.

Myra and I strolled along a path that wound its way between a series of flower beds. She took my arm as we walked, something I accepted with bad grace. Myra kept stopping to look at the flowers, many of which she surprisingly remembered the names. There was a scattering of other people on the path, including two elderly women being pushed in wheelchairs by nurses. The nurses greeted us as we passed, but their charges stared straight ahead, empty-eyed as if oblivious to everything around them. Soon, we reached a bench from where we could see the door to reception. We sat there so we could keep an eye open for Helen. She was in reception for at least twenty minutes, and during that time, Myra kept up a barrage of inconsequential chatter, stopping and changing the subject so often that I couldn't keep up. And she kept asking what Helen was doing. Every time she asked me, I told her that Helen had to talk to the people inside. The fifth or sixth time she asked, the door to reception opened, and Helen appeared. She seemed a little preoccupied as she looked around the garden. Then she saw us and walked over. She looked at me and gave a little shake of her head as she took her mother's hand, and we headed back to the car.

Myra happily chatted about the flowers she'd seen and how she'd enjoyed her outing, but otherwise we remained silent as we drove home. After lunch, Myra went for her rest, so Helen and I were able to talk.

'The staff were very friendly, but at present they don't have a place,' said Helen. 'The lady I spoke to even phoned the other homes on our list, but they were all full too.'

'There must be other nursing homes,' I suggested.

'I'm sure there are, but I'd rather keep to the ones Mr Masters recommended. We can wait.'

'I suppose.'

'Anyway, I've got Mum on the waiting list, and there's only two ahead of her.'

'So, how many inmates are there?'

'They're patients, not inmates,' she answered angrily.

'Sorry, but it did look a bit like a concentration camp with that high wire fence.' I remembered that when Helen had driven us out, she'd had to use a special card to get the gate open, one she'd been given at reception. Otherwise, we'd still be locked in. I figured that the security arrangements were pretty good, an essential feature of the place under the circumstances.

'After I'd put Mum on the waiting list, they showed me round,' she continued. 'Every patient has their own room, each one with an en suite. They're nice rooms too. I was impressed. And they have a big common room with comfortable chairs, a TV, and heaps of games.' Helen opened her bag and took out a brochure. 'This will give you some idea,' she added as she gave it to me.

The first thing I saw was a list of the rates. 'It's not cheap,' I said.

'No, it's not, but the interest on Mum's investments will cover the costs.'

'Well, that's a relief.'

'I don't want you quibbling about money. I want the best for her.'

'Fair enough.'

'It's bad enough having to put her in a nursing home. I feel so terrible sometimes, knowing I can't do enough for her myself.'

'Perhaps she'll make lots of new friends there.'

'I hope so, but it won't be easy for her. It was depressing going through that common room. The patients seemed much older than Mum, many of them in wheelchairs, just staring at nothing. It was like they were waiting to die. Quite horrible.'

It was already November when Helen had a call from Beechwood Gardens. Over the months since our visit to the nursing home, Myra had become increasingly difficult. She had to be watched constantly, and Helen was tired. She badly needed a break. Often when I returned home from work, she would cling to me in desperation, and I would need to comfort her and help her with chores round the house. By then, she was also having problems herself, suffering a great deal from morning sickness that had started in July, and from which she still suffered acutely. She was now five months pregnant and showing quite a bulge. There were times recently when she had felt funny little movements within her womb as the baby kicked, and she had got me to feel her stomach when the baby was active and producing such odd little blips under my fingers. Lately, I had even pressed my ear to her stomach and could feel the faint pulse of its heartbeat. It made me a proud father-to-be.

The call from Beechwood came while both she and Myra were out visiting the clinic where they had gone for her regular ultrasound. The doctor had pronounced that all was still well, the baby growing normally. Helen hadn't thought there was anything amiss, but she'd still felt a degree of relief at the news. When they entered the house, she noticed that the answering machine had a message for her. She called back immediately to be told that a place had become available and would be ready for her mother over the weekend. She still hadn't told Myra what was being planned but realised she would now have to do so. It was something she had been putting off, intensely worried by what she would be doing to her mother, and expecting an angry reaction. With a heavy heart, she made them both tea and went to the pantry for a packet of her mother's favourite biscuits. As they sat, Helen broached the subject. 'Do you remember Mr Masters, Mum?'

'Who?'

'Mr Masters, the specialist that examined you, gave you all those tests.'

'Oh, yes.'

'And, do you remember why I had to give up work, to stay at home and look after you?'

'Did you Helen?'

'Mr Masters said you had to be looked after because you forget things. You needed a full-time carer, and ....'

'I *do* forget things, I know. I'm sorry.'

'Well, Mum, the fact is that with the baby coming, I can no longer look after you, so I've found another place for you to live—a place where you can be properly looked after, where you'll

be better off. Do you understand?'

Myra stared at her. She looked puzzled. 'Oh, no. I don't want to leave here.'

'Sorry, Mum, but it's for the best. You'll be really happy at Beechwood. It's like a hotel, and I'll come and visit you whenever I can.'

By this time, Myra was sounding quite alarmed. 'No, Helen, I really don't want to go.'

'I'm sorry that I have to do this, Mum. But I can't cope anymore.' By this time, Helen told me later, she was almost in tears.

Watching her daughter's dejected expression, Myra must have experienced a change of heart, a degree of acceptance. 'I'll come home again once the baby is born, won't I?' she asked.

'Of course, Mum.' It was the only lie she had told her mother about her new home. She was honest by nature, and it was the only intentional lie she'd ever told as far as she could remember, and it haunted her long after the conversation was forgotten.

I received the news as soon as I returned home that evening. It came as a huge relief for I would finally have my wife entirely to myself. It was going to be a new existence, one in which I would at last have control of my marriage, as well as the house and everything in it. Of course, I could never put these thoughts into words. I would have to keep my aspirations and my objectives to myself for the time being, but I tried to be helpful as Helen got everything ready for Myra's impending move. Helen spent the next couple of days deciding what her mother would need and packing it all into two suitcases. It wasn't just a matter of clothes. Helen wanted her to have plenty of knick-knacks with which to decorate her room at Beechwood and a couple of pictures that her mother loved. She wanted to make Myra's room as homely as was possible, but it was difficult to choose the items that would make her happiest, and when she asked her mother, Myra seemed totally indifferent, perhaps sure that she would again return home one day.

Helen wanted me to come with her when she delivered her mother. 'I want you to see what it's like inside,' she said, so on the Saturday morning, I piled the luggage into her car and helped Myra into the back seat. As Helen got in behind the wheel, I could see she was once again close to tears. Then she suddenly winced, putting a hand on her distended belly. I thought the baby must have hurt her, but she said nothing, so I put my hand on her knee in an attempt to comfort her, and she gave me a wan smile as she started the car.

It was a thirty-minute drive to Beechwood Gardens. As before, the gate opened as we drove up, but this time there were many more cars in the parking area and a host of people out walking or pushing wheelchairs in the gardens. I could see that many of them were visitors, there being quite a few children, some chatting excitedly to their older relatives. I opened the car door for Myra, and she stepped out, looking around her with interest. 'I think I remember this place,' she said after a time. Helen took her arm and guided her to reception, while I followed carrying the suitcases. After Helen had made herself known to the lady behind the desk, we were guided back outside and taken round to another building, which was connected to the main part of the complex by a covered walkway, again bordered by beds full of shrubs. Evidently, every building was named after a flower. The one we were heading to was called Hyacinth, and the lady receptionist took us to a room named Hyacinth 3. She then fitted a tight-fitting waterproof bracelet round Myra's wrist with her name and room number printed on it, just in case she ever got lost and couldn't find her way back to her room. The receptionist left us then, telling us all to come back and see her when we had settled Myra into her room so that she could show us round the rest of the complex. But before she left, she pointed out a bell push that would summon a nurse should the occupant be in any sort of trouble, day or night.

It was a pleasant-looking room, though I noticed an odour that I couldn't place. Perhaps it was just the smell of old age, a mixture of hospital odours, and those of bodily functions. The walls of the room were painted a light-lilac colour, and its single window overlooked a small grove of beech trees. It was carpeted and furnished with a comfortable armchair and cushions, a bed with a patterned cover that matched the curtains, and plenty of cupboard and shelf space. A door on one wall led to the bathroom, which was fitted with a shower, a toilet, and a handbasin, again with plenty of cupboard space and safety rails that had obviously been designed for older residents. Myra was certainly mentally challenged, but she was still quite able physically and wouldn't be using any of those safety fittings. Helen and Myra set about unpacking the cases, hanging clothes and generally making the room as appealing as possible, and when they were finished, we walked back the way we'd come.

We were shown the dining room and the large common room. By now, it was nearing lunchtime, and the patients who had gone outside were returning. We were invited to stay for lunch on this first day. We were told that it helped to settle someone in, having a meal together in the new setting, so we stayed. I thought the food pretty good, but Myra only picked at hers. Afterwards, we were taken to the common room and introduced to some of the other residents, as we came to call them, rather than patients. We had also been told that we should slip away quietly once Myra was suitably involved in some activity there and that a nurse would be assigned to her for a time as soon as we were gone. We called in at reception again on our way out, Helen being needed to sign some documents, especially regarding the financial arrangements. When we got outside, I could see that she was emotionally drained. In fact, she was shaking and quietly sobbing, so I offered to drive us home.

Helen remained silent all the way back. When I stopped the car outside the garage, Helen turned to me with a wan smile. 'I'm absolutely drained,' she said, 'and not feeling too well. I think I'll go and lie down for a bit.'

'OK.'

'Would you mind doing a bit of shopping for me? I was going to do it on the way home, but I'm exhausted. Here's the list of what we need,' she added, pressing a piece of paper into my hand.'

'I think I'll just pop round and see Mum and Dad first. Haven't visited for a while.'

'Good idea,' she replied as she got out of the car. She turned back to me before she shut the door. 'You know, you're lucky to still have parents.'

So I drove off to my old home, but when I got there, my parents were both out. I remembered where the spare key was always kept, so I let myself into the house, intending to leave a message. There was a hastily scribbled note next to the telephone. I recognised Mum's writing and read that she'd gone off to visit Barbara for the afternoon but would be back by six. It was addressed to my father, so he must have been on the afternoon shift. I left another note next to it and relocked the front door behind me as I left. I felt at a bit of a loose end and wondered whether I should call in at the supermarket and go home but decided to first visit Hudson. I had rather neglected him. In fact, it was months since I'd seen him and wanted to catch up on his news. As luck would have it, he was out too, but Hudson's parents were at home. They greeted me like a long-lost son and apologised for their son's absence. 'He's out with his girlfriend,' said Mr Little.

'Would that be my old friend Nola Weston?' I asked them.

'The very one,' answered Mrs Little. 'Thick as thieves now, they are.'

'We think they'll be getting married before too long,' said Hudson's father. 'Anyway, come in and have a cuppa with us. Tell us your news. I heard you sold the Beetle.' They took me inside, and we spent a pleasant hour chatting about everything from the weather to Hudson's new job in IT, until I suddenly realised the time. It was already after five, and Helen would be getting worried. I hurriedly took my leave and drove to the supermarket, bought everything on Helen's list, and headed home. It was nearly six o'clock when I finally reached the house. I knew that I should have been back earlier, so I was expecting an irate wife as I opened the door, but the house was silent. I thought Helen must still be lying down, so I went upstairs to the bedroom, but there was no one there. However, the bed was in disarray, the bedclothes heaped on the floor, and when I looked closer, I saw a bloodstain on the sheets and a trail of blood on the carpet. I followed the trail downstairs where I found another pool of blood next to the telephone. By then, I was in a panic. I quickly came to the conclusion that Helen must have phoned for an ambulance, realising she must have thought she was losing our baby. I remembered her pale, worried look in the car and her need to rest. I should never have gone out for so long. I knew I had let her down, and I felt guilty, wondering where the ambulance would have taken her. So I dialled emergency and asked for the ambulance service. When I got through to the operator, I explained who I was, gave our address, and asked if they'd taken Helen Madden to a hospital, and if so, which one? The next moment, I was on my way to the Alfred.

I was told to wait, and after ten minutes of pacing, a short Indian doctor approached me. 'Mr Madden?' he enquired.

'Yes, that's me.'

'I'm Dr Gupta. Please follow me.' He took me to a small office and indicated a chair. As soon as we were seated, he spoke in a voice full of sympathy. 'I'm sorry, but we couldn't save her.'

I felt the blood drain from my face, immediately thinking I would never see Helen again, that she was gone for good. 'Oh my god,' I blurted out.

'She was a girl, a Down baby.'

'But my wife ....'

'Oh, *she'll* be fine in a day or two,' the doctor interrupted.

I was so overcome with relief that I nearly got up and gave Dr Gupta a hug. 'I thought you meant you couldn't save Helen,' I said.

'I'm sorry. I should have been more specific.'

'So, what's with this Down business?'

"Down syndrome is basically a chromosome problem that occurs in the foetus, actually an extra chromosome 21. Nearly 50 per cent of Down babies are miscarried before term, though most miscarriages occur much earlier than your wife's.'

I remembered having seen children with the syndrome on television, though I don't remember much of the programme. Quite honestly, they looked like morons, and possibly were. I realised they would be difficult to bring up. So perhaps it was for the best. I didn't want that sort of drag on our marriage. 'What are the chances of it happening again?' I asked the doctor.

'For a woman of your wife's age, it's well under one in a hundred, possibly as little as one in a thousand. You shouldn't worry. In your case, it was just a bit of bad luck, and if you are worried, there are tests that can be carried out in any future pregnancy.'

'You mean …., so one can get a termination if it doesn't look good?'

'Exactly.'

'Well, that's an out anyway. Where is Helen now?'

'We're keeping her in ICU for tonight, and then she'll be moved to a ward tomorrow. We want to keep her in for a couple more days, just to make sure the miscarriage is complete.'

'What do you mean?'

Dr Gupta smiled. 'Make sure there are no bits left behind. We also had to give her a blood transfusion, and we want to make sure there are no complications.'

'Can I see her now?'

'She's heavily sedated, so unable to talk. But you can certainly see her.' The doctor led me to the ICU, a familiar path for me now, and handed me over to a duty nurse.

'Thank you,' I said as I shook his hand. Helen was in a bed two cubicles away from where Mum had lain. She was pale but looked quite relaxed, and when I took her hand in mine, she didn't stir. I stayed for ten minutes, watching her chest slowly rising and falling. It was quite hypnotic. I eventually realised that it could be hours before she would wake and register my presence, so I told her sleeping form that I loved her, and I gave her hand a light squeeze in parting. Then I went to find the nurse, asking her to let Helen know, as soon as she woke up, that I'd been to see her and would return the next day, which, being a Sunday, meant I was not required at work.

When I got home, I did my best to clean up the house, soaking the soiled sheet in cold water and mopping up the pool of blood in the hall, but there was nothing I could do about the stains on the carpets. I doubted that we would ever be able to get rid of those, though I tried for a time with a bucket of soapy water and a sponge. When I was finished, it was late. I realised I hadn't eaten since lunch at Beechwood, but I didn't feel in the least hungry, so I made up the bed with fresh sheets and had an early night. As I was leaving the next morning, I noticed that some late spring roses were still blooming. I picked a half dozen or so, ready to take with me, and I collected a vase to put them in at the hospital. I was just about to leave when I remembered that Helen would be moving to a ward that day and I would have to wait for official visiting hours—namely, two o'clock. Since I'd missed Mum the previous day, I decided to go round and spend the morning there.

Both my parents were at home this time and were horrified at the news of Helen's miscarriage. However, they said it would all be for the best in the long run, the girl being a Down baby. 'A child like that would be a handicap for the rest of your lives,' added Mum. 'You don't want something like that hanging round your necks,' all of which I agreed with. 'And it could even ruin your marriage.' They asked me many of the same questions I'd put to the doctor, and I answered them to the best of my abilities, though I'd already forgotten all the medical terms. Both Mum and Dad warned me to go easy on Helen. 'It'll be very difficult for her,' Mum said. 'She'll be grieving for a long time. Give her plenty of love.' They wanted me to stay for lunch. I asked Mum if we could eat early as I dare not be late at the Alfred. She had made some soup, and I was amazed to see my father happily slurping his way through a bowl of it and then asking for more. How times had changed.

When I reached the hospital, I was directed to Helen's new ward, and as I came in the door, she saw me and held out her arms. I didn't know what to expect as to her condition, thinking that she might have been worn down by her experience and unable to do much talking. But she at least had some colour in her cheeks, and someone, presumably a nurse, had made an attempt to brush her hair. However, as I put my arms around her, she burst into tears. 'I'm sorry,' she said, 'so, so sorry.'

'It's not your fault,' I said. 'There's nothing anyone could have done.' I felt close to tears myself as she clung to me.

'I felt so alone. I tried phoning your parents' house, but there was no reply.'

'They were out, so I went to Hudson's instead.'

'I understand.' Helen saw the flowers that I was carrying and brightened considerably. 'That's lovely of you, John. Thank you.'

'They're out of the garden.'

She bent her head and smelt them. 'Still plenty of scent,' she said. I had given the vase to a nurse on the way in and had asked her to fill it with water for me. When she brought it in, she arranged the roses in it and placed it on the table. As soon as the nurse had left us, Helen spoke again. 'Did they tell you all about Debbie?'

'Debbie? Who's Debbie?'

'I decided our daughter needed a name.'

'Oh, I see. Well, yes, I saw a Dr Gupta. He told me the baby had Down syndrome. That's why you miscarried.'

'I don't understand how these things happen,' said Helen, shaking her head in disbelief. 'Everything was going so well.'

'I saw my parents this morning, before I came to visit. They send their love.'

'Thank you.'

'Mum said she thought it was for the best.'

'Why?'

'Well, you know, the problems we would have raising a child with a disability. It would be quite a handicap.'

'What handicap?' Helen cried out angrily.

I was taken aback by her reaction but needed to explain myself. 'You know, the problems we'd have bringing her up, the constant care she would need.'

'But I would still have loved her,' she cried. 'I *do* love her. She was part of my body for five months.' I hadn't realised before how deeply she would be grieving, how lost she would feel. In fact, I was quite shocked and a bit puzzled. I had expected that she would have been a little relieved at having such a terrible responsibility taken away. But by using the word *disability*, I had obviously said the wrong thing. I couldn't think how to extricate myself, so I remained silent. 'I'm sorry, John,' she went on. 'But men will never understand what it feels like for a woman to lose a baby. It's shattering. *I'm* shattered. I don't know how to get over it.'

'I'm sorry. I should never have repeated what Mum said.'

'It's *so* depressing.' With that, Helen burst into tears again.

'I know,' I said. I put my arms around her again and tried to comfort her. She clung to me for a long time as her sobs slowly decreased in intensity. I noticed that the two other women in the ward, who up to then had been following our conversation, were now busy pretending not to listen.

'Please bear with me, John,' pleaded Helen through her tears. 'It'll be a while before I'm back to myself again.'

I managed to change the subject, and we chatted on until the end of visiting hours, mainly about my parents and my visit to the Littles. Helen was happy to hear Hudson might well be getting married soon. 'Perhaps he'll return the compliment and ask you to be *his* best man,' she suggested. Helen was now sounding a little more relaxed now that we'd left the subject of Debbie. I hoped that it would not take her too long to recover from her trauma and realised that I would need to keep future conversations firmly on other matters.

Before going, I mentioned that I would have to be at work the next day so couldn't visit till the evening. Helen thought she'd probably be leaving hospital on Tuesday, so I said I would try and get that day off to collect her. She seemed a little happier at last, and I felt more at ease. I was looking forward to having her home again so soon and gave her a somewhat chaste kiss on the cheek as I stood to leave. 'You can do better than that, darling,' she suggested, smiling, and the next time we kissed, she plunged her tongue into my mouth. Her ordeal had not taken away her playfulness, I was glad to see. I hoped that I'd now been forgiven for my lack of empathy.

*   *   *

CHAPTER 10

1984–1985

Helen was still weak and in some pain for the first week of her homecoming. I treated her with kid gloves, doing as much for her as I could in the evenings when I returned from work, and over the weekend I undertook the heavier housework. But she slowly recovered, and after another week, she seemed more or less back to normal in a physical sense, though I had no idea how long it would take for her mind to heal. Occasionally, she would stop what she was saying in mid sentence and stare unseeing at some inanimate object. And there were times in bed when she would suddenly yell out in her sleep, the victim of some nightmare. I would gently wake her and ask her what was troubling her, but she was never able to give me a coherent answer. And it was difficult to get her out of bed in the mornings. In the end, I gave up trying, so my cooked breakfasts went by the board.

Helen wasn't yet ready to drive for a while, so on two weekends, she asked me to take her to Beechwood to visit her mother. On the second of these occasions, I went in with her and was introduced to an elderly man who, Myra told us, was a friend she'd just met. Boris Matthews, for that was his name, was tall, but he had a pronounced stoop, so he seemed about the same height as Helen's mother. He had thick white hair that defied a hairbrush and a slightly lopsided grin that seldom left his face. I rather liked the old codger, especially as he seemed to have overcome Myra's earlier homesickness and therefore lessened the chance of her wanting to return home. Boris didn't seem to be suffering from dementia. In fact, he was a very alert gentleman, well-spoken, and full of amusing quips about some of the other residents. I never saw him in a wheelchair, but he did use a stick to get around. Helen reckoned he was in his late seventies, so at least twenty years older than Myra, but that didn't seem to bother either of them. They appeared very caring of each other, and I wondered how close the two of them had become in the short time they had known each other.

On our way home, Helen seemed particularly buoyed by that visit. She commented that her mother seemed both happy and now settled comfortably into her new environment. During the first couple of weeks in Beechwood, Myra had frequently asked nurses and other residents whether they had seen Peter anywhere, but that had now ceased, to Helen's relief. Strangely, Myra never noticed the absence of Helen's bulge, and the miscarriage was never mentioned by either of them. Helen later told me she had wanted to put it all behind her, and since her mother hadn't said anything, she thought it best to let sleeping dogs lie. I thought that with Myra, it was a case of looking without seeing, and wondered whether that was simply a sign of her dementia. Perhaps she also listened without hearing and even touched without feeling, which could be dangerous.

It was a night soon after that visit when Helen turned to me in bed one night. 'Darling,' she said, 'I think I'm ready now.'

My mind was busy on other matters at the time, so, at first, I didn't appreciate what she was suggesting. 'Ready for what?' I asked her.

'You're a bit slow tonight,' she replied, laughing.

I suddenly understood. 'Are you quite sure it's not too soon?'

'Definitely not. I'm *sure* I'm ready,' and she reached out to touch me.

A month before Christmas, Bill Thompson announced that he would be shutting down the operation for four weeks, in line with most other construction companies, and the staff should all take leave. I was due time off anyway, having just about completed my first year, and decided to give Helen a surprise by taking her for a holiday. Donna told me that the previous year they'd gone off to the Motor Inn, a hotel in Bright, for a week and had really enjoyed it. 'They do a fabulous Christmas lunch, at least five courses,' she told me. 'You'd love it.' So I got the details from her, and one weekend, while Helen was out of the house, I phoned the hotel to make a booking. I was lucky, being told that they'd been full till that morning but had just had a cancellation, so I snapped it up.

'I've got a surprise for you,' I told Helen when she returned.

'That's nice.'

'How would you like to go to Bright for a week's holiday?'

She brightened considerably. 'Love to. When?'

'I've booked for a week over Christmas.'

She suddenly looked crestfallen. 'Oh, dear, not then.'

'Why?'

'We really should go and visit Mum on Christmas Day. If we're not there, she'd be the only person in the whole place without a visitor.'

'Well, it's booked now,' I said firmly. 'I can't change it. Anyway, she's got Boris.'

'Sorry, John, but you'll have to change it. Apparently, Boris has a huge extended family. They will all descend on him on Christmas Day, so he's not going to have time to be with Mum.'

I thought for a moment. There must be some way we could persuade Boris to keep an eye on Myra. 'I know, why don't we drop in again this Saturday?' I suggested. 'Take her out for the day. Boris too. Take them to the Botanic Gardens and buy them lunch.'

'OK,' said Helen warily. 'But I don't think they'd allow Boris to join us, not without his family's permission. And I still want to see Mum over Christmas.'

Her obstinacy was making me angry. 'That's just too bad,' I said.

'What do you mean *too bad*?'

'We're going to Bright and that's final, so stop arguing!' I shouted at her. 'Why must you always be so bloody difficult?'

'I'm not being difficult,' she whispered.

'Here am I trying to do the right thing, give you a bit of a holiday, and all you do is worry about your fucking mother.'

Helen started trembling, shocked by my outburst. 'How could you say such a thing?'

There was a fiery silence between us, but after a while, I realised I'd gone too far and resolved to try and make peace. 'I'm sorry,' I said. 'That was unfair. We'll just tell her we can't see her then because we'll be away. I'm sure she'll understand.' Helen remained silent, so I continued. 'We'll explain the problem to the staff before we go. Make sure they're onside.' I could see that Helen was still not happy, but I decided to leave it at that. I was sure she'd come round to my way of thinking.

When we visited Beechwood the following weekend, I slipped away to reception and asked if we could get permission to take Boris Matthews out to lunch. She looked in her filing cabinet and fished out a folder, opening it and looking inside. 'His son Stanley looks after his affairs,' she told me. 'He's the man to ask.'

I gave her my best smile. 'Can you ask him for me, please?'

She looked in the file again, dialled a number, and had a short conversation with a person on the other end. 'He says that's fine. Just sign him out when you go.'

'Thanks a lot.'

'His family seldom comes to see him,' she added with a smirk, 'so he'll enjoy an outing.'

I found Myra and Helen outside in the garden and told them we now had permission to take Boris as well.

'Oh, is that what you were doing? Well done.'

'Where is he anyway?'

'We left him in the common room,' answered Helen. I went straight in to find Boris, asking him if he'd like to join us for lunch. He looked very pleased at the invitation, and after signing the two of them out for the day, we all went back to the car. We had to let Boris sit in the passenger seat; he would have had difficulty fitting into the back with his long legs and lack of flexibility. I parked as near the Botanic Gardens restaurant as I could, and we walked slowly the rest of the way, finding a table under a large umbrella as close to the lake as possible.

Boris was voluble in his appreciation. He told us he'd been at Beechwood for three years, and it was the first time he'd been out of the gate in all that time. He had quite a story to tell. When his wife had died, he had tried to manage on his own, rather unsuccessfully, he added. His three children had persuaded him to move to a nursing home so he could be properly looked after, and once they had dumped him, as he put it, they had all virtually ignored him. They'd sold his house as soon as he was gone, and he had no idea where all the proceeds had gone. Only his daughter ever visited him, and he hadn't seen her for months. He paused in his story before continuing. 'I've got seven grandchildren I never see anymore, and I believe I now have two great-grandchildren whom I will never meet.'

I could see that Helen was horrified at his treatment, as indeed I was. 'Then you're not expecting any visitors on Christmas Day?' I asked him, taking a sideways look at Helen as I did so.

'Oh, no. They're far too immersed in their own lives to think of me,' he answered with a sad smile. 'I'm beginning to think of *you* as my family these days. My own is a great disappointment.' So I explained to them both about our planned holiday and apologised for the fact that we would also be absent on Christmas Day. We hoped they wouldn't mind and that they could keep each other company instead. 'Of course, we will,' he said. 'And, where might you be going?'

'Bright. Do you know it?'

'Oh, yes. Great place. Enjoy yourselves.'

We left Myra and Boris to chat, while Helen and I went to order the lunches. When we returned, they were holding hands under the table, much to my delight and Helen's surprise. We'd been sitting awhile when Myra suddenly spoke up. 'Boris and I want to ….,' she began, but then she stopped, a worried frown on her face as her train of thought vanished.

'Yes, "Boris and I want to …."', Helen repeated, but Myra couldn't recall what she'd been about to say, and Boris couldn't suggest anything either, so whatever it was that they wanted would never be known.

There were two musicians, flute and harp players, standing in the shade of a tree next to the lake and playing for everyone's enjoyment. They were selling records of their music, and Helen bought one to give to her mother, checking with Boris first that there was a CD player available in the common room at Beechwood. After our meal, we took a short walk along the lakeside before returning to the car. Myra kept stopping to admire the flowers and became quite animated when Boris took her arm. I couldn't help smiling.

It was after three o'clock when we dropped them off. Boris himself was effusive in his thanks. It was a most enjoyable and satisfying day, he told us. We were touched by Boris's sincere gratitude, and even more so by his account of his family's rejection. We felt angry, but at least he and Myra could enjoy each other's company over the festive season, and we would now be able to leave on our holiday without feeling guilty. 'I told you so,' I said to Helen as we drove out.

*

We decided to travel to Bright by first driving east to Bairnsdale then north through Omeo. It was a long drive, longer than either of us had done before, even further than Lakes Entrance, so we took turns at the wheel, stopping for lunch at a small cafe in Bruthen. The scenery was really picturesque, especially as the road weaved its way through the Alpine National Park beyond Omeo. In winter, the area would be full of skiers, but being summer, it was largely deserted. We arrived in Bright just after three o'clock, stopping at a pub in the centre of town to get directions to the Motor Inn. Our hotel turned out to be another kilometre out of town, and in ten minutes we had found it, a large building facing the road. Behind the main building, which contained the reception, lounge, and dining areas, were a series of smaller buildings surrounded by lawns and trees that housed the individual rooms. Behind that again ran the Ovens River, though it was little more than a slow trickle at this time of year. It was a lovely setting. We were both impressed and decided, once we'd dropped off our luggage in the room, to take a walk along the riverside path.

We turned left along the stream and soon found ourselves at a bridge that crossed above us. A sign told us that this bridge used to carry the old railway track to Bright, a line that had only been closed down the previous year. We retraced our steps, and when we reached our room, Helen suggested we go back into the town to explore and find a place for a meal. When we got there, Bright was still buzzing with sightseers and other pedestrians, even though it was nearly six o'clock. There were plenty of shops still open and other places to see, including the now redundant railway station that we were told was to be made into a museum one day. We came across a number of restaurants, as well as the pub we'd already visited, so there was plenty to choose from. We thought it a good idea to come into town every evening for dinner, if only to give us plenty of variety. Of course, Christmas Day itself would be excluded since we were booked in for lunch at the hotel, and this promised to be such a huge gastronomic experience that we wouldn't need anything later.

It was three days till Christmas, and we spent every hour we had exploring Bright and its environs, including long walks both ways along the Ovens River. On Christmas Eve, we took the car up the narrow winding road that led up to the Mount Buffalo National Park. There were many good walks around there too, and the magnificent craggy scenery was wonderful. Of course, we couldn't leave the area without a visit to the Mount Buffalo Chalet, a place that Helen said her parents had wanted to visit but never had. She was obviously thinking of them as we went inside for she became quite emotional. The place had a charm but was beginning to look a little seedy. However, it was still operating, so we stayed for a very English afternoon tea.

However, my abiding memory of that week in Bright will always be the Christmas lunch. The Motor Inn had a large dining room, and it was packed to capacity. We were one of the few couples there, most of the guests being in large noisy groups. Helen and I ordered a bottle of sparkling wine, and the food never stopped coming. When the wine ran out, we ordered another bottle, and the lunch went on till well past three o'clock. There was still a bit of the wine left when we finally rose to our feet, so I clutched the bottle with one hand, and Helen with the other, as we weaved our unsteady giggling way across the lawn to our room. Helen drew the curtains, and we collapsed in an unsightly heap on the bed. We were too moribund from overeating to take our clothes off. Instead, after a few moments of petting and kissing, we fell asleep.

It was already beginning to get dark outside when I woke, though Helen was still sleeping. I looked over at her. She was lying on her back and was so relaxed, it didn't seem right to wake her. I watched her features, now softened by sleep, and her chest rising and dropping as she quietly breathed. An irresistible urge began to build up in my body. After a moment of hesitation, I gently placed a hand on her thigh and then touched her lips briefly with mine. She immediately opened her eyes, almost as if she hadn't been sleeping at all. She smiled. 'I thought you would never ask,' she said.

'You've got too many clothes on,' I replied.

'So have you.'

'Race you.'

'You're on.'

It was like that day on Philip Island, and she won this time too. Once again, we were laughing so much that it took a while for us to stop and continue our intimacy. I remember feeling totally relaxed and very much in love, both with Helen and with the world at large. And I remember that the moon came up while we lay together and how I drew back the curtains so I could watch it making erotic patterns of light and shadow across Helen's precious body. We got up to all sorts of antics that night and managed to continue our joyous lovemaking for much longer than usual. In fact, we were still conjoined as we once again drifted off to sleep. That night was another abiding memory of our Christmas Day, and we never did get around to finishing our bottle of wine.

When we got home, there was a message from Hudson on our answering machine. I phoned back that evening to be told that I would be needed in January to act as his best man.

'We were going to wait,' Hudson told me, 'but now we can't.'

'Oh, dear! Have you left a bun in the oven?' I asked him.

Hudson laughed out loud. 'How did you guess?'

'Intuition. That and knowing you.'

'Nola wants the wedding before she's too big to enjoy our first night.'

'Doesn't sound like a *first night* to me.'

'Well, you know what I mean.'

'And I guess she wouldn't want to be too big walking up the aisle in case everyone thought it was a shotgun wedding.'

'Yeah, that as well.'

'You sound happy.'

'I am.'

'Well, congratulations, my friend.'

'Thanks, Johnnie. How was *your* holiday?'

'Brilliant.'

'Anyway, the second Saturday in January. I trust you're free.'

'Absolutely. Wouldn't miss it for the world.'

'Good, Johnnie. I'll phone in a couple of days to let you know the details.'

Despite all *our* attempts at conceiving another child, Helen announced one day in mid-January that her period had arrived. I was particularly saddened by the news on this occasion. Christmas night had been so special that we had both hoped to be looking back on it as the night of Helen's conceiving. The disappointment happened only days after we had together witnessed Hudson's marriage. It was quite a small wedding under the circumstances, but as I knew both sets of parents, and many of the other guests as well, it had been a most enjoyable get-together. Nola looked particularly lovely, and she appeared to have lost much of her frivolity. She was a lot more mature than I remembered her. She was going to be a good wife for Hudson. I had previously told him about Helen's miscarriage and had asked him and Nola to avoid mentioning it in her presence. In fact, the two women had quite an intimate natter about everything else regarding marriage but avoided the subject of babies.

It was the day after Helen had started her period, and we were sitting in the lounge room after dinner. 'If I'm not going to be pregnant for a while, I think I'll go back to work,' she announced.

I didn't know how to go about it, but I had to put a stop to that idea. I was horrified at the prospect, and I needed to stamp my authority on the situation. 'No, you mustn't,' I replied.

She looked at me with a puzzled expression. 'Why ever not?'

'I just don't want you to, that's all. I'm earning enough for both of us, so you don't need to.'

'It isn't for the money.'

'No?'

'I hate sitting at home all day doing nothing. I want to be useful, have a bit of company sometimes, people to talk to.'

'Your use is here, looking after me and the house.'

'I've proved I can do that *and* work, or have you forgotten?'

I hadn't forgotten but needed to change tack to make my point. I was entitled to make decisions regarding my family, and Helen would have to fall into line. 'Am I suddenly not good enough for you?'

'Oh, John, don't be silly. You know it's not that.'

'I reckon you just want to go and find another bloke, get pregnant, and then say it's mine.'

'What on earth gave you that idea? It's so ridiculous.'

'I've seen you eyeing other men, giving them come-hither looks.'

'What *are* you talking about? Surely you're not serious?'

'Well, you're not going back to work, and that's final. I won't have it,' and with that ultimatum, I left her. I was angry at the way she'd spoken to me. I'd felt like knocking some sense into her, putting her over my knee, and giving her a good spanking, like a naughty child, but I'd vowed never to raise my hand to her and so quickly walked out on her before I could change my mind.

An atmosphere of hostility lingered in the house, but I ignored it, and a few weeks later, I was back at work and had largely forgotten the argument. It took a while for Helen to get over her chagrin, but she slowly began to accept my decision. At least she started talking to me again, and she became more amenable and more loving. She began working out the dates on which she would be most fertile, marking our kitchen calendar with big red ticks on those special days. I always knew when they were coming up without looking at the calendar, because Helen would suggest an early night every time, and once in bed, she lured me close with erotic caresses. I was always a willing participant, of course. Something had to happen, and late in March, I once again came home to Helen's ear-to-ear smiles. 'It'll be a Christmas baby,' she announced. She had lashed out and bought a huge piece of fillet steak for our dinner, which she had made into a beef stroganoff, something she'd never tried before, but which was absolutely delicious.

Meanwhile, we continued making weekly visits to Beechwood. Poor Myra was losing her mind even more rapidly than before, and Boris was becoming ever more caring of her. On two occasions, Myra had strayed into another woman's room, Hyacinth 9, looking for Boris, but his room was Daffodil 9, in a different building altogether. And when Helen gave her a picture book to keep her occupied and had asked Myra to write her name in it so it wouldn't get mislaid, her signature was almost unreadable. There were many other signs of her lapses into early senility, including a lack of concentration and an inability to remember faces. She'd already forgotten my name, and I felt that it wouldn't be long before she forgot Helen's.

Then one cold winter's day in June, we arrived to be told that Boris had been taken to hospital. He'd suffered a heart attack and was not expected to live. Myra was distraught, and when we caught up with her, she was pacing up and down the common room, unable to comprehend his absence. She was becoming increasingly childlike and agitated, and the nursing staff were worried. She kept asking for him, just as she had done earlier for Peter, and wouldn't be comforted. Helen tried her best, but eventually we had to leave Myra with the nurses, hoping they would know how to deal with the situation. Back at home, we kept in touch with Beechwood, getting a daily update on Boris's progress. In the end, however, Boris didn't last more than three days. We were told that Stanley had given the hospital permission for his father's life support system to be switched off. Evidently, Boris's family felt a measure of goodwill towards us because of our befriending of their father, and they notified us of the funeral arrangements. I decided to ask for the day off work so I could attend, and we picked Myra up to take with us. Perhaps if she witnessed Boris's funeral, she'd finally stop asking for him.

There were not many mourners there, just a couple of nurses from Beechwood and Boris's two middle-aged sons and daughter, with their respective families, all of whom came up to introduce themselves. And there was one elderly lady there, someone to whom they all seemed to be showing considerable attention and respect. When I enquired from the daughter who she was, I was told she was their mother. I said that Boris had told us his wife had passed away, and they explained that it was his second wife who'd died. All the children were from the first marriage. We were further told that the first wife had divorced Boris. He was having an affair at the time with the woman who became his second wife and that the children had all taken their mother's side. We now understood how they had become alienated, and quite honestly I didn't blame them. In fact, my esteem for Boris took a bit of a hit, though a part of me had quite a chuckle. The sly old bugger. Myra remained largely silent while we were talking together, but at least she seemed to accept that the body in the coffin belonged to Boris.

We dropped Myra off at Beechwood before returning home. 'I hope you never do a Boris on me,' Helen said later that night as we lay in bed.

'I won't if you don't,' I replied, laughing.

'I often wonder what makes men abandon their family for a bit of instant pleasure,' she said. 'I often wonder whether men have a different set of morals to women.'

'Hold on. It's not only men who stray.'

'They're the main culprits.'

'Who said?'

'Well, aren't they?'

'No, they damn well *aren't*. Women are just as bad,' I said.

Helen clammed up after that. I knew that I would just about murder her if she cheated on me. I didn't think I was a jealous type, but I would be keeping a close eye on any changes that might occur in our relationship, changes that might indicate another interest, not that I suspected her of anything at this stage, and certainly not during her pregnancy. I'd accused her once of infidelity, or at least planning such a move, but now was not the time to do so again.

Her morning sickness didn't seem so bad this time around. It had lasted only a couple of months, so perhaps that was a good omen. She continued to get good reports back from her monthly visits to the doctor, having decided against undergoing tests to see if there would be a repeat of the Down problem. She wanted the baby regardless of any possible deformities. I thought that a bit stupid, but Helen would not relent. Luckily, with the new baby now well on the way, all thoughts of going back to work were forgotten.

A happy expectant atmosphere had descended on the house until one day, early in August, Helen received a phone call from Beechwood. Her mother, now becoming increasingly frustrated and belligerent, had attacked another resident and had had to be restrained. Helen rushed over there to get the full story. Apparently, Myra had been accustomed to sitting in a particular chair in the common room, and that morning, after breakfast, she had found another woman sitting there. World War III had broken out. It took three nurses to break up the fight and calm everybody down. The other woman had suffered severe scratches to her face and arms, while Myra had been banished to her room, to be visited later by the doctor and sedated. It was left to Helen to apologise to Myra's victim and the nursing home staff. But, of course, there was nothing she could do for her mother except beg her to continue taking the medication that the doctor had prescribed, medication that would hopefully prevent further outbreaks.

When we visited the home the following weekend, it appeared that Myra was indeed taking her medication, though, as it turned out, it was only because a nurse stood over her every morning while she took the necessary pills. But in the few days since Helen had seen her, she had become a zombie. She was now almost incapable of rational speech, and she was beginning to drool. She just sat in her chair and stared at nothing, a slick of dribble coming from the side of her mouth. However, what was worse was her inability to recognise and welcome Helen with any warmth. She did say 'hello' when we arrived but no longer knew her daughter's name or the fact that my wife was indeed her daughter. This hit Helen hard. In fact, she was so hurt by this apparent rejection that I worried for the baby. I was no expert, but I thought that anything that upset her like that might damage the foetus or at least impede its growth. She was depressed for days after the Beechwood altercation and our most recent visit, realising there was little point in making regular calls anymore.

However, there was one bit of news that bucked her up considerably. Hudson phoned. He was so excited, I could hardly understand what he was saying, but after calming down a bit, he told me that Nola had been delivered of a girl, and they were going to call the child Sarah Helen Little. I thought that was a lovely touch, and Helen agreed. It was another good omen. Meanwhile, she had another four months to go, and I realised it was at exactly this stage in her first pregnancy that she had lost Debbie, but this time she sailed through the moment without any trouble. Soon after Hudson's phone call, Helen said she would like to visit Nola and see the baby. My immediate reaction was to stop this happening, at least not let her go on her own, so I suggested she wait until Nola had the child safely at home. I said I would like to go with her, so it would have to be over a weekend. I phoned Hudson and made the necessary arrangements. Then, a couple of days beforehand, Helen visited our local baby shop and bought a growsuit as a present for Sarah.

Hudson and Nola were renting a small house close to his parents, and the following Saturday morning, instead of heading to Beechwood, we drove to their new love nest. It was a cold day in late August, windy but sunny, as we turned into their street. The house turned out to be a rather run-down weatherboard place, set well back from the road. It had an overgrown garden at the front with a solitary tree in the middle of what was once a lawn, its branches hanging low over the front of the house. The building itself was little more than a shack, its paint peeling and its windows grimy, and there was a broken-down car further back behind Hudson's Volvo. Helen parked out in the street, and we walked in. There was no bell or knocker on the front door, but it was slightly open, so I just shouted, 'We're here!'

A moment later, the door opened further, and Hudson stood there in an old pair of trousers and an even older-looking jumper, a grin on his face. 'Welcome to Chateau Little,' he said as he ushered us inside. The front door led straight into a small lounge room that had obviously been furnished from op shops. 'Lovely to see you both.' We went in and looked around. The paint was peeling in there too, but the room had a homely feel. 'And before you turn your collective nose up at our splendid accommodation, I must explain that it's only temporary.'

'Well, we were a bit surprised when we saw it,' I said.

'The alternative was to stay at Nola's parents' house, and with the baby on the way, we decided we should be independent.'

'So, where's permanent?'

'Our two sets of parents have put their heads together and have paid the deposit on a new house. It's being built just up the road. As soon as it's ready, we'll move in there.'

'So, how did you find this place?' asked Helen.

'It looks as if it's almost ready to fall down,' I added.

'The father of a mate of mine at the office. He bought this site and has plans to knock the old place down and build a pair of units in its stead. I managed to persuade him to let us live here for a few months till our house is ready. Only fifty bucks a week, though we had to get all the services reconnected, plus a telephone.'

Just then, Nola came in carrying their sleeping daughter. 'Sorry I wasn't here to greet you, but Sarah was in the middle of a feed.'

Helen had gone quite gooey-eyed. 'May I hold her?'

'Of course,' answered Nola. 'In fact, take her while I go and make us a cuppa,' and she handed over the sleeping bundle and went off to the kitchen.

'There is little point in doing anything to this place,' said Hudson, 'and our landlord doesn't expect us to. He won't do anything either, under the circumstances, though he did replace a few floorboards before we moved in. They were that rotten.'

'May I take her outside?' asked Helen. 'I'll keep her out of the sun.'

'Certainly,' answered Hudson. As soon as she had gone, he turned to me. 'So, how's it going, Johnny? With Helen, I mean?'

'Well, she's recovered from losing Debbie and is now four months on with the next one.'

'Yeah, I did notice. Good on you. And her mother?'

'Gone completely gaga.' I didn't say any more as Nola returned carrying a tray. 'And, how are you?' I asked her. 'Bit different from fixing cars?'

Nola laughed. 'I still fix Hudson's.'

Soon after that, Helen returned, and we all sat down to a morning tea, complete with a cake and a plate of Tim Tams. While sitting, Nola opened the gift Helen had brought and went into raptures over the growsuit, such a lovely shade of mauve. Afterwards, Hudson and I went out into the garden for a chat, leaving the mother and the mother-to-be to engage in their women's business undisturbed. I continued what I'd been saying to Hudson earlier. 'Yes, Myra's gone totally gaga. She doesn't recognise her daughter anymore and is now being sedated every day to stop her attacking the other inmates.'

'That bad, eh?'

'She could go on like this for years, soaking up all the money.'

'Are you paying for all this?'

'Not yet, but when the nest egg runs out, who knows?'

We discussed our respective jobs, Hudson being very pleased with his, and we went and looked at the old car wreck so that I could assess whether anything could be done to save it, but it was well past any remedial work. Then it was time to leave. Helen and Nola gave each other a kiss on each cheek, while Hudson and I shook hands. Helen was glowing; she'd really enjoyed the visit and her talk with Nola.

On the way home, I asked her about the money going to Beechwood, wondering if there was still plenty to keep her mother there, knowing that she could live another thirty or forty years. 'The interest on her investments will cover the costs for as long as it takes, providing the interest rate remains as high as it is now,' she answered. I didn't pursue the matter any further.

Spring arrived, the weather began to warm, and blossom began to coat the bare trees. The daffodils had been flowering for a few weeks by now, and the rose trees were beginning to send out new shoots. There was a feeling of renewal in the air, and alongside all this other growth, Helen's body was imperceptibly expanding. September became October, and October slid into November, and her face shone with healthy anticipation. Her increasing weight was a problem, but she managed our lives with composure and confidence, and she never once complained, saying that she wanted to continue doing everything she normally did around the house until the last minute.

Helen had decided to visit her mother one more time before the birth. She had gone that last time in early October, and she had made the trip during the week, at a time when she could still comfortably get into the driving seat of her car. She returned depressed at her mother's condition. Later that day, she told me there had been little change, for although Myra had seemed to recognise her daughter at first, and had even smiled, she was still not speaking coherently and had returned to her usual introspective self long before Helen had left. But Helen's low spirits only lasted a few days. I managed to jolly her along by reminding her of some of the good times we had all shared.

According to the doctor's calculation, the baby was due on December 8, or thereabouts, though he did claim that first babies are usually late. I wasn't sure if this one counted as a first baby. Bill Thompson had earlier in the year issued all his staff with pagers so that we could be contacted if we were out on a job. This would make it a lot easier if Helen went into labour while I was at work. She could simply phone Donna, who would then page me. Helen's felt a lot better with this arrangement. By early December, she had a bag packed all ready to take to hospital when the time came. Helen had booked herself into Cabrini Maternity in Malvern, a private hospital that was the nearest we could find in case there had to be an urgent dash. I had been asked if I wished to attend the birth, and Helen had answered for me. 'Yes, I want my husband there.' Evidently, I wasn't to be consulted, though I did agree that I should be there.

Back in September, we had gone back to the baby shop where Helen had bought the growsuit for Sarah and had purchased an expensive assortment of baby clothes, nappies, toys, and even a rocking crib suspended off supports at each end. We also acquired a pram, one of those fancy ones where the top can be lifted off the base and used as a carrycot. And the spare room, which had previously been used purely for the storage of suitcases and unwanted furniture, as well as some of our unused wedding presents, had been converted into a nursery. Helen had spent hours cleaning and repainting the room in warm shades of light yellow. Every evening, when I returned from work, I had been taken upstairs to approve her handiwork. The room looked really special.

All was ready, but the eighth came and went, and Helen remained intact. It was a bit of an anticlimax, and we settled down to wait. Then, three days later, at a little after two in the morning, I was awakened by a hand shaking me. 'It's starting,' Helen cried. 'I've had three contractions already.' She was breathing heavily, and when I turned on the light, I could see she was sweating profusely. But we had already had two false alarms, times when contractions had started and had as quickly stopped, so I was a bit slow to react and even wanted to try and get back to sleep. She asked me to time the next contraction. It lasted twenty-five seconds, and it was eight minutes before the next one started. She was gritting her teeth with the pain, and when the next one lasted thirty-five seconds, only six minutes after the last, she said it was time to go.

Between contractions, she managed to get her clothes on, and I quickly dressed too before helping her down the stairs and out to the car. Traffic was almost non-existent at that hour, and we made it to Cabrini in twelve minutes. She'd had two more contractions in the car, and the second time, she'd cried out. I parked at the entrance, grabbed the suitcase, and supported Helen inside. They must be used to women arriving at all hours of the day and night, for a nurse appeared out of nowhere and, after taking down our particulars, escorted Helen along a corridor. I followed at a distance. Another nurse took her hand and the case I was carrying and led her into a ward. Just before the door shut, Helen turned to me with a frightened, abandoned look. She looked intensely vulnerable. 'Good luck,' I called, blowing her a kiss, trying to comfort her.

The first nurse took me back to reception. 'Labour can take six to twelve hours,' she said, 'so you may want to go home and come back later.'

'She wants me here for the birth,' I replied.

'Well, we can give you a call once it's imminent.'

So I returned to the car, having made sure they had the correct number to call, and drove home. It was still not four o'clock, but it was hardly worth going back to bed, so I went into the kitchen and made myself a coffee. I was far too uptight to eat anything but thought coffee would at least keep me from getting drowsy. Then I went in the lounge room and sat waiting. But I couldn't sit for long. I kept getting up and pacing up and down the room, worrying about what Helen must be experiencing, hoping she wasn't in too much pain. I thought about the names we had chosen: Kevin Peter if it was a boy, and Megan Bianca for a girl. I knew Helen wanted a girl, if only to replace Debbie, whereas I would have preferred a boy, but really all we wanted was a healthy child.

I was still sitting, and beginning to nod off, when I heard the clock strike midday. I couldn't wait any longer but decided to go back to Cabrini and sit in the waiting room. When I got there and gave my name, there was a different nurse at the reception desk. 'Oh,' she said, 'I just tried to phone you, but there was no answer. Come with me.' I followed her along a different passageway and was led in through a door marked Delivery Room. Helen was sitting up on a narrow bed with her knees raised and her legs spreadeagled, while next to her a nurse stood, talking softly to her. She looked worn out and terrified, her hair matted and lank as it hung over her eyes. She saw me as I went in and held out a shaking hand to me. When I held out mine, she gripped it hard just as another contraction hit her. She screamed. I remember little of what followed during the next half hour or so. A doctor appeared and another nurse. Someone said, 'Head's showing,' and a nurse was saying, 'Push,' and, finally, with a loud cry from Helen, a slippery parcel appeared between her legs, a wet and slimy bundle that looked to me more like a lined and shrivelled old man than a baby.

Everyone's eyes focused on the little stub of a penis. 'It's a boy,' said everyone. I turned to Helen, who by now was grinning in triumph, and kissed her sweaty forehead. 'Well done. You're a star,' I said. 'We have a son,' I added, 'and he's beautiful,' I lied.

*   *   *

CHAPTER 11

1985

Once Kevin had been checked over by the doctor, who pronounced him free of any signs of Down syndrome, then washed, weighed, and wrapped, he was placed in Helen's arms. He had uttered a few cries during those first few moments but now appeared to be sleeping even though his fists kept moving, his fingers opening and closing as if he was trying them out or looking for something to grip on to. Despite her tiredness, Helen had a look of intense joy on her face as she looked down on his tiny face, then she looked up at me and indicated that I should take him for a bit. A nurse lifted him and gave him to me. At first, I was terrified of dropping him or not holding him properly; he seemed so small insignificant, and I was amazed at how light he felt. After I handed him back, a nurse told me that Helen must have her sleep now, so I kissed her, told her I'd drop in the next day, and left. As I walked past reception, I saw a calendar up on the wall. Today was Wednesday, December 11.

I felt both proud and happy as I drove home, planning on all the phone calls I would make that evening: my parents, Barbara, Hudson, my boss, and probably Helen's uncle Frank. But I'd only just got in when the phone rang. It was Beechwood, asking for Helen. 'Sorry,' I said, 'she's in hospital, just given birth,' I added proudly.

'Is that her husband?'

'It is.'

'I'm afraid I've got some bad news for you.'

'Oh?'

'There's been an accident. Mrs Madden's mother.'

'Oh my god. What's happened?'

'She managed to leave the premises. We're not exactly sure how she got out, but she went into the road. She got hit by a car.' My euphoria simply evaporated, and while I wondered what to say, the lady from Beechwood continued. 'I'm afraid she died soon afterwards. We're all very shocked. I'm terribly sorry.'

'When did all this happen?'

'Soon after midday, we think.'

'And, where is she now?'

'The ambulance took her to the mortuary. Will you tell your wife, or should I phone the hospital and talk to her?'

'No. I'll handle it.' There was no way that Helen should be confronted with a tragedy like this right after the birth. She'd be absolutely gutted, though my own thoughts were a lot more ambivalent. Of course, I was saddened, but at the same time I felt as if a weight had been removed from our lives. Myra would have been enduring a terrible life cooped up in that place. I had another thought, one that I knew would be inadvisable to repeat to Helen. Now we would no longer be haemorrhaging cash. She would have total control over all her money, and I hoped that ultimately I would too. My next thought was that something would need to be done about a funeral. I realised that, with Helen incapacitated, it would now be up to me, and I didn't have a clue what to do. I needed help. The first person who came to mind was Helen's uncle Frank. He'd always been a fountain of wisdom and had helped enormously with our wedding. I found his number and called his Sydney home, first telling him about Helen and the new baby and then explaining what had happened to Myra and asking for his help. Helen had told him some time ago about her mother's dementia and the necessity of putting her into a nursing home, but he still sounded really upset at the suddenness of her death. However, he was pleased to hear about the new baby and asked me all sorts of questions about Helen and the birth. 'Congratulations,' he said. 'Obviously, Helen won't be able to do anything under the circumstances. Would you like me to come down?' he offered.

'Yes, very much.'

'I can't come tomorrow, but I'll see if I can get a flight the next day. And please give my love to Helen.'

'Thanks. I will.' I realised then what a great help he would be if he actually stayed with us while in Melbourne. 'I was thinking, would you like to stay here?' I asked him. 'It might be easier.'

'That's very kind. Are you sure Helen won't mind?'

'I'm sure she'll be delighted to have you here. It will be a difficult time for her.'

'OK, then, I'll hope to see you in a couple of days.' Afterwards, I went straight upstairs to prepare Myra's old room. It was still full of all the junk that we'd removed from Kevin's new nursery, so it took me a while to get it habitable. Later, I phoned my boss at home, telling him both about the birth and my mother-in-law's death, a strange dichotomy of subjects, I realised later, and asking him for a few more days off, just till the end of the week, to sort myself out. He told me they were pretty busy at the moment, but, OK, as long as I was back on Monday.I knew that Helen would be devastated by the news from Beechwood, so when I went back to see her the day after the birth, I didn't mention it. I thought she needed to regain her strength before I told her. In fact, the full story of Myra's accident only came out after a few days. She had wandered out of the common room during the morning and had walked to the entrance. A van driver delivering goods to the home had activated the gate and driven in, and Myra had slipped through the opening just before the gate had fully closed again. The driver vaguely remembered seeing a figure in his rear-view mirror as he drove in but thought no more about it—that is, until ten minutes later when he'd finished making the delivery and was on his way out. The entrance to the main road had been blocked by a traffic accident.

Evidently, Myra had, after leaving Beechwood Gardens, walked straight out into the road without looking and had been struck by a car. When Myra had unexpectedly appeared in front of her, the female driver had braked sharply but couldn't stop in time, and a truck following closely behind had slammed into the car, pushing it over Myra's inert body. The car was so badly damaged that it could no longer be driven. It had taken a while for a tow truck to arrive and lift the car away so they could get to the person underneath, and by that time, Myra could no longer be revived. And it was only then that one of the bystanders saw the bracelet on Myra's wrist that tied her to the nursing home. The delivery van driver went straight back to alert the staff. Understandably, the whole place was now in an uproar, with nurses and other staff asking who was to blame. It seemed such a strange irony that Myra had lost her husband when *he* was struck by a car, and now she'd suffered the same fate. And it was another strange irony that she had been killed at almost the same moment as her grandson was born. I wondered whether she had, in some strange way, sensed her daughter's agony and this had deranged her even further, prompting her to go looking for Helen. We will never know.

Uncle Frank was waiting for me outside the house when I returned from visiting Helen two days later. He'd hired a car at the airport and had driven straight to the house. The first thing he asked me was 'Have you told Helen yet?'

'I thought I should wait until she comes home. She's still pretty weak,' I answered.

'Well, I don't think she'll be happy that she's being kept in the dark, but it's your decision.'

'She'll be home tomorrow.'

'The first thing we must do is to choose a funeral director and then settle on a date,' he said. 'We'll do the first today and then organise the date once you've spoken to Helen and we know where the funeral is to be held. Then we must inform everyone. Put a notice in the *Age* newspaper and so on.'

'Sounds like you've done this sort of thing before,' I said, smiling.

'Not since my parents died,' he replied. 'Anyway, first, I want to visit the nursing home that made this cock-up.'

I had to admit that Kevin looked far more like a baby when I brought him and Helen home. He'd filled out and was quite plump. This time, when I repeated my statement about how beautiful he was, I was no longer lying. Helen had initially had a problem feeding Kevin. 'He just wouldn't take a nipple,' she told me, 'but with the help of a nurse, I persevered, and now he's sucking like crazy.' In fact, as soon as we got home, Kevin was beginning to fret for his next feed. She took the baby into the lounge and heaved out a swollen breast. The sight of a mother feeding her baby must be one of the most glorious experiences imaginable. I was fascinated but decided to wait until Kevin had finished feeding before I broke the news to Helen. To be honest, I was scared of her reaction, knowing that I had hidden it all from her for three days.

'I could do with a nice strong cup of tea now,' she said a soon as the baby was asleep again.

'I'll get it for you, but, first, I need to tell you something.'

She looked puzzled. 'What?'

I went and sat next to her, putting my arm around her. 'It's bad news. Really bad. From Beechwood.'

'Mum. Something happened to Mum?' Helen was now sitting bolt upright, a worried frown on her face.

'Yes, I'm afraid so. She …. she died.'

'Oh my god.' She paused, shaking her head in disbelief. 'What did she die of? She wasn't ill, was she?'

'No. It was an accident. She managed to get out of the gate. She was hit by a car.'

Helen looked shocked, stunned, speechless. She'd gone pale but finally found her voice. 'Oh, no, not her too. I don't believe it.' She paused again, her eyes drilling into me. 'When did this happen?'

'The day Kevin was born.'

'What?' she cried. 'And you never told me.' Her outburst had unsettled Kevin, who started whimpering. Helen turned to him and rocked him in her arms.

I was saved from further embarrassment by Frank coming into the room. He must have been standing outside, eavesdropping. 'John thought it best to wait until you were home.'

Helen was shocked even further by her uncle's appearance. 'Uncle Frank! What are you doing here?'

'John phoned me for help, so I came down. Your mother was very dear to me, and I wanted to do everything I could to help. It's a difficult time.' He paused, walking over to where Helen held the baby. 'John invited me to stay here till the funeral. I hope that's all right with you.'

Helen continued shaking her head in disbelief. 'This is all so unexpected, the happiest time of my life, and suddenly .... now .... the shock .....' She lapsed into silence.

'I think I'd better make that cup of tea now,' I said and escaped to the kitchen.

When I returned five minutes later, Helen had put Kevin back into his carrycot and was standing, folded into Frank's arms, and sobbing her heart out. I stopped dead in the doorway and nearly dropped the tray I was carrying. It should have been me consoling her, so I felt somewhat hurt at the way her uncle had taken over. But, of course, I couldn't say anything. I was probably still in the dogbox for not having told Helen earlier, but I still thought I'd done the right thing. I stood for a time until her sobs subsided. I gave a little cough to announce my presence, and she pulled away from him and sat. I carried the tray over and placed it on the table. Helen looked up at me, her eyes red with the tears, but she did look more relaxed now, as though she'd recovered some of her composure. 'Thanks,' she said and started pouring the tea.

'I realise this won't be easy for you,' said Frank, 'but we do have to start talking about the funeral.'

'Of course,' answered Helen. 'When would be a good day?'

'I've provisionally booked it for a week today, eleven o'clock. If you are happy with that, I'll get a notice in the *Age*.'

'That's fine.' Helen seemed to be recovering a little now.

'And I'll let all the family know, and Myra's friends,' continued Frank. 'My wife will certainly be joining us, together with the children.' I remembered his wife, Brenda, and their three daughters: Nichola, Mandy, and Pippa, all of whom attended our wedding. 'Being a Saturday,' Frank continued, 'there should be quite a number of people coming.'

'Good,' said Helen.

'And there's a burial spot right next door to Peter, which I've claimed.'

'Thanks so much, Uncle Frank. I don't know what we would have done without you.'

'There's one more thing. The nursing home has agreed to return the last month's payment, purely as a gesture of goodwill, of course, but you may wish to take it further.'

'How do you mean?'

'They are legally responsible, and if a court were to find them guilty of negligence, they could be up for a lot more.'

'You mean ….' Helen paused, wondering how to put it. 'Are you saying we could sue them?'

'Indeed. Of course, it's entirely up to you whether you wish to proceed. I'm happy to find a good lawyer to take up the case if you want me to.'

Helen didn't have to think about it for long. She started shaking her head. 'Oh, no,' she said, 'definitely not. A court case would just extend the grief. There would be years of bickering and litigation, and, anyway, we don't need the money.'

'And that's your final decision?'

'Yes, I think so.' She turned to me. 'What do you say, John?'

I thought it best to agree. 'OK by me,' I replied.

'Fair enough,' said Frank. 'I believe you've made the right choice.'

He stayed with us for another four days, until the funeral arrangements were all complete. During this time, he asked us what we would like to contribute to the occasion. Helen agreed that she should do a eulogy, and then he asked me if I would like to read a poem. 'Myra loved poetry,' he said, 'and I remember how Peter used to read to her when they were first married.'

I was surprised at the suggestion, surprised and somewhat disconcerted. I'd only ever read poems in English class at school and had hated doing it, especially when asked to read out loud. I thought it a bit sissy, and I knew that I'd feel an absolute twat standing up in front of people and spouting poetry. 'Not really my cup of tea,' I said.

'Well, I think you should give it a go,' answered Frank.

'Agreed,' piped up Helen.

'Looks like I'm outnumbered,' I said despondently.

The lounge room had a large bookcase against one wall, full of books I'd seldom looked at. Frank went over and started scouring through the shelves. Eventually, after some minutes of searching, he pulled out a *Selected Poems* and started looking through it. 'Here. This'll do,' he said, finding the poem he been searching for.

I looked at the poem he'd selected. 'Who's Christina Rossetti?' I asked him.

'A nineteenth-century English poet.'

'OK,' I said tentatively.

'Just don't rush it when you read it aloud, so that it comes over clearly. And watch the punctuation. Where there's no full stop or comma at the end of a line, read on without pausing. It makes a better sense of the poem.'

He schooled me a couple of times over the next two evenings until he was satisfied with my delivery and that I fully understood what I was reading. And he spent a lot of time with Helen while I was at work, going through old photo albums and discussing Myra's favourite music. Finally, he left us and went to pick up his family from the airport, opting to stay with them at a nearby hotel. By then, it was only three more days till the funeral, and only a week till Christmas. I had been back at work from Monday, catching up on a backlog of jobs. Bill Thompson said they would be working right up to Christmas that year as there were a number of contracts that had to be finished before everyone took leave. So Helen had to cope with everything on her own, and she was always grateful to see me in the evening when I arrived home. She hadn't started driving again yet, so every morning she gave me a shopping list, which I filled on my way home. I did a fair amount of the cooking as well, and quite early on Helen showed me how to change nappies without sticking the safety pin into Kevin's stomach, though it was a job that nearly turned my stomach.

As the day of the funeral approached, I thought about what we should do with him. It didn't seem right to take him along, and Helen agreed to 'farm him out', if at all possible. I phoned my mother, but she said they wanted to attend Myra's funeral themselves. Then I thought of Nola. Helen phoned her, and she was more than willing. In fact, she said she was still feeding Sarah but had so much milk, there was enough for two, so if Kevin needed a feed during the funeral, she could oblige. She thought it might be rather fun being a wet nurse and having a child at each breast. And so it was arranged; on the day of the funeral, we left early and went via the Littles to drop Kevin off.

The funeral home was already quite full when we got there. Uncle Frank was welcoming people as they arrived, and he introduced us to a tall moustached man in a dark suit called William Steadman, who greeted us with an ingratiating smile, told us he was sorry for our loss, and ushered us to seats at the front. As we walked in, me with the *Selected Poems* carried self-consciously under my arm, a number of people turned their heads and stared at us, and in particular at Helen, with expressions of sympathy. The room was hushed except for some nondescript music that was oozing out of hidden loudspeakers. There was a printed 'Order of Service' on each chair, something else that Frank had been busy with. Helen had told him that she didn't want anything too religious in the ceremony. None of them believed in God, and they'd only ever been in a church for weddings and other people's funerals, like her father's.

In front of us was a low dais on which Myra's coffin had been placed, mounted on a low trolley and festooned with flowers. Ten minutes after we'd arrived, the ceremony got under way. The nondescript music ceased as William Steadman strode to the front. He welcomed everyone and explained that we were here to celebrate the life of Myra Deborah Sykes and not mourn her death, sad, though, it must be for everyone present. Of course, that was why Helen had chosen Debbie as our miscarried daughter's name. As I was thinking about this, some music started. My programme told me it was the slow movement of Mozart's 'Clarinet Concerto'. I've never been a fan of classical music, but that piece was great. It must have been a favourite of Myra's, and I could understand why. I was up next, so clutching the book of poems, I fronted up to the lectern and opened the book at the page I was about to read. My heart started beating frantically as I looked up into all those expectant faces. Then, when I saw Helen do a thumbs up and smile at me, I felt better. My heart slowed, and I started reading.

When I am dead, my dearest,

Sing no sad songs for me;
Plant no roses at my head,
Nor shady cypress tree:
Be the green grass above me
With showers and dewdrops wet:
And if thou wilt, remember,
And if thou wilt, forget.

I shall not see the shadows,
I shall not feel the rain;
I shall not hear the nightingale
Sing on as if in pain;
And dreaming through the twilight
That doth not rise and set,
Haply I may remember,
And haply may forget.

As I finished, there was a deathly silence; you could have heard a pin drop. Then there was a loud collective sigh, and the world around me returned. I went back to my seat, and Helen gripped my hand. I could see tears forming in her eyes. 'That was so beautiful,' she said. A moment later, another piece of music started: 'Air on the G String' it was called, by someone called J. S. Bach. What the hell was a G string? I wondered, though when the violin started, I realised what the title meant, though I still couldn't understand why they would only want to play on one string. Nevertheless, I couldn't help smiling. The only G-string I knew had erotic connotations. Trust me to think of that in the middle of a funeral, but, in fact, it was another lovely piece of music. Then it was Helen's turn. 'Good luck,' I whispered. She rose and strode purposely to the lectern. She didn't speak for long. She praised her mother's unwavering love, her integrity and sincerity, and her expectation that those around her should behave as she did. As such, she had been a wonderful wife and mother and had shown incredible fortitude after her husband died in such shocking circumstances. She had not deserved to suffer from the debilitating illness that overtook her, so soon after Peter's death, but Helen praised the staff at the nursing home, saying she didn't believe that the accident that finally took her life was their fault. 'I am really grateful for everything she taught me, and I shall always remember her with undying love,' she finished.

Finally, after yet another short musical interlude, Frank came to the front. William Steadman pulled down a screen that had been rolled up against the ceiling and then took up position behind a projector at the back. As a picture of Myra appeared on the screen, an old one going back at least twenty years, Frank started his commentary. I was amazed at the number of photos he and Helen had dug up: photos from her childhood, her teens, marriage, holidays, and finally ones of her holding Helen as a baby. As he gave a historical picture of Myra's life, he interspersed the talk with humorous quips, much enjoyed by the audience, and the show ended with a very posed picture of Myra, Peter, and Helen, which had obviously been taken just before I came on the scene.

The proceedings ended with the sounds of a choir singing 'Amazing Grace'. As the music soared, three more able-bodied men in dark suits joined William Steadman at the coffin. They lifted the trolley down from the dais, and as they trundled it out, we all rose to our feet, following the coffin outside and watching it being placed in the hearse. My parents joined me outside. 'I loved your poem,' said Mum. 'It was so moving.' Others, including Frank, came up and commented favourably on my reading, so it obviously must have gone down OK. By now, it was close to midday. In the 'Order of Service', there had been a mention of the subsequent internment, to which only family was invited, but it also named the hall where refreshments would be provided for all from one o'clock. It was the same hall where Helen had enjoyed her twenty-first celebration. I remembered it well. The throng of mourners were talking among themselves, greeting friends they hadn't seen all year, or making new ones. The conversations were all loud and a little garrulous, like that of kids who'd just been let out of school.

The hearse was now ready. Frank and his family went to their hire car, while Helen and I got into hers. The two cars followed the hearse out into the road and headed off to the cemetery, maintaining the subdued speed that seems a requirement of all funeral corteges. When we reached our destination, we parked adjacent to the prepared grave. A man in ecclesiastical clothing appeared next to us as we stopped. It was Helen's only nod to religion. He introduced himself to us as Father Benedict, while the four pall-bearers lifted the coffin out of the hearse and placed it on ropes across the grave. The priest said a short prayer, and as the coffin slowly sank out of view, he intoned the bit about 'dust to dust' and 'ashes to ashes', and we were invited to drop a handful of soil onto the coffin. It was all very quick and efficient. Helen was very stoical and only began sobbing as she dropped her handful of soil. 'Goodbye, Mum,' she whispered.

'I'd like to check on Kevin before we go to the wake,' said Helen as we drove out of the cemetery. I didn't think it necessary but agreed. I could sense that she was still upset after the funeral so thought it best not to argue. In fact, it was just as well that we did call in for when we got there, poor Kevin was screaming his head off. We could hear him from the road, and Helen ran in the moment the car was stopped. When we got inside, Nola was beside herself with worry. Helen rushed to Kevin and gathered him into her arms, rocking him gently till he began to settle. 'What happened?' she asked Nola.

'I thought the poor mite was hungry,' Nola answered, 'but he wouldn't take my nipple. Then he started crying and wouldn't stop. I must smell different or something.'

'Or perhaps he just sensed something wasn't quite the same. Anyway, don't worry. I'll take him away now.'

'He was absolutely fine till I tried to feed him.'

'I'm sure he was, and thanks so much for helping us out.'

'Anytime,' offered Nola. 'How did the funeral go?'

'A little nerve-racking,' said Helen with a wan smile.

By the time we got to the hall, the wake was in full swing. I got the pram base out of the boot and fixed the carrycot onto it. Kevin was sleeping now. Helen placed him inside, and I followed her, pushing the pram ahead of me into the hall. The noise of people talking was so loud that I expected it to awaken Kevin, but he slept on, oblivious to the racket. The wake was simply a stand-up event, though there were a few chairs around for those who needed to sit. Frank had managed to find some excellent caterers who were moving around dispensing plates of finger food, and there was a table at one end for tea and coffee. He'd decided to keep the event alcohol-free, to which I had agreed.

Some of the people, the ladies in particular, came over to make gooey noises over Kevin. Mum and Frank's wife, Brenda, who had managed to get introduced to each other and had already become friendly, were at the forefront of the admirers. I got talking to Frank's and Brenda's middle daughter, Mandy. Or rather she had sidled up and latched on to me soon after I arrived, and while I vaguely remembered her from our wedding, I hadn't spoken to her then. She turned out to be a very lively girl, with an attractive face, an unruly mop of red hair, and come-hither eyes. I didn't know how old she was, though I put her at about seventeen. 'What's it like being married to Helen?' she suddenly asked me. A curious question, I thought, so I just told her we were very happy, thank you. 'I'm very fond of her,' she added, 'but she was a bit of a know-all when she was younger, quite bossy in fact. She used to rule the roost among us cousins.' She continued in this vein for a few minutes before suggesting that I might like to keep in touch. I wasn't sure if this was some sort of veiled invitation, and she moved away before I could make any comment.

My father also came over to talk to me. He told me he was very proud of me, standing up in front of everyone like that, and he hoped I had taken full control in my marriage by now, to which I murmured something innocuous. There were numerous other well-wishers, people I'd never met, who came to talk to me about Myra. 'I knew her when she was much younger,' a white-haired old lady told me. 'We thought she would never get married,' said another. One man, a complete stranger, told me that the nursing home should be shut down. 'They're incompetent,' he claimed. Perhaps he knew more than I did. By that time, Kevin was getting restless, so I pushed the pram over to Helen and asked her what I should do. She decided to lift him out of the pram and show him off a bit.

After two hours, the crowd began to thin until there were just us and Frank's family remaining. As we were saying our goodbyes, Mandy suddenly approached me. She looked up at me, stood for a moment with a strange expression on her face, and said, 'I think you're cute.' Then she kissed me, full on the mouth. I was so surprised at her audacity that I stood rooted to the spot, my face burning with embarrassment. My first thought was, *What is Helen going to say?* She couldn't have missed it. But the moment passed, Mandy scuttled back to her family, and conversation resumed. But in some strange way, her behaviour had left its mark. I could still sense the feel of her lips on mine, so soft and giving and wonderfully erotic.

I stood there in a daze for a long moment. Helen was calling me. 'Come on, John. Wakey-wakey.' She was silent for much of the drive home, cuddling Kevin in the passenger seat, but suddenly spoke up. 'So, what was all that about?'

'I wish I knew,' I replied.

'What are you not telling me, John?'

'I honestly have nothing to tell.'

'Mandy has always been a brazen so-and-so, but you must have said or done something to make her hit on you like that.'

I could feel myself trembling, so I pulled the car over to the side of the road and stopped it. I looked at Helen with some annoyance. 'Are you accusing me of something?' I asked her.

'No. I just want to know what happened.'

'Nothing happened. She just came over to me and attached herself. She started asking questions about our marriage and talking about times she and her sisters had spent with you when you were younger. She reckoned that you were very bossy.'

'I wasn't,' protested Helen.

'She was very upfront. Quite honestly, I found her a bit embarrassing.'

'She's always been a problem child. Her parents worry she'll do something silly.'

'A flirtatious little minx, I'd say.' I turned to look at Helen. 'But quite attractive,' I added, smiling. I wasn't trying to make her jealous but reckoned it would do no harm.

'Do you really think so?'

'Yes. She's quite bubbly.'

'Well, don't get any ideas, will you?'

'Of course not, my love.' I put my hand on her knee and gave it a squeeze, just to get her back onside. Then I restarted the car and drove on.

But I still couldn't get the feel of Mandy's full soft lips out of my mind. I'd never been kissed like that before, not even by Helen. That night, I had a very erotic dream, most likely as a result of my daytime experience. In the dream, it was daylight, and I was lying on a deserted beach. A girl approached, and it was Mandy. We were both naked, and I was fascinated by her huge untidy mop of red pubic hair. Her mouth was open in a lascivious smile, and her lips were bloated, as if she'd had the full Botox treatment. She lay down next to me and played with me, kissing me all over. 'Fuck me,' she kept saying. 'Fuck me.' I pretended that I couldn't understand her, for I knew that if I did what she wanted, something terrible would happen, though I had no idea what. Eventually, I found I couldn't stop myself. I came the moment I entered her, my orgasm seemingly going on and on. As my last spasm finished, night suddenly fell. And Mandy disappeared.

During the early hours of the morning, Helen had to get up to give

Kevin a feed. I awoke as she got back into bed. 'John,' she said in a puzzled voice, 'the bed's all wet. What's happened? Are you bleeding?' She quickly turned on the light.

'Oh my god,' I said, feeling around me. 'The sheet's sopping. I must have had a wet dream.'

'A what?'

'A wet dream. An involuntary ejaculation.'

'Oh, yes, I have heard of them.'

'It's a male thing. I used to have them a lot, before we were married.'

'So, what brought it on this time?'

'Well, I haven't had sex for a couple of months now, so I guess it just built up inside me.'

'Did you know it was happening?'

'Well, yes, I did have an erotic dream, and I dreamt I was having an ejaculation, so that must have been the moment.'

Helen was getting really interested by this time. 'So, what was the dream about? Can you remember it? Who was in it?' I guessed she was still worried about Mandy, so I retold the dream, or what I remember of it, but I left out any reference to red pubic hair. However, I added in a few titillating details that could only refer to Helen. 'Crikey, no wonder you made such a mess of the bed,' and Helen laughed.

'Sorry. I can't help it. I couldn't stop it from happening, and it will probably happen again for as long as we can't have sex.'

'I understand, darling,' she said, as she then bent over to kiss me. 'I know it's difficult for you, but I'm afraid it'll be another three weeks before we're back to normal. Unless you want me to use my hand?' she offered with a smile.

'Or your mouth,' I suggested, knowing there was little chance of that.

Helen screwed up her face. 'No way,' she said.

I had two more days work to finish for Bill Thompson, and then I was on leave for three weeks. I decided that I should keep myself occupied by servicing our two vehicles over the break. Christmas came and went, but it was a bit of a non-event that year. We didn't bother with a tree or with decorations but strung up the dozens of cards that arrived from well-wishers. There was even a card from Mandy. It had a lipstick kiss on the inside, and luckily I was able to intercept it and destroy it before Helen saw it. Otherwise, there was little change in our lives. I think we were both far too tired to make a special effort, though we did buy in some special food to cook on our barbecue. Above all, we needed to recharge our batteries. Kevin helped. He was what is often referred to as a 'good baby', sleeping well and keeping to a routine. And Helen grew steadily stronger and more able to cope. We invited Hudson and Nola round for a New Year's Eve get-together, as well as their parents, but even that was a muted affair.

*   *   *

CHAPTER 12

1986–1993

Kevin was a happy baby, and he progressed normally over the first year of his life. At five months, he was able to roll from his tummy onto his back, and a month later he could sit supported, exploring with his hands, especially if there were toys close by. And another month later, he could sit unsupported and was beginning to crawl. For some reason, he had a fixation on the staircase and would love to try and mount the steps on his hands and knees. By nine months, he could pull himself up to a standing position, wobbling backwards and forwards till his legs once again gave way and he sat down with a thump. By then, Helen realised that it wouldn't be long before Kevin would be walking and furthering his wish to go up and downstairs, so she asked me if I could fit a gate at the top, one with a child-proof catch, to prevent accidents. I thought it probably outside my range of skills, so I said I'd ask around to see if anyone could recommend a good carpenter, failing which I'd check the yellow pages of the phone directory.

It was around this time that we acquired a cat. I don't like cats. In fact, at the time, I hated the damn things. I've never actually had a pet as my father refused to have one in the house. There was a knock on our door one weekday morning, and when Helen opened it, one of our neighbours was standing there holding a large cage. Inside the cage was a squirming mass of kittens. 'My cat has just produced these,' she said, 'and I'm trying to find a home for them.'

'Oh, no, I don't think so,' said Helen.

'I'll have to get them all put down if no one will take any of them.'

'How many have you got there?' 'Five.'

'I certainly don't want five.' But Helen was weakening. As she looked more closely at the cage, one of the kittens with ginger and white markings caught her eye. 'We don't have any pets, but perhaps my little Kevin should have one.'

And so we finished up with young Percy, though how and why Helen came up with that name, I have no idea. If I'd been at home, I would have said no, but I was at work the day the neighbour called, so I didn't have any say in the matter. However, Kevin seemed to be overjoyed, so I was in a minority. When he was introduced to the kitten, he got really excited, waving his arms and shrieking. He'd just started crawling by then and tried to follow Percy everywhere as the kitten explored every nook and cranny in the house. When I got in from work that evening, I walked into the kitchen and nearly trod on the wretched animal. When Helen explained how it had arrived, I was pissed off that she had brought it into our house without my permission. I was all for throwing the kitten straight back out again, but I could see that Kevin wanted it, so I swallowed my anger. However, I made Helen promise to toilet-train it or the kitten would be out on its ear.

Percy had taken quite a shine to Kevin, and they were almost inseparable. Quite early on, the kitten decided he would like to bed down with Kevin. One afternoon, once Kevin had been put down for a sleep, Percy sneaked into the nursery. Helen watched as he jumped up onto the side of Kevin's crib, but being a rocker, it swung away from him and threw him back to the floor. She had a bit of a laugh but didn't stop him. Percy started pacing round the crib, working out his next move. A light must have switched on in his little brain. The second time that he tried to join Kevin, he jumped up onto the end of the crib, and it hardly swayed at all. He was just about to jump down on top of Kevin when Helen snatched him up and removed him from the room. Later, she told me about Percy's exploits. She thought he'd displayed a considerable degree of intelligence in his problem-solving. I suggested that he'd just been lucky. At ten months, Kevin was taking his first tentative steps. By then, we'd found a carpenter, and he was busy building a gate for the stairs. He'd already been in to take measurements, and by the time Kevin was walking more than six steps without collapsing, the gate was operational. Soon, his first birthday arrived. It was on a Thursday that year, and I managed to get the afternoon off so I could attend his birthday party. We invited all the parents we knew who had small children, like Nola and Barbara, so it was as much a party for adults as it was for children. All the parents brought toys for their babies, and there was much swapping and fighting over them. Kevin managed to corner one of Amy's dolls and refused to let go. Helen was still breastfeeding him, though she'd augmented her milk with solids for the previous six months. She hoped to continue breastfeeding for another year at most, by which time she would once more become fertile. We'd never discussed the possibility of more children, and in our future years together, we would never make any extra effort to procreate them. And, in fact, Helen would never again become pregnant. We would always remain a one-child family.

Another four years passed. They were years in which I made considerable progress towards achieving my aim of total control. In the early years of our marriage, I had never felt the need to impose my authority over Helen, but for some reason, which I was unable to articulate, I felt the increasing need to do so. I suppose it was partly the way in which she always seemed to be making decisions without consulting me and the annoyance I experienced as a result. As our relationship had matured from those early carefree years, my confidence had increased. Without any conscious intention, I learnt how to discipline Helen whenever I found fault in her housekeeping or her meals or when she made decisions I didn't approve of. I did everything gradually so she wouldn't realise that the power was gradually shifting in our relationship, and, on the whole, she succumbed without complaining. On the odd occasions when we had an argument and she tried to stand up to me, I just had to threaten her in some way for her to become compliant. Once, I got so angry with her that I even went into the kitchen and grabbed the carving knife, telling her that I'd use it on her if she didn't shut up. I never had to do that again.

Every time I'd managed to bring her back into the right frame of mind, I would award her a kindness or praise her for something she'd done, such as buying her a piece of jewellery or complimenting her on her cooking. And I made sure she always showed me the necessary measure of gratitude afterwards. If we did have any difference of opinion and she had backed down, I would tell her how much I loved her, how my treatment of her was purely for the benefit of the whole family. I really did love her, very much, but wanted what I felt was best for all of us. During those years, I also managed to go some way towards separating her from her past attachments, belittling any of her of friends she still saw from time to time, separating her from the life she had led before I met her.

At the end of January, in the year after Kevin turned six, he was sent off to the local primary school. Up till then, Helen had given him a bit of homeschooling in addition to two days a week at a childcare centre, and Kevin was showing a fair degree of intelligence and curiosity, though he often appeared timid and withdrawn. As soon as he was safely settled there, Helen once again raised the prospect of her going back to work. 'Absolutely no,' I said when she first spoke to me about it.

'Why ever not?' she asked me.

'Because I said so,' I replied. I reacted somewhat firmly, refusing to discuss the matter further. She was so much easier to manage now she had no work colleagues interfering in our lives, and a work situation was likely to bring in plenty of unwanted confidants.

'I don't think it's up to you *alone* to make those sorts of decisions,' she said, her voice quivering.

'Are you questioning my authority?' She remained silent as I glared at her. 'A man knows what's best for his family.'

'Does he now?' she whispered.

'Yes!' I shouted, making a menacing move towards her.

She flinched and backed away from me, probably remembering the carving knife episode, and then, without another word, fled sobbing from the room. Another reason for my hard line was that I was beginning to lose my trust in her. Many times in the past year, she had gone against my wishes in the bedroom, and on a couple of occasions lately, she had refused to have sex with me at all, only succumbing once I'd forced myself onto her. 'A wife must submit'' I kept telling her, but even when she did give in, she refused to take any enjoyment. I began to think that she had a lover elsewhere, and the more I thought about it, the more I became convinced. I started going through all our phone bills, marking those numbers I didn't recognise, and quizzing her about them, not that I ever found anything to worry about. And every so often, I would do a search of her handbag when she wasn't looking, searching for incriminating evidence. I never did find anything, but I remained suspicious. So every evening when I got in from work, I'd make her account for every minute of her day and tell me whom she'd seen and whom she'd talked to. I thought she would be gratified that I was taking such an interest in the minutiae of her day, but it didn't seem to make her any happier. The happiest one in the household was Percy. Kevin was sleeping in a proper bed by that time, and Percy, who was now full grown and lazy as sin, liked sneaking into Kevin's room and sleeping on his bed. I reckoned that was unhygienic, and I chased him out every time I found him there, no matter what Helen said.

In the same year that Kevin started school, I commenced my eleventh year working for Bill Thompson. So far, everything had gone well, and there had been enough work for the company to take on another mechanic and more operators, as well as purchase more equipment. Further, Bill had awarded me another increase, now putting me well above the award rate, so I had no reason for wanting to leave. But in March, Bill had a stroke. It was a fairly mild one, but he was told to slow down. I don't think that, until then, anyone in the company realised how much the success of the company was due to his hard work, but it soon became apparent. His son Nigel took over some of the running, but he lacked both the expertise and the dynamism of his father. He was also lazy. Then three months later, just after his sixtieth birthday, Bill was struck down by a heart attack. He was dead by the time an ambulance could reach him. Donna was, of course, distraught with grief. I could tell they'd been really close, and I did my best to support her.

For a time, the company descended into chaos. One day, I arrived at work to find another man in the office, a younger man dressed in a suit and talking earnestly to Donna. She broke off her conversation to introduce me. 'This is my son Ronnie, John Madden,' she said as we shook hands. 'Ronnie is going to help us for a bit.' I never knew that she and Bill had another son, so I was quite surprised. When I got to the workshop, I asked Nigel about him.

'Oh, yes, Ronnie,' answered Nigel. 'My brother didn't relish the thought of getting his hands dirty, so he refused to come into the business. He joined a firm of bookkeepers instead, trained to be a number puncher.'

'He looks a lot younger than you.'

'Ten years actually. I think he was a bit of an afterthought for my parents.'

'You don't sound as though you like him very much.'

'Oh, we get along.' He paused. 'Although Ronnie's had fuck-all to do with the company, Dad's still left us equal shares in the business.'

'How about Donna?'

'She'll run the show initially, but once she decides to retire, we'll take over.'

'But Ronnie doesn't know the first thing about it,' I complained.

'Bloody right. So I'll do all the work, and he'll take half the profit.'

I later spoke to Donna, who told me that Ronnie wouldn't be interfering with the day-to-day running of the business but would just help her with the accounts and give advice as needed. She'd decided to reduce the business to its original size. No one would be fired, but if any workers left, they wouldn't be replaced. So my new boss was Donna. I was not unhappy about that; I would much prefer her to Nigel, and I made every effort to assist her whenever I could. However, I knew that when she finally did retire, I would be seriously thinking about another job. She was about the same age as Bill, so I thought I'd get at least another five years. But even with Ronnie's help, which didn't appear to be very effective, I could tell that the ship was sinking, if very slowly.

One day, some eight months into the new regime, Donna asked me if I'd like to have a drink with her after work. A couple of times during the preceding weeks, I had noticed her staring at me in a strange way whenever I went into the office, but it hadn't meant anything. And when she asked me to meet her after work, I thought she just wanted to discuss the job away from the work situation, so I agreed, but it turned out she was just lonely and wanted someone to talk to. We met at a nearby pub and sat in a corner of the lounge bar. She put some money on the table and asked me to go up and get her a gin and tonic, plus whatever I was having. She remained silent for a time as we sat nursing our drinks. Then she looked up at me and smiled. 'I don't really know what I'm doing here,' she started, 'but I just feel my life is falling apart.'

'It must be difficult without Bill around,' I suggested.

'Unfortunately, my sons are little help. They've got their own families now.'

'Don't they visit you at home?'

'Not unless I specifically ask them.' She didn't say any more for a time. I was wondering how I could help her during her time of obvious distress. I was almost about to suggest she come round and visit me and Helen sometime, but then she put out her hand and rested it on mine. It was totally unexpected. I should have taken my hand away, but I didn't. She didn't say anything for a while, and when she did speak again, it was on a new subject, one that I quickly realised she'd been leading up to all the time. 'I miss Bill so much, John—you know, in *every* way. He was still a very fit man.'

'He always seemed quite indestructible,' I said. I still hadn't grasped what was coming, despite being so affected by the warmth of her hand. I was immobilised, intrigued and not a little excited, wondering what she had in mind.

She laughed. 'Yes, I suppose he would appear that way.' She paused. 'Tell me, John, how is your marriage? Are you happy?'

I studied her, the office lady. I suppose I'd never thought of her before, not as a woman to be admired, and certainly not as a friend, a possible lover even, but that was exactly how she was coming over. I began to realise that she was still attractive. She had always seemed a bit slim for my taste, but she was still shapely and she'd certainly been looking after herself. Perhaps she was a gym freak. I thought about her question and wasn't sure how to reply. Granted that Helen and I had our differences, they weren't so much of a problem that I'd want to jump ship. 'Happy enough,' I said eventually, not wanting to divulge more.

'I really like you, John. Do you think you can forget that I'm your boss?'

'Is that what you want?' I asked her. She nodded. 'It wouldn't be difficult.'

'Well, then, I'd like to be your friend—outside working hours, I mean.'

She was being very forward. She had the benefit of age, and I supposed that gave her the right to be upfront with me. 'Certainly,' I agreed.

'Friends with benefits, I mean, if you know the expression.'

So that was it. I could hardly believe what I was hearing. My boss wanted me as a lover. I could hear my voice quivering as I replied, 'Yes, I think so, but you do realise, don't you, that I've never done anything like this before.'

'I thought not.' She paused. 'I'm not too old for you, then?'

'I haven't a clue. I've never had an older woman proposition me before.'

'But you want to try?'

'Who wouldn't!' I exclaimed in a moment of bravado. Donna clutched my hand, now in both of hers, smiling broadly. 'Good,' she said. 'You know, it wasn't easy for me to talk to you like this, but I've always liked you, John, so I decided to risk it.' She gripped my hand more tightly and smiled. 'Now let's get another drink.'

So this was to be my first affair; I was excited at the prospect. I just nodded in agreement and went up the bar. We made our plans over the next half hour then parted. As we rose to leave, she kissed me. Her lips reminded me of Mandy, but only because it was an illicit kiss, and I kept licking mine as I drove home, relishing the faint flavour of her lipstick. When I got home, life suddenly had to return to normal. Helen and I gave each other a chaste kiss, as we always did on my return, and which I insisted on even when a state of conflict existed between us, and Kevin came running up to me and put his arms round my legs, so I picked him up and gave him a cuddle, just as I always liked to do.

'You're late tonight,' said Helen.

It wasn't really an accusation, so I didn't say anything at first, but eventually I put Kevin down and told her I'd had some work to finish. 'And there's a fair bit of extra coming up, so I have to go in on Saturdays.' I was trying to subdue the faint quiver in my voice as I spoke my rehearsed and cheating lies. 'Just for the morning,' I added. 'Maybe for a couple of weeks.'

'All right, then,' she answered, apparently unaware of my deceit.

I'd survived the first hurdle. For the next few weeks, I had to make sure I didn't behave any differently. And I had to check myself that I didn't get excessively loving towards Helen that night, or on any succeeding night, in a way that might make her suspicious. I was worried that I might give myself away somehow, especially as Saturday approached, and I breathed a sigh of relief as I was able to slip quietly out of the house soon after six thirty that morning. Donna had given me her address and had made me memorise it, so I wouldn't get caught with a telltale piece of paper in my pocket. She had sold the family home when Bill died. There were just too many memories, she told me, and she'd bought an apartment closer to the business.

When I reached her block of flats, I drove past and parked a little way up the road. I found her first-floor apartment and rang her bell. The door opened instantly. Donna smiled at me but said nothing. She simply took my hand and ushered me inside, straight into her bedroom. She was wearing a light dressing gown with nothing underneath and a seductive perfume that wafted up to me as we kissed. My main memory of that first time with Donna was her incredible hunger, her unrelenting need, and her writhing body, that and the way her hip bones dug into me. She was quick to show me everything she wanted me to do to her, even though she was already fully aroused, and she talked a lot, obscene words interspersed with the happy sounds of her ecstasy. After the first coupling, she continued to cling to me. 'I wasn't expecting such a good fuck,' she said. 'Not the first time.'

'Nor was I,' I replied. I hadn't taken much notice of her body before beyond admiring her firm small breasts and wide hips. Now I had time to study her properly. She didn't appear to show any of the signs of ageing that I expected. 'You still have a great body,' I said. 'If you don't mind me asking, how old are you?'

'Sixty next birthday.'

'You could have fooled me. You look and behave like a teenager.'

'Thank you, John. That's good to know, but I bet you have never actually fucked a teenager?' she suggested, laughing quietly to herself.

'No, you're right. That's *not* part of my CV.'

'You should value experience.'

'Oh, I do. It was your suppleness and your animation that make you appear so young.'

We said no more for a time, then Donna suddenly sat up. 'I'm sorry. I'm forgetting my manners. Would you like a cup of something?'

'Love a coffee.'

'OK. I'll make us one. Then we must make love again. Slowly.'

It was midday when we finally surfaced. I left her reluctantly and headed off for a shower. Donna told me she'd put a bar of soap in there for me, same as the ones in the showers at work, 'just so you won't smell different when you get home,' she said. 'And make sure you wash your hair. That will smell too.' She seemed to have thought of everything, and I wondered whether she'd ever had a lover before me. I asked her once, a few weeks after that first encounter, and she told me that I was the first and only man, other than Bill, she'd ever slept with. 'Bill took my virginity,' she said. 'I couldn't stomach the thought of anyone else as much as touching me, but then he died and left a big hole in my life.' Before I left, we made the same arrangement for the following Saturday and had one last sensual kiss as she held the door open for me.

On my way home, I had a wicked thought. 'So I'm filling a hole, in more ways than one,' I said aloud and laughed joyfully. After three delightful Saturday mornings, I told Donna that Helen, though not yet over-suspicious, was asking me how long my extra work was going to last. I could have brazened it out for a while longer but thought we should try something different. 'I can't give up now,' she said. 'I'm feeling human again at last. How about lunchtimes instead?' Donna asked me. Thompson's had a forty-five-minute lunch break, and we worked out that, allowing for travelling time, we could still get thirty minutes together in her apartment, and perhaps we could manage twice a week. So we tried that. It was always a bit of a rush, and frankly it was unsatisfactory. As well as being a race against time, our trysts had to be abandoned frequently at the last minute, because of one of us being otherwise engaged. However, our loving continued for only another four weeks of fits and starts before being suddenly brought to a halt.

One Friday morning, as I arrived at work, Donna again asked me to meet her after work at the pub. She needed to talk to me. I was already seated when she walked in, a worried frown on her face. I'd bought her a gin and tonic and a beer for myself, which were sitting on the table between us. 'I'm afraid I'm the bringer of bad news,' she started. 'I have to end it.'

'Why? What's happened?'

'You aren't going to like this, but …. well, I've met someone else.'

My first reaction was one of anger, a perverse indignation at her duplicity, but underneath, and coming quickly to the surface, was a feeling of intense relief. At last, I would no longer have to lie. Also, as soon as I really thought about it, I quickly realised that Donna had every right to look around and find another life partner, one who could give her *all* of his time rather than fleeting moments. For a time, I remained tongue-tied. Then I looked her in the eye, shaking my head. 'I'm sorry.' I said. It was all I could think of saying.

'I met Tom at the gym. He and I both do yoga.'

So she *was* a gym freak. 'I hope he's a good lover,' I said with rather more acid in my voice than I had intended.

'I don't yet know if he is.'

'You mean you haven't tried him out yet?'

'We're moving slowly.' She paused. 'One thing I do know, John, is that no one will be a better lover than you. You press all the right buttons, and I just want you to know that. I shall treasure the times we've had together, but I must move on. I owe it to myself to find permanent happiness elsewhere, if and when I can.'

'I understand,' I said, and then, with more audacity than expectation, I added, "How about one last farewell fuck, then?"

Donna just smiled. 'No, John, that won't solve anything.'

'Well, enjoy your farewell drink, then. Cheers,' I said, lifting my glass.

'Cheers,' she agreed, taking a big swallow of her gin and tonic.

'And I hope that Tom Whatshisname brings you all the happiness you deserve.'

'Thanks, John. That's really nice of you.'

'My pleasure,' I said, though I didn't feel much pleasure at all.

Following this romantic interlude, life at work took a while to settle back into the completely humdrum. I tried to avoid the office as much as possible, but there were always times when I had to be there. When we did chance to meet, Donna and I pretended that there had never been anything between us, but occasionally she would smile at me in a knowing way. One Wednesday morning, as I was about to enter the office, I heard a man's raised voice, angry and belligerent, coming from inside. I thought it best not to interrupt the tirade, but then I heard Donna's voice trying to appease him, and she sounded almost tearful. I immediately felt the need to intervene, even though it really had nothing to do with me. The man, a bloke of about my age and with a few days' growth of beard on his chin, turned as I strode in. He stopped talking in mid sentence and stared at me.

'Oh, it's you, John,' said Donna. 'Perhaps you can help us. This is Sam Gould from Cedar Pools.'

'John Madden,' I said, holding out my hand in a gesture of goodwill. Surprisingly, he shook it.

'Sam has been waiting two days for us to get on-site and start a job,' added Donna. 'He says he spoke to someone here to arrange it, but I can't find any record of the call.'

This sounded to me like one of Nigel's cock-ups. It wasn't the first time he'd let us down with his laissez-faire attitude, and I didn't expect it to be the last. The idiot was costing us both jobs and money. 'What's required?' I asked.

'We're putting in a pool at a property near Seaford. The man I spoke to was supposed to start digging the hole on Monday morning.'

'Oh, dear,' I said not very helpfully.

'I've had men standing around for two days. It's just not good enough.'

'It certainly isn't,' I said. I realised I should do something to help, something that would improve my standing even further with Thompson's. 'Leave it with me,' I promised. 'Just give me the address, and I'll have someone down there this afternoon. What's the access like? And the ground?'

'Tight. You'll need a small digger.'

'Like a skidsteer excavator?'

'Perfect,' said Sam Gould. 'And the ground is quite soft. Not many rocks according to the builder.'

I turned to Donna. 'Is there an operator available?'

'Jason's just finishing a job down the road. He'll be back any moment.'

'I'll get the excavator up on the low-loader, and we'll leave as soon as he returns. I'll see you down there,' I told Sam.

It was good to get out of the workshop for a spell. In ten minutes, I had the excavator pumped full of fuel, checked over, loaded, and secured. Half an hour later, Jason appeared, and we were on our way. It had been a while since I'd gained my heavy duty license, and I hadn't used the loader very often, so I drove carefully down the Nepean Highway towards Seaford. Jason and I hardly said a word to each other for the first fifteen minutes or so, but then we got chatting about work. I didn't know him well, but the little I'd seen of his work had impressed me. He was a few years older than I was and had been with Thompson's since he'd left school, but as we approached our destination, he let slip that he was considering jumping ship. 'It's just not the same with Bill gone,' he said.

Sam Gould was waiting for us as we arrived, he and a couple of workmen sitting in a van marked 'Cedar Pools'. The site was a partially completed home, the owners wanting the pool ready at the same time as the house. The outline of the pool had already been marked out on what would be the back garden. I reversed the truck up next to the house and manoeuvred it close to the marked area. Soon, we had the excavator offloaded, and Jason was busy with the initial cuts in the soil. Sam and I watched for a time in silence. He seemed to have recovered from his earlier displeasure, and we chatted quite amicably. He told me about the difficulties that Cedar Pools had finding subcontractors, especially with regard to earth moving. 'And ours isn't the only pool company to be in trouble over this,' he added. In turn, I related the problems we were having at Thompson's because of the change of management and promised that we'd try to do better in the future, though, of course, I had no authority to make such promises. We parted as friends, and Sam left to go and visit another job. I stayed till late afternoon, by which time Jason had completed about a third of the hole. We locked up the excavator, leaving it there for Jason to finish the job the next day, before driving the loader back to the workshop. I had a lot to think about on my way home that evening: Cedar's dilemma with subcontractors, Thompson's management upheaval, and Jason's discontent. And there was my future to be considered as well. I began to get a crazy idea in my head, but the more I thought about it, the less crazy it seemed. The key was Helen and all the money she had tied up. I would have to be careful how I approached her. That evening, I waited until after dinner and we were sitting comfortably in the lounge room before I broached my idea. But, first, I told her all that had happened that day. 'There's obviously an opening for a specialist earth mover,' I started, 'someone who can dig holes for the pool companies.'

'And you think you're the right person?' said Helen in disbelief.

'Why not?'

'You actually want to start your own business?' She sounded incredulous.

'I'd love to give it a shot. I reckon it's only a matter of time before Thompson's folds. They'd have to sell all the equipment, and I might be able to pick some up on the cheap.'

'And I suppose you want me to stump up with the money?'

'Would you?'

'Absolutely not,' she replied with a decisive shake of her head.

I suppose I should have expected that response, but I was disconcerted that she wouldn't even discuss the matter. 'Why can't you be a little more supportive?' I railed at her, but she just looked at me without speaking. I would have liked to have said a lot more, to have accused her of disloyalty and even threatened her with some retribution, but I said no more that evening. But her lack of encouragement made me even more determined to prove her wrong. I wasn't going to give up my idea, but somehow I needed to get control of the money she had locked away. I resolved to wear her down, nibble away at her reluctance one bit at a time, though how I would do that, I had no idea. Ever since our marriage, Helen and I had lived comfortably on my wages, and I had even saved a little, though not nearly enough to even think about going into business on my own. I thought over the problem while at work the following day, and when I got home, I told Helen that since I would now have to save more, we'd have to trim our budget. To start with, I'd need to cut her housekeeping allowance and also postpone any immediate expenditures, such as reupholstery of the lounge suite, which she'd wanted, and new clothes for Kevin.

She looked at me in horror. 'A cut in housekeeping I can live with, but Kevin's growing fast. He must have clothes that fit him.' I just looked at her, waiting for her to say more, perhaps unbend a little. 'Anyway, what's the rush?' she added. 'It's not as though you're out of work.'

'No. Thompson's will continue to struggle on for a time.'

'And, in the meantime, you want us to struggle as well?'

'I just want to be sure that when the time comes, I can be first in line to purchase what I'll need.'

'Well, I think you should investigate the whole matter a bit more closely. I'm sure that starting a business requires a lot more than the cash needed to buy a few pieces of equipment.'

'Such as?'

'You need premises for a start, and there must be all sorts of legal requirements.'

'I guess so.' In my blind enthusiasm, there had obviously been heaps of things I hadn't thought of. I had to eat humble pie over that one, though I remained angry about the way that Helen had deflated my ego so easily. Anyway, I still didn't entirely relinquish my plan, and a few weeks later, I again found myself on a job with Jason and discussed the matter with him. He was keen on the idea and asked me to keep him in mind should anything develop. I promised he'd be the first to know. I also had a discussion with Sam Gould, who'd given me his card before we'd parted company at Seaford. He was also supportive. Cedar Pools was based in an industrial estate between Frankston and Kananook. We met in a pub near his office one day when I was working in the area. He told me that most of their work was around Frankston or down on the Peninsula, and that if I was serious about starting a business, I should base it in that area. He said there were a lot of small properties close by if I was interested. I just needed two things to happen: the final demise of Thompson's and Helen's agreement to finance the enterprise. The former seemed certain, just a matter of time, but the latter remained a problem.

*　　　*　　　*

CHAPTER 13

1993–1994

It was Kevin's eighth birthday, and Helen wanted to mark the occasion with a proper celebration. December 15 fell on a Wednesday that year, and it being a school day, we decided to postpone the party till the following Saturday. It was a happy day. Kevin was allowed to bring up to six friends from school, but in the end, he invited only three, all boys. Two of them were twins, and the third a shy little boy called Jackson, who Kevin said was his best friend. Jackson appeared to have a touch of Asian about his face, and it turned out later that his father was a Chinese Malaysian, though his mother was Australian. Helen also invited Kevin's two female cousins and Sarah Little, so there were equal numbers, though Florrie was fourteen now and Amy eleven, so a little bit older than the others. I asked Hudson and Nora to come, as well as Paul and Barbara, and I arranged a treasure hunt for the children in and around the garden. Kevin wasn't normally a person that ran everywhere, but on this occasion, he was caught up in the general excitement and raced around the garden like a puppy off the lead. In fact, it soon became apparent that all the other children were following him, which I suppose was only natural since he knew the layout better than anybody.

It was a warm and somewhat humid day, and once all the treasures had been found, the children went inside. They played hide-and-seek all over the house, while Helen laid the party food out on the dining-room table. When I called them, the children descended on the food like a plague of locusts, and, finally, once they'd slowed down, I ushered them outside again. Each child was given a large cone with two dollops of ice cream, one chocolate and one strawberry. I was quite proud of Kevin's behaviour during the day. In everything, he had waited his turn patiently, and he showed great gratitude for all the gifts he'd been brought. At five o'clock, the mother of the twins arrived and picked up all three boys, and while Kevin and the girls sat in the lounge room and watched cartoons on TV, the rest of us started clearing up.

I finally had a chance to chat to Hudson. He had recently changed jobs, though he was still in IT. I hadn't seen him for nearly a year, not since their annual New Year's Eve party. He and Nora had already been in their new house for seven years and were loving it, and Nora was obviously pregnant again. When I remarked on her condition, Hudson told me that the new baby was due in three months. He told me they'd been trying again for the previous five years without any luck, so her pregnancy was something of a miracle.

I also had a long chat to Barbara, who told me that everything was still fine with our parents, though Mum had let slip that Dad had started drinking again. Apparently, he'd attended a colleague's retirement function and someone had doctored his orange juice. After that, he'd gotten the taste for it again, though so far it hadn't been a serious problem. In the meantime, he'd received a promotion and was no longer working shifts. It was some troubleshooting job in the office, she told me.

We all sat around in the lounge room once the house was shipshape again. Percy emerged from where he'd been hiding all day. He wandered round the room then jumped up on Kevin's lap and lay there purring. We drank wine and beer, and Helen found enough leftover sandwiches and sausage rolls to keep us fed. I told them about my ideas for a new business. Helen kept silent, but both Paul and Hudson were very supportive. 'There's a lot of water still to flow under the bridge,' I said, 'before I can do anything.' Paul told me that his father had started a new business some years back. He was sure that his dad would be free with advice if I needed it, for which I was grateful. Paul said his father was a cabinetmaker and had opened a small factory making high-end furniture for 'discerning customers', as he put it. I thought my proposed subcontracting venture would be very different from that, but all advice would be welcome.

By seven o'clock, the little ones were getting fractious, and the party broke up. As the parents ushered their children out to their cars, they were lavish in their thanks. As soon as they had all gone, Helen returned to the lounge room to finish clearing up, while I took Kevin up to bed. Later, she and I sat together to discuss the day. 'Evidently, you are still serious about your new enterprise,' she said once we were settled. Some weeks ago, I had realised that my previous ultimatum regarding Helen's housekeeping allowance and other expenditures was somewhat counterproductive, and I had tried a softer approach. I rescinded the cuts and generally became more agreeable, and I had even proposed that we all take a holiday over the Christmas and New Year period. But it wasn't the holiday I wanted to talk about.

'Yes, I'm still serious. I'm sure I can make it work for us.'

'For *us*? Are you including me in this?'

'Absolutely,' I replied, though I'd actually been thinking about me and Jason when I'd referred to *us*. I quickly changed my approach. 'It's essential that you are onside,' I said, 'and I don't only mean with the money. I could try for a bank loan if it was *only* about money.'

'Well, that's a change.'

'How do you mean?'

'Asking my opinion. That's new.'

Of course, I'd been aware that I'd cut Helen out of any decision-making for some time. It was all part of my control strategy, but I realised that on this occasion I needed her input. 'We would have a completely different lifestyle, one you would need to agree to,' I told her.

'Well, I have to say, I'm not happy with our current lifestyle, so any change would be an improvement,' she said sadly. I didn't say anything, so she continued. 'Anyway, what would be so different?'

'It would no longer be a nine-to-five job, that's certain. I'm sure I'd have to work some weekends, so you would have to look after Kevin a lot more.'

Helen seemed happy with that idea. She had always said I was too hard on the boy when I was at home, too harsh a disciplinarian. 'At last, you're making sense, John,' she said, and she smiled, the sort of relaxed smile I hadn't seen in Helen for a long time.

'If I'm now making sense, does that mean you are prepared to discuss my proposal?'

'Possibly, but, first, you have to talk to Paul's father and put together a business plan.'

'OK. I'll be on leave at the end of next week. I'll phone him tomorrow and make an appointment.'

'Good,' agreed Helen. 'Now we're on the same page for a change, I feel happier.'

'Me too,' I replied.

'In fact, I might even enjoy a little gentle pleasuring tonight, if you want me,' she offered.

The main concern I had over my proposed career change was still the matter of cost. I had no idea how much I would need to get started and, in particular, how much I would have to outlay for the machinery I would need. During the week, I managed to persuade Donna to show me the details of Thompson's capital expenditures. At first, she was rather suspicious, wondering why I needed to know, but somehow I convinced her that I would be more use to Thompson's if I understood their financial pressures. 'I'd really like to know,' I told her, 'and I'm sure you won't mind helping me out, even if just for "old times' sake",' I added, winking at her. So, a couple of times during the next week, I studied the new and book values of Thompson's different assets. Some of the older pieces of machinery were almost completely written off, but others, like the skidsteer excavator, which was almost new, only had 10 or 20 per cent off their purchase prices. To start with, I would need a larger excavator as well as the smaller one, plus a low-loader for transporting them to various jobs. All that would set me back between $60,000 and $100,000, I reckoned. I also asked Donna how they calculated the costs of a job, how much they needed to charge a customer, and she explained about fixed and running costs. I was beginning to get a handle on everything. I went on leave at the end of the week feeling happier.

The start of my leave coincided with the last day of Kevin's school year. During the week, he had asked Helen if he could take Jackson with us on holiday. Kevin's friend was the son of a single mother, her Malaysian husband having deserted her. She, like most people in her position, had little money and certainly not enough for holidays. When Helen asked me, I consented immediately. Kevin and Jackson would keep each other amused, giving me and Helen more opportunity of being together, and when she phoned Jackson's house, his mother readily agreed. 'She sounded happy to have a break,' Helen told me. I had booked two adjacent rooms at the Princes Motel in Cowes for a week from January 1. It was the place we'd stayed before our marriage, and I wanted to see how it had changed in the twelve years since we'd been there. I'd even managed to book the same room number. I thought it would be romantic, and that would help Helen to overcome any further reluctance she still had regarding my business venture. I suspected that she would be aware of my ulterior motive, but I still had to make the holiday as comfortable as I could.

But, first, there was Christmas to navigate. My parents, Barbara, and I had an arrangement to take it in turns to host the rest of the family. That year, it was my parents' turn, and to relieve Mum of some of the work,

Barbara and Helen agreed to each bring a course for Christmas dinner. Helen decided to make a pavlova, and it looked magnificent. She balanced it on her lap as I drove to Mum and Dad's house, and at the other end, Kevin jumped out of the car and opened the passenger door for her. As we went in, I was worrying about my father. He'd been on the wagon for twelve years, and I could have cheerfully shot the idiot that got him started drinking again, but he seemed entirely sober as he greeted us all. 'Happy Christmas, Grandpa,' piped Kevin, and we all joined in with our greetings.

Paul, Barbara, and their brood arrived a few minutes after us. She carried a huge bowl of peeled prawns and sliced avocado, all in a seafood sauce. 'Don't worry,' she said, laughing. 'These have been well refrigerated.' Just then, Mum appeared out of the kitchen, wiping her hands on a dishcloth. She looked well, though older than I remembered, and she still carried the scar next to her eye.

'The turkey is browning well, and the potatoes are in to roast,' she said proudly.

'Anything I can do to help?' offered Helen.

'No. Everything's fine. But, John,' she called out to me, 'there're two bottles of bubbles in the fridge, if you wouldn't mind.'

After I'd poured the drinks and found a bottle of Fanta for the children, I watched my father closely. 'Are you having one?' I asked him.

'Just a small one.'

'Tell me about this promotion, Dad.'

'I've just been moved sideways, that's all. I had a run-in with some rowdy kids, a bunch of private schoolboys. They were effing and swearing, carrying on like they owned the tram, and being rude to other passengers, so I stopped and told them to get off or I'd call the police.'

'And, did they?'

'Eventually, but the bosses reckoned I was too old to be driving. Instead, they put me in the office, pushing papers around.'

'Doesn't sound much of a job?'

'It's not too bad. At least I'm off shift work.'

The children were eyeing all the presents surrounding the Christmas tree, one that Dad had bought and erected in the corner of the lounge room, and which he and Mum had decorated together. It made the place look homely, but it was another tradition that presents would only be opened after lunch, so they were only allowed to look and feel. As expected, the food was enjoyably received, and, as usual, everyone ate too much. As a result, most of the pavlova remained uneaten and would be divided up for people to take home and eat later. And the noise that had remained subdued during the meal reached a crescendo as the presents were distributed and opened. Kevin, being the youngest, was allotted the task of handing them out, though he became confused as to which John was which.

I had been keeping an eye on my father, but he'd only had the half glass of bubbles and a beer with his meal. Nevertheless, I felt I should have a word with him before we left. I asked him to step outside with me as there was something I wanted to ask him. 'Dad,' I started once we were out of earshot from those inside, 'I heard that some bastard spiked your drink at a work function. Is that right?'

'I'm afraid so, son. There must have been a shot of vodka in my orange juice, which is pretty tasteless, so I never realised.'

'And it started you off again?'

'Not really. Just a wee bit every now and then.'

'After all these years too.'

'I know, but I've learnt to moderate it. I never have more than one drink.'

'Dad, you know it could just be the thin edge of the wedge.'

'I don't think so, John. I'm fine now.'

'Well, I just want to warn you, in the kindest possible way.'

'How do you mean?'

'It's just that if it leads you back to your old ways, my threat still stands. If I ever hear that you've taken it out on Mum, I shall be fucking furious.' I paused for a moment then put my arms around him. 'Please, Dad, I love you both. Don't let me down.' When I released him, I noticed a tear on his cheek.

*

We drove down to Phillip Island on New Year's Day. We played a game with the boys, each of us making words using all three letters of the number plates of the cars we passed. The person with the shortest word won; IXZ 312 completely defeated us. Then we played I spy, and finally the boys slept. When we arrived at the Princes Motel, we could see that it had received a makeover. 'Under new management' read a banner over the entrance, and the lady in reception was new, both friendly and efficient. And the rooms, too, had new curtains and were freshly painted. At least the beds looked the same. The boys wanted to go straight off to the beach, so we got them into their swimming trunks, grabbed the buckets and spades, and set off down to the waterfront. Jackson had never been to the seaside before. At first, he was hesitant about going into the water, but eventually he followed Kevin's lead. Our son was already a strong swimmer, and we had to warn him not to take Jackson out of his depth. Helen tried to show him how to swim, but it was difficult in the waves, and after he'd twice choked on mouthfuls of seawater, he retired to the shore. We decided it would be better to teach Jackson in a pool somewhere, and when we asked the lady at the motel, she gave us directions to the Phillip Island Leisure Centre, just down the road in Church Street. We went there two days running, and before long, Jackson was sufficiently confident in the water for us to return to the sea.

Most days, we went to the beach in the morning, and in the afternoons went on drives. We visited the Wildlife Park a couple of times as we wanted to introduce the boys to Australian fauna, and it was good to go back and see the wombats, which had made such an impression on me all those years ago. Altogether, it was a splendid holiday, somewhat lacking in the lustful abandonment of our previous visit but still a great time of relaxation. We indulged in sex only when Helen indicated a wish to do so, and I gave her plenty of rope, allowing her to go off on her own whenever she wanted a break, though I had to make a conscious effort to do so. I was fully aware that I was surreptitiously making myself as congenial as I could in an attempt to get her to agree to the financing of my new business. And it appeared to be working. During our holiday, she let slip a couple of remarks that seemed to indicate her possible willingness to be a partner. I had spent two hours with Paul's father before Christmas, two very useful hours, and had made copious notes of our discussion. Then I'd weighed up all the pros and cons with Helen, and she had suggested we should go together to visit a lawyer. 'How about Candice Maybury?' she suggested. 'She was the person that sorted out all the powers of attorney for me. And her firm advised me on the investments as well. She's good.'

When we returned home, I had one further week of leave before I had to return to work. In that week, we had a session with Candice and another with the financial adviser. On both occasions, Helen had phoned Jackson's mother to ask if she would look after Kevin for the day. She was happy to do both; though, the second time, Kevin himself was less than keen to go. He had returned after the first visit with some rather bizarre tales of Jackson's household. Evidently, his mother had acquired a new boyfriend over the Christmas and New Year period, and the two boys had been left alone for hours at a time, getting increasingly bored, while the lovers had disappeared to another part of the house. And lunch just didn't happen. But the second visit was an improvement, we discovered from Kevin when we picked him up afterwards.

I returned to work on the Monday, expecting within a few months to put in my time and start on my own. However, matters were taken straight out of my hands. As I arrived, all Thompson's employees were called into the office. Ronnie and Nigel were already there as well as Donna. She was looking exceedingly anxious as we filed in. She stood up behind her desk and spoke, her voice breaking at times. 'I have to tell you,' she began, 'that, over the break, we've had to do some soul-searching. Ronnie has been going through the books, and it appears we have been losing money, that in fact we've been operating at a loss for most of last year. And with the lack of forward contracts, we've collectively decided to close the business.' There was a collective sigh of astonishment. 'I know Bill would have been horrified, but there it is ….' Her voice tailed off, and a hubbub rose around her as people started throwing questions at her. Eventually, she held up her hand to gain silence. 'We have two contracts to finish over the next month, and these will be honoured. In the meantime, all entitlements will be met, plus one month's extra wages for all employees as they leave for the last time.' There were murmurings of acceptance before Donna spoke again. 'We would like the following personnel to stay and help us finish the two contracts,' and she started reading out the names of a select number of operators, one of whom was Jason. She also wanted me to stay to help with necessary maintenance and stay for the final closing down of the business.

There was an air of disbelief among us as we left the office. We walked out silently, everyone lost in their own thoughts. I blamed Nigel for most of the problem. I'd looked at him frequently during Donna's address and could see that he was blind to his part in the demise of the company. In fact, he carried a silly smirk on his face. I could have hit him, but my mind was already working overtime on what it would all mean to me. As the crowd broke up, I spoke briefly to Jason, promising him a job in my new venture. He just nodded his acceptance, and as soon as I could, I caught Donna on her own and asked what was to be done with all the machinery that would now become redundant.

'We'll have to sell it,' she answered. Then she looked at me with a grin. 'Interested?'

'Actually, yes.'

'I thought as much, with you snooping around the books last month.'

I just laughed. 'Guilty as charged.'

'Well, all I can say is good luck, John. You're welcome to take your pick.'

'Thanks.'

'But you'll have to pay book value.'

'No problem,' I said. 'And I hope that all the relevant spares in stock are part of the deal.'

'Of course.'

'But, tell me, how is Tom Whatshisname coming along?' Donna just held up her hand to show me a brand-new wedding band. 'Oh. Congratulations. When was the big day?'

'Just after Christmas.'

'You didn't think to invite me?'

'It was quiet. Family only.'

'Well, I hope you'll be happy.'

'Thanks, John.' She looked around to make sure no one else was listening. 'And thanks for getting me over my bad patch,' she added with a smile.

'More than happy to oblige,' I said and left her still smiling.

I didn't really have a great deal to do in my last three weeks at Thompson's. I just had to be available in case of any breakdown or other maintenance job. It left me plenty of time to make sure that the two pieces of excavation equipment I had earmarked and the low-loader were in the best possible condition. At the same time, I went through the store and made sure there were sufficient spares.

When I returned home that first evening, I gave Helen a big hug. 'We're in business,' I announced.

'What's happened?'

'Thompson's has folded. I'm buying all the machinery we need in a month's time.'

'Wow. That's quick.'

'They reckon the company is no longer viable.'

'Are you getting what you're owed?'

'That and an extra month's wages.'

'That's all right, then.'

'We must go and find some premises, next weekend preferably.'

I had recently purchased a mobile phone. There were more and more of them coming onto the market, and I realised that one would be essential to my new business. Once we were operating, I'd seldom remain in one place for long, or near a landline. It was going to be especially useful in the coming weeks while I was setting everything up. The next day at work, I phoned a number of estate agents in and around Frankston, ones that dealt with industrial land. I told them I was looking for a small property to rent, preferably one with a large shed of some sort that could be used to house and work on machinery. Only two agents had anything approaching what I was after, so I made appointments to visit them on the Saturday. Then I made a call to Sam Gould, notifying him about the demise of Thompson's. 'I should be in business within six weeks,' I told him, 'so I hope you'll have some work for me.'

'Enough,' he replied.

Helen and I set out early. We bundled Kevin into the car and drove to Frankston in a state of some excitement and a growing confidence that hopefully was not misplaced. In the event, the first agent only wanted to show us 'greenfield' sites for sale, but the second had quite a few rental properties for us to look at. He gave us a typed list, and we drove round and had a look at each. Most were unnecessarily large, being a few acres in extent, but two were possible. They were both about one acre in size, had good solid fences around them with locked gates, and included a large industrial building. We drove back to the agent to pick up the keys for the two properties so we could make a closer inspection. We went first to the one that had looked the best from the outside and didn't have to look any further. It had everything I needed. A wide concrete strip ran from the road to the front of the building, a tall structure that was big enough to house all the machinery we would be using. A big sliding door, high enough to get equipment in and out, faced the street, and inside the concrete floor looked solid enough. As a bonus, there was a fenced-off area, which I could use as a store, and there was a small change room with a shower and toilet. A small office with a door facing the road, and another leading into the workshop area, was tacked onto the front of the main building. It seemed as though it had been built specifically for me.

When we returned to the agent, we took Kevin in with us, not wanting to leave him alone in the car. The agent told us that the company, which had previously occupied our favoured property, had gone to the wall. The building on it had been built specifically to their needs. 'What business were they in?' I asked him.

'Lawnmower repairs, I believe, but they were too isolated to attract customers.'

'Makes sense.'

'Anyway, what do you want it for?'

Before I could answer, I saw Kevin standing in some discomfort, his legs crossed and his face screwed up in misery. 'Excuse me,' said Helen, 'do you have a toilet?'

'Through there,' he said, pointing to a door.

'There's one other thing we will need,' I said. 'A fuel bowser. A diesel tank. Will it be OK for me to get one installed before I actually move in?'

'Shouldn't be a problem.'

When Helen had returned with a relieved Kevin, we spent some time discussing the terms and conditions of the rental. I told the agent I wanted the property available from March 1, and I wrote out a cheque to cover the deposit, promising him I'd deliver the first six months' rent before I took possession. That being acceptable, we headed back to the car. I was beginning to get a handle on all the costs, but it was time to make another visit to Candice, the lawyer. Helen had indicated that she'd be able to invest $200,000 in the company. That was the limit of her inheritance, and we would have to manage on it. To keep the outlay as low as possible, I thought we should operate as a sole trader, simply calling the company Maddens, so we didn't have to register a separate business name, but there were other registrations to be applied for, all free of charge, such things as an Australian business number and so on. I felt we would have quite sufficient capital, but I was very undecided about running costs and resolved to pick Donna's brain a little more, if only to establish exactly how much one should charge for different jobs and how one should calculate it. I needed a crash course in cost accounting.

I had a few small jobs to attend to in the workshop on the Monday, and once I was free, I went to the office. Donna was on the phone, and judging by her happy face and the words of endearment she uttered, she was talking to her new man. She smiled at me as she put the phone down. 'He's such a sweetie,' she said. 'Tom, I take it?' I answered.

'Who else? He's quite wealthy, and I'll never have to work again. I'm so lucky.'

'You'll be bored.'

She just grinned and shook her head at me. 'Now, my budding entrepreneur, what can I do for you today?'

'How much time have you got?'

'For you, John, all day.'

'You *are* in a good mood.'

'Yep.'

'Well, since you no longer need to keep your family secrets, I want you to tell me all you can about costing jobs.'

'Gladly.' I got a chair and sat beside her at her desk, while she got out a large pad of paper. She made two columns: fixed costs and running costs, and detailed all the expenditures under them. Then she got another piece of paper and showed me how to work out the amount of fixed costs, which should be apportioned to each job, before adding its running costs and a percentage for profit. I realised that if one could have two jobs running at the same time, the proportion of fixed costs on each job would be halved, and the job made cheaper, that or the profit increased. But there were a lot of intangibles, such as how many jobs one could attract in a month, say, and how long each one would take. I realised that that's where experience became essential. 'Or you could charge by the hour,' she said, 'though most people prefer fixed prices upfront.'

I took all Donna's jottings home with me that afternoon. I walked into a house in mourning. Helen came to the door with an expression of deep melancholy. 'Percy is dead,' she announced. 'Kevin's upstairs, crying his eyes out.' My antipathy to Percy had moderated a little over the years. I had even allowed him to perversely jump up onto my lap a couple of times lately without chucking him off, so I, too, was upset at the news.

'What happened?' I asked her.

'Kevin found him out in the road. He must have been hit by a car.'

I found Kevin lying face down on his bed. He was still sobbing, so I lifted him up and gave him a hug, holding him till he was quiet. 'Mummy told me,' I said. 'We'll find a special corner in the garden and give him a decent burial.' Kevin immediately started sobbing again. 'Don't worry, Kev. We'll get you another kitten, even better than Percy.' His tears stopped, but he remained silent. 'Come on,' I said. 'We'll go out and find a good spot for him.' He allowed me to lead him out into the garden, and we chose a place in one of the beds where nothing else ever seemed to grow properly. I fetched a spade and dug a hole, while Kevin went inside and collected

Percy's corpse wrapped in an old tea towel. Helen came out too, and the two of them watched while I laid him to rest and covered him over.

'Goodbye, Percy,' said Kevin. He was pale, but he had stopped crying. He stared at the little mound of earth for a long time, then Helen ushered him inside. 'When can I have my new one?' he asked. Helen looked at me with a puzzled frown.

'I told him he could have a replacement,' I told her. 'Perhaps you could take him to the RSPCA tomorrow and see what they've got.'

Once Kevin was tucked up in bed, I sat down with Helen and studied Donna's lists. I was able to start putting numbers against many of the headings, and Helen made a number of suggestions for limiting start-up costs. We went to bed that night with a little more belief in the successful birth of Maddens. And the following evening, I came home to be greeted by Kevin carrying his brand-new kitten. It eyed me balefully. It was another male, black with white markings on his face and his feet. 'His name is Socks,' Kevin announced proudly.

At the end of January, Kevin returned to school, and in the middle of February, Thompson's finally closed down. I asked Donna if she could keep Jason occupied till the end of the month as I wouldn't need him until then, so while all the other remaining employees left, he and I helped to make an inventory of all the firm's assets. While we were busy, I discovered that Jason's wife was a qualified bookkeeper, and I asked him to sound her out about looking after my books, coming in once a month, to get everything up to date. I pointed out to him the equipment I had earmarked for purchase, and once Jason had spoken to his wife, whose name was Pat, I took them both down to Frankston to show them my new premises, so they'd know where to go. But, first, I visited the estate agent to drop off a cheque for the first six months' rent and borrow the keys.

'Yes, it is in a bit of a mess. No one's been in here for a few months,' I answered.

'Well, I like to do all my work on a computer. So that and a printer. A laptop would be best, so you can take it home when I'm not using it, and a good printer, black and white only.' Pat also listed the software that would be needed on the laptop. 'Best to get the shop to set it up when you buy it.'

'And furniture?'

'A desk, couple of chairs, and you'll need a filing cabinet. A heater wouldn't go amiss, with winter coming. And, how about a kettle?'

'I reckon you should get an electrician in as well,' added Jason. 'Just to check that the power points are OK, as well as all the lighting.'

While they spoke, I was busy making notes. I added the necessary cleaning materials to the list, together with document baskets and stationery. I could see myself spending a few hours in the local Office Works, buying the laptop and arranging deliveries. Now that Kevin was back in school, I'd ask Helen to do some of the purchasing, and I could probably buy a lot more off Thompson's, more than just the machinery and spares. I had already obtained Jason's rate of pay from Donna, and I'd promised him the same rate when he started with me. But I had no idea how much to pay Pat, so I asked her how much she would charge per month. 'I don't know what's involved yet,' she answered. 'Put me on the same hourly rate as Jason to start with, just for the first couple of times. Then we can work out a fixed rate later.'

'Fair enough,' I said. 'I'll look forward to having everything ready for you sometime around the beginning of April.' With that, we locked up and returned to the car. I drove back, dropping them off at their home, which turned out to be a tidy little cottage between Carrum and Patterson Lakes. Being equidistant from Mordialloc and Frankston, Jason would have the same distance to get to work as before. I was glad for him, but in my case, I would have much further to travel. Each time I had visited Frankston, it had taken me between thirty-five and forty-five minutes each way. I enjoyed driving but wondered how long I would want to keep that up before needing to live nearer my work. I thought it best not to mention this to Helen. She had enough upheaval to get used to without her having to sell the family home.

On the last day of February, I loaded the largest excavator onto the low-loader, along with an almost-new bucket I'd found hidden in the store, and instructed Jason to drive it down to Frankston the next morning. Once offloaded at the other end, he was to return and pick up the smaller machine, together with the larger items of spares and some furniture I had persuaded Donna to let us have. In the meantime, I loaded my ute with all the smaller items of spares, and when I was ready to leave, I went looking for Donna. When I found her in the office, she was bent over an open filing cabinet. I gazed at her backside for a moment, remembering how sexy it looked when it was naked, then walked up to her and gave it a friendly rub. She jumped up and turned. 'Just came to say goodbye,' I told her. Then I took her in my arms and gave her a loving kiss. Her lips were as delicious as I recalled, and I could feel my body responding. She didn't hold back either. She thrust her body into mine, and we clung to each other in recognition of our earlier relationship. She finally pushed me away. 'I wish you every success,' she said, her voice soft and tinged with emotion. 'If there's anything I can do for you, just ask.'

'I will,' I said, 'and thanks for all your help.' Thompson's had been a major part of my life, and I was grateful for the start they'd given me in my career, as well as the send-off they were giving me now as I embarked on my new enterprise.

The next day, Helen came with me to Frankston, telling Kevin to make his own way to and from school. The estate agent was waiting for us at the site, and, once inside, we began the process of cleaning the office and change room, a job that took all morning. They were looking and smelling a lot better by the time we finished. I'd also gone back to the road and had fixed a large board to the fence adjacent to the entrance. I'd employed a signwriter to paint 'MADDENS' in large letters on its face, with 'for pool excavations' in smaller letters underneath. It wasn't much of an advertisement, but it would suffice for the time being. By the end of that first day, with the machinery delivered, as well as some extra furniture we had ordered and spares laid out on shelving in the storeroom, everything was in position. We were ready to start our first job for Cedar Pools the next morning. Maddens was ready to start work.

*   *   *

CHAPTER 14

1994

It was five months before I eventually got around to broaching the subject of the house to Helen. It had slowly become apparent, to me at any rate, that I should be living closer to work. It wasn't just the travelling time but also issues that kept arising, problems that required my immediate presence in Frankston, like the weekend when I had Jason working to finish an urgent job, and he called to say the excavator he was using had broken down. That particular job was on a property way down on the peninsula, so it was an extra half hour of driving to reach the place. I was getting exhausted, and there were other things that were making my life disagreeable. My friend Sam Gould had a new boss at Cedar Pools, a man who suddenly decreed that the payment of invoices would in future be paid in sixty days, instead of the usual thirty. Sam did his best for me, but I had started having severe cash-flow problems so that I, too, had begun to delay payments.

When I first hinted to Helen about my travelling concerns, she was less than sympathetic. 'I'm not moving anywhere,' she told me, 'and we're not taking Kevin out of school. He's settled now.' I had to tread carefully, being circumspect in how I approached the matter without upsetting Helen unduly. But I continued to pester her. 'You should have thought of all that when you based yourself so far away,' she said another time. But I didn't give up, and I even looked at a couple of houses in Frankston whenever I wasn't too busy. Property was certainly cheaper there than in the city. I even suggested to Helen one day that I should stay somewhere in Frankston all week and just return home at weekends. That went down like a lead balloon, and, of course, I would never make such a move. How could I possibly keep tabs on what she was up to if I wasn't at home every night?

I wondered what I would have to do to convince her. Then, one day in August, something happened that proved a catalyst for change. Helen received a phone call from Kevin's school. There had been some sort of altercation in the school playground, and Kevin had come out of it the worse for wear. He was currently being cared for in the sickroom, and Helen had to go and pick him up from there. Further, she was asked to make an appointment for the two of us to go together and see the principal. Helen drove to the school immediately, fearing the worst. She found Kevin stretched out on a bed in the sickbay, his face scratched and dirty, and a large plaster on his knee. He'd obviously been crying, but now he seemed quite relaxed. 'Can we go home now?' he asked.

'What happened? Have you been in a fight?'

'Some big boys attacked me,' he answered, and he wouldn't say any more, not even once she'd got him home and cleaned him up. Nor would he tell *me* anything further when I got home that evening, but I could see he was nervous about going back to school the next morning. Two days later, we arrived for the interview with Bea Hopkins, the principal whom Helen had met previously but I had not. We took Kevin with us, and he sat outside the principal's office during the interview. Bea was a no-nonsense lady with a rather severe-looking expression as she ushered us in. I realised later that her gravity was simply a front she put on for parents she was meeting for the first time, for she wasn't in the least bit forbidding when she started talking. She spoke with a rich Scottish accent and looked on us with a kindly smile as we settled into chairs in front of her desk.

'Thanks for coming in,' she started.

'Is Kevin in trouble?' I asked, thinking that I would give him a belting if he'd been playing up.

'No. Nothing like that'" She paused, looking down at a paper on her desk. Then she looked up at us, first, at Helen and then at me. 'Are you aware that Kevin is being bullied?' she asked.

It came right out of the blue and left me quite speechless. 'No,' said Helen. 'He's never complained about anything like that.'

'So, what happened the other day?' I asked. 'He just said some older boys had attacked him.'

'Quite right. They did, just when one of my colleagues, a teacher who was supposed to be patrolling the yard, was somewhere else.' We remained silent. 'I guess I just want to apologise for what occurred.'

'Has it happened before?' asked Helen.

'I think there's a bit of a story behind all this,' said Bea. 'Your son had a strong friendship with one of our more vulnerable boys, one Jackson Ong.'

'Oh, yes,' I said. 'We took him on holiday with us in January, at Kevin's request.'

'That was good of you. Anyway, Kevin had a falling out with Jackson a week ago.'

'He never told us,' said Helen.

'A gang of three year-five boys must have had the pair of them in their sights for a time, but there was some sort of relative safety in numbers when they were together, so the gang never did more than snipe at them, hassle them with verbal bullying. Kevin always protected Jackson, but when they found Kevin alone, they tackled him.'

'Divide and conquer,' murmured Helen.

'Quite so. Anyway, they roughed him up a bit, and I'm sorry.'

'Didn't any of his teachers realise what was going on?' I asked.

'Sadly, it was missed. We should have known.' Bea sounded truly sorry.

'And, what's being done about those wretched bullies?' I asked.

'They have been counselled and their parents told to reprimand them, but I doubt it will do any good Unfortunately, all three of them have been troublemakers for some time and come from family situations that are far from ideal. I want to reassure you that we will be keeping a very close eye on both them and your son from now on.'

'And Jackson too, I hope,' said Helen.

'Yes, of course.'

'Thank you.' Before we left, I asked the principal about Kevin's schoolwork. 'How is he progressing?'

'Very well. His teachers have given me good reports. His maths is going particularly well.'

'That's good to know,' I said.

'And he's one of the leading lights in the junior choir.'

I had often heard him singing at home. He'd always seemed good at holding a tune, so I wasn't surprised. We gathered up our son on the way out and walked with him to the car. 'You never told us that Jackson was no longer your friend,' I said. 'What happened?'

'Just stuff,' he answered.

'What stuff?' but he refused to talk about it, and we never did find out.

But a change was coming over Helen. 'I'm not happy about a school that lets this sort of thing go on,' she told me later that evening. 'They are culpable.'

'I know what you mean, but teachers can't be everywhere.'

'That's not the point,' said Helen sharply. 'It's no good counselling those morons. They should be told to leave and not come back.'

'Perhaps a different school is needed,' I suggested.

'We're not zoned for any other school.'

I just looked at her. 'Exactly,' I said. I had the impression that she had understood my point, so rather than push it further, I changed the subject. 'I know what it's like, being bullied at school. I got heaps, and I really feel for Kev.'

'Me too,' said Helen, 'and girls can be even worse than boys. Not physically, but they can get really nasty with their snide comments and put-downs.'

'You weren't on the receiving end, were you?'

'Not me, no, but I saw the effect it could have on the less fortunate.'

Another issue soon arose concerning all the extra travelling I was doing. My ute broke down on the Mornington freeway one dark evening as I was travelling home. I eventually managed to get it going again and limped home. The vehicle was twelve years old by now, and there were over two hundred thousand on the clock. I needed to trade it in and buy something with more room to carry spares and other items needed for my work, perhaps a van like the one Thompson's had for going out visiting jobs on site. I remembered that Bill had bought a new one for the company a couple of years back. Perhaps Donna hadn't managed to sell it yet, so I phoned her at the first opportunity. There was no reply from Thompson's old office, but I still had the number of her apartment, so I phoned there one evening. A man answered, her new husband having moved in after their wedding, and when Donna came on the line, she told me the van was still sitting in Thompson's yard. No one had made an offer, and she'd be more than happy to be rid of it. 'The keys should still be in the old office,' she added, 'but you'd better be quick. The new owners of the site are moving in next week.' I arranged to meet her there the next morning.

The van was still in good shape, and I took it round to the signwriter to have Thompson's name changed to mine and my mobile phone number etched in below 'MADDENS for pool excavations'. Jason was most impressed the first time I drove it to work, and Helen, too, thought it a good way to advertise. She had slowly been coming round to the idea of moving house, even though there had been no further incidents at Kevin's school. 'I suppose we should never get too fond of anything,' she said one day rather prophetically as it turned out. I moved quickly while she was still in a state of indecision.

Since schooling was one of the catalysts for a possible move to

Frankston, I suggested that we should search out the primary schools in the area, as well as the secondary ones, and find a house in the vicinity. So, one bright Saturday spring morning, we set out on our quest, having first studied a Melways. The nearest primary school to the Frankston High School was the Frankston Primary in Davey Street, so we drove there first. Although it wasn't a school day, there were a few people about in the grounds, so we went in and had a look around. 'Why are we here?' Kevin kept asking, so I told him what we had in mind. After that, he took a big interest in both the grounds and the buildings, though the latter were all locked up, and we only managed to glean an impression by staring in through the windows.

Frankston High wasn't too far away in Foot Street. We just looked at them from the car and then drove round the adjacent suburbs, getting a feel for the area. There were some nice houses there, but Helen was getting cold feet. 'I'm just not ready to start house-hunting yet,' she told me. So we drove down to the beach for a walk and to give Kevin a chance to paddle in the surf.

'If we are going to move, we must be here by the end of January,' I said. 'It's already October. We don't have much time.'

'I must go home and get my head around it,' she answered.

'It wouldn't do any harm to get our house valued as well,' I suggested.

'It's all a bit frightening,' she said, giving me a grim smile.

Two days later, my phone rang while I was at work. 'John Madden,' I answered. The man on the other end announced himself as Koos Bischoff, the owner of Glitter Pools. He had a strange guttural accent, which I later discovered to be South African, but on that first call, I had difficulty understanding him. He'd evidently seen my van down in Frankston, had written down my number. and now wondered if we could help him. For some time, I had worried about having all my eggs in one basket, especially now that the basket wasn't all that sound, so having a second swimming pool contractor to do work for would be a good move. I gave him my address and asked him to come and see me, thinking it would be good for him to see and assess my set-up before we talked business. Koos arrived half an hour later, a burly man with a prominent moustache and an easy-going manner. He had a strong handshake and a winning smile. I took to him immediately. 'How can I help you?' I asked him.

'Agh, man,' he started, 'I've been let down badly. Blerry subcontractor. Hopeless bugger.'

'I do pool excavations. Is that what you're after?'

'That's what I want. Ja.'

'We are just finishing a job for Cedar in Frankston North. I could start ....'

'Cedar,' he interrupted. 'Those bastards keep undercutting us.'

'The day after tomorrow,' I finished.

'Good,' he answered, the 'g' coming out as gruff as could be.

'Where is the job?'

'Not far. Out Langwarrin way.'

'We could go and look at it now, if you've got time.'

'OK. Ja. We'll take my bakkie.'

On the way, we discussed terms, and I gave him an hourly rate in case there wasn't time to put together a fixed price quotation. The site we visited had an ornate mansion built on the side of a steep rise with views of rolling farmlands. Behind it was a line of eucalyptus trees, and, further, seedlings had been planted at each end of the house and along the drive. A short distance from the near end of the house was a huge shed, obviously being used as a garage. Two very expensive cars: a Mercedes and a smaller Alpha Romeo, stood in front of the door. A man in a uniform was busy polishing the Mercedes. He glanced up as we arrived but quickly returned to his task.

'They must be pretty well-heeled,' I suggested to Koos.

'Ja. Money no object,' he replied.

In front of the mansion, Koos's workers had marked out a huge area where the pool was to be built. I was now quite skilled at guessing what the ground would be like just by studying the surfaces in the surrounding area. I could see that this area would be extremely rocky, and I pointed this out. 'There's a good two weeks' work here, if not more,' I told him. He didn't look at all perturbed by this. 'At least there will be no problem with access,' I added. As he drove me back to my workshop, he explained that when he'd quoted my part of the job, he'd told the owner it would have to be done on rates, so it didn't matter how long it took, within reason. When he dropped me off, he gave me his card and asked me to call him when I was ready to start.

As soon as I got in, I phoned Sam Gould and told him I was getting work with Glitter Pools. I wanted him to know that Cedar wasn't the only pebble on the beach. He told me that he'd met Koos a few years back and had gotten to know him quite well. That's when I discovered his South African background. 'Only been in Australia five years,' he told me, 'but already they're our main rivals.'

'That figures,' I said. 'He tells me you're undercutting him.'

'That's the new boss. No wonder he's only paying sixty days.'

'Do you know that site out in Langwarrin?' I asked him.

'Yes, and we wouldn't touch it with a bargepole.'

'Rocky ground, huh?'

'Yep.'

'Well, I'm doing it on rates, so I won't lose money on it.'

'That's the only way, mate.'

In the end, the job took three weeks, but Koos wasn't surprised. Nor was he particularly concerned. As Koos had told me before we started the job, he'd excluded the earthworks from his quote, simply because the owner of the property, a man called Jim Sutton, had warned him about the ground conditions. It was something that he had come across while the builder was digging the foundations for his house, so he expected to have problems with the pool excavation. In addition, Jim Sutton was extremely well off and wasn't in the least upset by the increased cost. In his turn, Koos was pretty impressed by our work and offered us more jobs anytime we wanted them. I could see that I might soon be required to have two jobs going at the same time, so I asked Jason to bring me up to speed with operating the machinery. By the end of the Langwarrin job, I was becoming quite an expert. There were some large rocks that we had excavated, and, as an extra, the owner got us to erect a huge rockery next to the pool. His wife came out to supervise. Rhonda Sutton looked about half Jim's age. She was tall and slim, though her belly was a little distended, and I had the impression from the way she walked and touched herself that she was pregnant. Rhonda knew exactly what she wanted. For two days, we were moving rocks around with the excavator bucket, placing them strategically, and adding earth and a few smaller boulders. At the end of the second day, she pronounced herself totally satisfied with the rockery. She told me she was going to plant the crevices with flowers and shrubs.

I came home one day during the Langwarrin job to find a For Sale sign erected in front of our house. I was amazed, excited, and not a little puzzled by Helen's sudden change of heart. 'Yes,' she said as I got inside, 'I've given it a lot of thought, and I realised it was for the best.' She gave me a piece of paper with a very large sum of money written on it. 'That's the valuation,' she said. It was another surprise, being considerably more than I expected.

'Did you want to go to auction?' I asked her.

'I think we should just see if we get an offer without it. I told the agent to advertise it for fifty thousand more. People always want to knock down the price.'

'Fair enough.'

'And I've been phoning agents in Frankston, and I asked if any of them had houses for sale in the area we looked at.'

'And?'

'Well, only one had properties on their books—three houses actually. They seem to have a bit of a monopoly in the area.'

'My love, you are a champion,' I said and gave her a big hug. 'We could go and look on Saturday,' I suggested.

'Shall I phone them?'

'Please do. And thanks for everything. I know it's not been easy.' I hugged her again tight against me. 'You've made my day,' I said, giving her a playful kiss.

'Well, as you said when we started Maddens, we're in it together. And while we're about it, you can do much better than that for a kiss.' It was like that time in hospital, after Helen's miscarriage, and I did, much, *much* better the second time, our tongues touching and entwining in an erotic dance. Only Kevin's sudden appearance and his request for help with some homework stopped me from dragging her upstairs.

What I couldn't tell Helen, or rather what I didn't want to tell her, was my third reason for wanting to move. Schooling for Kevin was one thing, all the extra travelling I was having to do was another, but the main benefit of a move, as I saw it, would be that the new house would be *ours* and not just hers. With a bit of patience, I could actually make it *mine*, stamp my authority on it in a way that I could never do in Peter and Myra's house. Soon, both Helen and Kevin would become my exclusive property,, living under my guidance and control in every sense of the words. As well as being my support team, they would happily become my resources, mine to lead and to manage, mine to prevail upon to act and behave the way I wanted, just as if they were part of my business. It was all falling into place.

I was tense with excitement as we drove down to Frankston on the Saturday morning. We went straight to the real estate agent, where we were introduced to Gus Smiley, the man who was to show us the houses. Gus was well-named. He seemed to turn his smiles, which were more like leering grins, on and off like a light switch. 'Shall we go in my car?' he asked with a sudden grin. I told him it would be better for him to drive, a comment that provoked another grin. We came to call him 'Grinning Gus'.

I remember nothing of the first two houses we were shown, except that one was ultra-modern and to my mind ugly, and the other far too large. But Helen and I both loved the third one. It had character, something that showed through despite its lacklustre exterior. The house was a three-bedroom home in Denbigh Street, almost midway between the two schools we had looked at. It had come onto the market quite recently and was part of a deceased estate. The house was a long low single-storey building with a veranda along the front. Its land had a slight slope down to the road so that, whereas the back of the house was level with the garden, the front was built up on brickwork, there being three wide steps up from the path onto the veranda and the front door. A single garage was tucked into the side of the house, with a carport in front of it. The garden was somewhat unkempt, but there were a couple of large trees and a few tall bushes in front of the house, which partly hid it from the road and gave it privacy.

We were met at the front door by a middle-aged man who turned out to be the son of the old lady who had lived there. He said he was busy getting all the furniture moved out, and in a week it would all be cleared. We had a good look around the house, and as we walked from room to room, I realised that it needed a fair amount of work to bring it up to a reasonable standard. It seemed structurally sound, but many of the rooms had walls covered in wallpaper that was fading or peeling. The house need painting both inside and outside, and the kitchen stove looked as though it was overdue for retirement. The main bedroom had an en suite, which had been modernised quite recently with a large shower cubicle and modern fittings and cupboards. The second bathroom, however, didn't look as though it had been used for years. It smelt musty, the old bath had stains under the taps, and the whole room needed stripping out and remodelling. But the house had enormous potential, I felt. By the time we had finished inspecting the house Kevin had already decided which room he was going to have, one that looked out onto the back garden. The owner kept apologising for the mess as he tagged along with us during our inspection, but as we left, he still seemed hopeful of a sale.

Having returned to Gus Smiley's office, we discussed prices. The asking price tag was little more than half of the valuation on our existing house, so, if we bought it, there would be more than enough money left over to bring it up to scratch. We would need to install air-conditioning, a better heating system for winter, and a new kitchen. On top of that, the second bathroom would need upgrading, and there was many weeks of redecorating to be done. However, at a rough estimate, we would be able to afford all this and have plenty of money left over, as well as buy Helen a new car, something she had been pestering me about for some months. Her father's aged car was over fifteen years old now and showing definite signs of senility. I put all this to Helen as we sat in Gus's office, while Gus himself, happy at the prospect of a sale, was busy switching his smile on and off. He told us that the house would *not* remain on the market very long, not at that price, but, of course, that was what all salesmen say. I asked him to give us first option and told him we would make a decision by Monday morning.

'This is a big decision, darling,' said Helen as we got outside. 'And if we're going ahead with the purchase, we should make an offer considerably less than they're asking.'

'OK,' I said.

'You really want to go ahead with it, don't you?'

'Of course. It has great possibilities. I'm sure we can make it into a really delightful home, and we can do a lot of the work ourselves, at weekends.'

'But you never told him about us having to sell the other house first. We can't work on the new house until settlement, and we can't settle until we get the money for the old house.'

'How about a bridging loan?'

'And, what happens if we don't sell?'

'We will. Or we can simply get a short-term mortgage on the new property. Do stop being so pessimistic,' I demanded.

On the Monday morning, I left Jason at the Langwarrin job and then went back to see Gus Smiley. I offered him the asking price, less a hundred grand. And I was prepared to settle on November 1. Gus said he was sure the owner would agree. He let slip that the old lady's son had a few money problems himself and that the early settlement date was bound to be an attraction. I had just enough cash in the bank to pay the deposit and said I would return later in the day to get his answer. Meanwhile, once she'd seen Kevin off to school, Helen went to our bank to talk money with the manager. He thought a bridging loan the better option; short-term mortgages could be a little messy.

Three days later, everything was complete. Gus Smiley's customer had agreed on our terms, and the bank had approved the loan for the difference, plus another eighty thousand to cover upgrades on our new house. And on top of that, Helen's agent had already brought two prospective buyers around to look at the Melbourne house, though, so far, there had been no offers. By November 1, our portion of the Langwarrin job was finished, and Koos Bischoff had started concreting the pool. On due date, the conveyancer, having received the money for the new property, notified me that the house was ours. Helen came with me to pick up the keys from Grinning Gus, and we went together to the house. The first job was to make a list of everything that was needed, especially those items for which we would need quotes. I left Helen to work out how she wanted to upgrade the kitchen, while I decided where we would place reverse-cycle air-conditioning units. I felt that the rest we could do ourselves, mainly painting plus a few small repair jobs. I was glad to see that the flooring, woodblock throughout except for the bathrooms, toilets, and kitchen, was in excellent condition, though all the floors could do with a good clean. I helped Helen measure the kitchen so she could draw a scaled layout of her preferred new set-up and take it to a firm that specialised in kitchen renovations. We had to move fast as everything had to be in place by the end of the year, with the possible exception of the second bathroom and the painting of the outside. We wanted to move in not later than the middle of January, and Kevin could use our bathroom in the meantime.

It soon became obvious, however, that our timeline was far too optimistic. No kitchen renovator would guarantee to have ours finished by the end of the year. We decided to settle for just having the new stove installed, together with as many of the new cupboards and working surfaces as could be managed in the time available. At least the kitchen would then be usable if we had to move in before it was completely finished. We had better luck with the second bathroom renovations, even though it wasn't a priority. One day, I saw a builder's van parked in a driveway just up the road. On the side of the van, it said 'Bathrooms a Speciality', so on the off-chance, I went in and spoke to the tradesman I found inside the house. It turned out that he was just finishing a job there and would be free to tackle ours the following week. I also found, once we'd started, that the internal painting would take considerably longer, working only at weekends. The problem was the stripping of the old wallpaper and the preparation of the walls before we could apply the paint. We decided to concentrate on those rooms we would need first, starting with the two bedrooms and the kitchen, once the old one had been stripped out and before installation of the new one had started. We spent a lot of time studying colour charts and deciding on quantities of paint we would need.

We'd just got started on the work when it all became increasingly urgent. In the third week of November, the agent for the old house found us a buyer, one who would give us our full asking price but only if we agreed to an eight-week settlement. We'd have to be in the new house by mid-January or we'd lose the sale. It was a deal we couldn't refuse, even if it meant literally camping at the Frankston house while the work was finished. The dates were set. We would move out of our old house on January 13, a Friday, with settlement the next day. I trusted that Friday the thirteenth wouldn't be a bad omen. In the meantime, Helen and I paid a call on the Frankston Primary School and registered Kevin into year three, explaining about our upcoming move into their neighbourhood.

We had eight weeks of feverish activity. For the first five, I was increasingly busy with pool work, wanting to finish all the contracts we were engaged in before closing down for four weeks over Christmas and New Year. I had already been awarded another job by Koos, and when I finished that, just before Christmas, he asked me to go out to Langwarrin to look at the new pool there, now finished. It was looking magnificent, its blue water sparkling in the slight breeze. 'This will be a great advertisement for me,' he said. 'For both of us,' he added. While we were there, Rhonda Sutton, now definitely showing, came out for a chat. She declared that she was very impressed with how it all looked. A shed to house the circulating pump, chlorine storage, and so on had been installed at the opposite end of the pool to the rockery, where she'd already started planting seedlings and shrubs. On New Year's Day, she told us they were going to have an official opening of the pool. Everyone who'd worked on it was invited.

'Do you have family?' she asked me.

'Wife and nine-year-old son.'

'Would you like to bring them along too?'

I figured that as long as I kept a close eye on Helen, I could make sure she didn't get too friendly with other guests. 'Love to,' I answered and wondered at this overt sign of generosity. 'Three o'clock, then, and bring your togs.'

I was about to mention that it was Jason who had done most of our work, thinking that he should have an invitation as well, but then I remembered that he was taking Pat off on a holiday and wouldn't be around.

Kevin's birthday and Christmas passed us by with little celebration, though we did attend Hudson and Nola's regular New Year's Eve party. And on New Year's Day, we headed off early in Helen's new car to our Frankston house, ready to do a morning's work before setting out for Langwarrin. We arrived at the Suttons' soon after three o'clock. The parking area in front of the garage was chock-full of expensive-looking cars, and the party was in full swing with some of the visitors already enjoying the pool. I spotted Jim and Rhonda as they greeted guests up on their veranda. They must have employed a catering firm, for a bevy of uniformed men and women were laying out tables and chairs, both on the veranda and round the pool. We went up, and I introduced Helen and Kevin to our hosts, and they welcomed us, inviting us to make full use of the pool. We were instructed to use rooms in the house for changing, and Helen took Kevin straight inside.

In the two months since I had first met her, Rhonda had grown considerably in girth; later, Helen told me she was five months into her pregnancy. Once introduced, she and Rhonda had, I noticed, spent a great deal of time talking together. They'd obviously hit it off well, which I found disconcerting. Friends could only be a distraction. When Helen later came to see what Kevin was up to in the pool, I introduced her to Koos Bischoff, whose wife, Catarina, clung to his arm everywhere they went. Her accent was even more pronounced than Koos's, though in fact she spoke very little, her understanding of English evidently being somewhat limited. It was a splendid day, a gay and carefree gathering, and it went on long into the evening. Few of the grown-ups went into the pool, but there were plenty of children enjoying the water, and Kevin joined in the inevitable splashing and 'bombing'. The tea, scones, and cakes, which were served around four, were replaced by plates of finger food savouries, wine and beer at six, and Jim Sutton announced loudly that no glasses were to be removed from the veranda and taken anywhere near the pool. 'We don't want accidents,' he said.

We made our apologies and took our leave at eight o'clock. By that time, it was dark. The underwater lights in the pool, as well as fairy lights mounted along the length of the veranda, had all been switched on, giving the whole place a wonderfully festive look. Kevin, for one, didn't want to leave, but I could see he was tired after all his time in the pool, and work on the new house required an early start the next day. Kevin was already asleep before we'd gone far, and Helen and I kept our voices low so as not to wake him. 'I like your new friends,' said Helen.

'They're more business partners than friends,' I countered. 'Rather out of our league, I would say. But you seem to have made a big hit with Rhonda.'

'It was a bit strange actually. She sort of fastened on to me as though I was a kindred spirit. Then, when we got talking, I realised that she was finding her whole new existence, living in that huge house and not having to watch the pennies, both strange and uncomfortable. I got the impression that she was in a bit of a dream world. She'd been thrust into the sort of wealth that she'd never known before. She just wasn't used to it.'

'So you think she was brought up on the other side of the tracks?'

'Possibly. I have no idea where she and Jim met. They seem to have lived in totally different environments.'

'She's well spoken anyway,' I said. 'Posh accent.'

'And she has a good dress sense.'

'I wouldn't know.'

'Then we got to talking babies ….'

'And that was that,' I interrupted.

Helen laughed. 'She's very much in love. And she feels very spoilt. I got the impression she's only been married a few months.'

'Shotgun wedding, do you think?'

'Possibly.'

'Anyway, good for her, landing such a rich husband,' I said. 'I hope it lasts for her.' As we drove on home, I thought long and hard about the Suttons. As I had told Helen, they were out of our league, and I didn't want her thinking she'd found new friends. She seemed over-happy that she'd met Rhonda, and I had to put an immediate stop to that. 'I really don't want you talking to them,' I ordered her. 'They aren't our type of people.'

*　　　*　　　*

CHAPTER 15

1995–2003

Friday the thirteenth came and went, and the sky didn't fall in, not immediately anyway. While I had gone to the new house every day of the previous week, to get things ready and to open all the windows to try and get rid of paint smells, Helen had been busy packing all the small stuff into boxes and our clothes into suitcases. Luckily, the new house was well equipped with built-in cupboards. I had taken down a couple of cases every day and had emptied them into the cupboards. Realising that Socks was becoming increasingly anxious about the disruption to his habitat, Helen shut him in the spare room for the last two days to prevent his escape and put him in his cat cage on the morning of the move. Now moving day had arrived. The removalist came at eight o'clock, and the two men had the truck loaded by eleven. Before midday, they'd arrived at the new house, and by three, the furniture was all in position.

The only problem had been the piano, a white elephant as far as I was concerned, a monstrosity that I would have gladly taken to the tip, but it was something of an obsession with Helen. Throughout our marriage, she continued to play it, but never when I was at home. She was aware that I wasn't musical and in fact hated the sound of it, so she'd always been careful to keep her playing to herself. Not so Kevin. From an early age, he had enjoyed banging on the keys, and Helen had started to teach him to play properly, an uphill battle as it turned out. Kevin had a good singing voice but didn't seem to have any aptitude for the piano. Anyway, it now had to be loaded onto the truck. For years, it had sat up against a wall in the lounge room, a solid immovable object making permanent indentations in the carpet. I never realised how heavy the damn thing was, and I had to help, much against my inclination. Luckily, the men had brought a sort of lifting device and a heavy-duty trolley, which made it a bit easier.

We'd arrived at the new house ten minutes before the truck. We climbed the steps up to the veranda, and I unlocked the door. However, before we went in, I suggested to Helen that I should carry her over the threshold in the time-honoured tradition. 'Do you think you can?' she queried.

'Ha ha,' I replied and grabbed her, one arm under her back and the other under her legs. I staggered into the house, and we both collapsed laughing, while Kevin looked on in astonishment. It was the sort of intimate moment that was all too rare in the Madden family, and Helen showed her appreciation by giving me a friendly hug. I took her and Kevin on a quick conducted tour before the truck arrived, and she was duly amazed at the progress I'd made in the week since she'd last seen the house. Our bedroom and en suite were complete and ready, as well as Kevin's bedroom and the second bathroom, now with the old bath replaced with a shower, a new basin fitted, and new cupboards installed. Also, the lounge room and passageway were all complete. Only the spare room and the separate dining room, which led off the kitchen through an archway, remained untouched, together with the remainder of the kitchen upgrade, which the contractor would complete the following week.

The piano, being the last item into the truck, was the first out. I had decreed that it be relegated to the spare room. There was no space for it in the lounge room, which was a bit smaller than the one in the old house. All the other furniture fitted in exactly as we had planned, and while I went out to pay the truck driver, Helen began unpacking the boxes that contained the bedding and started making up the beds. Socks was parked in the spare room with the piano until the removal truck had gone and was then allowed out. He dashed out of the room in a streak of fur when I opened the door, before suddenly coming to a halt in the passage. There he sat and began licking himself. Then, having been introduced to his box of cat litter, he prowled round the house on a trip of exploration. He would need to get used to the inside of his new home before he would be permitted to go outside.

That evening, we had a scratch meal seated round the old kitchen table, and afterwards we all sank into our beds, exhausted. Socks found his way onto Kevin's, and I was too tired to argue. I had planned on making love that first night in our new house, give it a fitting christening as it were, but Helen was asleep in seconds, and I wasn't far behind. I dreamt of a swimming pool, one like the Suttons', except that this one was so large, it continued out into the distance like an inland sea. In it, Helen was swimming, she and Rhonda Sutton, and they were going further and further out. I was swimming after them, chasing them, but couldn't keep up. I woke up shaking, and when I realised it was only a dream, I reached out to check on Helen, make sure she was still with me. I lay awake for much of the night, worrying that Helen might one day walk out on me and making plans to ensure this would never happen. Was the dream not some premonition of an impending departure? I realised that I would have to threaten to kill her if she did leave, telling her that if she left, I would follow her to the ends of the earth to enact my revenge.

It was agreed that I would go back to the old house for one last visit the next day, to do a final clean and make sure nothing was left behind, before taking the keys to the agent. On Monday, we should have settlement. We'd have the money to pay off the bridging loan with plenty left over for the kitchen contractor as well as a painter to do the outside of the house. There would still be a sizeable sum remaining, and, once we knew how much it amounted to, it was my plan to invest it in the business. Some of my equipment was getting old and unreliable, and it would soon need replacing. I had earlier persuaded Helen to open a joint account to handle all the recent transactions, so now I would be able to siphon off as much as I needed and transfer to my Maddens account. At the same time, I'd keep the balance of the joint account low enough to prevent Helen from absconding.

I only had one more week before Maddens was due to reopen. In that time, I wanted to complete the dining room, intending to have both it and the kitchen completed together. Helen was already planning the first meal we would have to celebrate the occasion. The dining room had a pair of French doors that led onto a patio at the back of the house. We had decided to paint it a dark olive green, with white woodwork, which would go well with the lighter green I'd used in the kitchen. By the Wednesday, the contractor had finished. Helen was very proud of the result and spent much of the next day unpacking the remaining boxes that contained all her pot, pans, cutlery, and appliances. A day later, the dining room was finished as well.

There was a flood of work waiting for us when Maddens restarted. Not only did we have jobs lined up with Cedar and Glitter, butthere was now a third pool company, Summertime, that specialised in fibreglass in-ground pools. A man called Dick Darcy had phoned me in the middle of January, asking me if we were interested in doing a job down in Mornington. I told him we would be very busy until mid February, but I'd be glad to help if he could wait that long. He said he'd be in touch, and a few days later, he phoned back and asked me to put his job on our waiting list. Fibreglass pools are smaller than the ones we normally worked with, often in small backyards where it would be difficult to manoeuvre an excavator, but I thought it worth a try. I mentioned all this to Jason as soon as I saw him. 'I'm going to have to buy a third machine, in addition to replacing the other two,' I told him, 'and hire another man.'

'I might be able to save you the trouble,' he said. 'I've got a nephew who's looking for a job: Jack, Pat's sister's boy.'

'How old is Jack?'

'He's just turned twenty.'

'Has he any experience?'

'None to my knowledge. Look, he's been a bit of a rebel, unable to hold down a job for long, but if I'm around to keep an eye on him, I'm sure you won't be sorry, and I can train him up.'

'I can't pay him full rate until he can handle a job on his own.'

'Fair enough.'

'Bring him in, then, and I'll talk to him.' Jason brought Jack in the next day. I found him a little arrogant, but he appeared to be keen enough, and he badly needed the work, he told me. After a short chat about what I expected of him, I told him how much I would pay him if he joined us. He seemed entirely happy with that, so I offered him the position. And so it was that Jack came and joined our little group. It took him a while to learn the ropes, and he was bit erratic in both his work and his timekeeping, but I put up with it for his uncle's sake. I don't know what I would have done without Jason's help. He not only was a steady reliable worker but also gave me a lot of good advice along the way. When Pat arrived for her monthly visit, she said how nice it was to have another member of her family around, and she gave Jack a few words of wisdom, telling him to make sure he didn't stuff up again with this job. He was lucky to get it and to have such a caring boss. I didn't think I was supposed to hear that last bit, but I felt quite chuffed. Pat used to bring her little radio into the office when she came to do the books, always tuned into the station Triple J. She always had it playing quietly as she worked. One day, once Jack had been working for a couple of months, she said we should call our outfit *The Three Js*, for John, Jason, and Jack. 'Better still, *Triple J*,' said Jason, who had just walked into the office. Pat laughed, but the nickname stuck, and soon the people we were working for started using it as well.

With all this extra work going on, plus getting Jack up to speed, I was unable to see Kevin into his new school, but Helen duly delivered him on the first day of the new school year. She was introduced to his year-three teacher, a Ms Forbes, who seemed to be far too young to be a teacher but who nevertheless welcomed Kevin into her class with sufficient self-assurance to put Helen's mind at rest. And Kevin was full of praise for his new school when I got home that evening. He thought Ms Forbes a 'grouse' teacher, and he'd already been inaugurated into the school choir. The music teacher was a Mr Weardon, who had already heard him sing and who held practices once a week on Wednesdays. Kevin told me that he hadn't made any friends yet, and some of the boys in his class were too boisterous for his liking, but he seemed happy enough and already settled. Helen, too, was pleased, and I was delighted. Everything about our move to Frankston had turned out well. Even Socks was happy, and the next morning, he presented us with a dead mouse he'd caught in the garden.

It was around this time that I found myself doing a bit of a self-appraisal, mainly to do with my attitude to my family, and in particular towards Helen. I loved her dearly, but in addition to showing her my love, I had to be a disciplinarian, to show her who was the boss. How else could I hope to control her, especially a woman as strong-minded as Helen? I had to convert her completely to my way of thinking, to my needs, make sure she appreciated what I was entitled to as the result of our marriage. I had, of course, thought all this through long ago and had made a good start, but now we were in our new house, I needed to make absolutely sure that she couldn't step out of line, ensure her obedience at all times.

The move to Frankston had made me extremely gratified. It wasn't just Kevin's new school. Nor was it the house or the proximity of my work, or even the fact that the new home was ours and no longer Helen's alone. The fact is that I had by now largely isolated Helen, separated her from outside influences, including all her previous friends and acquaintances. She was now mine to manipulate without external interference, transform into the sort of wife that my father had told me I needed, a wife who would do what I wanted and when I wanted it. She would now have to obey my every whim, and God help her if she didn't, not that I believed there had ever been a god or any other deity up there who could or would meddle in my affairs. In many ways, I still despised my father for what he did to my mother, the way he raised his hand to her when his anger was brought on by his drinking. I believed that, because I am not a drunkard, I would never do to Helen what he did to Mum, but I often wondered whether I had some evil genes that he'd passed on to me and that one day I would strike out if I was provoked. I hoped not. I loved Helen, and, so far, she had never aroused my anger to that extent.

As far as I am aware, the first time she did something that I hadn't sanctioned, and which I disapproved of, was the matter of the piano lessons. Kevin came home from school one day, early in his first term, and announced that the school's music teacher, Mr Weardon, or Weirdo as the children called him, had asked if any members of the choir would like to take piano lessons. He told them to ask for their parents' permission if they wished to put their name forward, which is why Kevin had raised the issue. It transpired that Mr Weardon was only employed part-time by the school, and taking students for individual lessons was something he did out of school hours to earn extra money. Remembering Helen's thwarted attempts at teaching Kevin the rudiments, I thought it unlikely that he would want to pursue the offer, and so it turned out.

I thought that would be the end of it, but two weeks later, I came home from work to find Helen looking at a book of piano studies. 'What's that?' I asked her.

'My homework,' she answered. 'Mr Weardon lent them to me.'

'Who?'

'I phoned the school and asked him if he also taught grown-ups. He's going to give me lessons. Half an hour every Tuesday morning.'

'You can't do that,' I said.

'Why on earth not?'

'Because I haven't said you could.'

'Since when do I have to ask your permission?' she demanded. 'I need lessons if I'm ever going to improve.'

'How do you know you'll be safe with the man? He could be some sort of predator.'

'Well, he's not. You're being ridiculous.'

'Don't ever call me ridiculous!' I shouted at her.

She didn't say anything for a time. Then she looked at me with a puzzled frown. 'You've changed, John. Your attitude. What's happened?'

'Nothing's happened. I'm exerting my authority, that's all.'

'Well, you don't have to worry about Mr Weardon. He's the most mild-mannered old boy. He's only a couple of years off retirement, and he's got a sweet wife.'

'So you've already met the whole damn family.'

'I went round to his house, yes.'

'Well, you're not going back there, and that's final,' I told her. As I walked out and left her, I could see she was shaking with anger, but she had more sense than to answer back. I felt entitled to make decisions for my family, if only to protect their welfare. I wouldn't back down. We hardly spoke for the next few days, and I was never sure if Helen would defy me, so on the following Tuesday, I hid her car keys. Actually, I just removed them from where she normally kept them and placed them in a kitchen drawer, one that was seldom used.

When I returned from work that evening, she stopped me. 'I seem to have mislaid my keys,' she said. 'So I couldn't do any shopping today.'

'Where have you looked?' I asked her.

'Everywhere I could think of.'

'Let me hunt for you. What were you wearing the last time you used the car?'

'I've searched through all my clothes. Nothing. I feel such an idiot.'

I went into the kitchen, opening all the cupboards and drawers, and while her back was turned, I recovered the keys. Then I went into the lounge, pretended to search under the cushions, and finally went upstairs, making a noise as I opened and shut all the doors and cupboards. Finally, I called out to her, 'I've found them.'

She came running up. 'Where?'

'In the pocket of your dressing gown,' I lied.

'That's one place I never thought to look. Why on earth would I leave them there?'

'It's the sort of thing your mother would have done.'

'I am *not* getting dementia.'

'Are you sure?' I said as I held out the keys for her.

And so it was that, almost by accident, I discovered how to make Helen yet more reliant on me. It was the episode of the keys that led me to it. I just had to hide something that she would miss and then find it again for her in some unexpected place. I did that with her favourite kitchen knife a couple of times, and then I took to putting totally unsuitable things in the fridge, like the book she was reading. And I hinted that I thought dementia was possibly hereditary. I worked on her fears very slowly, and there were many setbacks. However, within a few years, Helen was doing everything

I asked of her. She became very quiet, losing much of her self-assurance, and at night she never again denied me anything in bed. Sometimes, if she had argued with me or crossed me in some way during the day, I would let her know how angry I was. That night, I would force myself onto her, be intentionally rough, entering her before she was properly aroused. She sometimes screamed when I did this and whimpered long after I'd finished. I didn't consider it rape, but I did realise it was painful. I wanted her to know who the boss was. Then the next day, I would bring her a small gift. She never dared complain about the way I treated her, not out loud, though she kept strictly to herself and wouldn't speak to me afterwards. And I always apologised when I brought her the gift.

As the years passed, Maddens continued to make satisfactory profits, and Kevin completed his primary schooling. He had blossomed at his primary school, and we had high hopes for him as he moved on to the high school. He had just turned thirteen as he entered year seven. A year later, his voice started breaking, and he had to give up singing. When he'd started at his new school, he had once again joined the school choir. He had really enjoyed the experience and was one of the leading trebles, singing a solo in his school's end-of-year concert. The choir was under the tutelage of a Ms Baxter, a twenty-three year-old honey blonde that the older boys in the school fantasised over as they played with themselves in bed at night. The girls liked her too, though for a different reason. She appeared to be a kind and caring person, though she brooked no nonsense during rehearsals. She sounded quite sad as she told Kevin at the start of his year eight that his voice no longer had the purity it had displayed previously and that he should give up for a year while his voice settled down. 'Perhaps your voice will have adjusted to tenor by next year,' she told him.

What Kevin thought about her in bed, or at any other time for that matter, we never discovered, though by the age of fifteen, he was evidently having night-time emissions. Helen was forever having to wash his sheets, and when she complained to me, I suggested to Kevin that he use a towel to mop up if he felt it necessary to masturbate in bed. At the same time, he seemed completely indifferent to the female sex and made no effort to ingratiate himself with the girls in his class. He certainly never mentioned, either to Helen or myself, the name of a girl he liked or had become friendly with. He hadn't become mates with any particular boy either but rather kept strictly to himself and concentrated on his schoolwork. He was what in my day would have been called a 'swot', and much as we tried to draw him out, he became a bit of a hermit at home, shutting himself into his room for hours at a time, ostensibly doing school homework. Certainly, his marks supported that, and on the occasions when Helen and I attended parent/teacher nights, he was invariably praised for both his attendance and achievement.

The only exercise he took was his twice-weekly soccer practice. A year after we first moved to our new home, he had been persuaded to go along to a club that ran a junior training programme for would-be soccer players. He had taken to it straightaway, and it seemed to be a healthy outlet for him, so we encouraged it as much as possible. He had even made the under-twelve team a couple of times and would soon be trying for the under sixteens. And for his thirteenth birthday, we had bought him a new bicycle, telling him that he was now old enough to ride to school. We also got him a chain and padlock so it wouldn't be stolen from the school bicycle shed.

It was around this time that Helen started getting itchy feet again. 'Please, John,' she said to me one evening, 'I need something to keep me occupied. Why won't you let me get a job?'

'No chance,' I replied.

'Just part-time somewhere.'

'You must be joking,' and I laughed at her.

'I'm so bored sitting at home all day.'

'You were never any good at your job anyway.'

'What do you mean? I just about ran the place.'

'That's not what I heard.'

'Who from?'

'Your friend Di, for one. She was always having to cover for you, all the mistakes you kept making.'

'She would never say that,' claimed Helen. 'I don't believe you, John.'

I grabbed her wrist and shook her. 'Are you calling me a liar?'

'No,' she whispered, shaking her head.

'Always bloody arguing with me, aren't you!' I shouted at her.

She started sobbing. 'Sorry,' she said.

'Stick to your fucking piano instead, even though it's the most godawful noise.' She didn't say another word but went on sobbing, and eventually I got sick and tired of it. 'Oh, do stop blubbing, woman.' She just left me and went out into the garden, unable to stop her tears. I left her there for a quarter of an hour, and then I went out to her. I crept up behind her and put my arms around her. She froze momentarily then relaxed. 'I love you, Helen,' I said quietly. 'I'm sorry.'

She turned. 'Oh, John,' she cried, 'what happened to us?'

I didn't reply, but as I looked over her shoulder, I saw Kevin peering apprehensively out of his bedroom window. I smiled at him as though nothing had happened.

I felt that I now had full control of my family. However, to make sure, I continued to vet all our telephone accounts, making sure there were no numbers I didn't recognise. Every now and again, I would query a call, just so Helen would know I was checking up on her, but they all turned out to be legitimate calls. I began to think I'd been wrong to accuse her of infidelity; there was never a sign of it. I also continued to quiz her every evening about everything she had been doing during the day, and I started phoning her at odd times from the office, just to check up on her, make sure she was carrying out the instructions I had given her in the morning, and see what she was up to. I kept her supplied with money, but only enough to cover everyday expenses. If she wanted anything extra, such as clothes or items for the house, she had to ask for it and make a good case as to why it was needed and couldn't wait. It was just another control, a method of making sure she didn't get out of hand. And every so often, when Helen was otherwise engaged, I would surreptitiously go through her handbag and other possessions, making sure there was nothing incriminating.

Then, one evening, Helen told me she had bumped into Rhonda Sutton at the supermarket that morning. Anger started building up in me. I could see problems looming. 'I told you not to speak to her,' I said.

'Actually, I didn't,' she replied. 'She found me, came up to me, and said hello.'

'That's splitting hairs.'

'I couldn't very well refuse to talk to her, now, could I?'

'Where did this meeting take place?'

'At the Karingal supermarket.'

'Well, you are going to stop shopping there. Go to the Frankston supermarket.'

'The parking is so much easier at Karingal.'

'Will you stop arguing!' I shouted at her. 'Don't go near Karingal. That's an order.'

Helen shrank back then looked at me with a puzzled expression. 'Don't you even want to know how they are, she and the children?'

'No!'

'The Suttons have got three now.'

'I said no!' I shouted. 'That's enough. And if you do meet her ever again, ignore her. Do I make myself clear?'

*

When Kevin was in year nine, the under-sixteen team at his soccer club started their season with a match against one of their main rivals. One of the expenses that I was persuaded would be necessary was a new pair of boots for him. He had enjoyed a sudden growth spurt in the previous year. He was already as tall as Helen and would soon overtake me as well. Kevin was picked for the team, much to our delight, and we duly attended the match. As the game got under way, I was surprised at Kevin's sudden turns of speed and his nimbleness, not realising how much his game had improved since I had seen him in the under twelves. His team won by two goals, to our even greater delight, and I decided to take the whole family out to dinner that night in celebration. In fact, Kevin remained a team member right through the season.

In the New Year, he went into year ten. Early in the first term, he came home one day and told us of a new friend he'd recently made at school, a boy called Marcus O'Leary. Marcus was in the same class for a number of subjects, and Kevin thought it would be advantageous if they sometimes did homework together, so he asked Helen if he could bring his friend round a couple of days a week after lessons. She told him, quite rightly, that it was up to me to decide. So when I got home, he approached me. He seemed a bit hesitant as he sought my approval, almost as if he was a little unsure if that was what he really wanted, but I thought it would do him good to have a friend around. Kevin was becoming too much of a loner as far as I was concerned. I couldn't see any objection, so I told him that Marcus was welcome anytime, but I told him the arrangement was not to be reciprocated. 'That's OK,' he said. 'Marcus has a big family, so their house is often a bit noisy. It would be easier to work together here,' he added.

'So you've already been to his house?' I asked him.

'Just the once,' he answered. 'It's on the way home, and he wanted to lend me a book he had in his room.'

'I don't want you visiting other boys' houses,' I ordered him. 'Not without my permission. Do you understand, Kevin?'

'Yes, Dad.'

'Good boy,' I said. 'And I should meet his parents.'

That happened sooner than I expected. It turned out that Marcus's family had recently emigrated from County Cork in Ireland, and Marcus himself still retained the accent and some of the figures of speech associated with his homeland. I have always loved the Irish brogue, as well as the Irish sense of humour. Marcus had plenty of both. He was shorter than Kevin and a bit plump, but he had a jolly face and captivating smile under his mop of reddish-brown hair. I could see that Helen was also quite taken with him, so he was a good part-time addition to our family. We must have passed muster as well. A few weeks after he had started visiting, he told us his birthday was soon, and we were invited to come along to the party that his parents had organised to celebrate the occasion. 'We're having a lunchtime barbecue on March 3. It's a Sunday, starting around midday,' he told us. 'Very informal.'

'Is this invitation from your parents?' I asked him.

'Oh, yes,' he replied.

'Then we'll be glad to come. Thank you.'

I thought it right that we should take round a bottle of wine to the barbecue, and as we didn't normally keep wine in the house, I asked Helen to buy some the next time she went shopping. I gave her a ten-dollar note and told her to bring me the change and the receipt. Sunday turned out to be a warm day, settled as early autumn days often are, and as the O'Learys' house was only a few streets away, we decided to walk. I could understand what Kevin meant by a noisy household, for we heard the sounds of voices and laughter from a fair distance. There seemed little point in knocking; no one would have heard us. Kevin pushed the door open, and we walked in. The sounds were all coming from the garden at the back, so we made our way through the house. There seemed to be hordes of children of all ages cavorting around and bouncing on a trampoline that had been installed on the lawn. Kevin had told us that Marcus had two brothers and two sisters, all younger than him, but there were at least a dozen children there, so obviously many other families had already arrived. On the patio, a huge

212

gas barbecue sat with its lid open ready for cooking to start, and next to it, a table was covered with glasses and bottles of beer, wine, and cold drinks.

Kevin led us over to a group of grown-ups and introduced us to Marcus's parents, whose names turned out to be Sean and Maeve. Sean was a larger-than-life man. He looked like an older version of Marcus, but, unlike his son, he had a strident voice. 'Ah, yes, Kevin's parents,' he boomed when Kevin ushered us forward. 'Good of you to come,' and then added, 'you really shouldn't have,' when I passed over our bottle. Maeve was a lot quieter but had a sunny smile, which she dispensed to everyone. After they had welcomed us, they introduced the others, none of whose names I remembered later.

Kevin had found Marcus and had gone off somewhere with him. They reappeared moments later, in earnest conversation. Maeve had seen them too, and I heard her mention to Helen how happy she was that Kevin had taken Marcus under his wing. 'It wasn't easy for him, starting in a strange school, but he's settling in well now.' With that, she excused herself, needing to go and see to the food. I felt quite proud of Kevin after hearing that remark. I had always known that he was a caring boy, and just as he had done with Jackson, the friend from his first primary school, he had also now done for Marcus, though, of course, there the comparison ended. Jackson was the son of a single mother, whereas Marcus had a large and loving family round him. I wondered whether Kevin was perhaps a little bit jealous of the O'Leary family.

Maeve had prepared mounds of chicken pieces, most of them marinated in tandoori sauce, but some plain for those children that didn't like spicy food, together with a selection of chops and sausages, and these along with bowls of potato and green salads were placed on another table next to the barbecue. Under Sean's direction, we were asked to choose whatever we wanted to eat and cook it ourselves. I was lucky that I'd had some experience with cooking on a barbecue and didn't feel too much of a beginner. The other men with me all looked very expert as they tossed and turned the meat before it started getting overcooked, and they all seemed to know exactly when it was ready. Soon, the air was full of the tantalising smells. It was a delicious meal, and there were bowls of fruit salad and ice cream to follow. I kept a close eye on Helen, making sure she wasn't getting too pally with the other guests. Soon after three o'clock, some of the other guests, those with the youngest children, started drifting away, and it seemed a good time for us to leave as well. Kevin had once again disappeared somewhere inside the house, so I asked Sean to tell him we were leaving. I had noticed him earlier with a beer in his hand. Marcus had one too, so I didn't feel I could remonstrate with either of them in public. I let it pass, even though I had never given him permission to drink alcohol. I heard Sean bellow Kevin's name somewhere inside, and he soon came running out. 'We're leaving now,' I told him. He asked if he could stay on a bit. 'OK,' I said, 'but no more beer.' He nodded and went back inside.

Months passed us by. Kevin turned seventeen, and he and Marcus moved into year eleven. The two boys remained as thick as thieves, both out-of-school hours and in. Kevin's friend continued to visit two or three times a week, and occasionally Helen would ask him to stay for dinner. They appeared to be increasingly close, but I had never suspected there was anything inappropriate going on between them. Then one evening, after a somewhat harrowing day at work, I found Helen busy in the kitchen preparing a meal. There were four places set at the table. 'I take it Marcus is here,' I said.

'I've invited him to stay for dinner,' she answered.

I went out onto the patio to sit and relax until dinner was ready and happened to glance towards the window of Kevin's room. I was intrigued by movement inside the room, some activity that had nothing to do with schoolwork. I moved closer to see what was going on, and what I saw stopped me in my tracks. Kevin was kneeling on the floor in front of Marcus, whose trousers were down round his feet and whose very erect penis was firmly entrenched in Kevin's mouth. Our son was looking up at his friend with a devoted smile, whereas Marcus had his eyes shut and his hands round the back of Kevin's head. He was slowly rocking backwards and forwards. I remained frozen, totally immobile, horrified by the spectacle, but at the same time strangely aroused. Then, without thinking what I was going to do, I jumped to my feet and ran inside. I didn't bother to knock, just slammed open the door of Kevin's room and marched inside. The two boys were still in their compromised state. 'What the fuck are you doing!' I shouted at them. They'd frozen the moment I had opened the door, but when he heard my voice, Marcus quickly extricated himself. Otherwise, neither of them moved. They just stood rigid, like two rabbits caught in a car's headlights. And they both looked terrified. 'Get out. At once. Just get out!' I screamed at Marcus. 'Get out of this house and never come back again.' He grabbed his trousers, eyeing me warily as he did so.

By this time, Helen had come to the door. 'What's happening?' she asked.

I was livid with rage. 'We've been raising a poofta, that's what's happening,' I replied.

By this time, I noticed that Kevin was holding Marcus's hand. Then he picked up Marcus's school bag and gave it to him. 'You'd better go,' he advised his friend.

'Too fucking right!' I yelled. I felt Helen plucking at my sleeve, trying to guide me away from the scene. But I wanted to wait until Marcus had finally left the house, which he did as quickly as he could. 'Good riddance!' I shouted after him as the front door closed behind him. Then I strode back to the kitchen, still seething.

'What happened?' Helen asked again.

'Kevin was giving him a blow job. What a vile pair! I couldn't believe it. God knows how long it's been going on.'

'I'd no idea,' said Helen unhappily.

'I wondered why he never got on with girls. Now I know.' I was pacing up and down the kitchen, shaking with rage.

'Perhaps that's just the way he is.'

'What do you mean?' I roared at her.

'Well ....,' she paused, 'maybe he's one of those, you know ....'

'What? Queers?'

'I don't know. Perhaps, but please don't be too hard on him.'

'For God's sake, woman, why the hell not?' My anger was building even further. 'He's got to get over it. Start behaving like a normal human being.'

'I wonder what's normal to Kevin,' she whispered.

'Anyway, it's all your fault he's gone soft in the head.'

'Mine?'

'You've been mollycoddling him all his life. Now he's behaving like a spoilt girl.'

'How can you speak about your son like that?' she cried.

'You've turned him into a poofta.'

'I've done no such thing.'

'Do you think his behaviour is normal, then?'

'I've never thought about it. I've told you, I didn't know anything about it.'

'You must have realised something was going on. It's all your fault.'

I could see that Helen was also becoming increasingly annoyed at my continued recrimination, though whether from Kevin's perspective or hers, I wasn't sure. She suddenly stood tall, looked me in the eye, and spoke with unusual resolve. 'John, stop blaming me for your own failings. If I should have known what was going on, then you should have done too.'

'Bullshit!' I yelled.

'You are equally guilty, John.' She had given me her opinion quite softly, nervously even, but my unreasoning anger continued to churn during this exchange, and it suddenly boiled over at Helen's accusation. I lashed out with my fist. It would have caught her right on her chin, but she must have sensed its coming and turned her head. It caught her on the side of her jaw instead. She landed in a heap at my feet, hitting her head on the edge of the stove as she went down. I was shocked into immobility, frozen in time, not understanding what I was seeing.

Kevin came in the door just at that moment. He ran to his mother, bent down, and cradled her head in his arm. She seemed almost unconscious, her eyes open but unseeing. She uttered a slight moan of pain. 'Mom,' he called gently, 'are you all right?' Then he looked up at me. 'Why did you do that? It's me you should be angry with, not her.'

I had a terrible moment of regret, of actually hating myself, hating what I had done, wondering what had got into me. To be honest, I don't really know why I had lost my temper. I had always promised myself that I was better than my father, that I would never use my fists against Helen, but the very first moment my anger had taken over, I had let myself down. I had let us all down. I actually felt miserable, wondering how I could make everything right again. 'I'm sorry,' I said. 'I don't know what came over me.'

'Help me get her into a chair,' said Kevin. So, between us, we lifted her up and carried her to the sofa in the lounge room and gently laid her down. She was beginning to resurface, and Kevin went off to get her some water.

I took Helen's hand in mine and knelt down next to her. 'I'm sorry. So sorry. I do love you, really I do. I promise it won't happen again. Ever.' I realised that I was sobbing. Helen just looked up at me, her eyes not focusing too well, but remained silent. Every now and again, she touched her face where I had hit her, and when she moved her mouth, she winced with the pain. After a few minutes, I moved up and sat next to her, but when I tried to put my arm round her, she shrugged me off. Kevin came and stood in front of us. He obviously wanted to say something, for his mouth was moving but no words were coming out. Eventually, he left us, and I heard him talking on the phone, though I couldn't hear what was being said. He was supposed to come and ask if he wanted to use the telephone, but on this occasion, I had to let it pass. He spoke off and on for at least five minutes, and then I heard him put the phone down, and a few moments later, he returned and stood in front of us once again.

Kevin appeared embarrassed but determined. 'I've got something I have to tell you,' he announced. 'I've just been talking to Marcus, and he agreed that we should both explain ourselves to our parents, you know, come clean.' He stopped speaking for a moment as he gathered his thoughts. 'The fact is that Marcus and I love each other. I know we should have told you about our feelings earlier, but I'm telling you now. And today wasn't the first time we have enjoyed each other.' Kevin paused to allow this confession to sink in, perhaps expecting an outburst from me, but when I said nothing, he continued. 'Marcus and I discussed what we should do, and we decided that, to satisfy your prejudices, we should promise that we won't see each other again *out* of school hours till we've finished year twelve. After that, we are planning on living together for the rest of our lives. I do now promise that, and I hope you understand and won't create any obstacles.'

During this amazing speech, I remained silent; and when Kevin realised we weren't going to say anything, he turned and left us.

*   *   *

CHAPTER 16

2003–2010

Helen and I sat silently for the best part of an hour. I don't know whether she understood what Kevin had said, or whether she had even heard it. She seemed like a zombie, her face expressionless, while my mind was churning around in circles, unable to process any coherent strategy for making amends. Helen was obviously in shock, oblivious to everything around her, but eventually I managed to persuade her to take my arm and be guided to our room. I laid her down on top of the bed and stretched out next to her without touching. Neither of us bothered to get undressed. I was worried I might have broken something when I hit her or had dislodged a tooth or two, but at least there was no sign of blood where her head had hit the stove. I don't think that either of us slept much that night, and before six the next morning, I got up and had a shower before putting on clean clothes. I left Helen where she was, now also awake. I asked her if she would like a cup of tea. She nodded, still unable to talk without pain.

I made breakfast for Kevin and myself and prepared two packed lunches. Not a word was spoken on either side. After I'd seen him off to school, I went back to Helen to ask if I could get her anything to eat, but she just shook her head. I couldn't refuse if she'd insisted on seeing a doctor that day, but I knew it would be obvious to anyone examining her that she had been abused. Any worthwhile doctor would put two and two together, even without Helen dobbing me in. And if and when she did see a doctor, I wanted to be present so I could put a different light on her injuries. I would have to be with her, despite my not having any idea what I would say if I was accused of domestic violence. I was conscience-stricken by what I had done, but I still didn't want anyone to know about it, so I left for work without suggesting any such visit. That evening, when I got home, Helen was still lying down. At least she had gotten up at some stage during the day, had undressed and showered, and had gone back to bed. I also checked on Kevin, if only to make sure he was home and diligently doing homework, alone. Helen still couldn't speak without pain but indicated that she wanted to write something. I found a pen and paper, and she wrote 'packet of soup in larder'. So I made a cup of soup for Helen and resurrected some of the previous night's dinner, the one that she had partially prepared for the four of us, for Kevin and myself. He was quite chirpy once he realised that I wasn't going to bawl him out. I think he was relieved at having got his dirty secret off his chest. He chatted away about school and soccer, but thankfully he never mentioned Marcus.

Helen's jaw had been badly bruised, but she recovered slowly. She never asked to see a doctor, probably because she knew I would want to be there to stop her from telling her story. Despite the slow improvement, it was a week before she was able to eat solids, but only on one side of her mouth, and in that week, she indicated that she needed to see the dentist. One tooth at least was loose and giving her pain. They all needed checking. I made an appointment for the next day, telling the receptionist that it was an emergency. Otherwise, she would have had to wait two weeks for treatment. I hoped that by then the external bruising would be less noticeable and so wouldn't lead to unwelcome questions. In the event, the dentist had to remove one tooth, but he was able to save two others. By this time, Helen was talking reasonably well. She announced that the fitting of an implant to replace the missing tooth would cost around $2,000. It seemed a bit steep, but I decided that paying for it was the least I could do as reparation. She certainly needed a new tooth; her face was looking a little odd.

A distinct change came over Helen after that terrible moment of madness. She became distant, never speaking to me unless spoken to first, though doing everything I asked of her without complaint, and never smiling, certainly not for me. Two weeks after the altercation, she told me she had phoned Maeve O'Leary that morning. She wanted to try and smooth over any antagonism that might have arisen from their son being thrown out of our house. Apparently, Maeve wasn't at all alienated and had invited Helen around for a morning tea. I was told the whole story when I got home that evening. Apparently, Sean and Maeve hadn't been at all distressed, or even surprised, when Marcus had opened up about his feelings for Kevin. In fact, they'd suspected for some time that their son was either gay or heading in that direction. However, they had agreed that it was a good plan for the two boys not to get too involved while they were still at school. They would become the butt of jokes, and possibly bullying, if their relationship became common knowledge. 'Marcus's parents seem to have a very relaxed attitude about homosexuality,' Helen told me.

I could never be relaxed about it. To me, it was an abomination. After all, it was quite obvious that a man's genitalia was specifically designed to fit a woman's. That's the way everyone was made. The same thing could hardly be said about two men. Gays were an anathema, and I had a son going down that path, going rapidly to hell as far as I was concerned. I couldn't forget the scene I had witnessed in his bedroom. He claimed to be in love, and I found that ridiculous. What did he know about love anyway? Helen tried to tell me that gay love was just as legitimate as heterosexual love, that in fact it could be even more intense, but I wouldn't buy it. I reckoned that by keeping the two boys separate, they would get eventually get over it and return to normality. Helen never argued about it again, but I don't think she agreed with me. She became very defensive whenever I broached the subject, so we just agreed to keep off the subject.

As for Kevin, he kept very much to himself and during term time worked steadily at his studies. The problem was the school holidays, especially the long break over Christmas. I decided that while Maddens was closed down for our usual month's recess, I would take the family on holiday, as far away from temptation as we could get. Luckily, I didn't have to worry about finding a temporary home for Socks. The poor cat had suddenly died earlier in the year. At least we assumed he'd died, though actually he had just disappeared one day. He was never found. Kevin wasn't too upset, undoubtedly having more important things on his mind, so we decided not to replace the animal. I managed to book a two-bedroom self-catering apartment in Mallacoota for three weeks. It would be an all-day drive away from home, and I made a point of not telling either Helen or Kevin where we were headed until we were halfway there. I said it was going to be a surprise, but the fact was that I didn't want anyone to know where we had gone. As a result, once we were there and settled in, I felt we were sufficiently isolated for me to allow the pair of them out of my sight whenever they suggested exploring on their own. This they did frequently, usually returning tired and happy. However, we did manage a few walks together, as a family, usually round the lakes or into the town itself, where we would stop for a meal or to buy groceries. And sometimes we drove along the coast to a particularly lovely bathing beach and take a picnic to eat after we'd had our swim out in the surf.

As a holiday, it was not a success. Helen remained reserved towards me and, when I was with her, unresponsive towards the lovely scenery that abounded throughout the area. However, after the first week, she started getting a bit of colour back in her cheeks, and when she returned from her outings with Kevin, she was more animated as they talked about what they'd done and seen. Every time they did this, I felt excluded and angry, but I decided to say nothing. I felt that she was still punishing me for what I'd done to her earlier in the year, even though the subject remained taboo. I think we were all glad when the holiday was over. Not once did I hear Marcus's name mentioned, and I hoped he'd been forgotten.

Before we left Mallacoota, I spent a bit of time quizzing Kevin about his plans. I knew that his best subjects at school were maths and, to a lesser extent, physics and English, but I wanted to know what he intended doing once he'd left school. I had no idea what those people who were good at maths did for a living. 'Mum wants me to go to university,' he told me. 'My teachers too.'

'I'm not asking what *they* all want. What do *you* want to do?' I asked him.

'That's what I'd like to do too.'

I'd guessed that was coming, but I needed to find some way of changing Kevin's mind. 'And, how would you pay for it?'

'I'd get a loan.'

'Where on earth from?'

'HECS-HELP, it's called. One applies through the university.'

Kevin seemed to have all the answers, but none of my family had ever pursued such highfalutin nonsense, and I wasn't going to be a party to it now. 'You should get out to work, earn your living,' I told him somewhat harshly. Kevin clammed up, but I didn't want to leave it at that. 'You should listen to what *I* have to say, not just rely on your mother's opinions all the time.'

He again remained silent for a time. He looked uncomfortable and angry. 'OK, Dad,' he said at last. 'I'll think about it.'

I *did* realise that Kevin probably had the brains to do well at university. His teachers had said as much, but I couldn't afford the fees and wouldn't want to anyway. When I asked Helen why she was putting ideas into Kevin's head, she just shrugged her shoulders. 'I want what's best for him. That's all,' she said.

Soon after we'd driven home from our holiday, I was due to return to work. A couple of weeks later, Kevin was back at school for his final year. Obviously, I couldn't keep a close eye on him after that, but Marcus was never mentioned, not in my presence anyway, so I assumed that he really had gotten over his infatuation. Helen seemed to become ever more preoccupied now we were back at home, but she never crossed me, and I had little need to pull her up on anything. In fact, she became quite meek and docile and so submissive in bed that sex was becoming boring. She stopped getting any joy out of it. As a consequence, I didn't either.

The year progressed through the remainder of a hot summer. March 1 was the tenth anniversary of Maddens, but I decided to let it pass without any great celebration. However, I did invite Jason, Pat, and Jack out for dinner at a local pub to mark the occasion. Pat wanted to know why Helen was not joining us. 'She has a prior engagement,' I lied. The summer morphed into a cool autumn and a wet winter, but as spring approached, I sensed a tension building in the house. I put it down to Kevin's approaching exams. By the fourth term, he was spending long periods studying at home, only occasionally going into school for revision classes. The day of the first exam, English, finally arrived. I had an early start that morning as we were starting a job out towards Dandenong, but I remembered to wish him well before I left. Helen offered to drive him to school that day, but he declined, saying a walk in the fresh air would help clear any cobwebs out of his brain. In the event, Kevin came home smiling. The exam went well, according to him, as did all of them in the following weeks.

The day of his final exam arrived, a two-hour one starting at ten o'clock. It was a day that started much like every other, and I planned to take the family out to dinner that evening to celebrate. Unfortunately, that was the very day that one of my excavators broke down in the middle of a dig in Mount Martha. By the time I had found the fault, tracked down the necessary spare parts, and had fitted them, it was getting late. The celebratory dinner would have to wait. It was after seven when I got home and beginning to get dark. The first thing I noticed was that there were no lights on in the house. That was strange. And when I tried to open the front door, I found it locked. Normally, it was never locked until we were all inside for the night, though I always carried a key on my car key ring. I went in and called out. Silence. I checked the garage, only to find that Helen's car was missing. She and Kevin must have gone out to the shops, needing something for dinner. They shouldn't be long, I thought. I went into the kitchen. Everything was in its place, tidied away, and there were no signs of anything being prepared for dinner. I sat down to wait.

I must have dozed off, for when I next looked at my watch, it was already after ten o'clock. That's when I started getting worried. Perhaps they'd had an accident. I waited another hour and then, with increasing trepidation, phoned both the Frankston Hospital and the police to see if there had been any reports that might be relevant. There was nothing. Slowly, the truth began to dawn on me. Panic-stricken, I raced round the house, checking what might be missing, starting with the cupboard that housed Helen's clothes. It was quite obvious that she hadn't gone for just a few days. The cupboard was almost stripped bare. The suitcases had all gone too, and the bathroom cupboard was almost empty. Checking Kevin's room, I found that almost bare too; but unlike our room, which had been left tidy, Kevin's showed signs of a hurried departure. I searched for a note, some explanation, but there was nothing, not in our room, not in the kitchen.

I collapsed onto the settee in the lounge room, trying to work out what might have happened, but I was so angry, I couldn't think straight. How dare she just walk out? Where could she go? Helen had no money. I'd made sure of that, so she'd have to come back almost straightaway, and when she did, I'd give her such a thrashing. And she had no close friends in Frankston, with the possible exception of the O'Learys. I'd give them a call in the morning and find out if they knew anything. What the hell was she thinking of? And she'd stolen Kevin away. She had no right to do that. Kevin wouldn't have walked out on me without a word. This was all Helen's doing. She'd have a lot to answer for when she returned. Give her three days and she'll be back, begging to be let in the door. I felt better when I envisaged her tearfully imploring me to take her back, but I didn't sleep that night. I remained perched on the settee, gently fuming.

The next morning, I first drove to work, keeping an eye open for Helen's car. Of course, I saw many cars that resembled hers, but they all had the wrong occupants. As soon as I'd gotten the men started, I drove back to the O'Learys' house and banged on their front door. Eventually, the door opened, and Marcus stood there. 'Oh, good morning, Mr Madden,' he said very politely.

'Have you seen my wife?' I demanded. 'Or Kevin?' I added.

'No,' he said with a puzzled frown.

Just then, Maeve appeared. 'Can I help?' she asked me.

I didn't want to admit that Helen had walked out on me, so I just said that I needed to speak with her. I asked whether she was visiting them by any chance.

'No. Haven't seen her for months.' Maeve spoke to me with such a sincere expression that I had to believe her.

'OK,' I said, turning away. 'Sorry to have troubled you.' I was sure they knew nothing, so that was my only possibility dashed. To be honest, I couldn't think of anywhere else to look or even ask, so I'd just have to wait until they came back. I was sure they *would* return, their tails between their legs, in two days. Three at the most, but I waited a week, and there was still no sign of them. I went round to the O'Learys again, this time to be met at the door by Sean. I asked if he'd seen Kevin, or whether Marcus had.

'No, I haven't seen him,' he answered in his rich Irish accent. 'And Marcus is away at Schoolies Week, down in Lorne. Back next Saturday.'

'OK,' I said.

I was just about to turn away when Sean spoke again. 'Did you ever find Helen?'

I had detected a humorous sound in his voice and a faint smile round his eyes as though he was mocking me. I wondered whether they had discovered that I had been deserted by my family and were making fun of me behind my back. I hate being laughed at. It made me very angry, and I would gladly have wiped the smile of his face, but just then Maeve poked her head around the door and asked me if I'd like to come in for a cuppa. My resentment diminished slightly at this kindness, but I couldn't submit myself to either their sympathy or their wisecracks, so I turned down the invitation and went home.

Two days after my second visit to the O'Learys, I had a flash of inspiration. Perhaps Helen had not obeyed my order to cut her ties with Rhonda Sutton. She might have surreptitiously ignored my instruction and been seeing the sly cow behind my back. The more I thought of it, the more likely it seemed; and the more likely it seemed, the angrier I became. I started hunting again, all over the house, looking for something that would tell me that I was on the right track, but once again I found nothing. I resolved to go up to Langwarrin and check out the Sutton property. I'd go there the next weekend and confront Rhonda. Before I left, I spent much of the time rehearsing in my mind what I would say to her, and even more of the time thinking how I would punish Helen when I found her.

When I drove up to the Suttons' house on the Saturday morning, the place looked deserted. I realised that if Helen was there, I should be able to see her car, but the only vehicle there was the Alpha sitting in front of the garage door. Perhaps Helen's car was inside. I saw there was a window on the side of the building, and I tried looking in, but there was some sort of curtain over the window, and I could see nothing. Then I walked round to the garage door, but it was locked. There was nothing I could do but try the house, so I mounted the steps and hammered on the front door to see if anyone was around. All was ominously silent, but on my second knock, I could hear a child's voice, and then the door opened. A girl of about ten years old stood there.

'Hello,' she said. 'Sorry, Dad's overseas on a job.'

She was so self-possessed that I was momentarily hesitant. 'Then, is you mother in?' I asked her.

She looked over her shoulder and called, "Mum, there's a man to see you.'

Moments later, Rhonda came to the door. 'Yes?' she queried. She had a puzzled frown on her face, as if she didn't know me at all. Then, suddenly, a light must have dawned, and she smiled. 'Of course. I remember you now. You're John Madden, aren't you? The excavator man?' she added with a broad smile.

'That's right.'

'I haven't seen you for at least ten years. How are you?' she asked me in a friendly voice.

The whole conversation was becoming unreal, and Rhonda's affable mood totally unexpected if indeed she was harbouring my fugitive wife. 'I'm fine,' I lied and realised I would need to tread carefully if I wanted the truth out of her. She had completely disarmed me. I felt disoriented, no longer so sure of myself. In fact, I felt a bit of a fraud. I finally got my thoughts back together. 'I was wondering if you'd seen my wife lately? You know, Helen?'

'No. I haven't seen Helen for a long time. I remember meeting her in a shop one day a few years ago, but not since.'

'You're absolutely sure?'

'Oh, yes, and I remember something else. She told me she wasn't allowed to see me after that. I never did discover why.'

I realised then that I'd been on a wild goose chase. At one stage, I would have just shoved my way into the house and searched for Helen, but after such a friendly and innocent reception, I could no longer contemplate such a crass move. Rhonda was so obviously genuine that a home invasion was out of the question. I thought for a long moment what to do next but decided there was nothing I *could* do. I would just have to leave empty-handed. 'I'm sorry to have troubled you,' I said.

'I would have liked to invite you in for a cuppa,' Rhonda said, 'but I promised to take the girls to a film today, and we're a bit late already.'

'That's OK,' I said and quickly walked back to the car. I was disappointed but knew that I'd been clutching at straws. There had never been more than a very slight chance of actually finding Helen there. She'd obviously gone somewhere else, somewhere I would never think of looking. After that visit, I gave up the search.

Kevin's nineteenth birthday came and went and then Christmas, and he remained lost to me. The New Year got under way, and still there was no word from either of them. Maddens, as usual, closed down for three weeks, and for me, it was three weeks of total boredom. I had nothing to occupy me and was glad to get back to work once it was over. It was ironic that just when my personal life had fallen apart, my working life was blossoming. We had more work than I could have imagined earlier, and I was even having to turn down jobs. I did so with a heavy heart, but I didn't want the business to expand beyond its current size. It was comfortable the way it was and provided all of us with a good income. I had always been tight with money but never had ambitions to become rich. There were times when I got a bit shirty with my staff, times when my annoyance at Helen's betrayal boiled over into the workplace, but I always apologised afterwards and eventually told Jason what had happened, just so he would understand my moods. Both he and Pat were entirely sympathetic and sometimes asked me round to their house for a meal. They always made me feel welcome, and I was better for their company.

Then one June day, some six months after Helen had absconded, I received a letter from her. It was quite bulky, and I recognised the handwriting on the envelope as hers. It had a Sydney postmark. I didn't open it for two days, terrified of what it might contain, but eventually I could bear the suspense no longer. I sat at the table and picked up the letter. Outside, the beginnings of a storm was brewing, and the rain was sheeting down, as with trembling fingers I slit the envelope open and drew out the letter. There were six pages, covered both sides in Helen's neat writing.

*   *   *

CHAPTER 17

2010

My husband,

I have been meaning to write to you for three months but could never bring myself to do it, mainly due to the feeling of guilt that has been so much part of my life recently. For a long time, I couldn't even think, let alone get my thoughts together enough to write a letter. However, Uncle Frank, who I'm currently staying with, has persuaded me that I should. So here goes. You may think that I hate you for what you did to me, but I want to say at the outset that I don't hate you. In a strange way, I still love you, but I just can't live with you anymore.

You probably thought that my departure was a sudden impulse. Well, it wasn't. Granted that I was unhappy in our marriage, I had still resolved to stick it out despite the terrible things you kept doing to me and the times you raped me into submission, times that were so out of character. Then came that frightful day when you caught Kevin and Marcus making love, for that's all they were doing that day when you finally lost your temper and hit me with your fist. Everything changed after that. I knew I could no longer put up with your abusive control. Up till then, I had thought that you could never be as bad as your father, but after that I knew that you were. Like father, like son. I could no longer live with you if you were going to behave like the monster you had inexplicably turned into.

You may ask why I didn't move out straightaway. The fact is that I couldn't risk Kevin's life in your hands, not while you were so antagonistic to his preferred sexual orientation. And I couldn't take him out while he was still at school. There was no way I wanted to disrupt his schooling at such a critical juncture. No, I would have to wait until the end of the year.

Quite early on, I sounded him out about his feelings in the matter, swearing him to secrecy when I told him what I wanted to do. He agreed that I should leave you, and following that time when he learnt of your opposition to his going on to university, he wanted to leave home as well. He was not comfortable. I knew that if one word got out about our plans, you would have gone completely ballistic. We would fear for our lives, and I couldn't risk it. Kevin and I had many long discussions about his future and how we could arrange to get away. Most of our plans were made in Mallacoota when you took us on that so-called holiday. I am fully aware that you only took us away to separate him from Marcus. You shouldn't have worried. He was entirely truthful when he said he would keep away from his friend until school finished, even though that was still a whole year away. He is a very honest boy, our son, candid and serious. He will grow up well. And he loves you very much, despite everything. So the plan was to leave as soon as his last exam was over. We would just go without leaving any indication of where we were going. We would hide.

I now have to admit to a certain subterfuge. I was aware that you checked our phone bills to make sure I wasn't talking to someone you didn't approve of. How silly! Especially since you couldn't monitor my incoming calls. I expect you remember the day I told you I'd met Rhonda Sutton at Karingal, and you nearly lost your cool and told me never to see her again. Well, one morning, nearly a year or so after that meeting, I had a call from her. She wanted to know what had happened to me. She wanted to get back in touch. I found I couldn't be rude and just put the phone down on her, and after talking to her for a bit, she must have realised something was very wrong. She is a person one can talk to quite openly. She is totally non-judgemental, and I found myself baring my thoughts to her. I explained about the checking going on and the other things I was being subjected to, such that I could never phone her. She was horrified at some of the things I told her. We spoke for an hour, and then she suggested I simply get myself a mobile phone and keep it well hidden and then call her whenever things got too stressful for me.

I managed to save up enough over the next few weeks to buy one, and I stored it in a place you would never look: the inside of my piano! At least now I had free communication with the outside world, and I kept Rhonda aware of what was happening. One particularly bad day, when I was unburdening myself to her, she invited us to stay with them in Langwarrin, if and when Kevin and I ever plucked up enough courage to leave you. Our plans had the final piece of the jigsaw puzzle in place. Such a relief!

From the day we arrived in Langwarrin, Jim and Rhonda were absolutely marvellous. They made us feel very welcome, and they said from the outset that we could stay as long as we wished. They gave us free rein of the place, but Jim advised us not to stray too far from the house in case we were recognised and our whereabouts were reported back to you. And he said there was still a chance that you would come looking for me, so he hid my car in his garage, put a large sheet over it, and a thick curtain over the window. And he gave instructions that the garage door must be locked at all times. He was very protective. As you can imagine, I was in a state of shock, of total collapse at the time we moved. I don't know how I kept going, maintaining a silence as to what we intended doing and trying to appear normal. It was nerve-racking. Of course, Kevin wanted to see Marcus as much as possible. He had used my mobile to contact him a couple of times (they talked so much that he kept running down the battery!). Anyway, Maeve and I arranged for the pair of them to go to Schoolies Week down in Lorne, so as to give me a bit of space to lick my wounds.

Then came that critical day you showed up at the house. I was playing cards with the girls in the lounge room and happened to look out of the window when I heard a car. I saw you arrive. I panicked. Jim was away at the time, so I shouted at Rhonda, 'He's here!' and ran to the toilet and locked myself in. I sat on the toilet seat, shaking with fear, my heart beating so violently that I thought I would faint. It seemed like hours of terror before Rhonda came and tapped on the door. 'He's gone,' she said, but it still took me a long time before I found the courage to unlock the door and emerge. She had been waiting for me outside, and when I saw her, I fell into her arms and wept with relief that we were still safe. The one thing I didn't know about Rhonda was that she was a trained psychologist. When you arrived, she sized up the situation very quickly, knowing that you would be belligerent and possibly a little unhinged. She knew that the only way of fobbing you off would be to win you over with a mixture of solicitude and friendliness. Rhonda's oldest girl, a child who is wise beyond her years and who, like all the girls, had been told my story, agreed to greet you at the door in a sign of normality, and Rhoda did the rest, bless her. Thank God it all worked, and you left none the wiser.

Another thing: do you remember implying that I was showing signs of dementia? I was worried that you might be right, and I resolved, at the first available opportunity, to get myself checked out. Rhonda was adamant that your behaviour was just a part of your coercive control, but I still thought it best to get a second opinion. I got an appointment with Mr Masters, the specialist that saw my mother. He gave me all sorts of tests that showed I was entirely normal. When I told him about the way I had started losing things or misplacing them and the fact that it was getting worse over time, he asked me about you and our relationship. By the time I was seeing Mr Masters, I was becoming more able to talk about our marriage, so I related some of the worst incidents to him and the circumstances under which they had occurred. He was very sympathetic, and he said it sounded as though you had been 'gaslighting' me. It wasn't an expression I'd ever heard before, but what Mr Masters said made a lot of sense.

So, were you deliberately hiding things? Why would anyone do that? I can hardly believe it. You know, you completely undermined my self-confidence, and it has taken all this time for me to realise how I've been manipulated. You even accused me, in a roundabout way, of being unfaithful. I want to tell you here and now that I have never cheated on you. I am not like you. Yes, I know about your affair with your boss's widow. You weren't quite as good at hiding it as you thought, but I never raised it with you because I knew you would have got angry at being accused and would simply shift the blame to me, as if your deceit was all my fault. Anyway, it seemed to end almost before it started, and she was the seducer, or so I was informed. It's water under the bridge now, though at the time I was deeply hurt.

Well, I stayed with the Suttons for three whole months. They remained generous and caring throughout, and nothing was too much trouble. They wanted me to get my head together before they would allow me to move on. It took all that time, and I'm still not entirely right. I still have nightmares. Kevin returned and joined us for his birthday and Christmas, as well as the New Year celebrations. In the interim, he got his results. They were very good indeed, and we were all delighted. During his last two terms, Kevin applied for a couple of university courses up in the city. I know there is a Monash campus in Frankston, but he needed to get far away from home. Once he'd got his results, he was offered his first choice, a general science degree at the Monash campus in the city. He started three months ago. I hope you don't mind, but I have arranged for him to stay with your parents while he is studying. I pay them rent, money they welcome now your father is retired. Marcus has also started work up in the city, and they see a lot of each other. While we were staying at the Suttons, I taught Kevin to drive. Knowing that I could be of some use in this world was a great help in my convalescence, something my lack of self-esteem needed badly. He was quick to learn, and I promised him that once he had his licence, I would buy him a small second-hand car. After my three months in Langwarrin, I drove up to Sydney to stay with Uncle Frank and his family, though now I have my own little flat nearby, which I'm renting. He and Brenda were very upset about our split; both of them liked you a lot, but they understood my predicament.

There is one more deception that I hid from you. Actually, I don't like to call it a deception for it is something that was designed to help us both if a need should arise. I'm sure you are asking yourself how I've been able to pay my way over the last six months. The fact is that my parents left me far more money than I knew about. I wasn't deliberately hiding it from you. In fact, I never realised the extent of my parents' wealth until you asked me to finance your business. That's when I went off to see the lawyer and get some advice. A lot of investments were hidden away, and I couldn't find any paperwork that led me to them. Some of them were still in my father's name, and it took time to sort everything out. It was in places that no one had searched, but when I went to see Candice Maybury, the lawyer, she asked her accountant to check right back through the records. It's amazing what he found, and eventually the whole story came out. Even after paying all that money to Beechwood, there was still over half a million. With the value of the house, I was actually a millionaire! My mind continued boggling for some time!

I had absolutely no idea what to do about it but knew it would be rash simply to give it all to you for your business. If that had gone bust, we would have been destitute. Candice told me to take great care about divulging my wealth. Thank God she did. On her advice, I set aside one hundred thousand dollars in an education account for Kevin, and the remainder was split: two hundred thousand toward Maddens and the last two hundred thousand into term deposits for a rainy day. I thought little more about it until I started planning on leaving you. The rainy day had arrived! Please don't be sore at me for keeping this from you. At the time, it just seemed to make sense, and it was all done with good advice. You had enough to start your business, and we had plenty in reserve in case it should fail. I must congratulate you that it didn't. So many new companies fail in the first two years, or so I'm told, that I half expected yours to do so as well. You did well, and I'll always be proud of you for that. Of course, that was all ten years ago. With interest rates as they've been since, the sums have just about doubled, so Kevin has plenty to pay his way through university, with enough over to get him started in whatever he decides to do. And enough for me to make a new start in life.

I seem to have been writing for ages, but now I'm almost done. It has actually been quite a cathartic exercise, getting all this off my chest, especially all this last bit about the money. I feel much more relaxed now I've told you everything, and I hope this letter is not too upsetting for you. It is true, as I said at the beginning, that I felt guilty. The ruse over the money was the major part of that guilt. In fact, it was greater than my guilt for leaving you, so I hope you will understand my predicament at that time.

What of the future? I have to admit that I'm not entirely comfortable in Sydney. It took me a while to find my way around, though Frank and Brenda are lovely people and were very supportive, so my stay with them was an agreeable time. I often wonder about you and how the business is going. During our various visits to the Mornington Peninsula, I fell in love with the area and think that, once I can face another move, I will try my luck down there, get a job, and maybe buy a small property. As for Kevin, he and Marcus are as thick as thieves and are still planning a future together. He doesn't yet know what he will do with his degree. He still loves you and to some extent respects you. I would like him to come and visit you one day. He wants to do that, though he is worried about your reaction. If and when he does visit, please be kind to him. As you are aware, he is very sensitive and still sometimes needs a lot of reassurance.

I wonder if you and I will ever meet again. Currently, I have no wish to see you, though I don't mean that in a spiteful manner. However, times change, and perhaps you'll change too and be like the man I first fell in love with all those years ago. My love for you, which was both constant and unwavering, laid my heart wide open. As a consequence, I had no resistance to the evil you brought into our marriage, but I hope this letter will help you to realise how much you need to reform. We had some good times together, John, and I always try my best to treasure them without remembering the bad things.

With sorrow and the remnants of love,
Helen

*   *   *

CHAPTER 18

2010

I realised, as I finished reading the letter, that my cheeks were wet with tears. And my hands were shaking. I sat for a long moment trying to collect my thoughts, and then I went back to the beginning of the letter and read it again. My emotions kept switching between sadness and anger; sadness at what I had lost and anger at how I'd been duped—duped not only by Helen but by the O'Learys as well. They would have been party to Helen's plans, and I felt ashamed at having been fooled by their apparent honesty. Then, of course, there was the part played by Rhonda Sutton, the nasty bitch. I could kick myself for being so gullible.

I wondered how Helen could possibly have found out about Donna and how she could remain silent once she knew. It was all a mystery, but there was a certain logic to her letter, though her perspective in much of what she had said was so different from mine that at times I didn't recognise myself. And I found it hard to equate the vast sums of money that Helen had inherited with the somewhat unobtrusive standard of living enjoyed by her family. Peter and Myra were never extravagant, a feature that also remained part of Helen's nature. In some strange way, I wasn't jealous of her new-found wealth or angry at having been told nothing about the riches she and the lawyer had unearthed. I was just pleased that I wouldn't ever be asked to support her or Kevin again. I had half a mind to sit down and write a letter back to Helen, but, of course, there was no address on hers or on the back of the envelope. I reread the final paragraph, the one I realise now had brought on my tears. All I could do was wait for a message from Kevin, one to say he wished to visit. Of course, I would treat him kindly if and when he ever came. I realised that I had not been a good father to him, but that would change.

A month after receiving Helen's letter, I got another, this time from Mandy, Helen's cousin, whom I'd last met at Myra's funeral. It was quite a short note.

Dear John, Helen told me your sad news some time ago but swore me to silence until she had written to you. I saw her again last week. She released me from my obligation and gave me your address, realising that I probably still had the hots for you! She's not stupid. Anyway, you must be devastated and very lonely now you're on your own. I wondered if you would like me to come down and see you, hold your hand as it were (and anything else that would make you happy). I'm currently between boyfriends so have no commitments. I'd love to see you again. Just say the word and I'll come on down.

Lovingly, Mandy XXXXXXX

I thought back to the day of Myra's funeral. That was twenty years ago, so Mandy must be nearing forty. The reference to 'boyfriends' was a bit strange at her age, I thought. I wondered if she was still as flighty as she had been then. The tone of her letter made me think that she probably was. I remembered the exquisite feeling of her lips as she kissed me, and I chuckled to myself. The intent of the letter was rather too obvious, and why should I look a gift horse in the mouth? I hadn't had any sex for a long time, and the thought of Mandy in my bed was exciting. I also realised it would be good to get one back on Helen, let her know I was still a good prospect for *other* women, even if *she* didn't want me anymore. There was a phone number at the bottom of her letter, so I wasted no time and gave her a call. She answered immediately. 'Hello. Mandy Sykes here.' So if she had been married, she'd kept or gone back to her maiden name.

'Hi, Mandy. It's John. Your letter's just arrived.'

'And?' she answered cheerfully.

'Are you really free?'

'As the air we breathe.'

'Tell me, what are you doing these days?'

'Medical receptionist. Actually, I rather enjoy it.'

'Didn't you ever get married?'

'Could never find a guy that could keep up with me.'

'You're that fast, are you?' I asked her. I could hear her giggling. 'Anyway, most weekends I'm free,' I added.

'So you haven't hitched up again.'

'Not yet.'

'Then I'd love to meet up again, John.'

'OK. How about this coming Friday? Take a late plane down after work, and I'll meet you at Tullamarine.'

'Done,' she said. 'I'll enquire about flights and phone you tomorrow. What's your number?'

So I gave her the number, but when she phoned the next evening, she told me the flights were all full, being a Friday evening; could I manage the following weekend? And so it was arranged. She wangled an early getaway from work and a five o'clock flight down. I also took an afternoon off and drove to the airport to pick her up. She looked a lot older, of course, but hadn't lost any of her vivacity. Her red hair was cut rather shorter than I remembered it, but her body still had all the same sensuous curves. The kiss she gave me had all the promise of a very erotic weekend, but I decided we should call in for a meal at my favourite restaurant in Frankston before I took her home to bed.

When we got back, she said she'd like to have a shower. 'I'm hot and sticky from the flight down,' she told me. 'And I want to smell nice for you,' she added with a lustful grin. I found her a clean towel and showed her the en suite, and while I waited for her to finish showering, I started getting undressed. As I took off the last of my clothes, I thought back to the wet dream I'd had all those years ago after we'd met at the funeral: Mandy with a huge mop of red pubic hair, somehow intensely erotic. But, in the event, her private parts turned out to be almost bare. After fifteen minutes, she emerged naked from the en suite and stood there looking at me with a lascivious smile. She was shaved clean, with the exception of a thin line of hair that stretched from her hidden treasure almost up to her navel. It was so unexpected and so titillating that I couldn't take my eyes away. I just sat unmoving on the edge of the bed, mesmerised. 'It's the latest fashion,' she said. 'Don't you approve?' I didn't reply but sat silently, waiting to see what she would do next. She paused a moment, glancing down at my mounting erection and nodding with a smile of approval. Then she sidled slowly up to me, stopping right in front of me, her navel close to my eyes. She took my head in her hands and moved her legs apart. 'Kiss my pussy,' she begged, her voice quivering.

I was transfixed. 'You know, Helen would never let me do that,' I said.

'Why ever not?' she asked, moving away a little.

'There was a line we were never allowed to cross.'

'What!' she exclaimed. 'No oral sex? What a sad life.'

'I guess it was.'

'Sounds just like Helen. Anyway, wouldn't you like to taste the fruits of love now?' she suggested with a giggle, gently pushing herself back into my face. It was a part of the sex act that I had always aspired to, so I reached out my tongue, hesitantly at first, but soon came the sounds of Mandy's mounting pleasure, so I didn't hold back any longer. It was an exciting new experience for me, and it was good to have such an experienced guide. The fact that we crossed Helen's line in the sand was another source of satisfaction to me. I half wished she was a fly on the wall, watching us, so she would have realised all too late what she'd missed, what we'd both missed. Of course, Helen was far from my mind as Mandy and I continued to pleasure each other with gay abandon.

What a weekend it was. Never before had anyone thrown herself at me in such a lecherous manner. Mandy was exhausting, full of surprises and boundless energy. She kept asking for more, and she was upset whenever I called 'time out'. Then, after each break, her enthusiasm built up once again from one tireless orgasm to another as she cried out in passionate streams of four-letter expletives. I told her, during one of our few brief intervals, that I now understood why she couldn't find a man to keep up with her. She laughed uproariously and promptly continued as before. Helen had told me that Mandy had always been a nymphomaniac. So true! We did stop occasionally for meals, but as soon as she'd finished eating, she dragged me straight off to bed again.

When I drove her back to Tullamarine on Sunday afternoon, I was so worn out and my reactions so slow that I had two near accidents. However, we eventually arrived safely, and I took Mandy to a cafe in the terminal building and bought myself a long black coffee. 'I really enjoyed our weekend together,' Mandy said as I kissed her goodbye. 'Thank you, John.'

'Anytime,' I said, though in fact I thought such an interlude shouldn't be repeated too often. I would need plenty of recovery time after such an incredible surfeit of sexual activity. In fact, the weekend never was repeated. Mandy must have found someone else to screw regularly, someone who lived closer to home, someone who could fornicate for hours without getting tired. She never came down again, but by then my appetite was whetted. I decided to go online and find other willing bedmates, lonely and willing women who advertised themselves on the dating sites that I'd been told abound. I realised, too, that Helen was no longer the elephant in the room. Before Mandy's visit, I still had bouts of anger over Helen's deceit and sorrow over lost love. Now she no longer seemed important. I hardly missed her anymore. In retrospect, I realised that Mandy's visit was purely an act of resurrection.

The months passed, and at the end of that year, I received a call from Kevin. He had just finished his first year at Monash and was heading down to Frankston with Marcus to spend time with the O'Learys. 'Would it be all right if I popped in to see you one evening?' he queried. He sounded a little nervous on the phone, but I put him at his ease and asked him if he'd like to come to dinner. I told him that my cooking had improved a lot, and he accepted an invitation for the coming Friday evening.

He arrived in a little green Mazda 2, and when he walked in the door, I hardly recognised him. He had grown a luxurious beard and moustache, and when I commented on it, he told me that Marcus had asked him to grow it and that his friend really liked it. When he saw the unhappy expression on my face, he stopped in his tracks, looked very apologetic, and said he was sorry. He must have thought that Marcus was still "persona non grata" in my house and he shouldn't be mentioning his name. In fact, my mild irritation was not caused by his reference to Marcus but by his outfit. 'Where on earth did you get that awful shirt?' I asked him. It was patterned in an incredible array of snake-like shapes in every colour imaginable, most of which clashed so badly, they positively screamed at me. I found it distinctly off-putting, hideous even.

'It was a present,' he answered. 'Don't you like it?'

'Frankly, no,' I said firmly. A moment went by as I noticed Kevin's downcast expression, but then I suddenly saw the funny side. I began to laugh at the ridiculousness of both the shirt and my reaction to it. 'It must be the latest "in your face" undergraduate fashion,' I said. Then Kevin started laughing too, and the ice was broken. 'Anyway, as far as you and Marcus are concerned, I'm over it now,' I told him. 'I've come to accept your "odd couple" friendship.'

'Thank you,' said Kevin, and he put his arms around me and gave me a hug. We were both a bit teary as I went off to put the finishing touches to our dinner, and we enjoyed a good evening of chatter, mainly about his university course and the friends he was making. He told me that Granny and Grandpa sent their love and hoped I'd go and visit them soon. I felt guilty that I had ignored them for so long, as well as my other friends in

Melbourne, and resolved to do something about it. I think that Kevin was surprised at my acceptance of everything he was doing with his life, and he gave me another big hug when he left.

After that, he made a habit of visiting me every vacation during his time at Monash, and sometimes he would stay over. Once or twice, he even brought Marcus round. I felt a little uncomfortable in his presence but managed to welcome him without too much rancour. It was at the end of his second year that Kevin announced that he had decided what he wanted to do in life. He would become a teacher, but for that, he would have to do a one-year teaching diploma after his three-year science degree. That meant he'd have a further two years at Monash, but he was quite happy to do that. 'Mum has given me enough money to cover the extra year,' he told me.

'That's good,' I replied. 'Incidentally, where is she these days?'

He looked at me with a sad expression. 'Sorry, Dad, she doesn't want me to tell you anything about her life at present or where she's living.'

'That's quite OK,' I said. 'I understand.' Though I indicated my acceptance of Helen's wishes and wanted to continue appearing uninterested, I wasn't at all happy about her apparent need for such privacy. She was no longer part of my life, and she was no longer important to me, but a residue still remained with me of the time I had valued her as my property and had enjoyed total control over her, or rather had persuaded myself that my control was indeed absolute. This memory was something I didn't seem able to shake off. Consequently, I would love to have known what she was now doing with her life and where she was hiding, but why the need for secrecy? Did she really believe that after all these years I would go round chasing after her? Was she still frightened of me? Perhaps she believed that I was still really sore at her, that I still wanted to exact my revenge on her. I guess she had every right to be wary of me, for I was still angry at what she'd done. However, I decided to give the appearance of wanting to smooth things over, so I asked Kevin to relay a message to her, thanking her for the letter and her explanation. I had never written to her myself. There seemed little point.

At the end of his diploma year, Kevin got himself a job teaching maths at a posh private school down on the peninsula. He'd passed all his exams with flying colours and was eagerly snapped up by the school, since maths teachers were in short supply. Marcus was already installed in a job in Mornington, and they managed to rent a one-bedroom flat close to his work.

In the intervening years, my business continued to prosper, while my personal life stuttered along from one assignation to the next, usually women met through online dating sites, a number of which I'd joined, including one or two that turned out to be somewhat dodgy. A few of the matches seemed quite appealing at first, and of those whom I met, some even availed themselves of my suggestion that they spend the night with me. However, few of these trysts were satisfactory. I remember how one of the women couldn't sleep without the radio being turned on, albeit fairly softly. I couldn't sleep without it off, so she didn't last long. Another woman, an attractive redhead, used to suffer from strange nightmares, causing her to thrash her legs around in her sleep, as well as snore in a most disagreeable way; while a third would jump out of bed the moment we'd finished, dress, and rush off home. In the end, none of them lasted, and the ones whom I saw for more than a few weeks soon wanted some sort of commitment from me. That was never going to be part of my plans. I had a nasty habit of comparing them to Mandy, and not only Mandy. I started comparing them to Helen, the Helen that I'd married. As a result, I was often critical, or overbearing, and they left. I began to think that I was still in love with Helen, and perhaps I was, but I was still angry over her desertion, and I resolved never to let her into the house again, even if she came begging.

About that time, I acquired a new neighbour. The house next door had been quite run-down, rather like mine when we first saw it, and it had been on the market for a few months when a Sold sign went up outside. It had been purchased by a man named Martin, a confirmed bachelor by the look of it, for he moved in by himself and I never saw a companion or children there. He came round to see me the first weekend after he'd moved in, wanting to borrow some tools. He wore glasses most of the time, and he had a thick growth of beard. He loved to talk. We got to know each other well, and we spent many an evening solving the world's intractable problems over a glass of wine. Martin was a keen bowler, and he used to spend just about all his weekends at the local bowls club, and he was often there till late enjoying the equivalent of golf's nineteenth hole.

Then one day, the year after Kevin had started his teaching career, I met a lady called Silver. She was tall and willowy, and about my age. She was pretty, friendly, and outgoing, and she seemed a cut above the rest, well educated and always nicely dressed. And she told me that all three of her kids had flown the nest, so she was free of family commitments.

I really fancied her, and, most importantly because she didn't chatter on about inconsequential nothings like some of the other dating-site trollops I'd met. In fact, we had some interesting conversations, often about our children. She worked as a primary schoolteacher and said she got on well with other people's children, often better than with her own, she added with a smile. Silver also had an independent spirit and was mobile, having a small car, which she kept in mint condition. So I treated her much better than the others and hoped for something more permanent. We started meeting regularly, initially over a coffee at the local cafe and then for meals at weekends. At our third meeting, she told me that she had divorced her husband when she'd discovered his philandering. I was suitably sympathetic but didn't tell her about mine. I wasn't sure if she would enjoy the physical side of a relationship, but I was determined to find out. Once I'd got to know her better and we'd had a somewhat chaste kiss one evening, I invited her round to my house for the following Saturday, ostensibly for dinner, though once she'd been suitably wined and dined, I hoped she would have the inclination to stay the night. I gave her my address and asked her to be there at seven.

I went out on the Saturday morning and bought an expensive bottle of Sauvignon Blanc together with the ingredients for a chicken casserole. It must have been around four o'clock that I started preparing the meal, and it was almost ready for the oven when I felt a pain in my back. It was just a little niggle at first, hardly noticeable. But after half an hour, the pain had got worse and had travelled to my stomach. It was a feeling like the sort of ache one gets when one has eaten something bad. I went to sit down until it went away. I am normally a very healthy person, and at that stage, it didn't worry me overmuch, but as I sat there, the discomfort grew. There wasn't a huge amount of pain, but I began to feel nauseous. I was also getting weaker, as if my legs were about to give way whenever I stood, and my brain was becoming blurred. I was confused, unable to think clearly. I went out onto the veranda to see if a bit of fresh air would help and promptly vomited over the railing. It now dawned on me that there was something seriously wrong. My mind was playing tricks, and my body seemed to be giving up the ghost. I started panicking. I began calling out for help, but no one came. I hoped that Martin would be back from bowls, but it was probably too early for that. I leant over the railing and screamed out for help again and again, and in my depleted state, I eventually heard footsteps. 'Help me,' I managed to croak.

It was indeed Martin. He took one look at me, then rushed into the house. I heard him speak on the phone. When he returned, he told me I was as white as a sheet. He led me inside and made me lie down to wait for the ambulance. I drifted off into unconsciousness, but I vaguely remember two men coming in, lifting me onto a stretcher, and carrying me out, and, lastly, there was the sound of a metallic clatter as the stretcher was loaded into the vehicle.

*   *   *

CHAPTER 19

2010

I was incarcerated in a lunatic asylum, so I must have been certified insane, or at least found to be short of a few marbles. Or perhaps I had mysteriously arrived in a parallel universe, on a planet where nothing is what one expects, or is used to, for the strange things going on around me made no sense. There was no logic, no coherence. I was terrified, for I had entered a dream world, and the dreams all had a nightmarish quality. And I was being held against my will. I was captive, lying in a bed, fenced in by metal bars, confined to a world I didn't understand. I felt I was in a straitjacket. The bars imprisoned me, for they were barricades, obstacles that I was too weak to climb over, though I did try from time to time in frustration at my captivity. The guards, in their white coats, were full of hearty smiles. They had stolen my strength, as they had stolen my health. Whenever one of these white-coated people came close to me, I tried to tell them there was nothing wrong with me, that I was fine, that I wanted to go home, even though I wasn't sure where home was anymore. But no one listened. They just shook their heads and walked off. Or they stuck another needle into me.

One day, Kevin suddenly appeared. At least he looked like Kevin, but I was never sure; and when he spoke, it sounded as if he was speaking underwater. He soon went away again. And one of the white-coated men who kept worrying me was a clone of my neighbour, my friend Martin, complete with beard and glasses. In one of my nightmares, I was in a Russian Stalag, a place where they evidently operated on patients without the benefit of anaesthetics. I was being force-fed through a tube that made me choke and vomit. At other times, I was lying in what appeared to be a deserted underground bunker with a rowdy party going on somewhere nearby but out of sight. My surroundings were stark; the walls a bright white and the lights too intense. Proper sleep was impossible, so I was living in a weak and drowsy state, halfway between sleep and wakefulness, wishing it were morning when it possibly already was. As a final indignity,

I'd been positioned where there was an electric clock on the wall opposite my bed, and the hands were travelling anticlockwise. I thought I must have died and been sent straight to hell. Or else I really had gone mad.

Later, much later, after many days of convalescence, I discovered how close to death I had been. I was told that I was in the Intensive Care Unit at Frankston Hospital and had already been there a week, heavily dosed with morphine. Slowly, as my body began to recover, little snippets of memory returned, not in any chronological order but in unrelated chunks. It took me a while to piece it all together. One of the first things that came back to me was my name, John Madden, though it took me a day or two to remember even that. The next memories to return were the events immediately preceding my journey to the hospital. I remembered that I had been at home one Saturday afternoon, preparing to entertain a lady whom I had met online. Her name was Sable or Sybil or something similar, and I spent much of the day worrying that I'd get her name wrong when she arrived. I'm hopeless at remembering names. I sometimes think they travel in one ear and straight out the other. Then the memory of what happened later that afternoon returned: the strange ache, the nausea and the panic, the screaming for help, and finally the arrival of the ambulance. I was later told that when I'd been delivered to the hospital, I'd been sat on a chair in triage to await a doctor and had immediately slipped off it onto the floor, but I have no memory of this. And I was also told that when I collapsed, they had immediately checked my blood pressure and had found it to be so dangerously low that I was immediately rushed to surgery. I was diagnosed with a ruptured aorta, initially because of a 'bubble' on the artery, which had begun to leak, filling my stomach cavity with blood. The surgery was evidently successful, and I'd had two blood transfusions and been given huge amounts of morphine as my body was being stabilised.

I remained in the ICU for ten days, for the first week suffering the series of hallucinations brought on by the drugs. Some of the nightmares were truly frightening and the cause of much of my insomnia. Not only was I regularly hallucinating, but my fantasy world produced in me an abusive attitude towards those trying to help, especially on the many occasions when I'd tried and failed to climb over the bars holding me in. Finally, after a number of altercations with doctors and nurses, caused by my weird drug-affected and belligerent frame of mind, I slowly became more understanding and compliant. And once the hands on the clock opposite my bed were travelling in the right direction again, I was transferred to a single-bed ward.

I thought I would at last get some sleep now, but hospitals seem designed to keep you awake. There was a continual procession of nurses coming to take samples, measure my blood pressure, give me injections, feed me medications, and create other invasions of privacy. For some peculiar reason, everyone who came to my bedside kept asking me my name, my date of birth, and other damn fool questions. 'Do you know where you are?' was a regular one, and sometimes I gave them stupid answers, like 'On the moon'. At night, it was even worse. The staff seemed to be having parties outside my door, talking with loud voices and generally carrying on with no thought or regard for patients attempting to sleep. And somewhere not too far away, in another ward, some poor woman kept yelling out time and again, 'Help me, please help me!' It was torture, like a dripping tap, for it went on all night. The next morning, a nurse told me that the lady had dementia, that she had suffered a fall and was having surgery the next day, but was distressed not knowing where she was and not having any person with her that she knew. I don't suppose the hospital had any padded cells for the likes of her.

Even before I left ICU, I was getting worried about Maddens; but on my first evening in the ward, Kevin came to see me. 'Hi, Dad,' he said. 'How are you doing?' I was a little more compos mentis by then, and it was good to see a face I recognised. 'Did you pop in and see me earlier?' I asked him. 'I vaguely remember seeing you.'

'Yeah. You weren't making any sense,' he answered. 'You were right out of it.'

'That would be the drugs they filled me up with.'

'Anyway, you're looking better now. How are you feeling?'

'Like shit.'

'Well, there's one thing you don't have to worry about,' said Kevin.

'And, what would that be?'

'I've spoken to Jason. He says everything is under control. They've got enough work to get on with for this week at least.'

'Well, that's as maybe, but the sooner I get out of here, the better.'

'You haven't changed, have you? Always on the go. You should enjoy the rest.'

'I've really had this place,' I told him, holding my hand up to my throat, 'up to here.'

'Dad, you just can't leave yet. You aren't well enough. Who is going to look after you?'

'I'm OK.'

'Like hell you are. Anyway, that's the reason I came to see you,' Kevin says. 'Mum has offered to help.'

At first, I was struck dumb, and it took me a few moments to get my head around what Kevin had said. 'What the fuck? Helen?' I queried rather too loudly.

'Please, Dad, do keep your voice down.'

Just then, a nurse popped her head round the door. 'Anything wrong?' she asked. 'I heard shouting.'

'No, it's OK. Just my father getting excited.'

'Fine, but please don't upset the patient,' instructed the nurse as she retreated.

'I don't believe you. Why would *she* want to do anything for me?' I said. '"She wrote me off years ago. I don't want any woman smothering me again, especially not your mother.'

'Why not, Dad?'

'Because she did the dirty on me. That's why not.' I realised I was raising my voice again. 'Anyway, I've decided I don't like women anymore,' I added more softly. 'Well, not ones like Helen anyway. I guess you're not one for women either,' I added, trying to smile at Kevin.

'That's different, Dad. I still respect them.'

'And I don't?'

'No, Dad. Don't you remember why she left and took me with her?'

'Of course.'

'You damn near broke her jaw.' I didn't say a word. What could I say? Kevin remained silent for a time before continuing. 'I don't understand why, but Mum still has feelings for you, despite what you kept doing to her. Anyway, that's why she wants to help.'

'Perhaps she does,' I said, 'but I don't need help.'

'I've spoken to the doctor, and he says they can't discharge you unless there is someone at home to look after you. And I'm not in any position to help.'

'I don't expect you to.'

'So, what's your answer?'

'Not happy.'

'Why not, Dad?'

'Does she want to move back in? I mean, she's not expecting marital pleasures, is she?'

'I doubt it,' Kevin replied, laughing, 'but you'll have to ask her.'

I felt reluctant to see her again, let alone have her in my house, but I guess that needs must; so after another ten minutes of hesitation, I finally agreed to her visiting me. 'I'll see what she has to say for herself,' I muttered.

'Good. I'll bring her in tomorrow, then,' he said, and then, with scarcely a wave, he left me still pondering the fallout from his visit.

True to his word, at three o'clock sharp the next afternoon, they arrived. I expected Kevin to stride in first, followed by a cowering Helen. But it was Helen who marched in on her own. She stood in the doorway and stared at me, silently entreating me to make eye contact. I don't know how long she remained like that, because it took a while for me to look up at her face. She certainly wasn't cowering. She appeared to have a new-found confidence, and her gaze was unwavering. After a few moments of scrutiny, she came over to where I lay, bent down, and kissed my forehead.

'Wow,' I said.

'I would have kissed you on the mouth, but I can hardly see it among all the growth. You need a shave, John.' She spoke firmly, with no hesitation.

I had been shocked into silence. The last I had seen of Helen was six years ago. She had been a veritable mouse in those days before she and Kevin walked out on me. I suppose that, if she hadn't kept in touch with her friend and found that bolthole to fall back on, she would still have been with me, causing me never-ending angst. I couldn't get my head around the change in her, and I'd forgotten what a good-looking woman she was. Helen was again the woman I married, pretty and self-assured. And she was nicely dressed; her blonde hair was somehow very different to how it was before, very neat and perhaps a slightly different colour. She had drawn a chair up next to my bed and was still eyeing me quizzically, but she remained silent. I thought I'd better say something and was wondering why she was on her own.

'Where's Kevin got to?' I asked her.

'Oh, he just had to go and see the doctor, to discuss your progress.'

'OK, but I hope he's not too long.'

'Why?'

'I'm not entirely comfortable having you here on your own. That's why.'

'Well, you'd better get used to the idea.'

'I haven't agreed to anything yet.'

'Then you'll just have to lie there for another week or two. Or maybe more.'

Just then, Kevin came in, grabbed another chair, and sat next to his mother. 'Are you getting along all right?' he asked his mother.

'Your father hasn't changed much. He's digging his toes in, it seems.'

'Stop trying to rush me,' I told them.

'Well, the doctor says you can go home in three more days if you agree to Mum moving back in,' said Kevin.

'I don't know,' I said. Then I turned to Helen. 'Anyway, I don't want you sleeping in my bed.'

Helen roared with laughter. 'You'd be lucky,' she said. And once she'd stopped chuckling, she spoke again. 'I'll use Kevin's old room. Unless you've got someone else in there.'

'Of course not.'

'I'll sleep there until you're back on your feet. I'm not staying beyond a couple of weeks. I can only get that amount of leave.'

'Oh, yeah? So you've got a job now. What are you doing?'

'Working at Kevin's school actually, doing a bit of admin work for the principal.'

'Bully for you.'

'Anyway, I'll do the cooking and the housework till you can manage on your own. Otherwise, I'll keep out of your hair.'

'I suppose.'

'And one more thing,' added Helen. 'The first time you get stroppy and abusive, or try to push me around, I'm out of there. No second chances, John.'

'That's fair enough, Dad,' said Kevin. I nodded reluctantly. 'OK, then. I'll let the doctor know on our way out. I can't come in tomorrow. I've got a parent/teacher night. I'll come the next evening and make all the necessary arrangements for your transfer.'

'Please, Kevin, will you do one more thing for me?'

'Sure, Dad.'

'Just go round to my place and pick up my phone. I wasn't in a fit state to remember it when I was carted off. And I need to make some calls.'

'OK. We'll call in tonight on our way home. Spare key in the usual place?'

'I guess so. My keys will be in there too somewhere. Perhaps you could have a look for them as well.'

'Will do,' said Kevin as he rose to his feet and left to see the doctor.

A few seconds later, Helen also got to her feet. 'Goodbye, John,' she said. 'Just stop looking so bloody miserable. You've been granted a second chance of life. Make the most of it.' I silently waved the pair of them out, still unsure if it was going to work. I'd been enjoying my independence, happy in my avoidance of garrulous women. And, what was going to happen to Sybil or Sylvia or whatever her name is? As I lay there contemplating my future, it suddenly came to me. Her name was Silver. Damn fool name, I thought, but it did suit her, for that was the colour of her hair, or so it appeared when the sun shone on it, a very light blonde. I was looking forward to seeing her again. I wondered what had become of her. I wouldn't have been very popular when she pitched up to an empty house, and I wondered if I would ever be able to make it right with her. I'd better contact her as soon as possible and explain what had happened to me. I'll just have to wait until Kevin brings my phone in. I can't remember her number, but it'll be in the memory. And then I would need to put her off again until Helen was safely out of the way.

The three days were up. Kevin had brought my phone in the previous evening, and as soon as he had gone, I called Silver. Her phone rang for a long time before she answered.

'Hello,' she said somewhat doubtfully.

'Hello, Silver,' I answered with equal hesitation. I wasn't expecting an easy conversation.

'Yes?' she queried. She obviously didn't recognise my voice.

'It's me, John.'

There was a long silence on the other end, and I thought she must have hung up on me. Eventually, she spoke up. 'You've got a bloody nerve phoning me.'

'I'm sorry, Silver. I'm in hospital.'

'And, what might you be doing there? Are you sick or something?'

'I've been here two weeks now.'

'What? Ever since that day you stood me up? I don't believe it.'

'That very day. I collapsed that afternoon. Got taken to hospital in an ambulance. I nearly died. My aorta burst, and they had to operate.'

'Sounds bad.' Her voice had got a little less belligerent, and I realised I was winning.

'I was in intensive care for ten days then in a ward for a week.'

'Why didn't you phone me before you went in?'

'There was no time. It all happened very quickly.''I guess I'll just have to believe you, but I'm not happy.'

'I'll make it up to you, I promise.'

'So, how much longer are you in for?'

'I'm still very weak.' I didn't want to tell her I'd be going home the following day and that my ex would be looking after me, so I told a white lie. 'I'll be in rehab for a couple of weeks.'

'Oh, where?' she asked. 'Should I come and see you?'

'I'd love you to, Silver, but I'd be lousy company, so I think not.'

'If you say so.'

'I'll phone again once I'm feeling presentable, and I'll cook you that meal we never had.'

'OK, then.'

After we'd rung off, I felt a bit guilty for refusing her visit. She had seemed quite a caring person the first couple of times we'd met, and perhaps she would have looked after me just as well as Helen if I'd told her the truth, but the die was cast now.

I needed a change of scene, a bloke to talk to, so I put Silver to the back of my mind and phoned Jason, just to see how he was getting on. They would be running out of work soon. He answered straightaway. 'I believe my Kevin has been in touch,' I said.

'That's right,' answered Jason, 'but I'd already been round to your place to see why you weren't at work. I spoke to your neighbour, and he told me the news. How are you feeling now?'

'Better, thanks.'

'That's good.'

'I'll be off home tomorrow, but I'll still be recovering for a couple of weeks. Helen's coming in to look after me.'

'Wow! How did you swing that?'

'Kevin was responsible.'

'He's a good lad, John. Anyway, take your time. Jack and I will keep things going till you come back.'

'Have any more jobs come in?'

'There's one, but it's a fair way off, so I haven't agreed to it yet.'

'Could you pop round and see me one evening?'
'OK. We'll talk about it then.'
'Thanks, Jason.'

The following day was my freedom day. Early in the morning, I had a visit from the vascular surgeon who had saved my life. 'You look a lot better standing up than you did lying down,' he told me. And he explained how he had sewn a piece of Dacron hose into the damaged section of my aorta. 'The good news is that with this repair, your life expectancy is back to where it was before all this happened,' he added. I was also given a list of the medications I would need to buy on my way home, including iron supplements needed as a result of the blood transfusions.

It was a Saturday, so Kevin was able to pick me up from hospital and take me home. He arrived in mid-morning. The last thing I wanted was to go home in a wheelchair, so I'd spent a few minutes every day trying out my legs. I was given a walking stick to assist me, but I still couldn't walk more than a few paces at first. I'd never felt so bloody useless. But, eventually, after a couple of failed attempts, I'd managed to get through the door and hobble along the passage. Finally, I'd limped as far as a sort of reception area, where I was offered a seat so I could linger and chat up the nurses. They all seemed happy to see me up and about.

When Kevin arrived, he was on his own. I was already dressed and sitting in a chair next to my bed.

'Are you on your own today?' I asked him.

'Mum's already at the house.'

'What!' I shouted. 'You must be joking.'

'Why?'

'I don't want her poking around when I'm not there.'

'The house is in a right mess, Dad. She needs to clean it up, get it ready for you.'

'It's not right, Kevin. She should have ....'

'We went round there early this morning,' Kevin interrupted. 'The place really ponged, being shut up for so long. And it didn't look as though you'd changed the sheets on your bed for months. Or done any washing.'

'Yes, but ....'

'You've got to stop bellyaching, Dad. Let Mum do what she has to.' I didn't answer. Kevin just looked at me and shook his head. 'Come on,' he said eventually. 'Take my arm and we'll get going.'

It was a warm sunny morning in late February as Kevin drove me home. The roads were busy, but my son was a good driver, and we reached my house in less than fifteen minutes, after making a detour to a pharmacy for all the medications I'd been prescribed. The first thing I noticed as he pulled into my driveway was that the grass needed cutting, though it was no longer green after the hot summer winds had scorched it. My house looked welcoming in the sunshine as I gingerly extracted myself from the car and walked slowly to the three steps leading up to the veranda and the front door. This was my first challenge. While in hospital, I'd been made to climb three steps to make sure I would be able to manage it on my own when I got home. At first, even one step was difficult, and I couldn't find the energy to try the second. Even that little exercise had been exhausting. But I'd finally achieved two steps, and the next day all three, and I hadn't had a railing to help.

Helen was waiting for me on the veranda, smiling, as I heaved myself up. When I finally made it to the top, she spoke. 'Congratulations, John, and welcome home.' It was strange seeing her back here. She already looked at home, dressed in an old pair of trousers and an apron and carrying a broom, but I didn't say anything. She was obviously trying to ingratiate herself, and I wasn't about to foster that sort of nonsense. She stood back as I walked in. I sniffed the air. There was definite freshness about the place, and I could hear the sounds of the washing machine going through its cycles. I looked around. The furniture all seemed to be where I remembered it, where it should be in fact, and I could see that Helen had been ultra-busy cleaning everything up, so I managed a 'Thank you, Helen', though it was not an easy thing for me to say. I was still a little raw about the way she had taken over.

'My pleasure,' she said. 'The house was in a bit of a mess when I arrived, and there was a foul smell in the kitchen. You'd left a heap of chicken out on the bench. It had really gone off, and the stench was ghastly.'

'Yeah. I left in a bit of a hurry.'

'I decided to bury the chicken in the garden. No point in stinking out your rubbish bin.'

'Fair enough,' I said. By this time, I'd been standing for a while and needed to take the weight off my legs, which still felt a little weak after my exertion. Just then, Kevin came in and joined me on the couch.

'I've made a list of things you need for the house, including groceries,' said Helen. 'Have you got any cash salted away somewhere?'

'There should be a couple of fifties in my wallet,' I replied, 'but I haven't a clue where it is.'

'I retrieved it, along with your keys and phone.'

'Thanks, Kevin.'

'I'll go and do some shopping, then. OK if I use your car?' she asked Kevin.

'That's fine, Mum.'

'OK, and I'll make us all some lunch when I get back.'

'Make bloody sure you bring a receipt with you,' I called out to her retreating back.

She stopped at the door and turned to me, shaking her head. 'Still the old skinflint, I see. And don't forget this is still my house.' Then she smiled at me and was gone.

*   *   *

CHAPTER 20

2010

It felt like morning, for I could hear birds singing, a dawn chorus it must be, but the room I was in was still dark. In my half-awake state, I thought I was still in my hospital bed, but there was an eerie silence about the place, as though the nursing staff had deserted me and had taken all the other patients with them. But as the room got a bit lighter, I could see that there was no clock on the opposite wall, neither going clockwise nor anticlockwise. Then I heard it, the thin tinkling sounds of a piano being played in the distance. I looked around me, and only then did I realise I was in my own bed. My memory started clearing. The nightmare of the hospital was behind me, but who was playing the piano? The events of previous days came back to me in a flood: Kevin picking me up and bringing me home. Helen waiting for me at the top of the steps to the veranda. Helen greeting me. Helen going shopping, coming back, and looking after me. Helen kissing me and complaining about my hairy face. Helen cooking food for me and getting me to bed. With a smile. How did I deserve this?

I lay there for a while, my thoughts hovering between annoyance at the way Helen had wormed her way back into my life and gratitude that she had done so. When I tried to move, I realised how weak I was. It would need an effort just to get out of bed, but as I tried to lift myself, the sound of the piano ceased. Moments later, I heard a quiet knock on the door, and Helen put her head in. 'You awake, then?' she said. 'I came in before, but you were still out for the count. Did you sleep well?'

'Yes, thanks,' I muttered.

She went over to the window and drew back the curtains. 'That's better,' she said. 'I hope the piano didn't disturb you.'

'Not really.'

'It needs tuning.'

'That's not my problem,' I retorted rather unkindly.

'I'm not suggesting it is your problem,' she retorted equally sharply. 'But I'm going to take it when I leave here, and I'd like to get it fixed before I go.'

'Good riddance to it.'

'You're being a bore, John. Cut it out.' I didn't reply to that, and after a few moments of staring at me, she remembered her duty. 'I'll go and make us a cuppa,' she added.

After she had gone out, I resolved to be a bit more pleasant. She was doing her best, and, so far, she had proved to be a pretty good nurse. When Kevin had left us the previous day, he'd looked a little anxious. 'Are you sure you'll be all right, Mum, here with Dad?'

'Stop fussing,' she had said. In fact, Helen was the one who was being a bit of a fusspot. After Kevin had left us, she got stuck in, making sure I had taken all the pills I'd been prescribed and ensuring I was comfortable before leaving me for the night. And she had insisted that I take a shower and shave off all the facial hair that had grown while I was in hospital. I must say, I'd felt much better afterwards. Hospital smells lingered as Helen had been quick to point out, which is why she wanted me to freshen up. 'You smell nice now,' she had said once I was back in bed, and she'd given my cheek a light kiss as she tucked me in for the night.

I heard kitchen noises for some minutes before Helen reappeared, this time carrying a tray. 'I decided to bring you breakfast in bed.' She placed the tray on my legs as I sat up. 'Just some orange juice and a couple of slices of toast,' she added. 'I'll go and make the coffee and then come and join you.' Helen was obviously trying to insinuate herself, get in my good books as it were, and I wondered why. Perhaps she wanted us to take up where we'd left off, or rather back to the days before I'd lost my temper. Perhaps she was trying to sound me out. I was somewhat ambivalent on that score, so I decided not to react to her overtures. I still felt resentful, but perhaps a little less so than when Kevin had first proposed having her look after me. When she returned carrying two mugs, I was already into my second piece of toast. She perched on the bed next to me and smiled. 'So, how are you feeling?'

'Still a bit weak,' I said. 'I think I need some exercise.'

'Once you're up, we'll take a walk, a little bit further every day.'

'Sounds good.'

'You'll need every one of the fourteen days to get well enough to go back to work.'

We were silent while we sipped our coffee, and then I broached a subject that I'd been mulling over since I'd asked the same question of Kevin. 'I was told you're keeping your whereabouts a secret these days.'

'It's no secret anymore, John. I have a unit in Mornington, near Benton's Square.'

'On your own?'

Helen laughed. 'Checking up on me, are you?'

'No. Just interested.'

'Well, the answer's yes. So far.' We finished our drinks, and Helen put both mugs on the tray. As she took it to the door, she asked if I needed anything else. 'I presume you don't need help dressing.'

'Of course not.'

'I'll take all the clothes you had on yesterday and wash them if you like. They've also got a hospital smell about them.'

'Thanks,' I said.

I made progress quicker than I expected. On the third day at home, Jason called round at the end of his day's work. It was good to see him, a sign of normality, and we discussed the jobs coming up. He told me they were managing well despite my absence but hoped to see me back before too long, especially since one of the machines was giving trouble and needed me to look at it. It was good to feel wanted.

Helen and I went for a walk every morning, and after four days, we went out twice a day. For our second outing, she would often drive us out to places further down on the peninsula where we would walk along the beach till I got tired. *She* never seemed to get fatigued and always remained spirited. I wondered if she was trying to prove something. We always walked with a space between us, never touching, though there were many occasions when I wanted to take her hand. I knew that it was simply a case of misplaced pride that prevented me from doing so, but I wasn't yet ready to admit to any change in my feelings towards her. One day, we went as far as Somers, where we had seen the dolphins in happier days, but the beach was deserted, apart from one solitary fisherman casting his line hopefully into the waves.

On one of our morning walks, we'd just left the house when I saw Martin working in his garden. I wanted to thank him for saving my life, for if he hadn't summoned the ambulance, I'd be dead. He looked pleased to see me up and about. 'It was a bit of a miracle that you'd come back early from bowls that evening,' I told him.

'I don't really know why I did,' he replied. 'It was strange, a sort of compulsion. I just knew that I had to.'

I introduced him to Helen, who also thanked him profusely. Martin looked a little puzzled, for I'd told him that Helen and I were separated. 'She's just looking after me for a couple of weeks,' I told him, 'while I get back on my feet."

Helen had been with me for a week when I had an accident. I always had to walk carefully, especially in the bathroom, after my return from hospital. I suppose I was getting overconfident of my ability and wasn't careful enough as I emerged from the shower one morning. I slipped, my legs shooting out from under me, and I landed hard on my back, my arm thudding against the shower door. Helen came running as soon as she heard the noise. I lay there winded and unable to move. I felt like a stranded whale. 'Oh, John,' she cried out. 'What happened?' I saw her staring anxiously down at me and watched as her eyes swept over my naked wet body. Then she smiled, though I was embarrassed. I suppose that since we were still technically married she had every right to see me exposed.

'I slipped on the wet floor,' I managed to say at last, once I'd recovered a little. 'Could you help me sit up? I don't think anything is broken, though I hit the back of my head as I went down.' It was a struggle, but she put her arms under my back and managed to lift me to a sitting position. However, there was no way she could get me standing, though she did manage to get a towel under my backside and drag me so I could sit up against a wall. From there, once I had recovered, I managed to roll over and get back on my feet. Afterwards, I felt the bruise on the back of my head, which was rapidly becoming a lump. Helen wanted me to see a doctor, to make sure I wasn't suffering from concussion, but I managed to persuade her that it wasn't necessary.

Later that day, Helen looked at me with a wistful smile. 'Well, John,' she said, 'you've still got a great body.'

'You sound as though you might be missing it.'

'Perhaps,' she said with a grin. I was about to make some suggestive remark when we were rudely interrupted by a knock on the front door, and the possibilities of the conversation were wasted. 'Of course, it's Saturday,' remarked Helen. 'That could be Kevin. He did say he would try and drop round over the weekend.'

It was indeed Kevin. 'I've got Marcus in the car,' he said. 'May I bring him in?'

'Yes, of course,' I replied. 'You don't need to ask.'

Kevin went back out again and returned with Marcus, who was carrying a large box. 'We've brought an orange cake for afternoon tea,' Marcus said, 'specially made by my mother.'

'Thanks,' said Helen. 'That's very good of her.'

Kevin turned to his mother. 'And, Mum,' he said, 'I've spoken to the music teacher at school. She said not to have the piano tuned here but wait until it's in its new home.'

'That makes sense,' said Helen. 'I'll phone a removalist on Monday.'

My convalescence continued well, and as I gained strength, I was able to do more and more for myself. I was quite sure that by the time Helen had to leave, I would be capable of returning to work. Throughout her stay, I had gradually come to accept her presence, especially in that second week, though we remained distant. My heart had been so full of antagonism, and for so long, that I just couldn't bring myself to do or say anything positive. It was as if there was a sort of blockage in my lines of communication. On many occasions, I was about to say something, even tell Helen that I still loved her, that I wanted her back with me, but at the last moment, I shied away and remained silent.

After Helen had left, I convinced myself that she would return to me and that it wouldn't take long. I'd only have to wait a few days before she would come begging, asking me to take her back. As I waited, my love and my need for her continued to grow. The longer I waited the more obsessive I became, but I never paused to question my belief in her eventual surrender.

Then, after two weeks, I received another letter. It was less bulky than her first, and this time I ripped open the envelope immediately, expecting her to tell me of her decision to come home.

Dear John,

I hope you are now fully recovered and enjoying life to the full. I surprised myself by actually enjoying my stay and watching you slowly recover. You may wonder why I wanted to come and help in the first place. The fact is that I wanted to see if I still had feelings for you. Your visit to the hospital and subsequent convalescence seemed to be the chance I needed.

Well, I did find I had feelings for you, surprisingly strong feelings, which developed slowly over the two weeks I spent with you. I tried to show you my feelings without actually telling you how much I still loved you, hoping that you would show your hand if you still wanted me. I felt there was no point in making a big effort, trying to entice you back into my life, if you were not interested. It would just make me look silly. So I waited for you to say something. There were a number of times when you seemed on the point of welcoming me back into your life, especially on our last evening together, but you didn't, and I now know that it will never happen. You are too profoundly set in your ways and in a life that excludes me forever. So I left, deeply saddened.

There was a very good reason for sounding you out. I have met another man and now have quite a strong attachment to him. Lance is a fellow teacher at Kevin's school, where, as you know, I'm now working. He lost his wife to breast cancer three years ago and has been alone ever since. Now he has asked me to marry him, but I couldn't commit to anything until I knew for absolute sure that our marriage was finished for good. Now that I know that it is, I have told him that I will marry him as soon as our divorce is settled.

I'm sure you will have no objections to a divorce, especially when I tell you that, as part of the settlement, I shall relinquish any part ownership of our house or contents. I make one proviso, and that is that you make a will in which you bequeath the house to Kevin in the event of your death. This must be irrevocable. I also make no claim on anything to do with your business, despite the fact that I not only paid to set you up in the first place but also bought the house. You are welcome to both. I shall be comfortably off, as both Lance and I have secure jobs.

I am immeasurably saddened at having to write this letter, but it's all for the best. My love has been spurned, and I must move on. You will hear from my lawyer, Candice Maybury, in a week or two. I am pleased that you enjoy Kevin's company and seem to have accepted Marcus into your life as well. It augurs well for the future.

I wish you well, John. Take care and have a good life.

Your once-loving Helen

At first I simply could not believe what she was saying, so I read her letter again. The second time, as her words sank in, my anger and bitterness started rising like lava from an erupting volcano. I'd wanted a reprieve. I'd expected a reprieve, but I'd been duped. All was now lost to me, lost forever. I'd been too stupid to take my chance, too moronic to accept what Helen had offered that last night. Now she had slammed the door in my face. I'd been shamed, made to look a complete fraud. In a moment of torment, I grabbed a vase from the table and hurled it at the wall. It shattered, and the flowers that had been in it since Helen had left, now long since dead, landed in a wet mess on the carpet.

My wife had crossed a red line, and stabs of jealousy were eating into me. Wanting to divorce me was one thing, but offering herself to someone else was a step too far, one I could never accept. Her body was mine and mine alone. My earlier life with Helen swept through my fevered brain in rapid flashbacks, the memory of her lovely naked body mocking me. Deep down, I knew it was ridiculous, but I felt I'd been swindled, and I knew that I had to blame someone for ripping us apart. My mind immediately jumped to Rhonda Sutton. Of course. She was the person who started all this, the bitch who had come between us. She had stolen my wife, and she must pay. I paced the floor, gathering a cloud of fury round me, working out how I should retaliate.

It was dark and the rain had started when I got into my ute and drove to Langwarrin. I had no idea what I was going to do there, but I was ready for a confrontation. I drove much too fast on the wet road, and my rage at the world grew with every kilometre. By now the rain was sheeting down, and distant flashes of lightning lit up the sky, followed by rumbles of thunder. As I turned off the main road and entered the Suttons' drive, I realised that I was shedding tears, tears of outrage and antagonism towards the Suttons: their opulence, their extravagance, and their aloofness. My unreasoning mind was filled with hate, but their house was unlit, a huge bulk silhouetted against a lowering sky, a mansion of devils, and there was only a faint sheen of light coming from the pool in front of it. In a paroxysm of sheer fury I drove in a frenzy straight at the house, not caring about myself or the damage I would cause, but a front wheel of my ute must have hit a kerb-stone or some other obstruction. The steering wheel was wrenched out of my hands and I lost control. At that instant a shaft of lightning struck a tree less than fifty metres from the house, temporarily blinding me, and the explosion of sound that accompanied the lightning left me completely disorientated.

The next moment I was tearing across the immaculate lawn. I heard rather than saw the white picket fence as I drove through it with a splintering crash, and the next moment I was airborne.

*   *   *

AUTHOR'S NOTE

I first met John Madden when my neighbour was having a swimming pool installed in his back yard. The company doing the job had to remove part of our common fence for access, and I had a lot to do with John while the work progressed. There was something about his face and his demeanour that attracted me, for he often wore a dejected expression, as though he was remembering some poignant event in his life. I collect stories and other people's foibles, so I wanted to discover something about him and the life he had led, just in case I could use some of it in my writing. John was friendly enough when I approached him, but, at first, he didn't want to talk about himself, even when I invited him into my home for a meal. However, after a time, he lost his reserve, and over the months following our first meeting, he became quite open, voluble even. Eventually, he told me everything he could remember about his life, or certainly those parts he was willing to divulge. I'm really grateful that I did hear his story, though it took me many sessions, including visits to his Frankston home, before I could piece it all together.

One of my hobbies is a book group which I attend once a month, and a few years ago we all read and then discussed a book by Zoe Morrison called *Music and Freedom*, about a female pianist and her abusive husband. One of our members posed a question. Why is it that all novels about domestic abuse are written from the point of view of the victim? Why is it that no one has ever written one from the abuser's point of view? That question has stuck with me ever since, and I have often wondered if I could, or even should, write such a book myself. John Madden's story finally gave me the opportunity to do so, and the necessary motivation.

It was with great sadness that I learnt of John's death. When the Suttons, a family that up till then I had never met, returned from a holiday in Fiji, they found John's ute in their swimming pool with him still inside it. The water was up to the top of the windows, and he had made no effort to free himself for his safety belt was still fastened. Judging by Helen's recent letter, found later at his house, he must have decided that life without her was not worth living, though maybe he was knocked unconscious in the accident. Was it indeed an accident? And what was he doing there?

No one will ever know for sure. The authorities reckoned he'd been there, in his watery grave, for three or four days, and though his employees went hunting for him when he failed to arrive at work, their search had been in vain.

After his death, I managed to trace most of the main characters in his story, though it has taken me many years to piece it all together. His lovely ex-wife, Helen, was an enormous help, as was his sister, Barbara, his son, Kevin, and many of his work colleagues. I was unable to discover much about his childhood, though a onetime school friend, Hudson Little, helped me where he could, and Mr Little's wife, Nola, filled me in on his time as an apprentice, and his 'Beetle project' as she called it. What John told me of his early years was largely corroborated by his sister, Barbara.

Obviously, I have had to provide some of my own additions to the story in order to cover those parts which were missing, especially as regards John's last hours. After many hours of thought, knowing something of John's psychology and having read a detailed police report on the condition of John's ute when it was lifted from the Sutton's pool, I believe my conclusions to be reasonably accurate. Further, I did establish that there was a severe storm on the night in question, and one of the trees in the Sutton's garden was indeed destroyed by lightning. However, my interpolations are otherwise few and far between.

I decided to write John's story in the first person to make it more immediate. After all, it is his story to tell, and it is how he told it to me. And I decided to use words from Helen's first letter to John for the title. He was undoubtedly 'like his father', not only in his propensity for domestic abuse but also in the way he turned his life around after his dastardly act of aggression.

It was quite evident that John had been deeply in love with his wife when they married, and I often wondered what changed him into the monster he became. It also became obvious to me, speaking to Helen, that at the time of their marriage she too had been very much in love. She had idolised John, but was equally at a loss to know what had changed him. During the course of our discussions, Helen detailed many of the abuses she suffered at John's hand, including the instances of rape, but I have not included everything in the book. A complete account of everything John imposed on his wife as part of his coercive and abusive control would be far too gruelling. Helen has finally decided that there was a rogue gene in the Madden males, one that had been inherited by John. 'Thank goodness it never got passed on to Kevin,' she said the last time I saw her.

As for Kevin himself, he and Marcus were married as soon as it was legalised, which was some ten years after Helen remarried and nine years after Maddens was sold to Koos Bischoff.

Nicholas Day-Lewis
Somers, 2022

CPSIA information can be obtained
at www.ICGtesting.com
Printed in the USA
BVHW041512111022
649153BV00016B/539/J